20 YEARS YOUNG

LITTLE WHITE LIES...

20 Years Young is the second book in The Years Young Collection by Kathryn Louise.

15 Years Young reached the top 100 books on Amazon and voted The UK's Summer 2022 Must Read List.

"A fantastic read, can't wait for the next one.'
  - Nikki Scholl

"Page turning, raw, relatable and naughty! Loved it!"
  - Laura Ward

www.kathrynlouiseauthor.com
@kathrynlouiseauthor on all social media platforms.

Kathryn Louise has asserted her right to be identified as the
author of this Work in accordance with the Copyright,
Designs and Patents Act 1988.
This is paperback edition 2023 2.

First published in Great Britain by KLA Books in 2022.

A CIP catalogue record for this book is available from the
British Library. Printed and bound in Great Britain by KLA
Books.

For all the support and encouragement from my family and friends...

20
YEARS
YOUNG

Kathryn Louise

Little White Lies...

1

THE OUTCOME

The large courtroom smelled of old musty leather and rustic wood. As I took in every detail of our surroundings, I nervously fiddled with the rings on my fingers. Only my heart pounding in my chest and the sound of Daniel breathing heavily could be heard. We all knew I was guilty, there was no denying it, but it was the sentence I was about to receive that worried me.

The large oak doors creaked open. People hurriedly began to appear along with the sound of voices echoing as they chatted amongst themselves, making their way to their seats. One by one, the chairs arranged in a crescent shape at the front of the courtroom were filled with people carrying paperwork, briefcases, or both. I counted about twenty in total, plus the judge who took pole position on the front desk, above everyone else.

The fiddling of my fingers turned to toe-tapping. Daniel glared at me, prompting me to stop.

I couldn't help it—I was nervous as hell.

'All rise.' It was like the scene from a film I had watched. The judge banged his gavel as hard as he could on the sound block in front of him, bringing attention and focus to the ruling for the rest of the magistrates and tribunal members in the room. I stood up and so did Daniel. He was holding my hand the whole time like a pillar of strength.

The court clerk began speaking but the words just bounced around my head like white noise. I couldn't concentrate, my mind wandering onto matters that weren't important. I began thinking to myself, *What if I am arrested and jailed? How will Daniel cope on his own? Will he find a new girlfriend or a new mum for Jack? What kind of a mother am I to be recklessly drink driving?* Too late now, it was how I moved on from here that would make all the difference.

I felt Daniel shake my arm, bringing me back into the room. I looked up at him, confused. The court clerk was addressing me, waiting for my response, but I didn't know what he had said.

'Madam, could you please confirm your full name and address the court.' He looked angry and impatient.

'I'm sorry. Miss Rose Patricia Murrell, your honour.' I needed to concentrate for longer than five minutes, it was so important and serious, but as usual, my attention span got the better of me. I drifted away again, studying the pillar next to me. I looked at the carved wood detail on it and began appreciating just how beautiful it was. It must have taken somebody ages to achieve that. Daniel glared at me yet again. I felt like a naughty child at a boring church service.

'Rose, you have to listen,' he growled.

'I know,' I answered back as quietly as I could. The judge stared down at me but said nothing.

'I understand that the accused is on trial for the offence of driving under the influence of alcohol, careless and reckless driving, failure to stop at a red light, and failure to stop at the scene of an incident. Is that correct?' The court clerk was reading the list of convictions from the paperwork in front of him like a shopping list. He addressed my solicitor to confirm.

'That is correct, your honour.' He nodded his head.

I dropped my head in shame. Daniel looked at me—it was the first time that he heard about *all* of my offenses. He knew that I was arrested by the police for drink driving, but he wasn't aware of the other charges. To be honest, I didn't remember any of them as I was that drunk, but my solicitor had told me what I was being charged for and what I was up against.

I could feel Daniel's eyes burning a hole in the side of my face, but I didn't dare look up at him. He let go of my hand like he was ashamed and embarrassed of me. *Who wouldn't be?*

'And how does the accused plead?' the judge asked.

'Guilty, your honour.' My solicitor stood to address the courtroom. 'The defendant would, however, like you to consider a plea of mitigation based on the following... genuine remorse, a previously clean driving license, no prior criminal convictions, and the offer of alcohol counselling to help with her addiction issues following the case outcome. I would also like to add that the defendant understands the seriousness of her actions and is extremely apologetic. She is a mother and has the joint responsibility for a dependent son. The inconvenience of losing her license will be punishment in itself.'

My solicitor, Mr Davidson, or Alex as he asked me to call him, was extremely confident and I liked the way he was direct and to the point. That was his job, this was what he did and why he was so good. He had been recommended to me by a family friend.

Instead of looking at him and appreciating his professionalism and competence, I found myself wondering what he would be like in bed. He was quite an attractive man—dark in features, clean shaven, big strong hands... I could see that he worked out from his physique and the way his suit hugged his body. He was assertive, he took control. I liked that in a man.

What if I was locked up in a police cell for hours and he came to speak to me, just us all alone in the cell, handcuffs and a cold wall for him to press my body against?

'Rose, what the fuck?' Daniel pinched my arm, which made me jump instantly. 'Say yes.'

I had no idea what I was saying yes to since I was caught up in the moment of thinking about my solicitor, which was far more enticing.

'Yes, that is correct, your honour.' I nodded in agreement.

Alex looked at me. He was only a row in front of us, but it was close enough for me to smell the faint aroma of his alluring aftershave. He smelled gorgeous. There was something about a man's aftershave that made me want them. It had to be the right one, not too strong or overpowering, just enough to catch his scent and be drawn in.

Wow, Rose, you are something else, I tried reasoning with myself. *A few minutes of your life, this is super serious, and all you can think about is another man. Sort yourself out, you have issues.* My words of reasoning to myself didn't make the slightest bit of difference. I could tell myself till I was blue in the face that

I needed to behave but my mind had its own free will and no one was able to control it.

Right, back in the room and I was trying to decipher what was going on. What had been happening and what was still left to be said.

We sat through another thirty minutes of my solicitor providing evidence around me being a decent and responsible human being. He presented facts about mine and Daniel's hardworking attitude to life, being parents at such a young age, and the brief, mad moment where I let my hair down and had too much to drink resulted in the actions of the night that I had been convicted for. He made it all sound so innocent.

I was comatose into believing everything that Alex had said, I was hoping that the jury would see it as innocent too. The judge banged his gavel again and asked everyone to stand.

'The court will pause for ten minutes in order for me to make an informed decision on how to proceed with a verdict.' With that, he got up and walked out of the room, followed by two other magistrates and the court clerk. Everyone started chatting quietly and whispering to one another. Before long, the sound in the room rose and it was a bustling arena of legal executives. This was Daniel's opportunity to make a pop at me while Alex was sifting through his papers in case he had forgotten any small detail.

'What the fuck, Rose? When were you going to tell me about the rest of the convictions on the list or did you hope that I wouldn't find out?' He sat there staring at me, waiting for my response. I could see that Alex had swivelled on his chair and was also seeking my reaction. I hung my head low but didn't know what to say other than shrug my shoulders and raise my eyebrows.

'I'm sorry, Daniel. I don't really know myself... it was a total blackout. The only things I remember are small snippets and even those are blurry and confusing.'

'A red light. Failing to stop at the scene of an incident. What the hell?' Daniel seemed to be getting redder and angrier by the minute, but he kept the volume down on what he was saying to a loud whisper.

'I know. I know. I'm sorry, I...' I had no words. I didn't want to go over everything again, this happened months ago and here I was with history repeating itself. I just wanted to bury it under the carpet without the lectures from my perfectly behaved boyfriend.

The timing couldn't have been any better. The door swung open again and in walked the judge. The moment had arrived for them to pass judgement on me and give the verdict. I left Daniel hanging. Guilty or not guilty. Alex looked at me, giving a hopeful smile—at least he wasn't angry with me. I noticed that his hands were held behind his back and his right hand had his fingers crossed. *Is that for me?*

Daniel also looked at me. He smiled with hope, but I knew that the anger was still brewing and he was waiting to blow. I felt like he was watching the interaction between me and Alex. Jealous of another man showing me attention.

Bang, bang. There it was yet again. The judge turned the busy room into a quiet, patient atmosphere, tentatively awaiting his decision. The whole room sat down but Alex told me to remain standing. Like a performer on stage, I stood still, waiting for him to speak.

'Miss Rose Patricia Murrell, I have considered all the convictions along with the evidence that has been presented.

On that basis alone, I find you guilty of driving under the influence of alcohol and guilty of reckless and dangerous driving. I also find you guilty of failing to stop at a red light and at the scene of an incident.'

I swallowed heavily. Suddenly, my throat turned dry and I held my breath.

He continued, 'I have, however, considered your plea, and based on the fact that you are a mother, you have a dependent, and I think it is important for you to be there as a parent. Also, on the basis that this is out of character with no previous convictions or charges, I am sentencing you to a twenty-four-month ban, a fine of two hundred and fifty pounds, at least eight weeks of alcohol rehabilitation sessions, and community service for three months. You must surrender your license on leaving the courtroom.'

The judge was looking straight at me the whole time. 'Should you be convicted again of another drink driving offence or motor conviction in the near future, you will face imprisonment. Do you understand, Miss Murrell? Consider this a warning.' His words echoed around the room and hit me like a smack in the face. 'Should you successfully complete all the additional courses, your ban may be considered for early dismissal.'

'I understand, your honour.' I kept it simple. *Should I have said thank you? Am I supposed to say anything else?* I looked to Alex for reassurance, for guidance. He simply smiled back and nodded his head. Me taking that as complete and for me to sit back down.

'In that case, I would like to thank the jury for their time this morning. Court is closed, you are all dismissed.' Noise and voices began to fill the air once again as everyone got on with the rest of the day. For most, it was onto the next case.

'So, Rose, let that be a lesson learned today. The outcome could have been so much worse than it was. You also had a nice judge.' Alex held out his hand to shake mine. I looked down before I shook it back and felt his warm hand grasp and engulf mine, strong and firm. The hold was a little too long, as were our eyes on each other, but I kept it going. I quite liked the feeling of another man's rugged hand. Daniel noticed and looked at both of us in turn.

'I wanted to thank you for your time, help and support, Alex.' Daniel glanced at him, reaching out his hand so he could release mine and shake his instead. It was like a position of authority, both wanting to be top dog. Their handshake looked hard and dominating, both wanting to be stronger than the other.

'Not at all, it was my pleasure.' Alex looked at me and smiled. It was a naughty smile, one that almost seemed to tease Daniel. 'I do need your driving license before you disappear. There are some forms that need completing on your behalf. I will be in touch with the other documents, Rose, take care.' With that, he lifted his briefcase from the table, took my driving license that I handed him, and glanced at the time on his watch, quickly leaving the room.

I wanted the ground to swallow me up. I didn't think that there was going to be a good outcome from today, but I had been granted the better of two options. Two years of no driving, possibly reduced for good behaviour (whatever that meant), community service, a fine, and a series of drinking courses that I needed to attend. The upside to all of this was that I still got to be with my boy, Jack. Imagine him telling his friends that his mum was in jail... that was not something I wanted to ever happen.

We hadn't even left the room when he started.

'Will you finally wake up, Rose, and think about what you are doing,' Daniel started shouting at me, I could feel his rage.

'I'm sorry, Daniel, I should have told you.' I was genuinely sorry.

'You have no idea how small you make me feel, your little white lies, the things you forget to tell me and not to mention the flirting. I could see the way you were looking at Alex.' Daniel was angry, but more than that, his eyes looked disappointed in me. Time and time again, I treated him like he was an idiot.

'Daniel, I...' Before I could finish, he continued lecturing me.

'Rose, what do you want from me? I feel like you have such a hard shell that sometimes it's impossible to crack. I don't know who you are at times, so distant and uncontrollable like a child. You weren't even listening in there. Half the time, I want to shake some sense into you.' He was in my face, shouting and waving his hands, but I didn't care. My guard was up, and no one was getting in.

'Is everything okay?' Alex appeared in the doorway. 'Apologies, I didn't want to disturb you both, but I left my phone on the desk and I am late for my next client.' He gave me a look of reassurance, checking I was okay. I was in the wrong here, yet Alex was making sure I was alright, and he wasn't overstepping the line—Daniel had every right to be mad at me.

'Yes, everything is fine, thank you for asking, Alex. We were just leaving,' I replied.

Daniel said nothing. He dropped his arms and reached for my hand, pulling me along and whisking me out of the room and down the corridor like a child from a sweet shop.

As we walked out of the magistrate's court, I watched all the other people awaiting their trials, nervous and apprehensive. It made me think about myself as a person. *What am I turning into? Where am I heading?* As Alex said, if this wasn't a lesson in life, I didn't know what was.

2

SKELETONS IN THE CLOSET

There it was again. My phone buzzed on the sideboard and another text appeared. It was Tom. I glanced at the screen but dared not open it and read what he wanted. I had left abruptly last time... I was rude and dismissive, why would he want to contact me again? He was genuinely trying to warn me and be honest. Maybe I shouldn't have been so rude.

I flicked open my phone and clicked on the text.

'MEET ME AT NOON TODAY, SAME PLACE AS LAST TIME. T X'

That was it. No mention of what it was about—nothing at all. Not even his name, just an initial and a kiss. Short and sweet.

I didn't want to answer him. My mind had been playing games with me for weeks. *Do I tell Daniel or don't I? Am I a bad person for not telling him? Does he already know?* More and more little white lies that I thought were better kept quiet but tripled in reaction when the truth was finally out.

I tried to ignore Tom and what he told me. I shut it out time and time again, but I had a growing desire to know what he wanted that wouldn't go away.

'OKAY, SEE YOU THEN. R X.'

I texted back and finished it in the same way—my initial and a kiss. Oops, too late, I sent it without thinking. *Why did I do that?* I finished every text message with a kiss, except my boss, of course, but in this scenario, would he take it the wrong way?

I got ready, threw on my tight jeans, a vest top and trainers. Daniel was at work; it was a Saturday—he always worked at the start of the weekend. He would never know I went to meet Tom. Setting off in my car to the service station, it took me less than half an hour. I knew I shouldn't be going and should have ignored the text message but something inside me was excited. It was the naughty side of me, I liked being naughty and the thought of going to meet Tom made me feel alive.

Tom was so pleased to see me, he almost leapt out of his car as soon as he saw me pull up next to his. Last time, he looked flustered, but this time, he seemed the same relaxed, attractive man I met on holiday. The sun was shining but instead of my sunglasses sheltering my eyes from the rays, they were balanced on my head, holding back my hair so I could clearly see his dark and masculine complexion.

He walked over to me from his car and instead of kissing me on the cheek, he threw his arms around me and pushed against my body. The smell of his aftershave was intoxicating, something so powerful in it that it made me melt with seduction. Maybe it was the same aftershave as Alex wore in the courtroom, that's why I was so attracted to him... the same powerful scent as Tom and the same dark, seductive looks. The jet-black stubble on his face brushed against my cheek, sending shivers down my spine as he whispered gently, 'I've missed you!'

I didn't pull away, instead, I embraced his warm, strong arms around me. I knew little about him, but for some reason, he felt like a comfort blanket, I felt safe whenever I was with him. It brought back memories of Greece and being in bed with him. I knew it was wrong, I knew I shouldn't be here with Tom, but I couldn't help it. I couldn't resist him.

He stood back slightly, dropping his hands to my waist. Again, I let him touch me, his large hands felt warm against my sides. I stood there for a moment gazing into his rich brown eyes. They felt like warm pools of enticement, pulling me further and further into him. I studied his lips, his short, rounded nose and seductive features. Neither of us saying anything, just studying each other. Paying attention to every small detail of his complexion.

I didn't know what was racing around in his thoughts... *Is he thinking the same as me? Is he as attracted to me as I am to him?* Of course, he was, he had told me in Greece that he felt something between us, but I had shaken it off as I left him that day.

I liked danger... I liked the feeling of doing something so utterly wrong that I went with the moment. The thought of being caught out excited me even more—a sense of electricity that made you feel like you were living.

Without asking him what or why he even wanted to see me, I leaned in, giving him the green light to kiss me. Both our eyes stared back at each other until they couldn't focus anymore and closed. Our heads turned so that our lips could touch. His hands dropped even further to place them on my bottom as he pulled my groin into his until I could feel his erection pushing through his jeans.

Our lips met. I could taste him, his breath meeting with mine as we kissed passionately. My nipples were as hard as he was. My breasts felt so good next to his warm body, encased in his hold. I wanted him so much that I took no notice of the fact we were in a car park service station. I didn't care—nothing mattered. The only thing I was fixated on was this feeling of pure lust and desire. I went from being nervous to see him to wanting to take it further.

'Rose, get in the back of the car with me. Let me take you somewhere right now, just the two of us.'

How could I resist his request, his stunning brown eyes and spending an afternoon with him?

'I want nothing more right now.' I kissed him again, closing my eyes, blocking everything else out.

Tom moved me to one side of the car door so he could reach the handle, lifting it up and opening it. He guided me into the opening and gently leaned me back so I could climb inside. I fell back, he gently climbed in after me and hooked the door shut with his foot.

I shuffled back as far as I could so he had room. He lay between my legs, reaching for my face with one hand and the other grappling at the zip on my jeans.

I used one of my hands to stroke his cock, the other attempting to undo his zip.

'Rose, I've wanted this for so long, you have no idea,' Tom said as he whispered into my ear, his breathing more intense as he was becoming impatient.

'Me too.' I felt such an adrenaline rush just being with

him, but the thought of having sex with him in a car park seemed a bit desperate. *Maybe we should go to a hotel somewhere or find somewhere a little quieter.*

'Wait a minute. Why don't we...' I tried to put my hand against Tom's to stop him from undoing my trousers, but as I did, I felt like a window was open and a gush of cold air wafted into the back of the car. As I looked outside, it suddenly got dark. Impossible! I had only been there for about half an hour and it was mid-afternoon. I panicked and tried to push Tom off me but his hand looked different.

It wasn't Tom's hand... it was Daniel's. *What is he doing here?* Wait a minute. Confused, my heart pounded with the fear of being in trouble. I gasped as I looked up at his face in the dusky light. Daniel's face stared straight back at me. I quickly sat up and looked around... I wasn't in the back of a car, I was in my bedroom, the cold air in the room was the open window blowing the night's cold breeze.

I peered down at myself, not in jeans or a vest top, but instead, completely naked. I always slept naked unless it was especially cold.

I must have been dreaming. I had dreamed the whole damn thing. I hadn't met Tom, I was in my bed asleep, but it felt so real—the smell of him, the taste of him, everything.

'Are you okay?' Daniel asked as he rolled over and lay by my side.

'Sorry, I had a bad dream.' I rubbed my eyes and moved the hair draped from over my face. Looking around the room for a double take, I was so confused. Tom felt so real. I looked over at my bedside table. The light on my phone was on as though a text had popped up. I held it in my hand and flipped the screen just as I had done in my dream, but there were no messages. I sank back into my pillows. I wasn't sure quite what I was expecting.

'Rose, what's up? What are you doing?' Daniel whispered in a half-asleep, dusky voice. 'You kept saying you missed someone, who were you dreaming about?'

'Really? That's strange, I was driving in my car. Must have been all the commotion with the court case. I'm sorry I woke you. Go back to sleep, honey.' I motioned to him that I was fine, but his eyes were already closed. He was on his side facing me, so I placed my phone back on the side and slid back under the covers with my back against his stomach. Daniel's body completely wrapped around mine, I pulled his arm over my body so he was cuddling me. I closed my eyes but couldn't drift back off to sleep. Tom's face imprinted in my mind and me just about to kiss him.

It had to be a dream as there was no way I could just nip off in the car and meet him without a driving license anymore. If I dreamed about Tom, was it still classed as cheating? Was it a sign of something or someone that I was fighting feelings for? It wasn't the first time either, I'd had the same dream repeatedly and I woke up at the same place each time.

That morning, Daniel made me a cup of tea and brought it up to me just before he left for work.

'Jack is stirring but I didn't want to wake him until you were up. Just checking you were okay... what was your nightmare about? You seem to be having them more often now.' He placed the steaming mug on my bedside table and stood there, just looking at me.

'I'm so sorry I woke you last night, it felt so real,' I said, yawning and stretching.

'Is there something wrong?' he asked.

'Oh, I'll tell you all about it tonight when you're back from work. Just a silly dream. I'm fine.' I don't think he would be too impressed if I mentioned Tom or the fact that I was dreaming about meeting him, touching him or even kissing him and contemplating going further. I was hoping he would forget all about it by the time he came home from work.

'Okay, cool, I need to shoot, I have a lot to get done today and it's supposed to be raining this afternoon. I'll bring Jack in and head off.' Daniel made his way to Jack's bedroom and returned with him clinging to his back. His cute little arms wrapped around Daniel's neck like a cape. Daniel hurled him onto the bed, tickling him as he landed and Jack giggling away. They had such a lovely relationship, it made me smile watching them, more like brothers than father and son.

'Oh, Jacky boy, I love you. Thank goodness there aren't two of you. I would have to share my love with two gorgeous little boys like you.' He edged onto the bed, chasing Jack, catching him and giving him a big kiss on his head.

I suddenly realised what he said and instantly looked straight at him, but he was too busy with Jack, laughing and chuckling at his dad chasing after him.

It must have been an honest comment. I was reading far too much into it. Knowing what I knew about Michelle and the baby, I presumed that Daniel was hinting at something. *Does he know? Has he spoken to Michelle?* Maybe the dreams were all part of my guilty conscience trying to break through.

I hadn't done a single thing about the little secret that Tom had told me, and I wasn't about to either. If Daniel didn't want to hear from Michelle, then neither did I. As far as I was concerned, I knew nothing, and Tom hadn't told me anything. He couldn't prove that I met him that day and told me, so that was that.

'Okay, you two, enough is enough. Daddy is going to be late for work and we have a date with a dog that needs to go for a walk.'

'Ohhhh!' Jack was disappointed that he had to go to work, but I promised him we would go to the park whilst out with Harry to make up for it. He loved the park more than anything, we spent hours there just messing and playing around. It was lovely.

Daniel left the house; I heard the slam of the front door and him whistling as he walked up the front garden path towards his car. I did miss him on Saturdays, and he was always so tired from working six days a week, but we made up for it on Sundays.

I needed to get in the shower and get Jack dressed before we left the house, so I decided to bribe him with a cake and a cartoon comic book from the shops if he got ready all by himself. I climbed out of my warm and cosy bed to the fresher temperature of our bedroom, reaching for my towel, which hung neatly on a hook on the back of the door. I then noticed a light flash on my bedside table from the corner of my eye.

It was my phone. My mobile's screen flashed quickly off again. Rather than go to the shower and read it when I returned, something pulled me towards it. It couldn't wait. I'm sure it was probably Daniel saying to have a good day or my mum, but I needed to know.

I picked it up, flicking the screen open. It was Tom. How strange. Without opening the message, it showed just a question mark. Nothing else, no message, no nothing, just a question mark. What did that mean? I opened the message to look at the conversation before it. There wasn't anything. Of course there wasn't... *I delete everything each time I send some-*

thing to him, so there's no message history. But what was he replying to? It didn't make sense. I hadn't left my phone; it had been by my side the whole time apart from when I was asleep.

I suddenly filled with dread. *What if Daniel sent something? What if I had spoken in my sleep and Daniel heard the whole thing? Did he send a message to Tom?* I had no way of finding out. If I messaged Tom to find out, then it opened our discussion all over again and I didn't want that. It seemed odd that this appeared straight after I had been dreaming about him.

I stood there for a moment, pondering what to do. I hit the delete button and erased his question mark. I stared into the phone, not moving a muscle till Jack came running into the room.

'Come on, Mummy. I'm ready in less than five minutes like you told me to be. Let's go to the park.' His cute little face beamed up at me and he was trying to pull my hand so we could go to the park. I flipped the phone shut and threw it onto the bed.

'Okay, sweetie. Let me have a quick shower and I'm good to go,' I said as I made my way to the bathroom. It gave me fifteen minutes to think about everything. The secret, the feelings about Tom... I needed to tell someone, if I didn't, I may blow.

Sasha was my closest friend outside of George and, of course, Daniel, but was she so close to home that I could trust her with such a secret? It worried me that she may say something to Scott and him to Daniel. I couldn't take that risk, so I had to take this secret to the grave.

Sasha lived over the road from us and I had often seen her when out walking Harry. She commented a couple of times on how beautiful a dog he was. We instantly hit it off, so did Daniel and her boyfriend, Scott. They would regularly pop over to ours for a drink or something to eat and us to them.

I had only known her for a few years, but I felt like I had known her forever.

3

CLIMBING THE LADDER

W ork was going well. My new manager, Dave, was brilliant to work for. He was motivational, positive thinking and had a wealth of experience. All his team members loved working for him. For the first time in my life, I was excelling in my career.

This was also the first time that I started to get a taste for money, and I mean money that made a difference to the way we were living as a family. Each month used to be a balancing act—what bill did we pay first and how much. Clothes were limited to when we needed something new rather than looking at something we liked and buying it. Even Jack had to wait until he no longer fitted something rather than getting him something because it would look cute on him.

I was confident, sassy and outspoken. I made my career plans known to my manager, and exactly which direction I wanted to go in, and that was up.

Every month I had a target of profit that I needed to make the company. The more margin I added to a quote for a customer, the more I got paid. I was given key performance indicators, including how many cold calls I had to make and how many orders I received but that was the easy part for me. I knew full well that the harder I worked and the more effort I put in, the better my commission was at the end of the month.

Slowly but surely, we were up to date with our finances. We had a little leftover at the end of the month, which went towards activities for us as a family; holidays, weekends away, going to the cinema, more toys for Jack and even childcare so that we didn't have to keep leaving work early. It gave us a huge feeling of success and a buzz of adrenaline.

The one thing I never anticipated or expected was that the more money you earned, the more you wanted and there was a big hunger deep inside me that had been unleashed to go further and further each time. Every month I wanted to do better and better, to be the top salesperson, to accelerate more than I had ever done before. At work, it was all I could think about. Above all else, I wanted both Daniel and Jack to look at me and be proud. I wanted my friends to look at me and say, 'She works so hard, she deserves that.'

Or so I thought...

Every week on a Friday morning, I had a review with Dave. 10 am on the dot, I would hear him shout my name out like a queue in the doctor's surgery. He took thirty minutes with each of us in the team in turn. Dave would sit us down, ask how our week had gone, what was good, what was bad and how we could improve the following week. He finished with any questions we had for him and how he could support us, ending the session with, 'Great work, off you go.' We would leave his room, head back to our desks and it was time for the next person. Dave had management off to a fine art, and he knew all of us individually so well.

This week was no different. It was the first week of the month and I had smashed the previous one by 150%, so I knew my review was going to be good. He would be singing my praises for smashing my target and the last six months consecutively. It ticked 09.50 am on my watch, so I headed down to the ladies, went to the toilet, freshened up, straightened my hair and then headed back upstairs to grab my notepad, pen and phone. By this time, it was 09.56 am and I had four minutes to spare. He was as punctual as an army sergeant. Even though I hated being late, I had an uncanny knack of never arriving on time—it ranged from minutes to half an hour sometimes. Fashionably late I think they call it.

This time though, I heard shouting, raised voices and the slamming of fists on his desk. The rest of us in the office looked around at each other in surprise—Dave never raised his voice.

Our office was open plan, there were about sixty desks in total and the hustle and bustle of salespeople making calls, tapping away on their keyboards and pacing up and down created such a lively atmosphere that it made you want to be busy just to fit in. There was a large frame at one end of the office, which hung a heavy, gold gong. A hook on the wall next to it hung a mallet that was used to strike it when a deal was closed. It created a behaviour that praised success and a hunger for deals.

The high volume of their bellowing voices carried through the office as all of us sat in silence, wondering what was happening inside those four walls with Dave and Matt—one of our senior sales colleagues.

'Screw you and screw your job!' Matt shouted out. We could all hear it as clear as anything. The look of shock and gasps on everyone's faces, even though we tried to make out that we weren't listening.

There was an exchange of words from Dave that we couldn't quite hear in retaliation, then the door flung open. Keeping his head down and not looking anyone else in the eye, Matt continued to make his way out of the office and into the hallway. I'm guessing he also left the building as he didn't return.

Brilliant, I thought to myself. *I'm next up and Dave is not going to be impressed after the tension between the two of them. Should I give him time to calm down?*

It was now dead on the hour. *Make a decision quickly, Rose,* I thought.

'Rose!' Dave shouted out with regimented precision before it changed to 10.01 am.

I guess he didn't want time to calm down. It was the second time that I had felt nervous entering his office—the first time was my interview. I grabbed my things and walked confidently into the room, closing the door behind me and sitting on the chair across the desk from him.

'Morning, Rose, let's hope that our thirty minutes goes better than the last thirty wasted minutes.' He didn't look up at me, instead, he tapped away on his keyboard and looked at his screen, which I presumed had my sales figures for last month listed so we could discuss them.

'150% gross profit. 120% call volume achieved and 140% of meetings held. I'm impressed, Rose.' He sat silent for a moment, looking at me. 'Your thoughts?' He slid his glasses down his nose, folded his arms, swivelling on his chair at the same time and looked at me.

'I... um...' He caught me off guard. I didn't know what to

say, half expecting the same stern tone as he had directed at Matt before me.

'Nothing to say? Okay, again, better than the last salesperson in my office who had too much to say.' He smiled at his sarcastic comment even though I could tell he was still raging inside.

'Rose, how do you think you are progressing within the team?' His eyes still firmly fixed on mine, a bit more serious this time.

'Erm... I'm working really hard, and I like to think that I get on well with the other members of the team. I have learned an awful lot in the past six months working for you, and George always supports me.' I was hoping that was the right answer, but I couldn't disguise the nervous tone in my voice.

'I bet he does.' Dave sneered slightly. I wasn't sure what he meant by that.

'I think you are right, Rose, you are a valued member of the team, let's keep your figures going in the same direction they have been so far. Is there anything you need from me right now or anything I can help you with?' He seemed to relax, leaning back even further in his large leather chair. His arms uncrossed and instead moved both hands to clasp together, awaiting my response.

'Actually, there is, Mr Ashcroft.' I was slightly tense, but I was going to ask it anyway. *If you don't ask, you don't get, right?* I thought to myself.

'Dave.' He corrected me every time I called him Mr Ashcroft.

'Sorry, Dave.' I felt awkward calling him by his first name, it felt more personal than I wanted it to be.

'The thing is, I am doing well and hitting my targets, but I want to do better. I want to be the top salesperson here; I want to earn more commission. I'm ambitious and prepared to work for it. How do I climb the ladder?' I did the same—clasped my hands together, resting them on my lap, leaving him to answer.

He sat up in his chair. An awkward silence filled the room for a few minutes while I could clearly see him thinking about how best to answer. I wasn't wearing anything too revealing but you could see the outline of my bra through my white blouse. My tight-fitting pencil skirt had a side slit so high that it disappeared all the way up to my upper thigh.

He moved position and sat up. I began watching the direction of his stare, first at my chest and then to my side, tracing the line all the way up until his eyes returned to mine. It wasn't as if he did it secretly without me knowing. I followed his gaze and watched him process my entire body. Dave didn't seem to care that I was watching him either.

'So, you want to climb the career ladder, do you?' His hand on his chin, thinking, scratching the stubble on his face. He seemed to be planning his next few words to me like a decision in a game of chess.

'Yes, I do,' I replied. I was direct and to the point. I wanted him to think that I was confident and assertive.

'It's sometimes easier being a woman in a male-dominated industry, you know.' He smiled at me again, but I wasn't sure where this conversation was heading.

'Yes, I can appreciate that.'

'A young woman will get a better response dealing with men when it comes to information technology sales. They listen a lot more. Easier on the eyes, if you know what I mean. In fact, the men will be almost putty in your hands.' I caught him looking at my cleavage again. *What is he suggesting? Is he trying to make a move on me?* I couldn't read his body language or what he was getting at, but it made me feel slightly uneasy.

'Okay?' I waited for him to continue.

'The point I am trying to get to, Rose, is that with a little persuasion, I think you can talk most men into a sale. A young, attractive and intelligent woman like yourself. A little more work on your persuasion tactics perhaps and some more experience, but overall, I think you could be our top performer here. Where are you on Thursday evening? Can you make yourself available?' He placed his hands on the desk, switched off his computer screen, leaned forward and focused completely on my response.

I squirmed uncomfortably in my chair as if he was giving me an ultimatum. I had to make myself available, he was my manager after all, and I guess I had to do as I was told.

'I can be available. I just need to...' I replied.

He seemed to snap back into being professional again.

'Well, it looks like Matt has decided to leave the business. Stupid, I know, but that means that his clients, *our clients*, need looking after. This could be the career progression you are seeking, and I want you to meet some of them on Thursday evening for dinner. They are large, important customers for our business, so I expect you to be wearing something... well... I mean, appropriate for the evening. Perhaps something showing a little more leg or better cleavage perhaps—it may help your introduction.' His eyes turned to his phone as if he was checking something.

His suggestive words poured out of his mouth like they were a matter of fact. I hadn't acknowledged the fact that more revealing clothes were better suited to win business. Surely that was being seductive, enticing the client into spending money with you. I'm presuming that's what he

meant. I sat for a moment thinking about his recommenda-
tion. If that's what I had to do to win a deal or two, then so be
it... what harm could it do?

'Meet me at Waterloo Station, 6.30 pm on Thursday night
and I will escort you to the restaurant. There, you will greet
your new clients. I will make all the necessary formal intro-
ductions and then leave you in their capable hands. Are you
okay with this or do you want me to send the details by
email?' Dave looked up to check that I was taking it all in.

'No, it's fine, I've got that.' I wrote the information down
on my notepad.

'Right, is there anything else?' He was finished talking to
me. I could tell he was done.

'No, I think that is everything from me.' I was finished too.

'Great, then see you next week.' With that, he stood up,
prompting me to leave the room. I stood up too, turned and
went to walk out. I felt like saluting as I left but I didn't think
he would have seen the funny side.

'Rose?' he called out just before I reached the door. 'Close
the door please and tell George that I am cancelling his 10.30
am review.'

'Sure.' And with that, I closed the door and made my way
back to my desk. Dropping my book and pen back in its
place, I walked over to George.

'Hey, George. Dave just said that he is cancelling your
review this morning. He wanted me to let you know.'

'He what? He never cancels a review!' George looked
puzzled.

'Well, that's what he said. He asked me to close the door
and to tell you yours has been cancelled. Sorry.' I left George
confused and went to the ladies' toilets once again. I didn't
need to go, it was just somewhere I went when I needed five

minutes just to think, alone, out of the way of all the chaos and madness of the office.

I teetered along in my high heels, down the stairs of the building, back to the first floor and pushed the toilet door open. I always chose the third cubicle—I have no idea why, it was just my go-to. I swung the door open, closed the toilet lid and just sat down, locking it behind me.

Thinking back to what Dave had said to me. Was it my imagination or had he just asked me to wear something a little more alluring? Something to tempt our customers into placing an order with the company? I'm pretty sure he had, and I was quite sure that it was inappropriate.

Was I going to go through with it? Well, I had no choice, he was my manager. I needed my job desperately, everything counted on it—Daniel, Jack, me. He was giving me the opportunity to take on larger clients that would result in better commission, so I would need to go clothes shopping before next week.

The thing that kept banging around in my head was that I didn't see George wearing more revealing clothes and he was smashing his target, so why did I have to? They knew they could take advantage of me, of my situation, and that I needed this break so much.

I had to get on with it, talk some sense into myself and carry on.

That evening, I picked up Jack from nursery as I always did. Dave's comments were playing on my mind... I dare not say to anyone about what he had asked me to do, not even Daniel, but I planted the seed with him that I would be out with customers next Thursday night. He was fine with it; I knew he would be. The epitome of a trusting partner. Entertaining customers, wining and dining them, meetings and presentations, they were all part of my job. The more people liked you, the more they bought from you. It was how it worked. I knew that if I told Sasha, she wouldn't understand, she would be looking out for my best interests, whether it meant losing my job or not.

Thursday arrived and I was as nervous as I had been right at the start of my career, setting expectations and sometimes being a little more outgoing than perhaps I normally was. Choosing a dress was difficult. Too flirty, too revealing or not revealing enough?

I didn't want to appear too underdressed but nor did I want to seem too casual. It wasn't as if I could ask anyone either. High heels were easy, I always wore very high black patent shoes. The higher the better. As I was so short, they made my legs look longer, slimmer and more attractive. On this occasion, I thought maybe I should go for a different colour, something that would really stand out. Red, perhaps? Would they appear too slutty? They looked incredible though on my tanned, slender legs and transparent stockings.

My dress was plain black and strappy, low cleavage and short, just above my knees. Tight fitting to show off my curvy figure and accentuating my large breasts. It was smart but not too over the top. Hopefully, I got the memo right and I would impress both Dave and my clients. Finally, to complete the outfit, I chose a small clutch bag with a gold chain that hung nicely over my shoulder.

Standing in my bedroom in the middle of the afternoon while Daniel was at work, I found myself staring into the tall mirror propped up against the wall. *What a shame,* I thought to myself. I could imagine him finding me highly attractive in this. I began imagining him unzipping me, my dress dropping to the floor. Leaving me standing in just my underwear and red high-heeled stilettos. Daniel was the one I should be out to impress, not a group of strangers.

I had to get moving, I didn't want to be late. I peered out the window and the taxi I ordered was waiting patiently. I said goodbye to Harry and walked as quickly as I could in my heels to the car. It was a clear day so at least I didn't have to battle the elements.

Waiting patiently at Bracknell Station, the train to Waterloo was an hour long and was due at 5.22 pm—it would get me into Waterloo Station five minutes early at 6.25 pm, enough time if I needed a nervous toilet stop, but giving me enough time to meet Dave at 6.30 pm sharp.

My phone vibrated in my bag; I reached in to see who had messaged me. As I flipped it open, I could already see Dave A as the sender.

'ON YOUR WAY?' His typical short and sharp tone.

'YES, ETA 6.25 PM AT WATERLOO, SEE YOU THEN.'

'GREAT. I'LL BE WAITING OUTSIDE THE ENTRANCE ON THE STEPS. WE'LL GET A CAB.'

I quite liked his direct manner. No time for pleasantries, I knew where I stood with him.

'OKAY!' I responded, then flipped my phone shut and tucked it back in my bag for the journey.

The train pulled into the station; I walked as delicately as I could towards the second to last carriage. I was a creature of habit, just like the cubicle at work, I always had to sit in the same seat, same carriage and same direction—if it was free, of course. The doors beeped as they slid open, letting all the commuters disembark first, then making my way to a space next to the window so I could stare at the scenery as it passed. I enjoyed snooping into the houses that lined the tracks, their garden layouts and what I could see of their inside décor as it zoomed past.

Instantly, I could see eyes glaring at me from all directions in the reflection of the window. Most people in smart casual or just casual attire, I stuck out like a sore thumb. Uncomfortably, I tucked my breasts a little further into my revealing dress, tugging it up at the top so more flesh was covered but then also tugging at the bottom of it as I sat down so it didn't rise too high. I peeled the small bag from my shoulder and placed it on my lap so that I could fiddle with the golden chain the whole way there. There was no room for movement in this dress—beautiful but extremely uncomfortable.

There was an older gentleman—I would say late fifties, maybe early sixties—sitting opposite me and fidgeting awkwardly. First giving me a quick look, then continuing to stare out of the window. Each time I looked away, I could see him eyeing up my legs.

Stopping, pausing at my bright red, shiny shoes. They were stunning, even if I did say so myself. What was he thinking? He tried desperately to keep his eyes on the houses and buildings outside as they whizzed past, but something kept distracting and pulling his eyes back towards me.

Each time I caught him looking, he would sheepishly smile and then look away. I found myself wondering if I was asking for trouble wearing this dress on a train on my own, and again on the way home, late at night. *Am I inviting these looks from men? Is he thinking perverted thoughts?* Maybe it was an innocent distraction.

If I wanted to make a good impression, be successful and earn the amount of money that I've only ever dreamed of, then I had to put my assets to good use. He wasn't doing any harm by looking at me—it's called window shopping, right? I decided not to give a damn, concentrate on all the stations that we passed, and if people wanted to look then so be it. The train got busier and busier the closer we got to London. The seats began to fill up, shoulder to shoulder with complete strangers. So close that I could smell their personal aromas.

The train was grubby, the floor was dirty and the seats old and torn. I tried not to think about the number of bottoms that had sat on the same one I was sat on and instead to focus on why I was here in the first place. On the positive side, I was being paid to dine with customers—it wasn't all hard work, it wasn't strenuous, and after all, I had chosen this career and it had chosen me.

The final destination was close. As we approached Waterloo, the train slowed, waiting for signals to change so we could pull onto the platform. I started to shuffle in my seat, preparing myself to get ready to stand. I placed my bag back on my shoulder and checked my phone in case Dave had texted again—he hadn't.

I tried to be courteous and let most of the passengers off before me, but they insisted I went in front. Stepping off onto a busy platform, hordes of people making their way to the ticket turnstiles. Young men wolf-whistling and nudging one another as I tried to make my way through the crowds and out to the entrance at the other end of the station. It was flattering at first, but by about the tenth person, I was getting a little less tolerant.

Waterloo was a beautiful station, but I never really appreciated its beauty until I was caught waiting my turn to get through the turnstile at the end of the platform. Built in 1948, its grand Elizabethan-style architecture towered above me.

The glass ceiling and arches were incredible, food outlets and retail shops lined its foyer and the amount of people that visited it daily was staggering. I had been before as a young child and a teenager, but I had never really appreciated its grandeur until now.

I felt like a lemming, following the crowds to their next destination. The sound of so many people echoed through its expanse. I tried making my way to the main steps at the front of the building. I stood on the bottom step and strained to find Dave's familiar face. There he was standing up against the wall, talking on the phone as he was waiting for me. We both looked at each other and smiled.

As I approached Dave, he finished his conversation and slid his phone into his top inside pocket. He looked very dapper, dressed in a smart dark grey tweed jacket, white shirt, navy-blue jeans and polished brown shoes, holding out a deep red-coloured rose as if he was my date greeting me with flowers.

'Wow, look at you. Here, a rose for a beautiful Rose,' he said as he handed it to me.

It was a beautiful gesture, but I blushed from embarrassment. I was out of my comfort zone by a long mile. He was my boss and here he was offering me a kind gift.

'Why thank you,' I said and smiled nervously.

'Let's make our way to the taxi waiting area.' He led the way and I followed.

I had been to Waterloo many times but never had I sat in an official London cab. It was always by tube or walking as it was more affordable and easier.

'So, Rose, let's walk and talk,' he said, rushing me along. 'I like you... I think you are going to be a rising star in the team, but I want to get to know you a little better so I can guide you accordingly.' *Why did everything he say seem to be more like a riddle?*

I struggled to keep up with him as he tried to make conversation. Dave walked at such a pace that it was difficult to follow him in such high shoes. Experience taught me from then on to wear flat shoes to get to where I was going and then change into heels once I arrived. My toes felt like they had been squashed into a tight block like a ballerina by the time we stood in the queue for a taxi, and it was only the start of the night.

'What do you want to know?' I asked.

'So, tell me about family life, Rose. Are you in a long-term relationship? What does he do for a living, and your son, you have a little boy George tells me, is that right? It must have been hard having him so young, what with working, studying and fitting life in around everything?' He wasn't afraid to fire questions at me, one after the other, about my personal life.

'Erm... well, yes. Where do I start? My boyfriend is called Daniel. He works for a communications company during the week and then at weekends he also works for a family friend as a carpenter, so he is a very busy man. We have a little boy who is four, called Jack. He is adorable. They are both my world.' I wanted him to know how important the men in my life were. Everything I did, I did for them.

'That's lovely, they must be very proud of you,' he replied. 'And what about you?

'What about me?' I asked.

'What do you do in your spare time for you, outside of family and work? Hobbies, passions, interests, etc. There must be something you love doing? Tell me an interesting fact about you, Rose.' He asked a lot about me, but I knew nothing about him.

'Oh, I don't really have any hobbies. I don't have time.' I never really thought about myself in that way before. Daniel and I had committed every minute of our spare time together to make the most of Jack and had been busy working on the house, so we didn't have time for anything else. Besides, we never had the money to do anything else. Having a hobby would be a luxury.

Dave seemed to glance at me as if he didn't know what to say next.

'How about you, are you married? Children?' I felt cheeky asking but I wanted to know more about him as a person too. I didn't have a lot in common with him as he was more my dad's age.

'I was married but that didn't work out. She was the love of my life. I thought we were going to grow old together. Turned out all she wanted me for was my money and she took every penny she could when we got divorced. I've never found someone special since. I don't have children... I'm too selfish, so golf is my thing.' He shut me down. That was all he was going to tell me. I didn't know what to ask next and I'm not sure he wanted me to delve deeper into his personal life, so I left it there.

We eventually made it to the front of the queue. He told the cab driver where we wanted to go and we got in. Trying to be elegant, I climbed into the back, manoeuvring myself into the seat without my dress riding up, and crossed my legs. Dave sat down next to me; a lot closer than I would have liked, so I kept looking straight ahead. I wasn't the biggest fan of people invading my personal space, but again, as he was my boss and there was limited room, I didn't say a word. He placed his hand on the seat between us but accidentally brushed his palm across my thigh.

'Oh, I'm sorry, I do apologise, I thought there was more room than there is.' He sniggered quietly like a nervous schoolboy on a bus. I laughed too as I thought it was an innocent mistake, but it wasn't.

'You do have such soft and smooth legs though.' He brushed his hand back over my thigh, deliberately this time. I didn't know how to react. *Is he testing my patience or my reaction towards him?* Instead, I looked out the window and kept quiet. It was awkwardly silent, even the taxi driver didn't say a word.

The sky over London started changing from bright to dusk. Evening was drawing in as I soaked up the sights and lights of such a beautiful city.

In less than ten minutes, we arrived at the restaurant. He leaned over and paid the driver through the glass hatch that was there to separate us from the driver, so close that I could smell his expensive aftershave. Dave opened the door and then stood there with his hand out, offering to help me to my feet. I took his hand, noticing how hard and warm it was as he gently guided me to the pavement. I could see him look at my shoes first, then he took a long, paused look at my legs as they extended out of the door.

Again, I said nothing except thank you as he let my hand go and slammed the door shut. His eyes wandered up to the rest of my body, moving to my chest and settling on my eyes. We stood there for a brief second, looking at each other until I broke the stare, coughing and pretending to shuffle around for something in my bag. Dave suddenly snapped out of his trance.

'Okay, our clients are seated. Don't worry about saying too much, I will do most of the talking and you can listen and learn. The next time you meet them, you will be on your own. Understand?' His instructions were clear and concise—watch, listen and take note.

I nodded to confirm I understood. 'Uh-huh,' I said, feeling like it was another of his military operations, timings with precision and actions with strict instructions. It didn't sound too difficult. Sit pretty and only speak when spoken to.

I didn't need to do anything except follow him. Walking up the large stone steps to the main glass doors, he pulled the long vertical steel handle with ease and held it open for me to enter first. He spoke to the doorman, confirming the booking and arrangements. A group of five men were already seated, waiting for us and chatting amongst themselves. I smiled while waiting to be seated but I stayed quiet for fear of saying the wrong thing.

The restaurant was stunning—the most expensive looking one I had ever been to. Taking it in my stride, I looked around the room and made a note of all the women there and what they were wearing, their shoes, hairstyles, makeup, as well as their actions. To be fair, it was mainly men, but the women that were there sat with napkins on their laps, legs crossed, very elegant in demeanour. I noticed how all of them were laughing, but very few were talking.

There was a faint sound of music playing in the background as if someone was playing a piano in the corner of the room. A large, glass-walled bar stood at the back of the room filled with every drink bottle you could think of. The lights were dimmed but the flicker of flames from candles on every table created a pretty backdrop. The bartenders and restaurant staff were smartly dressed in fitted black dinner jackets, white shirts, black bowties and smart black trousers with shiny, polished, dark shoes.

Glass paintings hung on the walls along with sculptures

on pillars in sporadic places. About twenty round tables were dressed in glasses, plates and more knives and forks than I thought possible. I knew what cutlery to use and when for fine dining as my dad had taught me, but I was conscious that I didn't want to make a spectacle of myself or get it wrong. I suddenly felt like a fish out of water, out of my comfort zone, but it was time to learn.

Pay attention, Rose, I thought to myself. *Tonight, could either make or break my career and I have to be appreciative of Dave for giving me this opportunity.*

The head waiter approached us. 'Can I take any coats, bags or accessories and place them in the cloakroom for you?' he asked.

'No, I think we are all good thank you,' Dave answered for us both as if I had no tongue to speak.

'Excellent, in that case, I will show you to your seats.' He waved his arm in the direction of the table and led the way, allowing us to follow him. Even his hair was immaculately groomed, gelled and held in place. His neat moustache was trimmed just above his lip, and as he smiled, he showed a beautiful set of white, straight teeth.

Stopping just before the table, our guests began to stand as they noticed us approaching. In turn, Dave shook each one of the men's hands as he said their names out aloud. Brian, Adam, another Dave, James and Steve, I had to remember each of them throughout the night. As Dave walked around the table, I too went to shake their hands, but Brian, who was first to hold my hand, pulled me towards him.

He leaned forward and air-kissed the left side of my cheek, he shifted back and proceeded to air-kiss the right side. *What was that all about?* I thought to myself. I was expecting a handshake and instead got kissed twice. I moved towards Adam, doing the same again, two air-kisses as a greeting while he held my hand, so did Dave, James and Steve. Lesson number one learned—reach in and air-kiss in the future, that was the posh way.

So, with the greetings out of the way. Dave took a seat and I followed, sitting down on the chair to his right-hand side, Steve on my other side. I twisted, placing my bag on the back of my chair.

'No, no, sweetheart, place it under your chair, you never know who will whisk your bag off while you aren't looking,' Steve said, placing his hand on my shoulder to get my attention. I took his advice and tucked it under the tablecloth and held it tight between my elegant heels. I'm quite sure that no one in this restaurant would want my bag, or the contents of it for that matter. Looking around the room, even the women's dresses looked more expensive than my bag, but I took his advice anyway.

'Some champagne for you all?' the waiter asked before he left, almost bending over and curtseying.

'Yes, a couple of bottles of Laurent-Perrier, please?' Dave requested and then turned to our guests, ignoring the waiter.

'Gentlemen, firstly, apologies that Matt isn't here with you today, but I wanted to introduce Rose to you in his place. She will be looking after you from now on and is more than capable of dealing with all your requirements.' He turned to me and smiled.

I felt slightly uncomfortable with the way he introduced me but perhaps I was reading way too much into the situation. I sounded more like a hooker than a professional, but once again, I listened, nodded and smiled. Agreeing to everything that Dave said like a puppet on a string.

The waiter returned with his colleague and three large

silver buckets filled with ice and a bottle in each. He placed a stand sporadically around our circular table and stood the buckets on top. He returned with seven champagne flutes, starting first with Dave as chief organiser, pouring the smallest amount into his flute and handing it to him so he could be the first to savour the taste. Dave swirled his glass, took the smallest of sips, and finished it, placing it back on the table.

'Lovely, thank you, please carry on.' He nodded at the waiter to continue filling all our glasses, this time, just over halfway but not to the brim. Once they had all been filled, Dave raised his glass towards the middle of the table.

'To Rose.' One by one, they all raised a glass to me and so I followed. I wasn't sure why they were toasting to me, but I went with it. *No pressure,* I thought to myself as we all took a sip and placed them back on the table.

After my introduction, the conversation changed to general account discussions. Dave asked the clients what their plans were for the year, what they were looking for, what new investments they were looking to make in information technology and how the business could help them. There was a small amount of general chit-chat around golf and families, but it soon returned to Dave asking questions about their business and the roles they had in facilitating certain functions.

I learned a great deal, but I also had a lot to learn about business meetings. I wasn't familiar with finance, operations and infrastructures, or to some degree, the technology, but it would be something I would have to learn to work my way up in this industry.

All the men were polite and courteous. In fact, they were more than accommodating and always offered for me to go first at everything, from eating to drinking and choosing menus, treating me like a well-respected lady. It was a pleasant dinner with fine company, one that I could quite happily attend time and time again.

The time had whizzed by, and before I knew it, they were all wrapping up their conversations. One by one, they apologised that they needed to leave to start their journeys back home. They thanked Dave for organising and said how lovely it was to meet me, commenting on how they were looking forward to working with me in the future. It seemed to have gone so well.

Dave settled the bill and we started to get ready to leave the restaurant. To my surprise, another taxi was waiting outside the restaurant to take us back to Waterloo. I did the same as I had before, climbed into the backseat, this time with a stomach full of a five-course meal and several glasses of champagne.

The time had passed so quickly that I felt guilty I hadn't checked in with Daniel or said goodnight to my baby boy, Jack.

'Did you enjoy that?' Dave asked as the taxi pulled away.

'I did, it was lovely. Thank you for organising everything and giving me the opportunity of working with them.' I smiled pleasantly at him.

'Oh, you're welcome. You did well and you looked incredible by the way. I think they are going to like you.'

I blushed from such a compliment.

As I opened my bag to reach for my phone, I felt something warm run up my thigh and up in between my legs. I stopped in my tracks and looked up at Dave. He didn't smile, he didn't move a facial muscle, just locked his eyes on mine. His warm but firm hand was touching me.

'Oh, I'm sorry, I didn't mean to startle you.' But instead of stopping and noticing my reaction, he continued, reaching forward to try and kiss me. I pulled back until my head was against the headrest, but he kept moving forwards until his lips met mine. I didn't stop him, but I also didn't kiss him back, it was a motionless touch of lips. I closed my eyes, hoping that it would go away and he would get the hint. Dave realised that I wasn't enjoying it or responding. I lifted my hand against his chest to stop him, he looked at me confused, backing away. Yes, I had been treated like a lady, wined and dined but this didn't give him the green light to do whatever he wanted to me.

'Is this not what you want? I take it you don't want career progression then? You know I can only take you so far, but after that, it will be up to you and how hard you want it. Rose, you will need to make sacrifices if you know what I mean.' He raised his eyebrows as he spoke as if it was a statement rather than an option.

'It's not that... it's... of course I want career progression but...' I stopped. What could I say to that? I didn't want to offend him, but this was not what I signed up for. Yes, I wanted a successful career, but if that's what I had to do to get there then it wasn't for me. I didn't see George kissing his manager or his clients, why was it okay for me to?

'Well, you know that your customers are going to be expecting the same... you don't get anything for free in this line of work,' he stated in an almost matter-of-fact tone.

'I'm appreciative, I really am, but I have a boyfriend. I can't be doing this sort of thing,' I tried explaining but it seemed to fall on deaf ears.

'He will never know.' I felt like Dave had an answer for everything and he wasn't interested in listening.

Just as he said that, the taxi arrived outside Waterloo Station.

'That'll be £12.50 please,' the driver requested. 'You okay, Madam?' he asked me, he must have seen what was happening in the rear-view mirror, but before I could respond, Dave answered for me.

'She's okay. Is cash alright?' Dave rudely asked.

'Good with me.' He gave me a wink as he turned around to face us.

They exchanged the money. Just as before, Dave got up, stood on the pavement and offered me his hand. It was as if the conversation hadn't happened. The champagne had got the better of me and I tripped, trying to get myself out of the taxi and landed in a ball at his feet. He sniggered in a playful way but helped me to my feet.

'There you were saying that you have a boyfriend a few minutes ago, and now, here you are on your knees before me. Are you okay getting a train by yourself or do you need to stay over?' he asked.

'I think I can manage, thank you,' I said, straightening my dress, standing up, embarrassed and feeling ashamed of myself.

This time, he kissed me on the cheek, handed me back the rose that he had given me earlier in the night and said in a quiet voice, 'The pleasure was all mine.'

I watched Dave turn and walk towards the platform to get his train home. I stood for a moment, taking in everything that had happened. From the comments last week about revealing clothes to his suggestions at dinner and then the cab drive home. I didn't know how to feel about the whole thing.

Why did every man I had ever met have an ulterior

motive—except my dad and Daniel, of course? Was it me, was I teasing men? The way I looked, the clothes I wore, my attitude?

As soon as he was out of sight, I threw the rose into the first bin I could find.

Was I getting myself into something that I would later regret? What did he mean by having to make sacrifices?

4

AN UNWELCOME LETTER

It was a normal day at work the following week. I took Jack to nursery by taking the local bus. Leaving behind his beautiful, beaming smile and chirpiness and arriving at the top of the road to walk to the office.

I did everything as I usually would... you could predict my actions to precision. Walking the same route, saying good morning to the girls at reception, going to the ladies—the same cubicle, of course—and then sitting at my desk in the corner of the office. I turned on my screen and whilst waiting for it to load, I made my way to the kitchen to make myself a cup of tea. Stirring it five times clockwise, sitting back at my desk and holding it with both hands, blowing the steam to cool it down.

The entire office was in the kitchen every morning. It was a pleasant way to start the day and for us all to catch up with one another, making a brew and planning the busy day ahead. The usual jokers chatting as loud as they possibly could, the quiet ones waiting to one side until the others had finished.

You could tell which ones weren't morning people... I was one of them, I couldn't fully function until at least 10 am, but by then, I was on fire and carrying out tasks at a million miles an hour.

The sound of phones ringing out across the expanse of the office were ignored. If we didn't answer, they went to voicemail. As soon as we returned to our desks, there would be red flashing lights on the handsets that we would need to listen and respond to. Until then, the ringing sounds were buzzing away in the background as we caught up with the office gossip and pleasantries.

It was a great time to be in sales, you couldn't trust any of your colleagues as they were hungry for business and were so focused on hitting their targets, but overall, they were lovely people—they had to be, it was in their nature to please others and their job was to be liked. Vibrant, happy and outgoing people. In many ways, it felt like school, but you didn't get told off every five minutes and had the freedom to roam around and do what you liked, when you liked, as long as you were hitting your number.

Back at my desk, the home screen of my computer was asking me to log in and the desk phone flashing with voicemails. I moved all my papers over to my inbox and tapped away to start. I picked up the first couple of voicemails, jotted down their numbers to call them back, but just as I was scribbling away, I could see Sophie from reception making her way over to me.

'Morning, Rose, this letter came for you yesterday but, for some reason, it got left in the post room and I didn't have a chance to give it to you. I'm so sorry, I hope it wasn't urgent.' She smiled and placed it on the corner of my desk.

'Hey, no worries. Thanks for bringing it up,' I said, confused as I rarely received post.

With the phone handset balanced between my shoulder and my chin, I started to tear the corner of the envelope to open it. How strange, the letter was handwritten, and I didn't recognise the writing. No stamp so it must have been hand-delivered rather than posted.

Inside was a folded A4 piece of paper—again, hand-written but in capitals:

FANCY DRINKS AND FANCY DINNERS. DOES DANIEL KNOW WHAT YOU ARE UP TO?

I stopped reading and looked around the office. *Who is this from?* I expected it to be a prank, but no one was looking in my direction. I continued reading.

BE CAREFUL WHAT YOU WISH FOR, A DREAM CAN BECOME A NIGHTMARE AND YOU WILL LOSE WHAT YOU HAVE...

It took me a moment to take in what it said. I looked up around the office again.

Everyone was going about their day, not a single person watching for my reaction. My heart began to pound. For some reason, this letter had shaken me. I sank back into my chair. Was someone jealous that I had gone for dinner with Dave and taken on Matt's accounts? But wait a minute... I had worked hard and deserved that opportunity.

I looked at the letter again, flipping the page over to view the back. It was blank. I flipped it back to the front again and re-read the words. It wasn't signed by anyone, nor was it addressed to me at the top. Just the cover of the envelope.

I was half thinking that it was George playing games with me, but he was my biggest supporter... surely he wouldn't do something like this. *Who else could it be?* It definitely wasn't

Dave. Someone would also have had to know where I worked and who Daniel was. I sat staring at the screen, completely mesmerised by what I had just received.

If someone was trying to scare me, they were doing a pretty good job of it. It wasn't quite a death threat, but I found it threatening and intimidating all the same. What did they mean by 'You will lose what you have'?

'Hey, dreamer!' George startled me and I instantly turned to find him standing by my desk.

'Very funny,' I joked with him, expecting him to own up.

'Very funny what? You were staring at your screen. Hungover, are we?' he joked back.

'Erm, no, I didn't drink last night. Was it you?' I asked.

'Was what me?' He looked puzzled. I could talk to him about most things, but if it wasn't George, who else could it be?

'The letter... was it you? If it was, it's not funny,' I asked him again, but he still looked puzzled.

'Rose, I have no idea what you're talking about. What letter?' He leaned against my desk with his hand on his hip, waiting for me to explain.

'Shhh... keep your voice down. I don't want the whole office knowing, but look, I got this in the post this morning,' I whispered, handing the letter to him. It took him a few moments to read the words, he flicked the paper in his hand to check the back of the page, just as I had done, and frowned.

'Hey, Rose, you know I jest with you at times, but this was definitely not me and I was the one that suggested to Dave that you should pick up those accounts before they even had the argument as Matt wasn't doing anything with them, so why the hell would I send that? It makes no sense?' George reached across my desk to pick up the envelope, studying the handwriting.

'Plus, I don't write like that, it looks like a child has written it.' He placed them back down on my desk and seemed offended that the thought of it being him had even crossed my mind.

'Hmmm, then who the hell did?' I had a bad feeling in my stomach. Someone was intentionally trying to scare me.

'Look, don't let it worry you. Probably someone jealous of your hard work. Screw it up and put it in the bin.' He picked up the wastepaper bin beside my desk and held it in front of me. 'Besides, I wouldn't let anyone harm you.'

'Yeah, I know.' I nodded in agreement with him, but it still worried me. *Was there anyone that I had upset, other than Jim?* I couldn't think of a single person that would want to threaten me.

'Anyway, I came over to ask what you were doing for lunch today. I fancy a trip to the pub. Only one drink, of course, so if you want to join a few of us, we are leaving at 12.30-ish.' He winked at me and walked back to his desk.

George was like an older brother to me, but I always still checked out his bottom in his tight work trousers and wondered if I would ever sleep with him.

'I know you are checking me out, Rose,' he shouted back at the top of his voice so everyone in the office looked at me. He laughed out loud, returning his look to me quickly, just to make sure I was embarrassed. I was—my face had flushed bright red and I shook my head. He was the office joker, and nine times out of ten, the joke was on me, but I think I loved him more for it. I laughed; the rest of the office laughed with me as he sat back at his desk. The office would be a very dull place if it wasn't for George.

Instead of screwing up the letter, I put it back in its envelope and tucked it back into my desk drawer, underneath all the other things I had in there, and kicked the wastepaper bin back underneath.

Now let's get on with the day, Rose, I said to myself, trying to forget the letter and the effect it had on me.

Apart from lunch, the day was busy. I had quotes coming out of my ears, the phone hadn't stopped ringing and my inbox was piled high with price requests. It was good in a way because I knew the more quotes that went out, the more orders I hoped to get, and that meant one thing... more money in my bank.

My mobile phone buzzed on my desk. It was Daniel, I flipped it open to read his message:

'SORRY BABES, HAVE TO WORK LATE TONIGHT, DON'T WORRY ABOUT DINNER. LOVE YOU. D X'

I sighed in disappointment; I hated it when he worked late, but equally, he hated it when I did.

'OKAY HONEY, SEE YOU LATER. R X.' I replied to him and flipped my phone closed.

Daniel was such a hard worker, ever since the day when we found out we were having Jack, he had worked six or even seven days a week. He hated working in an office, he was too practically skilled and smart to be working behind a desk, but it was where the money was and he did it for us. He did it for our family and I couldn't fault him one little bit. He doted on me and our little boy.

There were so many things whirring around in my mind that made me question what we were doing. By having a career, it was distracting me from home life. *Should I be the housewife who waits hand and foot on her partner and the stay-at-home mum for Jack so that I wouldn't miss his every milestone?*

If I was, we wouldn't have the money to be able to pay bills or do the things we wanted to, so it was a constant balancing act between work and home life.

It made me think about the letter and question it all. *Am I jeopardising things with Daniel?* Whoever wrote that letter was right, but they had to know me or us to write that. Daniel wouldn't be happy that I was wining and dining with other men and he most definitely wouldn't be happy about Dave trying to kiss me or touch me in the back of the taxi. It was lie after little white lie that I had to keep hidden to save our relationship, but at what cost if he were to find out? The person who wrote that letter was close to me. From now on, I couldn't trust anyone.

I finished up the day absolutely shattered. I packed away the quotes I hadn't managed to get through into my inbox and switched off my computer. I pushed my chair under my desk, collected my bag and began to walk out, waving goodbye to those still working away at their desks.

There was a small walkway between our building and the bus stop, so sometimes if I was in a hurry, I would take that route rather than through the front main entrance. The back exit was a bit quieter, it was dark, no lighting, the door was underneath the building and opened out onto a path with hedges on both sides. It was completely concealed but it had never bothered me before.

I slammed closed the back exit door from the building and checked my phone as I walked—no messages and no missed calls, but before I went to flip it closed, I felt something behind me. I turned suddenly but couldn't see anything. The gentle spit of rain as it fell was dropping onto my hair and face. I rummaged around in my bag for my keys, trying to tuck my door key between my fingers for security, but before I could reach them, there it was again, a shuffling noise from behind me. I looked back. This time, the shadow of a man appeared along the alleyway beside the building.

I couldn't make out his face as he had a dark hoodie pulled right up and over his face. Dressed all in black from head to toe, he moved against the wall and stopped, still. Thinking it was a co-worker, I carried on walking but something didn't feel right, and he was rapidly getting closer. I turned again, he stopped a second time, playing a game of musical statues... why didn't he just keep walking instead of stopping? I didn't know whether to run or to call someone, my heart pumping like it was earlier when I got the letter. He stood still, motionless, quite tall, but I still couldn't make out his face, it was just too dark.

I pretended to call someone, hoping that it would scare him away, but as I looked at my phone, pretending to press the wet keys, I looked back up and he had gone. *Gone where?* You needed a pass to get access to the building. There were no side alleyways or places he could hide; the only way would have been to pass me. I picked up the pace to the well-lit bus stop, shaking and with such speed, I joined the others standing in line, waiting for the next bus to arrive.

I had clearly watched too many horror movies as I was expecting a mass murderer to be following me, getting the same bus as me and ready to raise a hammer to my head or to suffocate me. When I reassured myself that everything was clear, I stood patiently waiting with the others. Was I thinking too much into it? First, the letter this morning, then this strange guy in the alleyway... what was going on? I couldn't tell Daniel, no matter how much I wanted to. He would ask too many questions about what the letter said and that would open a whole can of worms. George was the only one who knew.

As soon as I arrived at the nursery, Jack's little face was peering through the glass pane in the door, making me forget about all the dramas of the day. His innocent, happy-go-lucky personality was all I needed right now. He only had a few months left of nursery and he would be going to start his first year at big school. How on earth had that happened? My once tiny little baby, cuddled and wrapped up in my arms, now had his own little character. He was perfect in every little way possible.

Every day, I felt guilty that I wasn't spending the time with him like the stay-at-home mum I should be or wanted to be, but the hours we spent together, between me picking him up and going to bed, were so precious. I wasn't eager for him to go to bed, we didn't argue, we didn't get fed up with each other's company, it was three to four hours every day of just quality, him and me time.

His nose was pushed against the glass and the steam of his breath was clouding the window like a caged puppy. He smudged it away a couple of times before his teacher unlocked the door, setting him free.

'Afternoon, Rose. Good day at work?' his nursery teacher asked. Lucy was a small 5ft, 4in (I was guessing), petite young lady. Very pretty, brown hair, brown eyes and the sweetest person with children. Jack absolutely adored her, but he also had her wrapped around his little finger.

'Ugh, a day at work... not necessarily good, but thank you for asking, how was yours? How has he been?' I continued the conversation despite being shaken up.

'Same as always, an absolute dream to look after.' She

smiled down at Jack and ruffled his hair. He jumped through the door, ran at me, wanting a big hug.

'Hello, gorgeous.' I bent down to his height. 'I'm thinking fish fingers, potato waffles and baked beans for dinner, or would you prefer roast chicken and cabbage? Daddy is working late so it's just us, baby.' I knew what the answer was, but I wanted him to choose.

'Fish with fingers.' Jack tugged at my hand to leave. We both laughed and said goodbye as we left.

As we finally arrived home, Harry's reflection in the front door was a silhouette of a barking dog. I struggled to open the door as he was too busy jumping up with excitement for us to get in.

'Okay, okay, okay. It's lovely to see you too,' I called out to him to let us through the door.

Poor Jack was only a little taller than Harry, so he got the full brunt of his slobbery kisses as he greeted us. Jack just giggled and firmly pushed him away.

'Right, let's get Harry fed and then I can start on cooking our dinner. Film on the sofa before bath and bed me thinks, I...' I paused whilst I was rushing round the kitchen doing a few things. As I looked at Jack, he had a letter in his hand. I noticed the handwriting on the front of it. I stopped instantly and froze.

'Sweetie, where did you get that from?' I asked, reaching towards him to get the letter.

'It was by the door, Mummy.' He smiled and handed it to me before taking off his shoes and placing his rucksack on the stairs.

I held it in my hands, paralysed and unable to move. There it was again... the same type of envelope, the same style handwriting as the letter I had received today at work. It had a stamp on it, so it hadn't been hand-delivered but it had my full name and address and the same childish font (as George had called it). Whoever sent the one to work also had my home address.

'Sweetheart, would you mind getting changed for me while Mummy quickly does something, please? Pop your pyjamas on and grab your favourite book from your room.' As he ran off up the stairs to do as he was told, I quickly tore the envelope open. Shaking with dread, I found the same again—an A4 piece of paper and the words just as I had received it at work.

FANCY DRINKS AND FANCY DINNERS. DOES DANIEL KNOW WHAT YOU ARE UP TO?

BE CAREFUL WHAT YOU WISH FOR, A DREAM CAN BECOME A NIGHTMARE AND YOU WILL LOSE WHAT YOU HAVE...

Now I was scared, really scared. Imagine if Daniel had been home first and asked what this was all about. What did it even mean? Was someone trying to scare me or just warn me? Was it the same man that was in the alleyway today? The first person that sprung to mind was Jim. Was he back? What did he want? What did he care if I lost everything anyway, he was the one trying to take everything from me all those years ago. I hadn't seen or heard from him since the last incident. I had the same creepy feeling that I felt all those years ago. Was he back? Had he found our new address and was trying to blackmail me? I didn't feel safe in my own home.

Maybe I should get Sasha over. She would know what to do and keep us company.

Jack returned, bouncing down the stairs, his navy pyjamas scattered with little red racing cars. I quickly folded up the paper, threw it in the envelope and stuffed it in my handbag in a panic.

'Well done, little man, that was super, super quick! You are such a good boy. Let's give Harry his dinner and take him for a quick walk before our dinner, shall we? Then we can read your book on the sofa together.' He nodded, picking up Harry's silver bowl from the floor to help me.

We fed Harry, and as always, he finished his dinner like a hoover sucking up dust. He ran towards the door and waited patiently. Even if I said it quietly, he knew the word 'walk' instantly. Jack wasn't the slightest bit bothered that he was in his pyjamas to go walking, in fact, he complemented his outfit with bright red wellies and a thick winter coat to keep warm.

Trying to get Harry on his lead was always troublesome, he would dart all over the place in excitement but, finally, with Jack's hand in mine, we closed the door behind us and set off on a quick walk around the block to let him stretch his legs and go to the toilet. It wasn't fair on him being cooped up all day. We did take it in turns to come home at lunch and our neighbours popped in frequently to let him out for a small fee, but it wasn't the same as a good walk with us. Jack was talking away to me about what he did at nursery during the day and the conversations he had with his friends as we passed Sasha's kitchen window. She saw us walk past and waved at us, but she seemed busy cooking dinner, so we didn't stop.

Struggling to concentrate on what Jack had to say about his day, I nodded occasionally and showed interest, but I couldn't help but worry if we were being followed or watched or if someone would suddenly jump out on us. My priority was making sure we were safe.

Once again, I felt like I was trapped somewhere with

someone trying to stalk me, just like Jim had made me feel, and here it was happening all over again. This time, I couldn't escape to my parents' house with security and comfort. I was too scared to mention it to Daniel for fear that he would think I was overreacting again, so I had to shut it down and try not to think about it.

It was more difficult than I thought. Every person I passed on the way during our walk, I thought to myself, *Could it be them?* I began trying to sift through all the people I knew and see whether it could be them. Narrowing down their likeliness like suspects in a murder enquiry. *Who knows both my addresses and why have they gone to the trouble of handwriting a letter and posting it to me? Why not say it to my face? They clearly don't want to share their identity.*

At this precise moment, I had to get through the rest of the day. Get Jack his dinner and spend some time with him. Daniel would be home soon and then tomorrow is another day. A fresh start, forget all about what happened today and hope that the letter was just a warning and would go away.

We sat down at the table with our favourite meal together, the television blaring out in the background, Harry sitting patiently by our side in case any small amount of food was dropped or being offered.

He said he wasn't, but I knew Jack was tired. His eyelids were heavy and he let out yawn after yawn.

'Have you had a busy day?' I asked. His mouthfuls of dinner had got slower and slower, and his chewing was almost non-existent. 'Shall we move to the sofa?'

He didn't say anything, he just looked at me and nodded with his lovely green eyes that matched mine. He was born with the most beautiful sparkly blue eyes like the Mediterranean Sea, but as he got older, around six to seven months old, they gradually turned from a mixture of blue and green to their current colour—emerald. They twinkled at me sleepily.

I took his plate out to the side, grabbed his small blanket from the downstairs toilet where it had been folded up and put away in the shelving, and led him to the sofa. The best feeling in the world was cuddling up after a hard day's work and him snuggling into the gap by my side. There would be a time when he would no longer want to do this, but up until then, I would enjoy the moment as much as I could.

I tried to read him his favourite book by Julia Donaldson, but his eyes got heavier and heavier and I watched him drift off. We only made it to page four, but I didn't care, I watched his perfect little face snore as he sunk into a deep sleep, his head resting on my side.

The following morning, I was nervous going to work. *Will that same man be lingering around? Will I get more letters?* I thought to myself. Getting off the bus and walking down the road, I felt bullish. I would walk down that same alleyway and confront him. I wasn't scared this time and I wouldn't let him bully me. I would ask him what he wanted, what the letters were all about and how he knew where I lived and where I worked. I threw my bag over my shoulder, my house keys wedged between my fingers so that if he did approach me, I had a weapon.

Step after step, I got closer to work's entrance, my heart racing. I could feel my whole body heating up ready for action. It felt dark, even though it was morning. The alleyway seemed closer than it was the day before and appeared to be closing in on me.

I stopped, I waited, looking all around for him to appear, then out of the corner of my eye, I saw something in the distance. There he was—he must have been stalking me to know I was going to be here at that time. Lurking in the shadows of the building like a sick animal waiting to pounce on me, I edged towards him. He did the same, getting closer and closer. I felt like running but my feet wouldn't move. I wanted to scream but no sound came out. I stood there motionless, weak and unable to do anything. He was tall, a big burly man, big feet. I could see arms within his hoodie but no hands, so I had no idea if he was holding anything.

My whole body was shaking with fear, anxious about what was to happen next. Closer and closer he slowly got to me, yet I still couldn't make out his features. His hoodie was too far over his face and too tight. My eyes strained and squinted, trying to notice something familiar about him.

Suddenly, I knew it was him. Jim was walking towards me, his face as clear as I had remembered it from before. Something shiny, glinting in light of the streetlamp as he turned it. It looked like a knife but I couldn't be sure. Why couldn't I move? Why hadn't someone come out of the office? It was always busy. Surely someone would appear, but with every step that he got closer to me, I just stood there, stuck to the pavement.

I could hear him muttering something under his breath. He seemed angry. Something white like a piece of paper was just about poking out from the pocket of his dark jeans. The letter... it was the letter he had written me. I could see the handwritten capital letters. Suddenly, he lunged towards me, his full force threw me against the wall, one arm pushing me against the cold bricks, the other around my neck. He was shouting at me, but I found it too difficult to make out the words.

'Does he know what you've been up to? Naughty girl.' His voice was deep and stern.

I was trying to struggle but he was strong, too strong for me to hold off. The fight against him seemed to be in slow motion, and as I tried to defend myself, his grip became stronger and stronger until I could wriggle no more. I looked down as he drew the knife from his sleeve and held it to my neck, the pressure felt like it was piercing my skin. I stood as still and calm as I could so he didn't draw blood. I didn't dare talk in case it made him angrier.

Tears began rolling down my face, I begged him to stop but he seemed possessed. Angry and infuriated by what I had done. I tried to move my head or my body slightly to free me, but with the cold knife blade across my neck, one wrong move and I could be dead. Visions of Jack and Daniel were flashing before me—maybe I was better off dead and I should just let him do it. I was shaking with fear. What did it matter to him what I was doing? Why was he so concerned about our business anyway? My hand was on his, trying to hold the blade away from my skin. I could feel my pulse on the cold metal. I would have done anything he told me to at this point.

Just as he went to raise his other hand, I felt something grip my shoulder and shake me. I screamed instantly.

'Rose, Rose, it's okay.' I turned my head to see Daniel standing there looking shocked. *What the hell is he doing here?* I didn't want Jim to suddenly stab Daniel, so I screamed in fear. 'No... he's...' Then I stopped.

Opening my eyes in a panic, I checked my surroundings —I had been asleep on the sofa. I sat up in a cold sweat, tears filling my eyes, shaking and unable to calm myself down. I checked around the room again, making sure I was at home and not in the alleyway. I must have fallen asleep with Jack, but it seemed so real.

'Rose, you had a nightmare. Are you okay?' Daniel said again. 'I took Jack up to bed; you were both fast asleep, but when I came back down, you looked really upset and crying out for help. What was that all about?' He sat down next to me and hugged me. It had never felt so good, thinking instantly that I may not have had the opportunity to do that again if it was real.

From the cold blade on my neck, the fear, the panic, his face and the trauma of it all, it seemed so true to life. The emotions from the day had got the better of me. Still shaken and traumatised by what had just happened, I sat still, wiping my eyes, taking a big deep breath in. I was sitting in a pool of sweat, hot and heavy breathing. *Why are my dreams so vivid and realistic, so confusing?*

I had found it difficult recently to distinguish between what was happening in my dreams and what was real life, the stresses and strains of reality playing tricks on me. Neither of which I could talk to Daniel about. It wasn't the first time that this had happened. My fantasies of Tom were realistic too.

'Do you want me to make you a drink? What were you having a nightmare about?' Daniel asked.

'Oh, nothing... just something crazy, it was stupid really.'

I felt like my dreams were trying to tell me something. Or perhaps I was going crazy, delusional perhaps. At least when I dreamed about Tom, they were nice. This one was horrific. The image of Jim up against me with a knife would be imprinted in my mind forever. I didn't want to go back to sleep for fear of dreaming it again. *What will happen tomorrow at work? Was it a sign of something about to happen to me, a premonition perhaps?*

'I'll go and get you a water.' Daniel got up and walked to the kitchen. I sat in a daze, contemplating everything.

'How was work?' I asked as he returned.

'Busy.' That was all he replied with—a man of many words.

'Oh, why did you have to work late? Did you get food?' I fired more questions at him.

As I waited for Daniel to answer, I noticed how strange I felt. My voice box squashed and painful, my neck sore and tight as if someone had been holding it for real. My throat was restricted and I couldn't breathe, I had to concentrate to calm myself down. I focused on Daniel to try to ease my dizziness.

'Uh-huh.' Daniel seemed preoccupied. *What is up with him?* It was late, maybe he was tired, but I was selfishly in too much of a confused state to read too much into what was happening in his world.

'I'm shattered, Rose, I'm going to head up to bed, are you coming?' He grabbed a glass of water for himself and made his way upstairs. Kicking off the blanket and reaching for my glass, I followed.

I couldn't wait for the comfort of lying in bed next to him, feeling the warmth of his body, and slowly but surely drifting off into hopefully a better dream than I just had. I felt safe next to him, I always had. The last thing I wanted was to hurt or lose him. *Tomorrow will be a better day.* I needed to get Jim out of my head and focus on all the positives in our lives right now. If it got too serious, I would have to call the police.

5

ANOTHER MILESTONE

Who would have thought that turning twenty-one would be so uneventful. My family were more excited than I was. In the grand scheme of things, I already had a child, bought a house with the love of my life and work was going great. Turning twenty-one just seemed to be another milestone to tick off my never-ending bucket list. I successfully made it this far without killing myself.

I didn't want to go away as I wanted to spend it with family and friends. I didn't want to be too hungover as it ruined the day after with Jack and Daniel, so I thought I would celebrate with a quiet dinner on Sunday and go out with friends on the Saturday night. One thing was certain, when I least expected things to happen, they ended up happening in a truly dramatic way. My twenty-first birthday was one that I will never forget, and for so many good reasons.

It started with a few drinks around our house with Alfie, Zoe, Sasha and Scott. Jack was with my mum and dad, and

Harry was fast asleep after a long run in the fields. Daniel cranked up the music so that the walls at home were shaking and walked into the room with a bottle of prosecco in each hand.

'Happy twenty-first, baby,' he said, smiling at me in such a doting way.

'Ahhhh.' Looking at the bottles, I ran at him, hugging him tightly in appreciation, conscious of the bottles in each of his hands so he didn't drop them. With no warning at all, I jumped up and held onto his body, my legs wrapped around his waist, my arms tightly gripping his neck and shoulders. He moved towards the kitchen so that the side could take the weight of my body and he could set the bottles down safely. He returned the hug, one hand on the back of my head, pulling it into his neck and the other right around my body. You couldn't buy a moment like this—two people who loved each other so much and felt so much for each other. I could imagine that we would be able to still do it when we were eighty years old. Although, I wouldn't be able to jump up and hold on and he may not have the strength.

Sasha joined in the love, hugging the pair of us and laughing at our group hug.

'Right, Rose,' he said, looking at me. I was still sitting on the kitchen side, and he was standing between my legs.

'We have a tight schedule and places we need to be, so when I say let's go, we need to go. Okay?' He was giving me strict instructions like a child. I was intrigued as to what he meant by a tight schedule and places we need to be. *Where are we going?*

'Okay.' I nodded and agreed whilst getting out five wine glasses from the kitchen cupboard for each of us. I would have got out champagne flutes, but we didn't have any. I even struggled with five matching glasses. I managed four tumblers and a pint glass for the fifth person.

Daniel held the first prosecco bottle in his hands and carefully tore off the silver foil wrapping from around its neck, then gradually untwisted, loosening the wire that was holding the cork firmly in place.

'Pop'. It shot up and hit the ceiling with a boom. We all looked up to check it hadn't made a hole. It hadn't. Concentrating on filling our glasses with bubbles and downing them so that we were ready for what Daniel had planned next, I had to stop myself from getting so drunk that I spoiled the night ahead.

'Right, we have six minutes to get our coats and shoes on and finish our drinks. There will be a taxi waiting outside at 7.30 pm. If we aren't there and ready, it will leave without us.' I liked Daniel being bossy and assertive, I found it attractive when a man took control and told me what to do. I looked at him in such a seductive manner that I wanted to fuck him right there and then. He returned my look with the dirtiest of smiles and a wink.

I got to it, my knee-high black leather boots took a while to put on and zip up. It was January and cold outside, so my thick black overcoat hid my scantily dressed body. I had chosen a revealing, low-cut, short, strappy black dress. It was tight and figure-hugging. My white, untanned legs were the only things on show from below my coat.

One by one, we picked up the glasses from the side. I was left with the pint of prosecco in hand. Gulping down the entire glass, I launched it back on the side and ran to the car park outside. I knew I would regret it later, but it felt good. I had been trying to behave myself after the drink driving conviction incident, but tonight it was my birthday, and I was going to celebrate.

'Come on, guys, let's get organised. Are we all here?' Daniel started counting us like a teacher on a school trip. Checking us all in and making sure no one was left behind.

A big, black, six-seater Mercedes van with tinted windows was waiting patiently outside for us. Daniel had organised it, but where it was taking us to, I had no idea. The five of us climbed into the back of the vehicle. I was already quite merry after drinking the prosecco so fast that I was now in the mood for partying.

We had all snuck drinks into our bags, *Well, I didn't want to be wasteful.* Taking the other opened bottle of prosecco from the kitchen, I held it, hidden inside my handbag and occasionally sipped the contents from it without the driver seeing us or telling us off. We were laughing and shouting at each other as he drove off. The night in full swing.

'Happy Birthday, beautiful,' Daniel said as he reached in for a kiss.

'Thank you. Are you going to tell me where we are off to?' I asked.

'Nope,' he said and laughed back. 'It will be full of nice surprises.'

It only took us about twenty minutes to reach my birthday destination. As the taxicab pulled up into a medium-sized car park, we arrived outside the entrance to a funky club that I had driven past many times before but never been in. They ran a lot of functions and events there, the posters were frequently plastered around town. *Nice,* I thought to myself. It was something different and unusual to where we had gone before, but what did he mean by full of nice surprises?

The building was quite old. It looked like it dated back to the 1920s—very square and boring. All the windows had been boarded up and covered with what looked like large pictures from previous events. The sign above the door was all cracked and barely hanging from its rusty hinges. I had heard that they ran some great events, so I was hoping the inside looked a lot better than the outside.

One by one, we fell out of the car and waited until Daniel had paid the fare, but our attention was caught by the metal side door of the club as it crashed open against the old brick wall and two performers bumbled their way outside to smoke. I looked at them both in such admiration, their outfits were incredible.

Two men with the most incredible legs I had ever seen stood against the wall, their heels hitched up behind them, resting on the bricks and mortar to steady them, lighting their cigarettes. They had the most flamboyant blonde wigs, makeup so well done that it put a lot of the women's makeup to shame, and their dresses the shortest and tightest fitting that I was surprised they were able to breathe. Their fishnet stockings and suspenders complemented their shiny, platform heels.

'Good evening, darlings. Welcome, welcome!' they both shouted and laughed at us.

'Thank you,' we replied.

'Hope you enjoy the show, it'll be a blast.' They crouched down and giggled together, I wasn't sure if it was a private joke or genuine.

Just as we were about to make our way into the club, I got a tap on the shoulder. I tried glancing around to see who it was, but before I could, their thick coat wrapped around me, long dark hair draped over my shoulders, blocking my view, and the beautiful smell of a lovely perfume wafted over me.

'Happy birthday, my lovely.' I knew that voice... it was my wonderful eldest sister, but what was she doing here? We hadn't planned to meet or for her to be here, and how did she know this is where we would be? Then I thought to myself for a moment, I bet Daniel invited them along. Sure enough, as her hug eased and we broke apart, I noticed my other sister standing next to her, waiting for a big kiss and a cuddle.

Although we didn't see each other all the time, my sisters meant everything to me. They were always there, supportive, loving and as encouraging as sisters could be. I got another hug from my middle sister as she leaned in and pulled me close to her. I wished I could see them more, but being so wrapped up in the house, work, Jack and Daniel, there simply weren't enough hours in the day. I needed to make more of an effort to see them. They also had busy lives with work and family commitments.

Before I could get any more love and attention from anyone else, Daniel grabbed my arm and pulled me towards the entrance. 'Come on, you... we need to get you inside otherwise we will never get to the bar and get seated in time for the show. You can say hello to everyone once we're in there and we have a few more surprises for you,' he said as he guided me towards the main doors and the ticketing booth.

A large queue of people on a short red carpet greeted us —two rope barriers on either side to keep everyone in line. Daniel just pushed past them all and spoke to the main man guarding the ticket booth.

I could hear him saying reservation but not much more than that. The man ushered for us to join him, we followed and walked in, just the six of us.

'If you would all like to wear one of these wristbands, this will entitle you to free drinks all night and the show. There is a cloakroom to the left-hand side of the bar that will take any coats, bags or belongings that you would like to leave in there. No glass bottles or smoking inside the venue please.' The man in the booth pointed to the bouncer to the side—a big burly bodybuilder with no neck and nearly 7ft tall. He began opening the large black doors ahead of us and let us through.

Inside, there was a busy bar, lots of lights flickering on and off, a main stage and a busy, bustling vibe. I imagined it to be similar to the Moulin Rouge. Then I saw a familiar face... a cousin, another familiar face, an old school friend and more people I knew. Daniel had invited all my friends and family.

Overwhelmed with all the hugs, kisses and birthday wishes, I felt grateful for all the effort he had made. So many people that I didn't get to see that often and should do. Everyone except the one person that I would have really liked to have seen there that night. The one friend that I got to see every day and for longer than I even saw Daniel. George. He wasn't there—he wouldn't have known, and Daniel wouldn't have thought to invite him.

I quickly said hello to everyone but made my apologies so I could put all my belongings in the cloakroom.

Returning as quickly as I could, I found everyone chatting amongst themselves at the bar. How nice it was that everyone had turned up for me. Up until then, I didn't think I had that many friends, but around fifty people in total had graced me with their presence that night. Slowly edging my way into the crowd and joining in the conversation with everyone, I felt a squeeze of my bottom cheek and turned quickly to find out who it was. Of course, it was Daniel, who else would squeeze it?

'I have one last birthday surprise for you,' he said.

'Oh.' I was intrigued.

'You need to close your eyes, no peeping.' He stood in front of me and made me purse them together, placing his warm hand over them so I did as I was told. 'And no peeping as you will ruin it.' He held my hand and led me forwards, walking us past the bar and onto somewhere else.

It went quiet for a while, then I heard a door creak as we entered another room and then silence.

'Okay, you can now open your eyes.' He lowered his hand and held mine.

'Happy Birthday to you. Happy Birthday to you. Happy Birthday dear Rose. Happy Birthday to you,' broke out in a beautiful chorus around me.

I opened my eyes to find the whole cast of the cabaret show in full swing of the birthday song and singing to me. I looked around to see that I was in what appeared to be their dressing room and all the performers in various stages of getting dressed. There were men with just women's under-wear on, some with wigs on and some off. There were women with no tops on, their breasts completely free and sat in front of mirrors preparing their makeup. No fucks given in this room; it was the way I wish the world could be. Everyone happy, smiling, humming and singing whilst getting ready.

'Oh my god, thank you so, so much.' I cheered and clapped in gratitude. Being in that dressing room was euphoric. Costumes hung from every hook and hanger there was. It was a dark room, pictures and posters plastered every-where, the desks were laden with brushes, hairnets and underwear... it was a messy and chaotic space, but I loved it.

'Okay, my lovely. My name is Steph. Would you like to get dressed or are you coming on stage as you are?' The most beautiful drag queen of them all came over to me and stroked my back. His gentle but calming eyes made me feel at home but his suggestion of me coming on stage filled me with dread.

'On stage? Oh no, no, no... I couldn't possibly. I...' I tried backing away, but he wasn't having it.

'Why you must, we just want to introduce you to everyone and obviously for everyone to wish you a happy birthday. Twenty-one is such a wonderful young age, cherish it before you get too old like us.' He waved around the room as everyone else laughed and nodded their heads in agreement.

'Oh, don't be so mean, she doesn't have to go on stage.' A stunning young lady who had been sitting at the desk to my right stood up and made her way over to rescue me. She only had a pair of knickers, a suspender belt and stockings on. Her perfect breasts sat neatly as she walked towards me. I could see Daniel watching her, his eyes dropping to her chest rather than her face. I smiled as I watched his gaze.

'It's okay, honey. We won't make you go on stage if you aren't comfortable, but you must join us afterwards in the dressing room for drinks, I insist. It's where all the fun and magic happens.' She picked up my hand and stroked the back before holding it. Her fingers and hands felt so soft, smooth and delicate. My heart felt light and inquisitive.

She had stunning features and striking blue eyes that sparkled against her blonde hair. It flowed onto her shoulders with a little wave at the bottom. Her small nose and thin, petite lips accentuated the gap in her front teeth as she smiled. There was something about her, something naughty, something enticing and magical. I found her gaze encapsulating. I stood there still and was drawn into her spell for a moment. There it was again... the second time since Greece that I had been attracted to a woman as well as a man.

Is it possible to feel equally attracted to both genders?

I'd never thought about it before as I hadn't looked for it, but I definitely felt something deep inside as she stood before me half-naked. There was something elegant and stunning about a woman's naked body, each and every curve was so graceful.

Daniel noticed our connection but didn't move. He continued to watch us as we stood there in silence, both of us fascinated by the other. I didn't notice whether the rest of the room was loud or quiet, it wasn't important.

'Thank you,' I finally said. Our hands broke free and she smiled at me again. *Is she Daniel's surprise or is it the after-party that he organised?*

'Give me five minutes to quickly get dressed and I will walk you both back to the bar. There is a bottle of champagne there waiting for you.' She resumed to her station, popping on a white vest top, her nipples still clearly visible underneath. Daniel and I glanced around the room, watching the hustle and bustle of the others getting ready.

'I'm Amy, by the way,' she said as she led us from the changing rooms back to the bar. 'Nice to meet you both.'

'I'm Rose and this is Daniel, nice to meet you too.' I smiled back at her.

'What a nice boyfriend organising this for you.' She looked back at Daniel and naughtily winked. I guessed that they had previously spoken about the night and possibly met before, but it didn't bother me. He looked bashful and she seemed like she enjoyed playing with him.

It was only a short walk back to the bar, but we stood

there whilst waiting for the champagne, trying to get to know one another. She asked many questions about me, about us and our relationship. She genuinely seemed interested, or perhaps she was just testing the trust between us as a couple. I felt a connection like she was an old friend that I hadn't seen for a few years, and we were catching up on lost time. I couldn't help but wonder what was in it for her. Did she really like us or had Daniel paid for backstage access and the champagne? Either way, I couldn't care less.

From behind us, music began to play on stage. The large red curtains that draped down from the ceiling looked to be twitching and the bar was getting busier and busier. The whole room looked like the scene from a fairground, large signs with bold writing, lightbulbs were strategically placed everywhere, lighting up the bar area with bright colours. Even the bar staff had the most seductive and sexy-themed clothing on. It created a dark and enticing atmosphere.

'I'm sorry, I must head backstage. We will be on in a minute but promise me you will join us afterwards for drinks. You must.' Again, she held my hand gently, applied a little more pressure than before, then released and looked deep into my eyes.

'We will, I promise.' I peered at Daniel, trying to gauge his appetite for drinks afterwards. He seemed fine with the situation, so I took it as a given and nodded. With all our friends and family at the bar and drinking amongst them, we joined back into the conversations—they were oblivious to where we had just been.

'Ladies and gentlemen, I would like to introduce to you our Cabaret spectaculars for this evening's performance.' The announcement rang out around the room, everyone silent and attentive, turning to face the main stage. The room was heaving with people all drinking, chinking glasses and chatting quietly as the performance was about to begin. A large, silver metal bucket full of ice with a champagne bottle submerged in it was heaved over the bar and placed between Daniel and me.

'Compliments of Amy to a Miss Rose,' the bartender said as he placed two champagne flutes next to it for us.

'Why thank you,' I said, receiving it. 'And thank you, Daniel, tonight has already been amazing. What did I do to deserve you?' I held his face and kissed him lovingly on the lips.

'Ugh, you two... get a room, none of that in here please,' Zoe said as she laughed with the others.

For ninety minutes, we watched a show of singing, dancing and parading. The performance was incredible. It was witty, funny and entertaining, nothing like anything I had seen before and one that I would go back to watch. Men with the most talented voices sang songs and hit notes that even the most famous of singers probably couldn't hit. The highest of shoes and uncomfortable-looking clothes, I praised them for their stamina. My feet would have hurt if I had danced around on those for hours. The whole cast was outstanding, but I still couldn't peel my eyes away from Amy each time she was on stage.

I watched her perfectly toned body move around. The way she flicked her hair, the way she bent over when she was dancing and the way she seemed to be looking at me the whole time. Was she doing it deliberately? I looked at Daniel, he was the same, fixated on her every move, drawing us in.

Before we knew it, the show finished, all the performers bowed whilst we clapped, and the curtains drew.

In all the commotion of the end of the show, everyone

heading back to the bar, I felt a tap on my shoulder. Turning around to catch Amy walking away behind me, our eyes met again with intrigue, her dirty smile directed at me and a sparkle in her eye, she motioned for me to follow her. I spun around to look at Daniel, who had seen what just happened and shrugged his shoulders.

'Go and see what Amy wants. I need the toilet first, then I will come and find you.' He almost pushed me in her direction whilst the others queued for a drink at the bar.

Amy kept walking without looking back at me to see if I was following. Had the after-party in their dressing room started already? I kept my eyes on her the whole time, watching where she was heading. Back past the main stage I went, the double doors to the side were partly open with a door stop holding it slightly ajar. I ignored the sign above the door saying, 'No access, private, keep out' and looked through the gap before walking in.

I could see all the performers scantily dressed, music on loud and their voices singing at full volume. They were all dancing and laughing and enjoying themselves. I couldn't see Amy until the door opened wider and she stood there smiling at me.

'Too scared to come in?' she asked. I suddenly felt like a vulnerable little lost lamb in a field full of sheep. It was unlike me as I was normally so outgoing, so loud and vibrant, but this made me feel slightly out of my comfort zone. I had nothing in common with them. I didn't know what to say, I was lost for words.

'I... err... wasn't sure where you went.'

It was as though Amy knew I was shy and was playing with me, just as she had played with Daniel earlier. I think she liked the fact that she was teasing me. Standing in front of me with nothing but her underwear and the shortest of skirts wrapped around her waist, she held a lit cigarette up to her mouth, inhaling the tobacco deep into her lungs and then blowing it straight into my face seductively. The smoke swirled in front of my face, lingering, then clearing to reveal her naughty face locked onto my reaction. I stood there caught up in what was about to happen next, completely in her awe.

I couldn't help but look down at her entire body as she stood there before me. I didn't feel like I was being judged by studying her, she seemed to like it. Amy's curvy body had the cutest patches of freckles at the top of her breasts and on each shoulder. Black, silk finished, see-through underwear showed her perfectly hard nipples and at least a size D cup.

It was as though she was encouraging me to touch her, but I stood there motionless, using my eyes to do all the talking.

Where is Daniel? I thought. I could feel myself being pulled into Amy like an alluring wave of lust bringing me closer to her body, but I couldn't do anything without him... *could I?* She brought the cigarette once again to her mouth, but instead of inhaling and bringing it back out, she kept it between her lips, holding it so tight that the bright red lipstick she had left was now on the cigarette butt. The hand she had holding it moved down to greet mine and she led me to her booth where she got changed and ready. It was a small cubicle with a draped black curtain hanging from the entrance. She wanted privacy with *me*.

I couldn't hear the loud music playing in the background anymore, or the singing and dancing happening around me in the room. I had even forgotten all my friends and family at the bar, enjoying themselves without us. The only thing I realised was that Daniel was now stood, towering over me from behind. *What does he make of me being here with Amy and just about to go into her small room?*

Amy looked up at him and smiled. He smiled back, the same dirty look as if they had planned everything between them. She pulled us both in and tugged the curtain shut behind us. I felt hot and extremely sexual. There was something so wrong and so naughty being in a situation knowing that your next move could either go horribly wrong or so right. Judging someone else's body language and reactions was like a fine art. My heart was racing in a good way, my senses heightened and I had a feeling of pure lust towards her.

There was hardly any room in this tiny space—a table strewn with makeup, clothes and a few other essentials at one end, and a small, battered leather chair at the other, some hooks on the wall again with clothes hanging and a bare lightbulb that expelled the dimmest light possible, just enough for us to see each other. It added to the moment and the tension of what was looming.

I looked at her again in anticipation, she was truly stunning. If there was ever a type of woman that I would lust after, it was her. With Daniel behind her leaning against the wall, she leaned into me, closing her eyes, I leaned forward too so that our lips could touch. She had the softest, most gentle lips I had ever felt. Her hand ran through my hair and held on to the back of my head, pulling me into her kiss.

I kept my eyes closed, feeling the passion and lust in the both of us connecting. Our tongues met and it felt so good. Her kiss was incredible, but I wanted more. Never had I felt such passion with someone other than Daniel.

I had a feeling of distraction, the same feeling you get

when you know that someone is watching you. Opening my eyes, I found Daniel had got closer and was standing almost between me and Amy. *Is he angry? Is he trying to intervene? Surely it isn't cheating if he's involved?*

He smiled at me approvingly. Amy released her grip on the back of my head and slowly turned to Daniel. Without warning, they both leaned in to each other and began to kiss right in front of me. Maybe I should have been mad or jealous, but instead, I liked it. Watching Daniel with another woman was erotic and sensual, sharing our feelings with another person didn't bother me at all. Again, maybe the fact that it was naughty and not something that most couples did made it all the more appealing, to watch the way he kissed another woman, touched them and me being a part of the moment.

The two of them kissing only seemed to electrify the situation. Something happened to Amy, she began moaning in pleasure and her body moved in such a way that she craved to be touched in more places. I could see Daniel's trousers tightening as he grew an erection.

Amy lifted her head backwards and away from Daniel. She pushed me back against the wall, leaving me to slide down onto the table. Her hands both on the straps of my dress, peeling them off sideways as well as my bra straps, pulling them both down so that my chest was exposed and out in the cold, my dress resting on my hips. Her eyes widened as she saw the size of my breasts, covered in goosebumps and waiting to be touched.

Amy bent down and began to circle my nipples with her warm, wet tongue. I could feel her flicking them in her mouth as she sucked and teased them. I took hold of her head, keeping her gently in place with both my hands as

Daniel moved around to stand directly behind her. He had full view of us, fixated on her bent over, her skirt rising, showing the tiny string of cotton that was resting between her pussy lips.

Daniel reached a hand forward, underneath her skirt and pulled the string out and to one side, feeling the wetness of her. He dipped one finger in first, then two as she looked at me and let out another moan. I wanted more, way more, and the thought of Daniel and what he was doing to her was driving me insane.

Amy's head buckled backwards, her eyes tightly closed. Enjoying the penetration from Daniel, she pushed back on him in rhythm. I began lifting my skirt, watching the two of them enjoying the pleasure before pulling my wet knickers to one side, and like Daniel, I took a finger and began to play with myself.

I could feel the pressure building inside me, the three of us twisted up in a threesome of ultimate passion and lust backstage at a nightclub—what could be more exciting? The fact that anyone at any time could whip open the curtain and catch us all there at any moment was adding to the heightened tension. Sex in a public space with a complete stranger shouted danger... that's why I liked it even more.

With one hand behind her, Amy was stroking Daniel's cock through his trousers until he could take it no longer and began to unbutton and release his length, his trousers falling to the floor around his ankles, resting his cock on the small of her back. He looked at me the whole time, checking I was okay.

Amy leaned forward, closer to me, one hand on the wall to steady herself, the other between my legs. She closed her eyes, kissing me, ready for Daniel to fuck her. He leaned in, grabbing her hips and entering her with full force. I could feel every thrust he was giving her as her fingers slipped inside my soaking wet pussy, in and out. She knew how to bring me to climax better than any man could. Her thumb on the outside of me, rubbing, touching and circling, the other two fingers deep inside. Her breathing in time with mine, her tongue swirling with mine, Daniel's thrusting sending both of us into euphoria. All three of us close to cumming and unable to control our bodies, we moved together, each of us focused entirely on our own selfish feelings.

Amy placed her hand over my mouth, I did the same to her as we muffled the sound of our orgasms. Daniel's legs buckled and shook as he shot his load deep inside her. His hard moan was hidden by the sound of the loud singing and laughing from outside the cubicle. He took a big deep breath in to steady himself before stepping back against the wall, his pulsing cock resting in his hands. Daniel looked up at the ceiling as if the release was too much for him. Amy looked at me for a moment as if she was deep in thought before standing as I sat there, pulling my dress back over my hips and adjusting my bra and dress back over my shoulders.

Each one of us remained speechless. I'm not sure there were any words that could have captured the moment. It would have been rude to say thank you or well done, so I kept quiet. Daniel leaned forward and kissed Amy quickly on the lips, more of an informal kiss than the one he had started with, and held out a hand for me to grab as I got to my feet. Amy did the same and re-adjusted her clothes, still in her see-through bra and short mini skirt, but she made sure it was neat before pulling back the curtain to the chaos outside.

'I best get dressed; I have a lift coming to get me in half an hour. Here's my number if you ever fancy...' Amy's voice trailed off as she handed us a card with her number on it.

'Thank you, Amy... you...' I stopped myself from saying anything else. From saying the wrong thing or perhaps too much. As I took the card from her, our fingers touched as I looked at her beautiful, blushed face. The build-up to what had just happened seemed to last for ages, but as soon as it was over, it was a quick reality check and out as quickly as we could like we were running away from a crime scene. Daniel and I walked out of the changing room, not glancing back, not saying anything about what had just happened, just making our way to the bar to find the others.

The club was empty, it looked like everyone had left except a few bouncers that were standing at the door to make sure there were no problems. He gave a wry smile as if he knew what had just taken place.

'Where has everyone gone?' Daniel turned to me.

'We must have been in there for a while... I didn't notice the time. Maybe they thought we already left?' I looked across the car park—no sign of any of our friends or family. Twisting my arm to read the time on my watch, it said 1.59 am. No wonder no one was there, we had been backstage for over an hour, but it felt like minutes. No wonder Amy needed to get dressed and away in a hurry.

'Come on, let's grab a cab, we have to get Jack in the morning.' Daniel pulled me towards the queue of taxis waiting on the side of the road just outside the club.

I felt strange. Strange in a good way... strange in a way that I couldn't describe. *Am I a lesbian? Am I bisexual? What just happened in there? Did Daniel set that up or was it something genuine that naturally took hold?* I felt bad that we didn't even know her, I only knew her name and that was it. I found women beautiful, I was highly attracted to their curves, their breasts, their intimate areas but I was also equally as drawn to men, their masculinity, their cocks and everything about them.

Is it possible to like both men and women?

We sat in the cab on the way home; we didn't speak a word about Amy ever again. I didn't ask questions and neither did he. Daniel just sat in the back seat next to me, his hand placed on my upper thigh. He gave me a smile—a loving, satisfied smile that I wanted to last forever, but I worried that this scenario might cause us problems in the future.

The following morning, I got a message from Sasha:

'HEY! WHAT HAPPENED TO YOU TWO LAST NIGHT? COULDN'T FIND YOU ANYWHERE, DID YOU GO HOME EARLY? HOPE YOU HAD A GOOD NIGHT. LOVE YOU. SASH X'.

As much as I wanted to reply to her and tell her what really went on, I couldn't. Our secret was safe between me and Daniel.

'SORRY, HAD TOO MUCH, HAD TO DASH BACK. SORRY I DIDN'T SAY GOODNIGHT. LOVE YOU TOO.'

6

IN IT FOR THE MONEY

Since the last meeting with my new clients in London with Dave, I had provided a few business presentations and participated in meetings. I was getting to know them quite well.

My favourite of all of them was Steve. He reminded me of George—a real character. I felt comfortable with him as if I had known him for a lot longer. He was quite a short man, around late thirties to early forties. He was married and had two boys aged eight and ten.

He had placed a few orders with me in the past few weeks but nothing major. Out of the blue, I got a call from him at work and he explained to me that there was a large project coming up. He needed me to quote on a lot of products but that we needed to discuss the terms and conditions and whether I would be interested in bidding. Of course, I said yes. I needed the commission and wanted to plan a nice holiday for Jack, Daniel and myself, and there were a fair few bills that I needed to catch up on.

He asked if we could meet in London again, same place as

last time. I agreed. This time though, it would just be me and him. It was fine, I felt safe in his company. I told Daniel that he needed to collect Jack from nursery as it would be a late one for me and that I would probably need to get the last train home. Being as understanding as he was, he stepped up as usual.

On this occasion, my dress wasn't as revealing as it was before—I didn't need to impress. Or at least I didn't think I needed to. I took the train from Bracknell to Waterloo and met Steve outside the Royal Exchange just by Bank Station.

The tube trains were absolutely packed, shoulder to shoulder of busy city workers enjoying a drink or two in town, or tourists that were trying to work out their way around the London transport network. A mixture of smelly armpits and old material seats that hadn't been cleaned since they'd been made filled the air.

Steve was standing there waiting when I arrived. He was quite a short but stocky guy, wearing smart grey trousers and a smart cotton shirt, unbuttoned down to the second button, exposing a dark hairy chest from beneath.

He smiled as he saw me. Brown hair, hazel eyes. I didn't find him attractive in the slightest, but he was such a nice, friendly guy.

'Evening,' he said as he leaned in to air-kiss me twice, just as we had done in the restaurant. I was used to it now and knew what the protocol was.

'Nice to see you again,' I replied. It didn't seem awkward going for dinner with another man—it wasn't a date, it was an innocent business discussion over a bit of food. Exactly the same as if it were two men meeting for a business lunch.

'I've booked a really nice restaurant; I hope you like it.' He led off in the direction towards Leadenhall, a quirky and fun part of London. This was all quite new to me, I hadn't been here before, so I followed his direction and listened attentively to what he had to say.

I was amazed at what a place Leadenhall was. In the middle of a busy, bustling part of the city stood this grand, gated market dating back to the 14th century. He knew all the history of the area from its cobbled small streets to its ornate roof made from intricate glass detail and decorated in beautiful green, maroon and cream. It was stunning, he watched my face as it lit up and I studied every minute detail. It was like stepping back in time to historic London and the way it was back then.

There were cheese mongers, old butchers' shops, eateries and barbers. The streets were lined with businessmen and women stood outside under the shop canopies, drinking and laughing. Thursday was *the* night to be in town. I felt like a puppy that had just left the house for the first time and was soaking in the sights around them. He smiled with pleasure at showing me around a new place, it was clearly somewhere he liked to go to, and he enjoyed being a tour guide.

'Let's grab a drink or two first and then head for dinner. We are a little early, so it makes sense.' He dived into a rustic-looking pub. It had what appeared to be an original black swinging sign with large gold letters saying, 'OLD TOM'S BAR' above the archway. Outside, the building was painted with deep reds, gold and silver. Very grand and extremely old-fashioned. Chalkboards scattered across the front with white chalk fancy writing.

It looked dark inside, but once you walked in, it opened into a dimly lit and cosy drinking area. Still with the original green and white tiled walls, a row of Chesterfield seats and small round tables around the edge of the bar with antique-looking bar stools against old-fashioned beer pumps, shelves and shelves of every alcohol you could think of. The glass mirrors looked scratched and worn but gave it its authenticity, I could imagine back in the day that the room would be filled with thick smoke and the chatter and chink of men drinking with pint glasses. Even the floorboards looked like the original ones that had been laid, it felt like a scene from Harry Potter.

I didn't want Steve to think I was ignoring him—I was simply quiet because I was soaking in the sights around me.

'Sorry, Steve, it's just such a great place, I've never been here before.' I looked around to see him standing at the bar, waiting to get the bartender's attention.

'Hey, no problems, take your time. What are you drinking?' he asked.

'Erm, I think I will have a prosecco, please? Hey, wait a minute, I should be getting these. You are my customer.' I stood next to him at the bar, interrupting his order.

'I think I can manage to buy you a drink this time.' He smirked. 'You can get dinner, how about that?'

'Okay, deal,' I agreed. I was supposed to buy the food and drinks for customers, I would then keep all the receipts and claim them back from work as expenses. As long as we didn't go silly and order the most expensive item on every menu, work would sign it off. It wasn't bribery for him ordering with our company, it was about building relationships with people. Getting to know them, understanding what their business was and how we could work better together. I guess you could call it networking.

Steve ordered a pint of beer. I settled the bill, took the receipt and he picked up both glasses, walking to one of the nicer leather seats and sat down, leaving me an obvious seat to sit next to him.

He didn't look me up and down, studying my chest or legs like other men had. He seemed genuine and I felt comfortable.

'So, do you tend to come here a lot after work?' I asked.

'Erm, a fair bit, I guess. It's just quite a nice, social place to come to for a drink when I am in town,' he returned.

'Any plans for the weekend?' I started by making general chit-chat. I didn't want to suddenly dive into work talk, but to be honest, it was the only thing I was interested in. As soon as he said he had a big work project that he wanted me involved in, I fell hook, line and sinker. I was thinking of the commission I would get and what I could do with the money. It would make such a difference at home. I felt a little cold and heartless that I was there to do my job, the drinks and the dinner were a necessity, my role was to bond with the customer, get an order and move on to the next one. I didn't care to some degree what he did in his personal life, what his circumstances or hobbies were, but I listened anyway and looked interested. So, thinking about it, how did that make me any different to the men who wanted to touch me? In return, I wanted their business—an exchange of goods you could say.

'Yes, the wife and I are going for a few days to the Lake District. A bit of walking, a nice dinner somewhere, that sort of thing. If we can manage the weekend without arguing that is,' he said in a way that he felt he was talking to a close friend. I wasn't expecting that.

'Oh, walking in the Lake District sounds nice. But why would it turn into an argument? Does it normally?' Maybe I shouldn't have asked that, but I thought it may have made him open up to me a little bit.

'Oh, god yes. We can't do anything without an argument these days. When you have been together for as long as we have, things tend to turn bitter, you lose the spark between you and it's just easy to stay together. You know how it is.' He picked up his pint and took a large gulp.

'That's a shame. How long have you been together for now? How did you meet?' Again, I fired questions at him, but I now wanted to know more.

'Fifteen years married, but we've known each other for more like twenty. Feels like an eternity.' He seemed to chuckle into his beer, but I felt like he was itching to say more.

'Is there nothing you can do to spice it up a little? Maybe couples sometimes get a bit tired as it is all work, kids, house-work, etc. Just needs a little excitement perhaps?' The words fell out of my mouth before I could think about what I was saying. I was implying that sometimes things just become stale. It was hard keeping a relationship alive, but I was by no means suggesting that I had anything to do with it. Even I knew that, and Daniel and I hadn't been together for half as long as he had been with his wife.

'Got any ideas?' he bluntly asked.

'Well, maybe surprising her with some flowers or a gift?' I proposed.

'I don't think that would work, she would think I was up to something or felt guilty. It needs something a little more than that.' He shrugged his shoulders and looked at me as though he wanted another suggestion.

'What hobbies does she have? Is there anywhere that she would like to go?'

'She doesn't have any hobbies; she just sits and watches

television. It was her idea to go to the Lake District, so that's why we are going there this weekend. I think it is one last ditch attempt at rekindling things or we call it quits.' He didn't seem to be too bothered either way.

'That's a shame. I'm sorry. I hope things work out for you this weekend.' I really was sorry, it was a long time to be together for things to just fizzle out.

'Thanks, I'm not hopeful.' He smiled and took another gulp.

'So, Missy, how about you? Married, kids?' he asked.

'Yes, I have a boyfriend, Daniel, and we have a son, Jack, who has just turned five. We are childhood sweethearts. Jack is adorable, he is our world.' I beamed as I always did when talking about them.

'Oh, that's nice, give it time,' he said pessimistically.

I looked up at him from taking a sip of my prosecco, shocked that he had even come out with that. How could I ever get bored of Daniel? We were going to grow old together. That was the one thing I was certain about.

'Oh, I'm sorry, I didn't mean to sound so cynical but it's the sad truth. I don't think any marriage or relationship can keep the spark for so many years or at least not have its problems... it's a fact of life.' Steve seemed to be so matter-of-fact. He wasn't being nasty or horrible, that was just how he felt. Of course, Daniel and I had our fair share of issues, but I loved him to death, as he did me.

'It's okay, I get what you're saying.' I smiled back to show him no hard feelings.

'So, you mean to tell me that you haven't slept with anyone else except your boyfriend and you are how old?' He sat there completely still, his hands interlinked as he waited for me to answer. I wasn't sure if I should answer that question, especially as he was my customer. Imagine if it got back to Dave that I'd been talking about sex with a prospective client, I could get fired. Besides that, how would he react to me talking about me being bisexual and our experience of threesomes or even foursomes. He may start to get the wrong idea.

'Come on, we are friends, aren't we? I won't say a word. Talk to me.' He seemed very forward for someone that I had only met a few times before and knew absolutely nothing about, apart from that he was married and going to the Lake District at the weekend. Hardly an in-depth conversation I wanted to have with a stranger.

On second thoughts, fuck it. I want to know what he thinks...

'Well, no, he's not the only person I have slept with. There was this one guy when we were on holiday in Greece together, all of us went back to the room and... well, you know. Then on my twenty-first birthday, there was a woman backstage at the club and, well, the three of us were in the cubicle together and...' I trailed off, not sure what more information I should have put in there or that he wanted to know.

'Oh, so you like a bit of both, do you? You like to savour the taste of women as well as men?' This seemed to excite him. I had his full attention. Maybe I had given away a bit too much information.

'But, technically, both of those were with your boyfriend, so you haven't really slept with anyone without your boyfriend present?' Typically speaking, he was right, but I'm not sure this was a competition. Nor should I be discussing this with him.

'I guess not, no.' I twisted in my seat and downed the glass of prosecco. I needed alcohol in me to cope with the way the conversation was going.

'Am I making you nervous? I'll stop at any time,' Steve said, cocking his head to one side.

'No, not at all.' *Why did I say that?* I could have ended the conversation right there and then and started on a different topic.

'So, would you?' He waved his hand at the bartender, signalling that he wanted his attention. He mouthed that we wanted another round of drinks and the bartender got to work.

'Would I what?'

'Would you sleep with someone else... without your boyfriend, of course?' The bartender came over with our fresh drinks just as he asked me the question. Nervously, I gave him my empty glass and took the fresh one.

'No.' I shook my head.

'No, not now or not ever?' Steve was testing me.

'I don't know, I haven't really thought about it... who knows what will happen in the future.' I gave a sneaky smile as the prosecco started to kick in.

'Hmm, I like your optimism. I think you're a bit of a dark character, Rose. You give off this air of innocence, yet I think you are a bad girl deep down.' Steve had a naughty look on his face. After only meeting him twice, he seemed to have me completely summed up. That was exactly who I was, but I didn't want him to know it just yet.

I looked into his eyes and tried to understand who he really was. You can tell a lot from someone's eyes, and I was fascinated. If there was one thing I noticed about a person, it was the colour and intricacies of their eyes. If you carefully studied an iris, you would notice the minute detail and colours of pigmentation that varied from person to person.

His hazel eyes had the occasional flick of brown, green, gold and yellow.

'Maybe I am,' I finally spoke.

'Let's go and get dinner, our table should be ready now.' He stood, finishing the last of his pint and slid it towards the middle of the table as we left. I did the same and followed him out of the dark, damp-smelling pub.

We walked a couple of doors down and entered a restaurant called Chamberlains. It was a fine dining place serving fish and steak, and it looked exquisite. I gulped at the prices, even though I could claim them back from work. I had to pay for them first and wait to be reimbursed, so I was sat there wondering if I had enough money in my account to cover it all.

Chamberlains was vast, it spanned four floors and was already hustling and bustling with people eating, drinking and chatting away. It was only 7.30 pm, but as the light of the day dulled, candles were placed and lit on each of the round tables. Smart brown leather armchairs were sporadically placed around the tables. The menus, cutlery and napkins were already there and waiting for us.

A beautiful young lady wearing black tights, a short tight-fitting skirt and a white blouse tended to us, sitting us down and taking our drinks menu. This was the third prosecco of the night, and already I was starting to feel its effects. Yes, I could drink but I hadn't eaten all day as I wanted to be hungry for this dinner, so the bubbles had gone straight to my head. Steve didn't have my full attention.

I think he knew that the drunker he could get me, the more I would bear all. How the tables had turned... there was me wanting him to talk to me so that I could get to know him and be a better supplier, and all that had happened was him taking full advantage of me. I was now in a really difficult situation. Dave had given me these accounts to look after, the customer was clearly hitting on me, and I had to be careful that I didn't mess everything up. At the same time, all I kept thinking about was Daniel and Jack and how I had to be extremely careful not to lose them.

The menu looked incredible. I ordered the sautéed foie gras, garnished with rhubarb and elderflower with spiced bread for my starter, so did Steve, and the roasted Rose County fillet steak for my main. Steve opted for the pickled mackerel instead. That was food ordered, so we handed our menus back to the pretty waitress and the conversation continued. *Damn it,* I thought. *I could have dragged that out for a little longer before the conversation started again.*

'So, Rose, I'm intrigued... what kind of a dark person are you? Are you a dark fetish type of girl or are we talking passion, rough and adrenaline?' Steve was almost infatuated by my pending response. He shuffled his armchair closer to the table as if to get more comfortable, leaning in and waiting for me to answer.

I hadn't been asked these questions before, and whilst it was totally inappropriate, I felt slightly warm and excited. *A stranger,* I thought to myself. He could be a serial killer or a rapist for all I knew and yet here I was talking about what type of person I am in the bedroom, encouraging him even more.

I couldn't help it, I felt drawn to answering his questions.

'I wouldn't say I have a fetish per se, but I like lust, passion, excitement—anything naughty. Something different. I like it rough but not too rough. I want to feel desire in its true form.' The words poured out of my mouth like I was spilling a long-kept secret.

'Go on,' he said, leaning into the table as if he was watching a gripping episode of a film, waiting to find out what happens next.

'There's a difference between love and lust. Love is sensual, meaningful, there are feelings and a sense of emotion. Lust is pure animal, almost drunken sex, the heat of the moment, driven and powerful. Yes, it's possible to have both, but they are entirely different. In my mind anyway,' I said with such enthusiasm and meaning.

'Wow.' That was all Steve could say. He sat there almost gaping at me. 'They are strong words for such a young lady. You have my attention. Go on...'

I didn't want his attention, I was just giving my opinion— fuelled by alcohol, of course—but I meant every word I said.

'And this lust,' he continued. 'Is this something you have already or want?'

'What do you mean?'

'I mean, Rose, do you have lust in your relationship with your boyfriend? Does he fulfil your needs?' Steve was waiting for me to answer.

'Yes, of course I do. Of course, he does.' It was hard keeping lust alive in a long-term relationship, but I meant it when I said yes. I just wished that lust would make an appearance more often. *Is that possible?* With someone different, it was exciting, naughty and adventurous.

Steve looked disappointed. 'That's what I want, Rose. I'm missing the lust in my life.'

The waitress appeared with two plates and a towel in her hands. She was completely oblivious to our conversation.

'Your starters,' she said, placing them in front of us both.

'Thank you,' we said in sync before looking at each other and smirking.

As the waitress walked off to attend other tables, I could see Steve was itching to find out more.

Was it my high sex drive or my inquisitive nature that kept me captivated and wanting Steve to ask me more questions? Maybe it was just the prosecco, but I followed his actions, picking up my knife and fork, placing my napkin seductively on my lap and taking the first savouring taste of my foie gras. As the first piece entered my mouth, the rich, creamy taste of liver activated my taste buds. There was something inside me that night that made me feel alive. The huddles of people around us loudly talking, the chink of glasses and the sound of cutlery meeting plates was adding to the atmosphere.

Go on, ask me another question, Steve, I thought to myself. *I dare you.*

'I like you, Rose... you are fascinating,' he said to me. 'I don't think I have met anyone quite as interesting as you before. Especially not a supplier.'

Was he saying that just because he wanted to get into my knickers, or did he genuinely mean it? He wasn't someone I would normally go for but there was something about him that was fascinating me too. Of course, I didn't return the compliment, that would be me inviting him in.

'Why thank you.' I smiled as I finished my starter, placing my knife and fork together and gently resting them on the plate. 'I'll take that as a compliment.' I dabbed the corner of my mouth and slowly ran my tongue around the outline of my lips, removing any residue that I may have left from eating. Steve watched as I did so. I had an idea of what he was thinking.

He had a wife and I had a boyfriend, but there was something building—I could feel it.

'I should really mention it before I get back to work tomorrow and can't remember what it was that you needed.' I quickly shifted the conversation back to work.

That was ultimately why we were here, and if I didn't ask him about his project before I was too drunk, then I wouldn't be able to run through it with Dave in my review tomorrow morning. Surely Steve wouldn't think it was rude of me to ask about his project, especially after the conversation we just had.

'Ah, yes... my project. You almost had me forgetting all about that, Rose. Our prior discussion was so much more interesting.' He too dabbed at his mouth, pushing his plate forwards and clearing his throat.

'So, I'm building a data centre over in the Docklands on the east side of the bank, and I am going to need a lot of servers, approximately 100. Not only that, but I am also going to need configuration, installation and testing. It will mean engineers on site 24/7 along with a full project plan. Now, I really like you, Rose, but I need to be sure that you and your team can handle this. I can't have any fuck-ups. I have other suppliers that I could go to, but after today, you are my favourite.' He smiled at me.

I'm presuming he meant the conversation about sex and desires. Is that really what men want? They wanted an honest, open conversation, someone that they could talk to about their needs and wants, not a guy that they could get completely drunk with and get taken to strip clubs. Boy, was I learning this industry quicker than I really wanted to. I was basing all my customers on this one man.

'Of course, of course,' I said, nodding and agreeing with everything he had just said.

'I'm going to need full back-up, failover and resources to

complete this project. Do you understand?' He squinted as he explained, making sure I was following him.

'Absolutely, we can do that for you, I can get you a full quotation over tomorrow,' I responded assertively. I had my fingers crossed under the table, hoping that I would still remember everything he was saying to me by tomorrow morning.

'Are there any minimum specifications for the servers or are you happy if I give you a couple of options?' I impressed myself, sounding like I knew what I was talking about.

'I will email you first thing in the morning with a list of the technical specifications that I want, but ultimately, it depends on the pricing. If you can do me a good deal, then I will go with whatever you recommend.' His lips pursed together as if he was thinking about my question.

'Okay, sounds great, I will pull it all together as soon as you send me the specifications in the morning.' I felt quite excited. This was what sales was all about—a pleasant dinner (slightly too in-depth conversation) but the potential of an order, and a big one at that. I was already working out the costs and the profit I would make in my head. My commission alone would be around ten thousand pounds, minus tax, of course. I had to win this deal, I needed it.

'So, Rose, getting back to our conversation because that was way more exciting than talking about servers. You haven't told me about the women you have slept with yet. Do you prefer men or women?' Steve had a slight smirk on his face.

'Well, that's a difficult question to answer.' I placed my elbows on the table and rested my chin on it, thinking hard but carefully. 'They are so very, very different. I like the curves that a lady has, the sensual way that her lips feel—so much more delicate and gentler. A woman knows how to and where to touch because she is a woman herself, yet another man would know how another man felt. Men are more powerful, strong and subtle. I like the energy that a man brings and being dominated by a man. So, I couldn't compare the two I'm afraid.' After explaining in depth, I looked up to find him mesmerised. I don't even think he was listening to what I was saying. He appeared to be locked on my voice and my lips moving, but not the words coming out.

'I could listen to you for hours,' he finally said.

'Well, that's good because I talk for hours too.' I was never short of talking, even if it was nonsense. I always had something to say.

Everything I told him was true though—men and women were so unique. An experience with either was so extraordinary.

'I couldn't speak for being with another man, but I agree with what you're saying about women. I would love to have two women in a bed with me.' Steve was deep in thought.

'How do you know if you've never been with another man?' I questioned his remark.

Steve screwed up his face. 'Not for me I'm afraid.'

'Why not? You only live once, you must try everything to know you don't like it. I'm open-minded and up for trying anything.' I sat back in my chair, a little more relaxed than I had felt the whole night.

'Anything?' he said.

'Well, most things.' I laughed out loud.

Our main meal was served, and we both tried to eat as we talked. I was a slow eater, but I tried to be as ladylike and polite as I could as I ate and spoke at the same time. The food was delicious, and the company was... well, different.

'Rose, I have a question for you. I have a proposal.' Steve

turned from calm and relaxed to serious. I wondered what he was about to ask me. I thought tonight and the project seemed too good to be true.

'Okay, I'm listening.' I cleared my plate and listened in.

'I'm confident that you could run the project for me, but as I said, I have other suppliers that I could go to.' He paused, swallowed his last mouthful of food and sat there studying me.

So, this is how he's going to play it.

'I've told you about my relationship and that things aren't going as well as they could. I need more, I want more from a sexual partnership, and after our conversation, I can't help but think...' He stopped again and paused. *Where is this conversation going?*

'It got you thinking what?' I prompted him to continue.

'Well, it got me thinking that we could be quite compatible. You scratch my back, I scratch yours, kind of agreement.' Either his words weren't clear or I wasn't getting what he was trying to explain.

'I'm not sure I get—' I started but he cut me off.

'Okay, I'm going to throw this out there. You spend a night with me, and the project is guaranteed yours. I won't go to my other suppliers. It's a done deal. You get me? I'll sign the order for you.' He launched the proposition straight at me like a tennis player batting the ball into my court.

I couldn't quite believe what he said. And if I didn't spend the night with him, I didn't get the deal, was that what he was saying? The business could fire me and Dave would be angry. If I spent the night with him, I would never forgive myself. Things between Daniel and I would never be the same, not to mention it being totally immoral that I was going to sleep with my customer for a deal. I sat there speechless. I didn't even find him that attractive, it was only the money that was appealing to me.

'I can be a gentleman, you know. You have needs, so do I. It's a win-win situation, but you get to walk away with the commission, and I'm satisfied. What's there to think about? You said try everything once, they were your words.' Steve was trying to persuade me and make out that it was completely normal. That it was my suggestion.

Think, think, think! I thought to myself. I had to make my mind up and think on the spot. *I can't believe I am actually contemplating this.*

It should have been a straight no... so what if I lost my job, I could get a new one. I wouldn't be able to get a new boyfriend like Daniel, that was for sure.

'I... um,' I stuttered, biding my time, shuffling the remaining cutlery around on the table in front of me.

'No one would ever know. A total secret, just between me and you.' It was almost as if he was pleading with me. 'One night... just one night, that's it and all over and done with. Am I that unattractive, Rose?' he asked, he sounded like Dave —*no one would ever know.*

'It's not that, I have a lot to lose,' I replied.

'So do I. I'm married,' he quickly added.

I sat back in the chair, fidgeting uncomfortably and perspiring. The room was starting to spin gently, I had double vision from the prosecco. *Fuck it,* I thought. *One night with a man that I had absolutely no feelings for... it won't mean anything. It's a business deal, right?* The minute it was over, I would have the commission and I could move on. One night only. We were talking about a couple of hours here surely. Daniel would never know.

'Okay, okay...' the words exploded out of my mouth quicker than I had time to think twice.

'It's a yes?' Steve looked surprised but elated.

'It's a deal... BUT I need the order signed first,' I said, bargaining with him.

'How do I know you will go ahead with it after I sign?' He frowned.

'I'll bring the paperwork with me to the room, you can sign it then and there and email it whilst I am with you, then we both keep to our sides of the agreement. Deal?' I couldn't believe that I was going ahead with this. I had turned into a professional prostitute. Sleeping with a man for a deal. This wasn't how business should be done but he had turned it into a seedy engagement. I held my hands up to my face with just my eyes showing. The expression behind my hands was inconceivable.

'Deal!' He held out his hand to shake mine.

I agreed and shook it.

What just happened? Rose, you absolute moron! I said over and over in my head.

'Can we grab the bill please?' Steve called over to the waitress. She nodded and quickly walked off to get it. He seemed in a hurry now that he had got the answer he wanted. My heart pounded; I took a couple of deep breaths, but the adrenaline was pumping around my body like a fuelled engine. I felt horrendous but I also had a wave of naughty excitement running through my veins that I just couldn't explain. It felt good—I was alive *and* I had a done deal. The commission would be mine for the taking.

I settled the bill, left the tip, tucked the receipt into my purse and got to my feet. I was a little wobbly, my next mission was to get to the train and sit down.

'Here.' Steve reached out to steady me. 'I'll get us a cab back to Waterloo... I want to make sure you are safe and then I'll get my train home. Will you be okay from the other end? Is someone coming to get you?' he asked.

Despite the conversation we'd just had, he seemed to be concerned about my welfare. He didn't come across as an arsehole or creepy. In fact, he seemed quite the opposite. It's funny how looks aren't everything. Someone with the right personality can count for so much more.

I held on to his arm as we left the restaurant and kindly accepted his offer of getting a cab back to Waterloo together. At the station, he air-kissed me twice like I was now accustomed to, and we parted ways.

I sat on the train in silence looking out of the window. A million thoughts running through my mind. *What should I expect? How do I act when I get home? What consequences could this have for me? What have I just signed up to?*

What a complete mess I had gotten myself into. Why was I always drawn into situations like these? I should have just kept my mouth shut and declined his offer. I wouldn't have got the commission; I may have lost my job, but Daniel and Jack were worth everything to me and that was all that mattered.

7

THE AGREEMENT

I hadn't thought about anything else for the past week. The deal of all deals had been playing on my mind.

Could I back out now? How would I go through with it? If only this was another one of my vivid dreams and it wasn't true after all... but it was.

Now that I was sober in the cold light of day, I questioned everything about that night. It's one thing to end up in a tricky situation when steaming drunk, but to plan something and knowingly sleep with someone without a drink was unbelievable. What kind of girlfriend was I? This was on a level with having an affair.

I kept saying to myself that I was doing it for Daniel and us as a family. The money could mean so much, but really, it was dirty money. What I was having to do for it was incomprehensible. I don't think Daniel would understand if I said that I was doing it for him and Jack.

I told Daniel that I needed to stay over in London as I had a very important dinner and there was a conference that I needed to attend early the next morning. It didn't make sense for me to travel home and then back again early to get there in time, so I asked if he would mind if I stayed overnight. Of course, Daniel being Daniel was fine with it... he even offered to drop me at the station. That's what made me feel worse than I was already feeling.

I had spoken to Steve on the phone since and he emailed me all the details the following morning, just as he said he would, but we didn't speak about the rest of the conversation we had that night. He asked if I was still in agreement with the full terms and conditions, which I said I was. He told me to be back at Bank Station on Thursday—same place, same time as last week—and that was it. He was going to take care of everything else.

It took me a whole day to work out the figures, get the technical team to check the design and specifications of the servers. I submitted the proposal, and it was lower than the price he was expecting. Dave was over the moon.

'I'm impressed,' he said. 'If you can manage to pull off this deal, it will be the biggest they have placed with us to date. I should have put you in charge of this client earlier. Now, don't mess it up.' Little did he know that the real reason why he was impressed was because I had a vagina.

His words stuck in my mind. If I didn't go ahead with our agreement, I could kiss goodbye to any credibility at work. I wanted desperately to speak to George and tell him all about what had happened and ask for his advice, but I simply couldn't. It had to be kept a secret between the two of us, then that way I knew if it got out it was him and not me. I knew that if I told George, he would try to talk me out of it and be quite defensive.

I had butterflies in my stomach as Thursday approached. A bit apprehensive maybe but not worried at all. My only concern was being caught out and my dirty little secret finding its way back to Daniel.

I did as we planned. I made my way from Bracknell to Waterloo and then onto Bank. I stood below the tall pillars of the London Exchange, just as I had before. The building towered over me and the steps that stood beneath it. I looked all around but couldn't see him anywhere. I had expected him to be stood patiently waiting as I arrived.

Sitting down on the cold steps, I pulled my phone from my pocket and flipped the front—no messages, no missed calls. What if he was the one who had second thoughts and changed his mind and I was sat here looking like an idiot? It was only 6.32 pm. He was only two minutes late, I had to give him a chance. I took out the paperwork from my handbag, ensuring that it was all there, in order and correct. It was. I had stuck to my side of the bargain, now all that was left was to complete the transaction. *Gosh, it sounds like a secret mission.*

In a way, I was secretly hoping that he didn't show up, but equally, it meant that he didn't sign the papers.

I looked up towards the tube station exit... there he was. My heart sank. Almost running up the steps from the underground tube and onto the large square courtyard pavement before me, Steve was sweating profusely as he approached. *Should I stand up? Should I stay seated?* I suddenly felt nervous, like a first date. Apprehensive about what was to happen next.

'Sorry, sorry, sorry,' he said, out of breath. A couple of trains were delayed and then the tubes were rammed so I had to wait for two or three to pass before I could get on.' He bent over, putting his hands on his knees and taking big deep breaths in.

'It's okay, I was just checking everything was in order anyway,' I replied.

'Look at you, Miss Efficient.' He laughed in a jesting manner.

I laughed too, breaking the icy atmosphere.

'So, you want to grab some food or drinks or head straight there?' he asked.

To be totally honest, I didn't want to go anywhere. In fact, I wanted to go home but that wasn't an option now, there was no turning back, I was in way too deep to back out now. *Actually, I could do with a drink... a little bit of Dutch courage to get me through this episode.*

That was the only way I would go ahead with this. Maybe the more drinks I had, the easier it would be. That's it. Get hammered and it would be over quicker than I had imagined, and I might not remember it.

'Yes, let's grab a drink,' I said.

'Okay, great, let's head over to the Pitcher & Piano. It's quite lively in there and has a great atmosphere. They also make lots of jugs of cocktails. Should be a great night.' I followed his lead as he walked us down the street to the pub. He was right, it was quite a big bar, lots of groups of people huddled together and socialising. You had to shout to be heard as it was so busy.

'Shall I order for both of us?' he shouted at the top of his voice for me.

I nodded. It was a lot easier than shouting back.

I stood patiently behind him whilst he ordered at the bar, paid and then carried two enormous jugs of bright red and orange liquid. He pointed to the glasses left on the side for me to collect and take his lead. We made our way to a slightly quieter end of the pub so we could at least hear each other speak.

'So, what cocktail is this then? It looks amazing.'

'Just like you, you look amazing.' He smiled. 'You like vodka, right?'

'Yep,' I said, ignoring his previous comment, not wanting to encourage him or make this more than it was—a business agreement.

'Well, this is a Cosmopolitan. It is a mixture of vodka, triple sec, cranberry juice and erm... I think a bit of lemon or lime juice. Try it, you will love it.' He was still half-shouting so that I could hear.

Steve pulled the glasses closer to him and began to fill them to the brim. He slid one back towards me and smiled, waiting for me to take a sip and see what I thought. I did, lifting the glass up to my lips, trying carefully not to spill any.

'Mmm,' I said before taking another sip. 'Wow, that is lovely, really sweet but so, so good.' Steve was watching me the whole time as I drank.

'Good, we aim to please.' He smiled as he began to fill his own glass. I placed mine back on the table and he refilled it right up to the top. *Is he trying to get me drunk?*

'Excuse me for a moment, I need to go to the toilet really quickly,' I said as I got up from my chair and made my way to the ladies in the far-right corner. I was feeling a little tipsy but not too bad, I'd only had a couple of drinks and hadn't eaten, so the alcohol went straight to my head. Trying to be quick, I washed my hands and made my way back to Steve again, but I couldn't help but stand for a moment, looking into the mirror, wondering what on earth I was doing.

Instead of the jugs I had left him with and my glass of Cosmopolitan, I found another cocktail on the table.

'Compliments of the barman, apparently.' Steve smiled and pushed the drink towards me.

'I'm sorry,' I said, confused.

'The bartender brought it over and said it was on the house. I wish I was a woman sometimes... I never get free drinks.' He raised his eyebrows and smiled. I thought it strange, but at the same time, I would never turn a drink down.

As I leaned back in my seat, something behind Steve caught my eye... I found it strange. Most people in the bar were in big groups, crowds, laughing, enjoying each other's company. There in the corner was a man in a dark black hoodie, on his own, slightly hidden by the people around us. He had the hood so tight and drawn up around his face that I couldn't make out who he was. I thought it was odd because he was on his own and appeared to be hiding. Trying not to be rude and ignore Steve, I picked up my glass again to sip, but as I glanced back, the man was gone.

I shook my head as if trying to bring myself back into the room and concentrate on our discussion. *Was it real or was I imagining it?*

The drink was nice but it tasted odd, not at all like the first Cosmopolitan. It didn't taste like alcohol at all, more of a bitter taste. Mouthful after mouthful, I sank them down, and the more I drank, the more he refilled. Even though we were there under peculiar circumstances, it was quite enjoyable, and we had a laugh. Steve was asking about my career, what I wanted to do in the future, what my life plans were, whether I wanted more children and about my family, my sisters and my parents. He knew a lot about me already.

Steve spoke about his weekend in the Lake District with his wife, his plans for the future, all about him travelling the world when he was younger and how he wanted to retire abroad at some stage. He genuinely seemed like a nice guy. I didn't find him sexually attractive one little bit, but as a person, he appeared lovely. It was going to be difficult sleeping with someone that I wasn't attracted to.

'I've booked one of the best hotels in London, I hope you like it. Views over the city and such unique, beautifully decorated suites,' Steve threw into the conversation. I suddenly looked up, forgetting the real reason why we were there, bringing reality crashing back to the room. I was having a better time just talking but I knew the inevitable was looming. He mentioned the word 'suite', not bedroom—that sounded expensive to me.

'Oh, really? Thank you so much, I'm looking forward to it.' I smiled but quickly downed another glass. At this rate, we would have finished both pitchers in less than an hour.

'Would you like some food? You must be hungry,' he asked.

'No, no, I'm fine, but if you are hungry, we can go and grab something. I'm totally easy with whatever you'd like.' I smiled back at him, waiting for him to decide. I felt bad that he had paid for the drinks since he had organised and paid for the hotel. *Wait... hang on a minute, this was his suggestion, so why shouldn't he pay?*

The more drinks I had, the more all sense of reality slipped away from me. I lost all perception of where I was, who I was with and what I was doing.

'Shall we make a move, or do you want more drinks?' Steve wasn't being pushy, but he appeared nervous too, acting fidgety and distracted.

'Erm... yes, we can make a move. I'm fine if you are?' I was intoxicated but trying to act as sober as I could.

Steve walked us to a large building block about ten minutes away from the bar. Large lit-up letters saying Threadneedles. Huge planters full of bright pink flowers lined every windowsill and alcove along the building's exterior.

As we approached the entrance, its grand hallway was jaw-dropping. Marble floors, a large dome with a stained-glass roof was impressive. I gazed up above me and stared into its beauty. I felt out of place. *He should be taking his wife here for a special anniversary or I should be here with Daniel.* I felt seedy and dirty. That nagging voice at the back of my mind saying, *You can't let the business down... do it for the money, do it for Daniel, for Jack, for the commission.*

Steve checked us both in, the reception staff looked me up and down in disgust. He turned to me with an amazed expression, taking my hand in his and leading me towards the lifts to the left-hand side of the reception desks.

'Come on, there is more to show you.' He smiled, pulling me towards the buttons so he could call the lift to our floor.

It wasn't a busy hotel, but the few people I saw were smart and elegantly dressed. You could tell there was a lot of money being spent here. The looks that I was getting from others in the hotel made me feel worse. The sense of cold, hard stares were burning holes in my back as I stood waiting patiently. I was being treated like a hooker... to be fair, I pretty much was, but it didn't help the way I felt.

As I took in the views of reception, I noticed elegant antique vases filled with lavish displays of flowers alongside expensive-looking ornaments. A stunning classic piano and accompanying chair stood in the centre of the room and the strong smell of fresh aromas filled the air. One thing was for sure, Steve liked to watch my reaction. He was studying my every move. Each time I looked back at him, he was following me with his eyes and smiling to himself. He liked to please.

He never once grabbed me or tried touching me inappropriately. Everything was with consent, the only thing he ever really tried was to hold my hand and pull me in the direction of the hotel. I couldn't fault him for his courteous and gentleman-like approach. If I was single and dating, I could imagine him to be a real charmer.

The lift chimed and the doors slowly opened. An older couple stood there in the middle of the lift. Faces blank, she had her hair piled high in a neat bun, a tight-fitting long dress, an overcoat and a handbag hanging from her forearm. He had a full suit, polished black patent shoes, holding a leather wallet in his hand. They didn't look like they had spoken at all during the lift journey, nor did they seem to be enjoying each other's company. Both leaving at the same time, very close to each other, giving us both a look up and down before making their way out of the hotel.

As I watched them leave, a man in a black hoodie and dark jeans walked into reception and made his way around the other side of reception. He glanced at me briefly in a strange manner—I couldn't make out his face, but he looked panicked as if he wasn't expecting me to turn around. Trying to hide behind the large pillar. It was the same man from the bar, but why didn't he want me to see him?

I wanted to glance back and see if he had taken a second look, but Steve tugged at my arm to get me into the lift, so I moved in, losing sight of him. He pressed the button for the third floor and waited for the doors to close again. There was a nagging thought in my mind that I had seen him before. The man from my dreams, the man at work. Had he followed me all the way to London? The same man that was sending me the letters and knew where I lived and worked. No, he couldn't possibly be the same person. I was going crazy—I'd had way too much to drink and, once again, was thinking more into something I really shouldn't. It couldn't possibly be Jim... what would he be doing here?

Behaving like the child I was and perhaps to lighten the mood a little, I pushed every button I could in the lift for every floor—there were fifteen in total. Chuckling to myself, I peered at Steve, taking in his reaction. He seemed amused, but instead of laughing, he took my hand from the buttons and held it close to him so I couldn't press anymore.

I liked his stern but patient hold on me.

As the doors opened on the third floor, he gently pulled me along by my hand, down the corridor, the room card in his other hand, looking up occasionally until the number on the door matched the key card. He stopped, me trailing along behind him. Steve held the card out to the door, expecting the small light to flash green and let us enter the room.

The locking mechanism clicked as he pushed open the door and we both walked inside. The air conditioning system whirred away as background noise, the see-through curtains were flapping in the wind as the floor-to-ceiling windows were slightly ajar, and a small metal balcony kept us from the drop below.

The room was spinning and I had double vision, but it was self-inflicted... I had to continue with the plan and get myself back in the room. I didn't know why, but this time it felt different. Yes, I was drunk but my legs felt abnormally weak, my body limp and my head spinning uncontrollably. No matter how hard I tried, I couldn't sober myself up.

'Can I... erm... use the bathroom quickly, please? I...' I tried asking Steve, but I struggled with the words.

'Of course you can, you don't need to ask, it's your room for the night too.' Smiling at me, he threw his wallet and keys on the bedside table and sat on the edge of the large king-size bed with the television remote in his hand. He was beginning to flick through the music channels as I made my way to the bathroom.

I would have given anything to leave the hotel room there and then. If there was a window, I would have climbed out and run far, far away. Screw work, forget the deal and the money. My family was the most important thing and there I was betraying both of them. I looked around but there were no windows in sight, only in the main bedroom.

I sat on the toilet for probably longer than I should have, my head in my hands, resting on my lap, deep in thought. Feeling like a different person in another woman's body, almost an out-of-body experience.

Right, pull yourself together, Rose. You are here to get your papers signed and do whatever you have to do to get it done. I pulled my knickers up and pulled my dress down, straightening it as I did so. I couldn't splash my face with water as I had a tonne of makeup on, so instead, I reached into my bag, pulling out my brush. I quickly aligned my hair, checked the rest of my face and took a deep breath. *Let's do this,* I said to myself.

I opened the door to find Steve had removed all items of clothing except his boxer shorts—everything else was folded in a neat little pile on the desk that was conveniently placed in the corner of the room. *That's a turn-off for starters,* I thought. *Isn't the idea to get each other slowly undressed instead of me touching a half-naked man while I'm fully dressed?*

'Everything okay? I was starting to think...' He stopped and paused what he was going to say.

'Yes, of course! Sorry, I was just freshening up.' I think he could see the look of surprise on my face as I appeared from the bathroom and noticed he was half-naked.

I know I had said that I didn't find him attractive, even though he was a nice guy, but I was amazed to see that his physique was in pretty good shape. His chest was well-defined, covered by a perfect amount of hair. I found hair on a man extremely attractive. My thoughts on hair was that it was what defined them as a man rather than a boy. Well-seasoned and experienced, they could teach you so much more than a young man could.

His stomach didn't quite have a six-pack, but it was nice and flat and tight... you could tell he worked out. Steve had strong, thick-set hands, and without him noticing, my eyes suddenly darted down to his boxers. I noticed the size of his cock through the material. *It just goes to show that you shouldn't judge a book by its cover,* I thought to myself.

Why on earth did his wife not want a piece of this? If I closed my eyes and laid back, maybe I could enjoy this. At a moment of madness and complete out-of-body experience, my mind went blank—any thoughts of guilt, bad feelings or a conscience left me. It was as if I was someone else, in some-body else's room with another woman's husband. The last part was correct, but for some reason, it didn't matter right now.

I walked over to the bed where he was sitting. He stood up as I approached and reached out for my hand. Pulling it into his body, he moved it behind him and placed it on his lower back for me to embrace him, which I did. He moved his large hands to the back of my neck, my hair entangled in his hold, and he pulled my head towards his. I closed my eyes and let the moment take control. He had an incredible, passionate and captivating kiss. His lips were fully locked with mine, and as they sealed, his tongue worked its way into my mouth. As he moved closer to my body, I could feel his groin pushing against the top of my thigh. I felt my body tingle in a way that it had never done before.

I was still fully clothed. Steve began to move his other hand to the neck of my dress and tugged at the zipper. The whole time, he was kissing me and holding me so tight, it was like his hands and body moved completely independently. His fingers worked the zip and the dress slid seamlessly all the way to the bottom, leaving my entire back exposed.

He stopped kissing me but kept his eyes firmly locked on mine. Both of his hands moved to each of my shoulders and he peeled the dress from my body as it fell to the floor. He looked down slowly, not at the dress but at my semi-naked body. He used his fingers to trace a line around the top of my bra as it sat cradling my large breasts. As his fingers touched my skin, goosebumps ran down my entire body. I couldn't help it, but I sighed in anticipation of what he was going to do next. I was completely in his control and beholden to what he wanted to do to me.

Normally, it was me leading the way in sex. I was the instigator, the dominant in all scenarios, but this time, it was different. I liberally stood there, open to whatever he wanted to try, a moment of hypnosis.

Giving in to raw adult pleasure with someone I knew very little about. This time though, there was no love or attachment. I had no feelings or care for him as a person, I didn't care what he thought about me or my body, or whether I was good in bed or not. It was just pure consensual sex filled with ultimate lust.

Again, he raised both his hands to my shoulders and ran

his fingers under my bra straps, slowly, gently feeding them down my arms and undoing the clasp fastener against my back, letting my bra drop to meet my dress on the floor. Taking his time with every touch and caress. His eyes were deep in mine. I was drawn into them, leaning forward to kiss him again, I could feel my heart pounding, the adrenaline running through my veins and the most incredible feeling of naughtiness. Something so ultimately wrong but it felt so good, I couldn't describe the fire inside me. It was as if I was on a high of attraction, passion and tension. I closed my eyes and moved back into his strong arms, my nipples pushing against his hairy chest, heightened and hard to the touch.

I could feel myself getting wetter and wetter as his hands moved down to my bottom, tingling with every inch that he drew closer. Steve was grabbing and squeezing my cheeks with such force that it turned me on even more.

'Turn around. Keep your eyes closed,' he whispered in my ear as he stopped kissing me.

I looked confused but I trusted his requests for some reason. 'Turn around,' he said again, keeping hold of my left hand the whole time as I slowly turned to face the wall. I was intrigued as to what he was going to do to me.

He reached around, grabbing a breast in each hand, gently cupping and squeezing them. I threw my head back and gasped, his rough hands felt good as he massaged them. Freeing both hands, I could sense him doing something behind me as his right hand slid down to the top of my knicker line. He teased the lace detail around the top—first, at the front, then at the back.

He leaned into me and said quietly, 'Keep those eyes tightly closed, let your senses do their magic. Let your body feel every touch, imagine pure ecstasy. You are safe, I promise.' I wasn't sure exactly what that meant, but I did as I was told. Closing my eyes, I felt his fingers slide my knickers slowly over my hips, dropping instantly. I was completely naked, stood with him behind me, the gentle cold air of the room flowing over my curves. I felt vulnerable, never had I been in a situation like that before. He could do anything to me right now as I stood there waiting.

I felt his body press up against my back. I could feel the full force of his erection against my young and tight bottom. I could feel the size of his cock, I didn't need to see it to know that it was impressive. He took his hand and slipped it down between my legs. He could feel how eager I was but just played gently inside my lips. My head fell back and leaned perfectly on his shoulder, my mouth open, breathing heavily in pleasure. I moved my arm up and held onto the back of his neck as he picked up the pace.

'Oh my god, don't stop, that feels so good,' I said in sheer pleasure. He knew exactly where to touch and circle at precisely the right point.

'Really? How good?' he said quietly into my ear. I couldn't answer him, I was caught in the moment. I threw a hand down and grabbed his thigh, digging my nails into him enough to know that he was incredible but not enough to pierce his dark, muscular leg.

He stopped instantly. I thought there was something wrong, but before I knew it, he brought his hand up and slid the same fingers that he had used to touch me into my mouth. I could taste myself on him. He smiled in pleasure as he watched me suck his fingers, focusing on me swirling the tips around my mouth like I was tempting him for more.

Steve moved his hand to my nipples and pinched them hard, which made me jolt suddenly. A quick, short, sharp pain. It hurt but I liked it, forcing me to take a deep breath in. Still facing the wall, my eyes closed. He did it again to test my reactions.

'Ugh!' I let out a moan, he knew it was a good moan. I didn't tell him to stop or not to do it, I let him know that it felt incredible. I think this was the sign he was looking for. Whether I was open and whether I had spoken the truth before when I told him I was open to anything.

His hands withdrew from my breasts. *Should I open my eyes or turn around?* I was waiting for his next command, but one didn't come. Instead, as I stood there, my arms hanging by my side, my nipples standing to attention and all my senses on full alert, I felt the full force of a whack to my bottom. He used his left hand to hold my left arm and his right hand to smack me across my cheek.

Without thinking, I let out another moan of pleasure. I liked it. I liked him hitting me... the more he did so, the more turned on I was. He smacked me again and again until my cheek felt like it was on fire, throbbing. I turned around suddenly. I opened my eyes and pushed him back till he fell on the bed. I was ready for sex now. Never had I had that type of foreplay before, it was unbelievable. I felt like I was ready to burst, hungry to reach my climax. He had selfishly been giving me pleasure for what seemed like hours.

As we both fell onto the bed, Steve used his whole body to flip me over from straddling him to me being on the bottom. He grabbed both my arms and lifted them over my head, holding my hands as tight as he could, passionately kissing me. I moved my thighs apart and brought my legs up, wrapping them around his waist, linking my feet together and squeezing him tight as his cock hovered above my aching opening. He had easy access to gently ease it in, but instead, he seemed to like me holding him tight with my legs. The harder I squeezed, the more electric he became. Him teasing me the whole time. He entered me like a hard, dark force, penetrating me deep and rough. The bed moved in time with us, the headboard banging against the wall and both of us moaning in pure pleasure.

It wasn't long before he had me begging for him to stop. He seemed to last for ages. Harder and faster than I had ever taken it before. My whole body clenched, my legs shaking. Both of us hot, sweaty and exhausted. I didn't want this feeling to ever end. It felt like a drug and I wanted him repeatedly.

It didn't feel awkward—it felt amazing. No emotional attachment, just steamy, hot, animal sex. We lay and cuddled for a while, my eyes still closed and completely in the moment, feeling everything with my body instead of my eyes just like he had told me to. I felt dirty. I felt naughty and needed to freshen up.

Dropping my legs to the side of the bed so I could get to my feet, there was a loud buzzing sound coming from my phone. As I opened my eyes, I noticed that my phone alarm was ringing and vibrating on the bedside table next to me. *That's strange,* I thought. *Why is my alarm going off?* Then I noticed something even more strange... it was light outside the window. *Had we really been having sex for that long?*

Suddenly, I noticed next to my phone was the paperwork I had taken with me. As I looked closer, I realised it had all been signed and completed. The pen just placed next to the documents. Steve had signed it all for me.

I turned around to thank him for doing it, but he wasn't there.

'Steve?' I called out, thinking that he was having a shower

in the bathroom, but he didn't answer. Nothing but silence in the room. I got up to go to the bathroom, dazed and confused about the night. Almost a blur, a gap in my memory of what happened between getting here and this morning.

I found a small white piece of paper that had the hotel room's name etched at the top and a handwritten message.

'Thank you for an interesting night. I knew you were dark but not quite how dark... you are an incredible person, Rose, don't change. Deal done! Steve.' What did interesting mean? Or dark? What did I do? Was it good or bad?

I carried the note back to the bed and just sat there and stared at it. *What on earth have I done?* For my own selfish reasons, last night was totally incredible. What a lover, but the guilt riddled my mind. Disgusted in myself but also thinking about the hours I had shared with Steve. Why had he left the room without saying anything, why couldn't I remember what happened? My mobile phone screen flashed.

'HOW WAS YOUR EVENING HONEY? MISS YOU. D X'

Daniel had messaged me. I didn't have the heart to call him, the guilt was crippling me like a disease. He would know from my voice how deceitful and untrustworthy I had been—he would know something was up and different about me. I hated myself for what I had done and the night I'd had. I didn't deserve him at all.

I felt like Cinderella—one moment, I was having an incredible night with another woman's husband in my bed, and the next, I awoke in a hotel room, him gone and no explanation as to how it ended. Did he feel as guilty as me and just pick up his clothes and leave? How would I speak to him the next time at work? Would it be awkward? How would I look at him again knowing that I had seen him completely naked and had sex with him? I was so drunk by the time I got to the room that I'm surprised anything happened at all.

I decided then and there to block it out, push it into the safe in my mind where all the other shameful things I had done were locked up. Remove it from my memory and give it no more time or space in my mind. That way, I could continue as normal, face Daniel thinking or knowing that last night didn't exist, and everything would be back to normal.

It took me a few moments to compose myself. I took a long shower, contemplating every action from last night... the way it felt, the way he touched me, the way he seduced me. It was like a dream, closing my eyes, trying to take myself back to the moment. As the shower ran its course, I patted myself dry with the fresh white fluffy linen from the hotel and stepped out of the steamy bathroom. I picked up the hairdryer from the fixings on the wall and began to blow dry my hair. I stood in a daze, filtering any memories from last night as I hit the erase button like a cold-hearted, emotionless woman.

I could hear my phone buzzing again from the bedroom, but I dared not look in case it was Daniel or even Steve. I needed a little more time to get myself ready before I called him back.

Getting dressed into the clean clothes and trainers I had packed, I placed all the paperwork carefully back in my handbag so I didn't lose them, then read my text message.

'HEY, STUPID, YOU GET THE DEAL DONE LAST NIGHT?'

I knew it was George instantly and he knew that I was meeting Steve to sign the paperwork but not the rest of the deal we had agreed to. He was like a brother to me, and because of that, I knew full well that he wouldn't be happy with what I'd agreed to, and more importantly, disappointed in me.

Another message bleeped in.

'ROSE, WE NEED A CATCH-UP. HAVEN'T SEEN YOU IN AGES. SASH X'

I felt guilty that I hadn't seen her in a long time, but everything recently had taken over in my life. I needed to make time to see her.

'YEP, ALL GOOD. SIGNED AND SEALED. WOOHOO.' I texted George back.

'MISSED YOU TOO, HONEY. EVENING WAS OKAY. LOOKING FORWARD TO CUDDLES WITH MY BOYS WHEN I GET HOME THOUGH. R X.' I meant every word I said to Daniel.

'MISS YOU TOO, SASH. LET'S CATCH UP SOON. R X.' I wished that I could confide in Sasha about the night I'd just had, but it wasn't safe to tell anyone at all—including her.

I flipped my phone closed and threw it in my bag along with everything else. I needed to get some food, something to drink and catch the train, then go to work. Dave would be so pleased that it was done, and I had closed the biggest deal in work's history.

Mission complete.

8

CELEBRATING SUCCESS

I managed to make it back to work just after everyone started to arrive back at their desks by lunchtime. George bounded over to me like a proud parent with a big grin on his face. He held up his hand to high-five me. I did the same back and a whack rippled through the office as everyone looked up and wondered what was going on.

'You need to go and bang the gong, you absolute legend!' George shouted at me.

'The gong, really?' I didn't want the embarrassment of everyone in the office looking at me. With the attention of it all, and more importantly, me knowing deep down how I really got the order in, I just wanted to hide in the comfort of my desk in the corner and forget it all.

'Come on, up you get, Rose.' George went around the back of my chair and lifted me up from under my arms to stand. Giggling and blushing a bright scarlet colour, I got to my feet. George walked me over to the other corner of the room, right outside Dave's office in full view of everyone.

Together, we held the mallet and smashed the gong as

hard as we could. I couldn't help but laugh out loud. The whole office clapped and cheered, it created such an atmosphere. The same bubbling feeling inside that you get when you are at a concert or a sports game. You look around to see everyone singing, chanting or cheering together. It felt so good, I was elated, proud and enthused all at once.

Looking up at George, he was also enjoying soaking up the mood in the room and I couldn't help thinking that if it wasn't for him, I wouldn't be standing here right now, and I certainly wouldn't be in this job. Yes, I worked hard, but he was the one who always pushed me further and encouraged me to do everything I had done. I owed him so much. Whilst the whole room was euphoric, I stood there looking at him, wondering why he helped me so much. I would remember him for the rest of my life.

Just as things started to quiet down and resume to the normal noise of the office, Dave walked over to me.

'Rose, can I see you in my office please?' With those nine words, it completely killed our celebrations. George looked at me out of the corner of his eye and raised his eyebrows. Sinking back into my more reserved character, I followed Dave to his office, still not feeling right from the night I had. This wasn't a hangover, this felt strange, but I couldn't put my finger on it. I was now panicking that I had to speak to Dave. I needed to keep calm, but my guilty conscience was over-taking my body.

Uh oh, I thought. Did Dave know what had really happened? Maybe Steve had called and told him all about our agreement and wasn't happy. That's why he had left... because I was too drunk and had put in a complaint to take me off the account. Would I be fired?

Oh no, please don't do this to me, Rose, I said to myself. Just when I thought that everything I had done would at least have a form of upside to it. Well, I could kiss goodbye to any type of commission I was hoping to get.

'Take a seat,' Dave said with his back to me, twisting his chair around to face the desk so he could sit in it and face me.

I didn't say a word, I just sat quietly in the chair, legs crossed, hands on my lap, waiting for him to speak. Just as I had done the first time he interviewed me.

'So, Rose, I understand you had a very successful night,' he said bemusedly.

'Erm, yes, I did.' I didn't want to let onto a single thing. Simple, one-word answers—that way, he wouldn't catch me out.

'And the contract, you have the signed document and purchase order, right?' Again, he asked me in a very confused manner as if I hadn't got it.

'Yes, it's on my desk, I'll go and get it right now if...' I placed both hands on the arms of the chair as if to stand up, but he stopped me in my tracks. This time, he had a big smile on his face and reached out an extended arm towards me. He wanted to shake my hand.

'Don't look so scared, Rose, you should be extremely proud of yourself. Well done! This will be the biggest deal in our company's history. The directors will be so pleased,' he said, shaking my hand, which, in turn, shook my whole arm and shoulder.

'Oh, well, I thought I was in trouble when you asked to see me.' I let out the biggest sigh of relief.

'Why would you be in trouble, Rose? Unless you have done something wrong? It's not as if you had to sleep with the guy or anything, so just enjoy the moment and look forward to the commission.' Just as he said that, I looked up, shocked and completely guilty.

Did he know and was hinting at something? Maybe he did know? He couldn't have done, could he? Had Steve called him?

'Oh, haha, of course not.' I laughed nervously. 'He was a true businessman and I like working on his projects.' I tried to back up my story.

'Well, that's great news, Rose, because he called me first thing this morning and said that he has another project he wants you to work on. Apparently, it's double the size and he thinks you would be very interested in working on it with him.' The words fell out of his mouth as he shuffled the papers on his desk.

At that same moment, my heart raced and my jaw almost hit the desk as I gasped in disbelief.

'I'm sorry... he said what?' I had to ask Dave to repeat himself as I couldn't believe what I heard.

'That's right, Rose. You must have made such a good impression that he said he wants double the servers you supplied this time and obviously more consultancy in addition.' Dave continued to talk but I couldn't quite process the words. 'Do you know what that means to the business and what that will mean to your figures? I really should have put you on this account a long time ago. I'm even considering giving you a few of the other large clients to work with as you clearly seem to be able to handle them.' He looked up at me, a big grin on his face as he waited for my reply.

'I... erm... don't know what to say... I.' The room suddenly felt as hot as an oven, I was melting with panic. I couldn't quite believe what he said.

'Well, in that case, I suggest you give Steve a call and ask him about his next project before he changes his mind. Take the contracts and the purchase order down to admin for them to process and make sure they do it all this afternoon so that it gets invoiced before the month's end. That way, you will get paid on it this month.' With that, Dave began tapping away on his keyboard, concentrating on his screen and signalling for me to get up and leave his office.

I should be happy that my client asked me to work on other projects for them, I also should be proud that my manager wanted me to pick up other bigger clients and work on those too, but instead, I felt numb. I did what I did last night thinking it would be that project and that project only, then I would be done and finished. What was I thinking? Who was I kidding? That I wouldn't have to see or speak to him again? I didn't see this coming, not one little bit.

The only thought that was whirring around my head like a bad storm was what would Steve want me to do for the next project. What did he have in store for me next? I hadn't even thought about the commission payout—it wasn't important. I suddenly didn't care about the money, it was irrelevant. I didn't want this turning into a regular occurrence.

'Thank you, Dave, and thank you again for your encouragement. I really wouldn't have been here without your support in the first place, and George's, of course,' I said as I got up to leave his room.

'You're welcome,' was all he managed to reply, but I knew he was happy with me and that's all that mattered.

My feet felt like dead weights as I made my way back over to my desk to collect the papers and head downstairs. Approaching my desk, I panicked.

Frantically, I moved all the papers on my desk, picking them up, sorting through them and checking them. The contract wasn't there, nor was the purchase order. It wasn't where I had placed it thirty minutes earlier.

Where the hell is it?

'Oh no, no. Shit, shit, shit.' I began muttering under my breath. 'This really isn't good... without this, I don't have anything. No commission, no bonus. The night was pointless.' I felt like crying. Maybe it fell out of my bag as I got into work. Kneeling to check through my bag, the chair shot out and George was curdled up in a ball under my desk.

'What the fuck are you doing?' I glared angrily at him.

'Missing something?' He waved the papers at me. 'Now, you really should be more careful, Rose. If I were you, I would be guarding these with my life and never let them out of my sight. Like gold dust, they are.' Before he could finish, I snatched them out of his hands.

'You really are a dick, do you know that?' As soon as I had the documents, I whacked him across the head with them. George held up his hands to cover his face but laughed the whole time. I think it excited him more than it should have done that he made me so angry at times. It did teach me a lesson though... without those papers, I would have been screwed and he knew that. Relieved that I had them, I sat back in my chair and laughed with him.

'I'll walk with you down to admin if you're heading down?' He began to uncurl himself from under my desk and got to his feet. I was surprised he managed to fit under there but agreed he could come with me. A grown man behaving like a five-year-old child in an office, ridiculous but funny at the same time.

'Oh... and, Rose. This came for you. I saw it downstairs in reception so thought I would bring it up for you. Obviously, I'm not prying but it looks like the same weird person that sent the last letter.' George frowned as he handed me a white envelope.

The minute my eyes caught sight of the same letter, I began shaking. I felt instantly sick. I didn't want to take it from him. I didn't need this right now, not with everything else that was going on. I was dreading what it would say and wished it would all go away. If I decided not to open it then I would be constantly wondering what *was* written. I had to read it.

I snatched it in anger. Not at George, but at the situation. The frustration. I stood completely still, staring at the letters on the paper. George stared at me, waiting for me to do something.

'I don't want to open it.' I looked up at him. 'Will you do it?' I asked.

George didn't ask questions and took it back. Without delay, he started tearing at the corner to reveal the letter within.

'You sure you want me to?' he said, checking with me before proceeding.

'Yes.' I nodded. 'Read it to me.'

ONLY DIRTY WOMEN STAY IN HOTEL ROOMS WITH MARRIED MEN. WHAT WOULD DANIEL SAY?

I suddenly felt sick to my stomach. My legs turned to jelly and I wanted to crash to the floor. I felt faint, the colour draining from my face.

'Rose, are you okay? Rose?' George put his hand on my shoulder to steady me.

'I... um... don't feel so well,' I said, staring down at the floor. I genuinely felt like I was going to pass out.

'Rose, what does it mean? A hotel? Who is writing these?' George looked hurt that he didn't know what was going on.

'I don't know...' I fell backwards into my chair. The wheels shook beneath me and it shuddered from the force of me sitting down. I buried my head in my hands, not wanting to see or talk to George. I didn't know what to say to him and I didn't want to have to explain what was going on.

The only two people who knew about our agreement was Steve and I... unless he had told someone, but who? There was no way on earth that Jim knew unless... but he couldn't! It must have been Jim following me in London—the man in the hoodie. In the bar, in the hotel reception. What was next? A ransom otherwise he would tell Daniel? Did he need money and was just waiting for the right moment to demand it from me? I couldn't bear it if Daniel found out. He would leave me for sure. Then what about Jack, how would that affect him? Maybe I had to come clean, be honest and tell Daniel what I had done and ask for his forgiveness. I don't think he would forgive me in a million years, nor would he be able to trust me or my job ever again.

Is he following me everywhere? Watching me at home? With Jack? With Daniel? I just don't understand.

'Rose? Come on, Rose, talk to me.' I heard his voice but ignored what he was saying. My head in my hands still, I pushed my chair backwards, stood up, flicking my hair backwards and taking a deep breath in. Trying to compose myself and get out of explaining last night's chaos.

We both made our way out of the office, into the corridor and down the concrete steps to the floor below. It always made me feel good going back downstairs, it made me remember the time when I worked there and had worked so hard to make it up to the first floor. Like career progression within the same building. George followed behind me... I knew he was itching to find out what was going on.

'So, Rose, are you going to tell me what happened last night?' George paused, hoping that I would do the same, but I continued without him.

'What do you mean?' I replied, making it further and further down the stairwell.

'You know what I mean, are they talking about yesterday in London? Did you stay with Steve last night?'

'That's a lot of questions in one go,' I added, trying to get out of answering.

'Well, you aren't answering me. What the hell is going on? You know you can talk to me.' He looked at me with empathy as he managed to catch me up.

'Do you care though?' I knew that he did, I just couldn't work out who I could trust and who I couldn't right now, and the letter had really shaken me up.

'Of course I do. You know me—you can tell me anything. Anything at all.' He smiled reassuringly at me again. How much I was going to tell him though, I wasn't sure.

'Look... we went to the Pitcher & Piano near Bank Station. We stayed there most of the night, had a few nibbles and then he went home early. Said he had an early morning and an important meeting to get to.' I felt terrible lying to George, it was as if he could read me like a book and knew it wasn't the whole truth, but I needed the secret to be as closed as possible.

'Really? I thought Steve was a bit of a party animal. Fair enough, as long as you had a good night and he didn't try it on with you.' George shrugged and left it there surprisingly. I should have left it there too, but instead, I carried on the conversation.

'What do you mean? Why would he try it on with me?' I

had to ask. What did he know? Was Steve known for being a bit of a sleaze with women?

George stopped mid-flight and turned to face me. I stopped in response.

'Rose, look at you. Why would a guy not want to...' Just as he was about to finish what he was saying, the door to the office flung open and one of the admin girls burst through on her way up the stairs, stopping our conversation halfway.

We both smiled awkwardly but it made us refocus and continue to the office. The discussion about last night ended and was never mentioned again. I wasn't about to raise it again. As far as I was concerned, nothing happened and it stayed in the past, where it belonged.

Once all the paperwork was safely with the administration team, the afternoon seemed to go so slowly. I tried desperately to delay talking to Steve, but as the day ticked by and it was nearly 5 pm—time for me to go home—my desk phone rang.

Stunned and unable to move my arms, I just stared at the receiver. The red light at the top of the display flickered as it rang. I tried to let it time out, one more time and it would go to voicemail. Without picking it up, I knew who it was, I knew the numbers on the display off by heart. Steve... it was Steve ringing.

'Do you want me to get it for you?' Kim asked from the desk next to mine.

'No, I... um... it's okay, I will get it. Sorry. Thank you for offering,' I said politely. I had to pick it up and speak to him. I swallowed nervously as my fingers gripped the hand piece to lift it.

'Hello, it's Rose. How can I help?' I said in a very professional manner.

'Hello, you,' he answered quietly.

'Oh, hey, Steve. How are you?' I tried to act completely normal and surprised it was him.

'Sorry I had to leave you this morning. I needed to be back in the office early and you looked so peaceful asleep. I didn't want to disturb you. I made sure you were okay before I left.' I could tell he was smiling through the phone; he was trying to be nice and clear the air. *Why did he need to make sure I was okay before he left?*

I looked around the office to see if anyone was listening. No one was looking in my direction or remotely interested but I couldn't help feeling apprehensive.

'It's okay, I had a lovely night. Thank you again.' I had to be careful what I was saying in case I was in earshot of anyone.

'I know you are in the office, Rose, and it's difficult to talk. I just wanted to let you know that I spoke to Dave this morning. I told him that you did a great job of looking after me last night and that the paperwork was all signed. I also told him that I have another project if you are interested but I will leave you to think about it. You can come back to me next week.' He went silent.

'Dave told me. Thank you. I have the papers; they are being processed as we speak, and I will come back to you next week if that is okay?' I was really struggling to have an honest conversation and say all the things I was thinking.

'Our secret is safe, Rose... you have my word. You know that, don't you? After seeing the state you were in, I couldn't...' The line crackled and I could make out what he was saying. 'I didn't say anything to the...' There it was again, a gap in his words. Frustrated, I banged the handset on the edge of the desk, thinking that would help, but instead, as I placed it next to my ear, it went quiet.

'Well, in that case, Rose, I am going to wish you a lovely weekend and I hope to hear from you next week.' He seemed to be waiting for my response before hanging up. It took me a few moments before I replied. So many questions I wanted to ask. Should I get him to repeat what I missed?

'You too, Steve, I hope you have a great weekend.' I buckled. That was all I could manage. I didn't ask a single thing. I held the phone to my ear, but the line went dead. Within seconds, silence was replaced with beeping tones. He was gone. I sat staring into space, the noise ringing in my ears, but I kept it there anyway. For a good five minutes, I had no thoughts, the phone was like a comfort blanket. I clutched at it till my ear went warm and numb. The only movement was the occasional blinking of my eyes.

What did Steve mean by he couldn't? He couldn't what?

The clock ticked 5.09 pm. I slammed down the phone, remembering I had to go and pick Jack up on the way home and enjoy the evening with my boys. Like clockwork, I switched off my computer and slid the keyboard to meet the screen. I placed all the papers on my desk into my tray and tucked my chair under my desk.

Even the thought of that strange, creepy man from the alleyway couldn't stop me from seeing Jack and Daniel tonight. I practically ran down the stairs.

'Bye, girls, have a great weekend,' I shouted to the ladies at reception as I flew out the main doors, across the road and waited for the bus to arrive. I used to hate getting the bus home to collect Jack, I felt embarrassed that I couldn't drive, but instead, I now enjoyed the quiet time of sitting on my own at the back of the bus, staring out of the window at all the traffic passing by. Reflecting on all the madness of the past twenty-four hours.

It must have been a record, all traffic lights on green, little to no traffic jams on the road and the bus was empty. It felt eerily quiet like an early Saturday morning.

That handsome, grinning face greeted me at the main doors as he always did. Jack's perfect little smile. He launched out from behind the door as it was let open and gave me the biggest hug of all.

'I missed you last night, Mummy,' he said.

'Oh, I missed you too, sweetheart, and I've got a big, big surprise for you,' I said, reaching into my bag.

'What is it?' He was almost bursting with excitement.

I vowed that if I ever left him at night then I would come back with something as a surprise so that he was all that more eager to see me. I pulled out a box of Lego. One that he had been wanting for a while. It was a car that he could build, it even had a motor that went in it when it was complete. I could imagine him racing it around the house. If there was one thing that Jack loved (apart from his dad and I), it was Lego and cars. He would spend hours building all types of cars, then hours racing them around the house.

'Oh, yes!' he said as he took it from my hands. 'That is the one that I have wanted for ages, Mummy.'

'Is it? That's good then. We can spend tonight building it together then, can't we?' I said, smiling.

Nothing gave me more satisfaction than giving him the things he wanted after so long of not being able to afford anything. If I couldn't be with him all the time and we missed out on quality moments together, then at least he had something to show for it. I wasn't trying to buy his love, but I needed him to know that I loved him so very much.

Jack said no more than a couple of words back on the bus home, he sat staring at the box of Lego, desperate to open it. We approached home, Daniel's car was already in the car park near our house.

As soon as I got in, I heard the scurry of paws running to the door. Harry jumped at me, eager for a stroke and fuss. I could hear the television on, Daniel must have been on the sofa.

Jack came running into the house. 'Daddy, Daddy, look what Mummy got me. Can you help me build it please?' He sat down on the floor without even taking his coat or shoes off and showed the box to Daniel.

'Wow, aren't you a lucky boy!' Daniel looked up at me, smiling. 'Hello, baby. How was work? I missed you last night.' He tapped the sofa next to him so I could sit down.

'I missed you too,' I said, kicking off my shoes and curling up on the sofa and into the arms of Daniel. Now this was happiness. Not a pay cheque, not money or commission. It was being with my two boys and my dog on the sofa having a cuddle.

Why had it taken a situation such as last night to finally appreciate that?

9

ON THE ROCKS

I t was a Saturday morning and I lay in bed after the whirlwind of a week. It was early, I couldn't hear Harry's footsteps tapping across the floor downstairs, nor could I hear Jack stirring. Daniel's snoring was keeping me awake. It was nice just doing absolutely nothing for ten minutes or so. I knew that the minute I stepped out of bed and peeled back the covers, I would be running here, there and everywhere, making breakfast, taking the dog out, going shopping, housework and many other things until later tonight and then bed again.

The only downside to not doing anything physical was that my mind was in overdrive.

I started to think about all the things that had happened at work with Dave, Steve and George. It made me wonder that if Daniel didn't know about all the secrets I was keeping, maybe he was keeping secrets too. It made me feel extremely paranoid.

Imagine there was a more attractive and stunning woman at work that was trying to seduce him. What if they had already gone that one step further and were having an affair. I had no idea what was going on—he never spoke about work like I did.

Is she more beautiful than me? Is she funnier? Oh my goodness... what if she is better in bed than I am.

It's one thing to like someone, but if you are sexually attracted to them, that's worse. Everything that was happening at work was making me read a lot more into Daniel and our relationship with each other. How I felt inside my own head was impacting the way I saw us.

I didn't want to be that needy, jealous girlfriend but I couldn't help but think about whether I was good enough for him. He was quite a charmer; incredibly good looking and I could see other women falling at his feet.

Stop it, Rose! Stop thinking about Daniel with other women and worry about it if and when it happens. There I was talking to my inner demons again. There weren't any signs. I had so many things happening in my life involving other men and sex that I began projecting the same scenarios into Daniel's secret little life. Evolving it into something that it potentially wasn't.

'Good morning, beautiful,' Daniel whispered in a groggy morning voice. He made me jump while I was trying to talk sense into myself. I rolled over gently to face him and smiled at his stunning blue eyes.

'Morning, honey.' I slid my hand up his warm body.

'What were you thinking about?' he asked.

'Oh, nothing, just daydreaming.' Well, that was a lie. What I really wanted to say was, *'How many people have you slept with, Daniel? And who is the best person that you have slept with?'*

'Well, you looked very deep in thought.'

'Creepy, watching me daydream.' I laughed.

'I could watch you all day long.' He said the cutest of things, but I wondered if he said it to other women. Maybe I was reading too much into it... why couldn't I just be satisfied that he loved me and our little family?

'Daniel...' I seized the moment. *Stop it, Rose, don't do it,* I thought to myself, but it was too late.

'Yes...' He knew a question was coming and his eyes tightened.

'Do you think you will ever get married?' Wow, I even surprised myself as to where that came from.

'Do you mean me in general get married or were you referring to us?' He seemed to be a little more alert, lifting his head up from the pillow to look at me.

'Erm, I guess I mean us. That's the next thing, right? We have a child together, a house, and a dog. Getting married is next, isn't it?'

I'm not sure what I was expecting. A proposal, perhaps?

'I suppose I want to get married one day but I wouldn't want it to change anything. What about you?'

'Why would it change anything?' Now he had me thinking. I loved him with my whole heart, he was my world, but getting married and saying that he would be the only person I would have sex with for the rest of my life seemed like a huge commitment. Sounds harsh but that was basically what it meant. I wonder what he was thinking.

'Let's talk about it when we have a bit more time.' He leaned forward, gave me a kiss and rolled backwards out of his side of the bed. I watched his perfectly toned, naked bottom walk around the edge of the bed and into the bathroom.

So, did that mean he didn't want to get married, or did

he? More importantly, why did I even mention it? Maybe I was looking to see how committed he was to me, and the fact that he didn't give me an answer didn't help.

I decided to get up and get on with the day, the thoughts whirring around in my head like a fairground ride. My own insecurities plagued my life and anyone that was important in it.

My plan was to be the best woman he had ever slept with, to carry out more desires than he could ever imagine so that he wouldn't want to touch or even think about anyone else other than me. I had to go all out, do things that a normal girlfriend wouldn't do. Find out his biggest fetishes and act on them. Or were they my desires and fetishes? Or even my guilt playing games with me.

My first act would be that of surprise, one of exhibitionism.

That Saturday, Jack had a birthday party for one of his nursery friends that he was invited to and that meant I had two hours free whilst Daniel would be at work. Plenty of time to carry out my plan.

I managed to dress Jack in his favourite smart jeans, polo t-shirt and his new little trainers. We had wrapped his friend's present in Toy Story wrapping paper. I helped him write his card as he still managed to get some of his letters back to front and upside down, so at least it was legible. All set and ready to go to his party, I needed to distract him for a few moments whilst I got myself ready.

'Hey, Jack, why don't you grab Buzz from your room and find some more of your favourite toys and pack them in your rucksack to take with you?' I asked, patting his back and placing his card and present on the kitchen table.

'Can I, Mummy?' He beamed up at me with a big smile on his face. 'Can I really?'

'Uh-huh. Quick, up you run.' I followed him up the stairs and into my bedroom to get changed.

While Jack was crashing around in his toy cupboard, I rummaged through the top drawer of my bedside cabinet. Unravelling a new pair of black stockings and a matching suspender belt. I sat on the bed and slowly started to slide them over my toes and then up onto my freshly shaven, silky-smooth legs. The thinnest, sexiest pair of knickers I had just purchased sat neatly underneath my suspender belt. Finally, I slid one arm, then the other, into a new underwired and padded black bra that I purchased in the week and fastened it behind my back.

I glanced at myself in the long mirror, first looking at my figure and my cleavage, then my bottom and how the knickers wrapped around my cheeks perfectly. 'I'm going to make him appreciate this new purchase,' I said under my breath. Opening my wardrobe, I reached for the longest coat I could find and threw it on. My hair pinned up into a pony-tail high on the top of my head. I slid my stockinged feet into the most comfortable trainers I found in a row underneath my bed, but I also picked up my only pair of hot black shiny heels and popped them into my handbag, draped over the handle of our bedroom door.

I sprayed my favourite perfume—Jean Paul Gautier—in my hair but not on my neck as I would want him to kiss me without getting a taste of it, just the smell that would linger on every strand. Another squirt onto my wrist so that the scent seeped out from under my sleeves.

No other clothes, no dress, skirt or blouse. Just my underwear and a coat. My heart was already racing at the thought that I had no clothes on underneath, leaving the house and making my way to see Daniel. I wondered if anyone would notice, I had to get the bus and make my way to Daniel.

Just as I buttoned up the last button under my chin on my long grey overcoat, Jack came running into the room, his rucksack bulging with as many toys as he could fit into it.

I gulped—it was now or never. What would Daniel do when I got there? Be angry or pleased to see me?

It took me at least thirty minutes to leave the house and drop Jack at his party. I left all my contact information so they could reach me in an emergency and then got the next bus to where Daniel was working. I only knew the address as he had told me the previous week that it was the road adjacent to the woodland area in the next village. He had said that it was so quiet and there was nowhere close to him where he could get food or drink, so he needed to take it with him. *Perfect,* I thought. *A nice quiet, secluded area to entice him.*

I didn't think much of it on the first bus with Jack, but as I climbed aboard the second one, I sat uncomfortably on the first seat behind the driver. I felt him looking at me in the large rear-view mirror. Did he know? Did he suspect that I had nothing on underneath apart from my underwear?

It felt strange. It felt naughty. Even though no one could see under my coat, the feeling of the coat on my half-naked skin was a huge turn-on.

The last bus stop was at the end of the road, but I still had a few hundred yards to walk to reach where Daniel was working. It was time to text him.

'HEY, IT'S ROSE. CAN YOU TAKE A BREAK?' I typed and then waited for his reply.

It took a few minutes, but my phone beeped as soon as I pressed the button for the bus to drop me at the next stop.

'YES? WHEN? ARE YOU OKAY?' Daniel replied.

I thought it would be easier to call. The bus slowed, the doors automatically creaked open, and I got to my feet. Slowly walking off the bus and checking my phone at the same time. I smiled back at the driver and thanked him as my feet hit the pavement by the bus stop. I scrolled down my list of contacts until I reached Daniel's number and began to dial.

It rang twice before he answered. I was shaking with anticipation and excitement, the wind blowing up the underneath of my coat and between my legs.

'Rose. What's going on?' He answered quickly.

'Nothing. I just thought I would meet you quickly. Can you take a break?' I asked, not giving too much away.

'Where are you? He seemed confused and impatient.

I was at the start of what I hoped was the road he was working on. I stopped, dropped my handbag on the floor and started to swap my trainers for my heels. I only had a short way to walk now, and I wanted him to see me walking towards him in those shoes, knowing that I had nothing on. Sauntering down the road. I had it all planned out in my head.

'I'm at the top of Asprey Avenue... and guess what?' I waited for his reply.

'Rose, I'm not playing your games, I'm busy as I have to finish this job today.' His stern voice put me in my place.

I ignored his reaction. 'I'm not wearing any clothes under my coat.' Just as I said that, walking down the road, I saw his angry face standing at the end of his customer's driveway, his mobile phone to his ear. He turned to look at me.

'For fuck's sake, Rose. What are you doing?' His face was red and flustered. 'I haven't got time for this right now.'

Completely killing any passion that I had built up in my head.

I laughed quietly to myself, I had to turn this around and make it sexy. I flipped my phone closed, cutting him off, and placed it in my pocket and continued walking towards him. Daniel's face turned from an angry to a naughty slight smile as he looked first at my heels, then up my body and finished at my eyes.

The closer I got to him, the more uncomfortable it became but in a good way. I wanted to tear off my coat and have sex with him in the middle of the street, but I knew I had some teasing to do to get him in the same frame of mind.

Daniel grabbed my hand as I reached him and pulled me to one side, behind the tall hedge that surrounded the driveway and out of view of his customer's house.

'Seriously, Rose, what the hell are you doing here, and more importantly, why do you have no clothes on like a pervert?' he asked, tilting his head to one side

'I wanted to surprise you. I want you to see my new underwear and I want you to fuck me in the woods.' I smiled.

'Are you crazy? Where is Jack?' he asked.

'Don't worry, it's okay... he's at a party. I have an hour.' I started to undo the top button of my coat, exposing my bare chest. I went to reach for the second, but he grabbed my other hand and stopped me.

'Rose, you really are something else. Not here. Come with me.' I couldn't make out if he was angry or pleased. He walked over to his car parked on the corner of the road. He fumbled around in his pocket for his keys and walked me to it.

'Get in the car.' That's all he said but I liked it. Short, sharp and demanding. I followed, opening the passenger door and got in. As I sat down, my coat rode up and showed more of my legs. Daniel got in the car and noticed immediately, turning to look at me.

'Surely, you can't turn me down after I've come all this way?' I looked up at him with my *come to bed* eyes, hoping he would give in.

'You do smell lovely and I'm wondering what you have on underneath. I have twenty-five minutes but I'm not sure where we can go.' He started the car and put it into first gear, lifting the handbrake and checking his mirrors as he did so.

'Take me to the woods and fuck me there or are you turning me down?' I said, giving him an ultimatum.

'Rose, what has got into you?' He laughed, turning the car around and heading into the woods car park behind us.

The car park was quiet, there didn't seem to be many dog walkers around and it was late morning, so I think most people had already been and were heading off before lunchtime.

Even though Daniel and I had been together for many years, this felt different. It felt spontaneous and naughty. I was attempting to put the lust back into our relationship, just as Steve and I had spoken about. I looked at him as he drove the car to the end corner of the car park. He had a glint in his eye and a smile on his face. I liked it.

By the time we reached the corner and he had backed up into a space covered by the towering oak trees, I had unbuttoned nearly my whole coat, leaving just one. It was a secluded and quiet space with only one other empty car around us.

Daniel turned the engine off, it was silent. He turned to me and smiled again.

I gave him a dirty look in return. We had never been in this situation before, but I quite liked it.

His hands were filthy from working but I liked him that way. He raised a finger and slid it between the opening of my coat, flicking it open. The cold air wafted across my half-covered breasts, sending a shiver across my skin. I sat still, waiting for him to do what he wanted next.

He ran his hand down to the bottom of my coat and did the same, teasing the edge of it open to reveal the top of my suspender belt into his view before dropping it down to the top of my thigh.

'Oh, you seem to be warm and moist down there. I'm guessing you came all this way to see me so I could pleasure you?' His voice turned to a smutty tone.

'In fact, I wanted to pleasure you.' I smiled, gently removing my shoes one by one and climbing over the hand-brake, onto his lap in the driver's seat. Daniel reached for the lever and jolted the chair back as far as it would go.

I didn't need to undo his trousers; I could already feel his erection beneath me. I peeled off my coat, side by side until I was straddling him in just my underwear in the middle of the car park.

'Rose... that's...' I stopped him talking and held my finger up against his lips.

'Ssshhhh,' I said before smiling and then closed my eyes. My lips touched his. This time, his kiss felt different, it felt like I was kissing someone else. There was a sudden spark—a spark that I hadn't experienced in so long. It rippled through my veins like a drug. The feeling I got when I was in a sexual drive was so powerful, I craved it time and time again.

Daniel held my hips and held me up so I could quickly unzip him. It was as if we were in a mad hurry to have sex, scrambling to free his shaft. The windows started to steam up, the dampness in the air filled the car as the passion fuelled our deep breathing. I couldn't keep my hands off of Daniel, wanting to feel him deep inside me. He didn't have a chance to touch me or for us to have foreplay, he ripped my knickers to the side and pushed me hard down onto his length, making me exhale fully.

Both of us breathing in time as I rode him back and forth, harder and harder. One hand against the window, the other holding onto the seat's headrest. I could see movement outside of the car but the more I could make out the figures of people as they came closer, the more I enjoyed every thrust of my hips. I couldn't have cared less if anyone could saw us. In fact, it made it even more exciting.

Daniel's face became emotional, he groaned and frowned as if he was about to pass out. His big forearms helping me to keep the rhythm on top of him until he could climax were gripping on tight. I could feel his whole body's tension. I took one last breath as he pushed backwards, hard into the seat beneath him. I couldn't take it anymore— my legs began shaking and my insides pulsing with pleasure.

Daniel held me still for a moment so that I couldn't move. I sank into him. My breasts were the perfect height for him to rest his head between them while his breathing slowed. Instead of holding me, his arms wrapped around me, giving him a chance to resume his composure. In an instant, he had gone from a strong man to a weak, shaking mess. Exhausted.

'Dammit, I love you, Rose,' he finally said.

'I love you too, baby,' I replied.

'Shit. There are people outside, Rose.' He looked panicked, trying to get me back into my seat and cover up. He slipped his cock back into his boxer shorts and held my coat over my semi-naked body.

'It's okay, the windows are steamed up, no one can see in.' I tried reassuring him, but I found it funny that he was so worried about being seen.

'Exactly, they know what we are up to. Quickly get dressed and I will drop you back off at Jack's party to pick him up. Where is it?' He was busy trying to adjust himself.

I laughed. Seeing him in a fluster was amusing. I liked having sex in an open place, the danger of being caught or someone finding us was adding to the excitement of it all. Looking at Daniel, I saw the face that I originally fell in love with, the young boy that I fancied and the man that I had always lusted after. But occasionally, it was nice to add a little bit of spice back into our relationship to keep the fire burning between us.

'Rose, for fuck's sake. Where am I taking you?' Daniel raised his voice, waking me from daydreaming about him.

'Sorry. The Memorial Hall on Ashbridge Hill.'

Daniel started the car and began driving me back, but I couldn't help laughing as I fidgeted in the chair, putting my coat back on and doing it up. He did the same until we were both laughing together.

'So, is this going to happen every Saturday? Surprise visits at work wearing next to nothing?' he asked.

'No, but I'm thinking of something else equally as exciting.' I smiled cheekily back at him.

'I like the sound of that.' Daniel pulled up outside the hall as I quickly changed from my heels to my trainers again.

'If you are quick, I can drop you both back at home.' It frustrated me not being about to get around as independently as I had been able to before I lost my driving license, and I hated having to rely on Daniel to ferry me and Jack around. He said he didn't mind but it must have been such a big inconvenience for him.

My second plan was for Daniel and I to have a night away from home in a hotel room where I had pre-arranged a few surprises for him.

The following weekend, I asked my parents if Jack could have a sleepover at their house. Of course, they accepted— they always did. Jack was the son that they never had and, of course, Jack was excited to stay there because he was always spoilt rotten.

Instead of heading there together, I went on ahead and left him some instructions. I had a medium-sized carrying case packed with a set of spare clothes for the following day, a see-through fishnet stocking corset and a variety of sex toys that I had ordered from Ann Summers the week before. Some for me and some for him. This bag would now be referred to as the 'sexcase'.

I had ordered a taxi for 7 pm and told Daniel to meet me at the hotel at 7.45 pm. That would give me enough time to check in, get the room cards, set up the room and be ready for his arrival. After paying the taxi driver, I reached over for the long handle of the carrying case and flung it over my shoulder. It was quite heavy, but it made me laugh to think about what I was carrying inside it.

The hotel was an old picturesque country house in what looked like beautiful landscaped gardens. I had never stayed there before so wasn't quite sure what I was expecting. A large oak-framed door stood as the opening to reception with a vast circular iron knocker in the middle of it. I pushed at it gently and walked in. The time was 7.10 pm and I had to check in quickly, leaving me thirty-five minutes to get ready.

The lady behind reception greeted me and asked for my name and booking reference. I quickly gave her all my details as she tapped away at the screen that stood upon the desk. The hotel had a strange smell to it, an almost stagnant beer-type aroma mixed with a floral scent that was trying to disguise the musty stench. It looked clean though and had great character. The décor seemed to be late century, although I wasn't a historian so my guess could have been completely wrong, but the plush armchairs and ornaments around the room gave it a grandeur.

Trying to hurry the woman along without appearing rude, I tried not to engage in too much of a conversation, eager to get my allocated room and door card.

'There you go, madam, you are on the first floor in room 14, here is your room card. If you head to the end of the corridor, take the stairs and turn left. It's the second door on your right. Do you need any additional room cards, or will you have any guests?' she asked inquisitively.

'No, I'm okay, thanks,' I answered as I took the cards from her gently.

'Enjoy your stay,' I heard her say as I made my way down the corridor. It was 7.19 pm and I had less than half an hour left. By the time I reached the room, it was 7.22 pm and I needed to let Daniel know the next step. I had already told him the name and address of the hotel but nothing from thereon.

'HEAD TO RECEPTION AND THEN TO ROOM 14. I WILL BE WAITING. DOOR WILL BE OPEN. MY NAME IS SCARLETT.' I didn't wait for him to respond, I flipped my phone closed, unlocked the door and went inside the room.

It was beautiful. A free-standing tin bath, a walk-in shower and a four-poster bed. Elegant velvet curtains draped across the windows and dark wood furniture. I didn't have the time to admire more of the room, it was already 7.25 pm and that left me twenty minutes. Five to have a quick shower and freshen up, five to get changed and into my corset, five to lay the room out and five to get into position—perfect.

I did everything on time. The finishing touches were two tea lights that I placed on each bedside table and lit them using the lighter from my bag, careful not to set off the smoke alarm in the room. I then took the wedge from behind the door and placed it between the door and the frame so it didn't lock closed and stayed slightly ajar. Making my way back to the bed, I lay across it in my lingerie, one leg slightly raised in front of the other and my left arm propping my head up. I froze in position, waiting for Daniel to arrive.

I waited patiently, trying not to fidget. I wanted Daniel to find me sprawled across the bedsheets in a sexy position. I told him to call me Scarlett like it was the first time we had met and were strangers. The way you make love to a stranger for the first time, the excitement of being someone different rather than the same boring person had got to be better, hadn't it? Just like last week, it felt good.

I kept quiet, watching the door, waiting for him to come. Each minute seemed to last forever. He was five minutes late. I could hear my phone vibrating, but I dared not look.

I could hear footsteps, someone coughing and then a small tap on the door. Hoping that it wasn't housekeeping or room service, I called out, 'Come in,' in a sexy, alluring voice.

I could hear Daniel laughing quietly as he walked in and threw his bag on the floor. His dark handsome face appeared as the door clicked shut behind him and he stood there looking at me.

'Oh, wow... hello, Scarlett.' He sniggered again as he approached the bed.

'Why is this funny?' I couldn't understand why he didn't find it so sexy and seductive.

'Rose, I don't get what you are trying to achieve. What with last week at work and now this... what has got into you?' He sat on the bed next to me.

'Don't you like my outfit?'

Daniel held out his hand and ran his finger along my side, following its curve, feeling the texture of the mesh and studying my body from head to toe.

'I love your outfit, Rose, but what is this? Why did I have to follow you here and the different name?' He leaned into me and kissed me on the top of my head as he always did. He wasn't jumping all over me as I hoped he would.

I took a moment to think about my response. *Should I be honest with him or keep up the charade?*

'Daniel, I thought it would add some spark to our relationship. You don't look at me the way you used to. You don't lust after me or touch me the way you used to when we first met. I couldn't bare you desiring another woman.' There it was, I had told him the truth so he could do with it what he wanted.

'Oh, Rose, is this what it's all about?' He touched me on the shoulder.

I didn't agree or disagree. I waited for him to say something else.

'You think I don't love you anymore.' He shrugged.

'I didn't say love. I know you love me. I just don't think you lust after me anymore.' The last thing I wanted was for this night to turn into an emotional rollercoaster, it was supposed to be an uncomplicated night of passion, but I had to say how I felt.

'Of course, I lust after you. How can I not find you sexy? Look at you. Life just makes me tired—work wears me out and sex isn't always the first thing on my mind. Never think it's you, it's sex with anyone.' He did seem genuine as he spoke, but I couldn't help but doubt his response.

'You're a man, you think about sex *all the time*.' I raised my eyes—the moment had been ruined.

'Is that what you think?' Daniel smiled.

'Yes, that's what I think.' I hung my head, not knowing what to say next.

'Right, Rose. I'm going to go back to the door and I'm going to come back to the bed, but this time, we are starting again and I'm going to have sex with my girlfriend who I adore. I don't want sex with anyone else and you need to understand that. No more shenanigans. You had better get ready though as I am going to kiss and touch every single part of your body all night long until you can't take it anymore. The filthiest and dirtiest night we have ever had together.' Daniel got up from the bed and turned around, making his way back out of the room.

The words that he said and the way he reassured me made me feel so much more at ease, I almost felt stupid for doubting his feelings for me, but I still found it important that we kept that spark alive between us. The whole conversation with Steve last week had made me doubt our relationship just because of the way he felt about his own marriage.

I picked myself up and got back into position on the bed. Daniel approached the bed once again. He kneeled beside me and stopped and smiled.

'So, my beautiful, Rose. What is in the bag? What do you

have in store for me?' He pointed at the opened bag on the bed behind me, showing a glimpse of brightly coloured toys.

I gave Daniel a dirty smirk, taking my middle finger to my lips and pushing it in and sucking it slowly in and out as if to tease him. It was a sign for him to start. He threw me backwards on the bed and laid on top of me. Kissing me. Touching me. Stroking me.

That night, we spent hours in and on the bed with each other until both of us could take no more. The early hours of the morning had made us tired—our loud noises had kept the entire hotel awake and we were both satisfied. We'd never had sex like that before, the heat of the room was intoxicating. He touched me in a way that I dreamed I would never be touched again.

I honestly felt as though we were untouchable as a couple. The love and lust that we once had was still there, we had just forgotten it. I vowed to make sure that we did something special or different every so often to keep us alive, but that it wouldn't eat away at my thoughts if life got a little too busy.

10

IT HAPPENED FOR A REASON

Four weeks later, I woke suddenly. Looking at my bedside clock, the digital neon numbers read 3 am. I felt sick to the stomach, my headache was pounding like a strong pulse behind my eyes, and I just couldn't settle. If I got up to go to the bathroom, I knew I would wake Jack. I fidgeted, moving from side to side under the covers. I thought that somehow lying on my side would ease the nauseous feeling.

Breathing slowly in and out, I concentrated on the street-light outside my window, but it didn't make the slightest difference. Sweat pouring from my body. The sensation got stronger and stronger and the need to be sick was building, I could feel the pressure rising until I could stand it no more. I flung back the covers and bolted to the bathroom. I didn't have time to turn on the hallway lights, instead, stubbing my toe on the doorframe, I ran down the hallway and crashed onto the cold tiled floor next to the toilet. I flipped the lid up quickly, smacking it against the cistern and just let my body do what it needed to do.

My body had turned into a hot, convulsing volcano that erupted repeatedly. My chest on fire and my head pounding more than ever, tears ran down my cheeks. I sat back against the bath panel, wiping my mouth clean and giving myself enough time to rest before the next wave of sickness. I was exhausted and tired. Jack hadn't woken yet but I was mindful of him stirring in his bedroom opposite so I tried to be as quiet as I could.

I imagined this feeling to be similar to what being poisoned would feel like. Was it something I had eaten? It wasn't a hangover as Jack and I had cuddled up on the sofa together watching television, so I knew alcohol wasn't the culprit. I did have the same feeling that I felt when I was pregnant with Jack. *Could I be? Surely not...*

I needed to calm myself down, get a glass of water and get back into bed. I sat for another fifteen minutes with my arms slumped over the toilet seat, my chin resting on the side feeling sorry for myself.

Things between myself and Daniel were incredible—we had never been so good. All we needed right now was a spanner in the works or something to test our patience. It was hard trying to be the perfect woman for Daniel. A mixture of fun, sexy and hard-working with an extra quality of being a housework goddess. Attempting to hold down a full-time job, being the perfect mother, girlfriend and looking after the house was too much at times.

'Rose, for the sake of Jack, get your shit together, you are twenty-two and an adult for goodness's sake!' I whispered to myself under my breath.

Flushing the toilet seat, dropping the lid and steadying myself on the sink basin, I turned the cold tap on full. The reflection of myself in the mirrored cabinet showed a dishevelled view of my normal self. I felt twenty-two going on fifty-two. Scruffy hair, a blushed face, watery eyes that looked like I had been crying and rosy, red lips.

I lowered my head to meet my hands full of cold water and splashed my face a couple of times. I opened my eyes and looked again at my reflection.

'The only person that can change things is you, Rose. If not for yourself, do it for Jack!' I tried to talk sense into my reflection.

I find it surreal looking at yourself in the mirror and staring into your own eyes. Deep into your soul and understanding your own mortality. The only person that truly knows you is you. Even your closest friends or partners don't know every minute detail—memories, experiences or past secrets. Everyone has a background and a past—good or bad —or things that you regret (I had more than most people's fair share), but having someone that can accept you for who you are and someone you can truly trust is what really counts.

Daniel had my back, he loved me for me despite all my many flaws, and yet I hurt him time and time again. The truth behind my business deal was eating me away inside and the thought of having to do it again for the next big deal. The stalker... when would it all stop? Yes, I could trust my parents and my sisters but even they would be disappointed in a lot of things I'd done. Daniel was the only one who loved every part of me unconditionally. He deserved so much more than me.

At times, I felt like I had been born emotionally mute with no conscience. The inability to show how I felt or even that I felt anything at all. I know I'm a cold person, but surely, I did have a conscience if this was bothering me so much. I always made sure that Jack knew how much I loved him and cuddled him constantly.

I had to sort my life out. What was I going to do about it all?

Switching off the tap and patting my face dry with the hand towel that was half hanging on its hook, I wandered slowly back to bed. I still felt ill but not half as bad as I did earlier.

For the next few hours, I lay with my eyes closed, hoping to drift off but the constant heavy, sick feeling in my stomach that was lingering was stopping me from doing so.

6.30 am buzzed on my alarm like an earthquake had arrived in the room. Loud and unannounced. I reached over with one arm and heavily thumped it to stop. It made a strange crackle-like sound and then stopped. I'm pretty sure I had broken it from the force, but with the room spinning, it made me feel better.

Once again, I threw back the covers and hurled myself into the bathroom. This time, Jack was sat up in bed, he rubbed his eyes and watched me wearily launch myself next to the toilet and be sick.

'You okay, Mummy? Why are you poorly?' Even at such a young age, he was such a caring little boy. I couldn't answer because with every breath I took, it just made me feel worse and I was sick repeatedly.

'Shall I get Daddy, Mummy?' Jack appeared in the doorway with his cute little pyjamas on.

'No, no,' I mustered. "Mummy will be okay in five minutes, just something I ate.' I looked up at him, watery-eyed, and tried my hardest to smile to show I was okay and not to worry.

'Oh, okay, Mummy.' He grinned and patted me on the back, gently pulling my hair back out of my face.

'If I put the shower on for you, can you get undressed for me and I'll help you in?' As soon as I said that, Jack ran to his room, pulled his top off and threw it on his bed and his bottoms he pulled down as far as he could. Using one foot, he kicked them as high and as far as possible in the other direction. They landed in the corner of the room somewhere. To him, it was a game to make his room as messy as possible. In less than two minutes, he was back in the bathroom and waiting for me to help lift him into the bath so he could stand under the shower.

At his age, he was quite independent. He liked a little help but if he could do it himself, he would. I would show him most things once, quickly picking it up, he was then known as 'Mr I can do it myself!'

He showered and washed himself, but I had to help him get over the edge of the bath by lifting him up, and once he had washed his hair, I would quickly check that all the shampoo was out or give him a bit of a hand before we turned it off. Even teeth brushing was easy, he had a little plastic stool that he would stand on to reach the sink basin and the cabinet. Jack would squeeze children's strawberry toothpaste onto his toothbrush and brush away at his perfect milk teeth smile. Then, when he was ready and had swallowed most of the toothpaste, he would turn to me and ask if they were alright.

'Do they look clean, Mummy?'

I would kiss him on the cheek and reply with, 'What beautiful white teeth you have!' He would grin and then run off, leaving me to rinse his toothbrush, place it back in the holder with ours and put his stool back around the side of the sink.

I loved that boy more than anything in the world.

I had to stop being sick. Jack would be late for nursery, and I would be late for work, so there was no time for being ill. I couldn't take time off work, nor could we afford it. I didn't want help from Daniel or my parents, I had to do this by myself. I checked Jack's hair, then as I turned off the shower, reaching for the large bath towel, I rubbed his hair first to take off most of the water and then wrapped it around his whole body, lifting him out and placing him on the floor. I used the towel to dry him all over and then asked him to get dressed in his underwear, t-shirt and shorts from his room. I said he could choose whatever he wanted to wear from his chest of drawers. He raced off, leaving me to quickly get showered and ready.

I could hear the faint yaps of Harry downstairs waiting for me to let him out and take him for a walk before work. Daniel was stirring in bed; I could hear him stretching and slowly getting up.

'Jack, sweetheart?' I called out from the bathroom.

'Yes, Mummy.' He came running and stood by the shower curtain.

'Do you think you can do me a huge favour please like a big boy?' I got out of the shower with one towel on my head and the other wrapped around me.

'Uh-huh.' He nodded at me like it was a game.

'Can you let Harry out into the garden for me please?' I tried to lean forward but I had to get to the toilet quickly before I was sick on the floor.

'Okay.' Jack couldn't quite run down the stairs, he had to step one at a time as they were still a little too steep for him, but every morning, we would let Harry out together so he knew what to do.

This is ridiculous, I thought to myself. *I don't have anything left in me to be sick, I am just heaving and nothing is coming out.* But it didn't stop the urge or my body's automatic movements. My chest was hurting, and I couldn't even keep water down. I needed to keep myself composed enough to get Jack to nursery, then I would work out getting to work.

Between the two of us... well, mainly Jack doing everything with my instructions, we made it out of the house, much later than normal but we did it, nonetheless. We got to the bus stop, but I had to stop several times on the way to be sick. Thank goodness I didn't see anyone I knew on the way.

'You okay, Mummy?' Jack seemed to look worried now. This morning was almost a little game, a challenge for him, but now he realised I really wasn't well. *Should I call in sick to work?* I couldn't... Did I phone his nursery and say he wouldn't be in today and we sit on the sofa all day? He would be bored, and it wasn't fair... Did I tell Daniel? Did I call my mum?

Nope, I had to get on with it. I could see the bus in the distance and I smiled at Jack. 'Mummy's okay. Just feeling a little poorly this morning. I'll feel better by lunchtime. Let's get you to nursery so you can see all your friends.' I just had to try and not be sick for fifteen minutes during the bus journey, that was the first challenge.

He smiled at me, held my hand tightly as we climbed aboard and bought our tickets. Jack chose the two seats right at the back so that he would watch out the back window as well as the side window. He loved getting the bus. I, on the other hand, hated it and just wanted my license back.

It was as much as I could do to hold my sickness down. I

clutched at the seat in front of me and the metal handrail to my side until my knuckles turned white with tension. All I wanted to do was go back home and give up, but I had to get him to nursery and me to work. The journey felt like a lifetime. It was only a fifteen-minute journey, but every traffic light and every queue seemed so much longer this morning. I should have stayed in bed and let Daniel take Jack. Mistake number one of the morning.

We pulled into the bus station opposite his nursery. Jack and I got off the bus quicker than we had got on. I sighed with relief and took a few minutes to breathe in the fresh air outside. Holding it down, I then checked that he still had his little rucksack, which had some of his toys and favourite things in, and held his hand again. He didn't have to take a lunch box in as he had a cooked meal there every day at lunchtime. It was Daniel's turn to pick him up after work today as he was on an early shift.

We rushed across the car park together, Jack pulling me along like he was trying to get me past the finishing line in a race. I lifted him up to press the security buzzer like I did every morning. Normally, I would give him a kiss at the door and his nursery teacher would take his hand from mine and lead him in. Jack waving at me through the glass door panel as he walked down the corridor and off to see his friends. This morning, instead, I was quite impatient. I rang the buzzer again, desperate to use their bathroom.

As they opened the door, his nursery teacher, Lauren, appeared and looked at me a little shocked.

'Are you okay, Rose, you look...' she asked, then stopped.

'Erm, can I use your bathroom, please? I think I've eaten something maybe I shouldn't have,' I asked before brushing past her and hurrying to their toilets, leaving Jack standing there with her. I didn't even wait for her response.

It took me over ten minutes to feel like I could compose myself again and make my way to Jack's classroom. I felt embarrassed, ashamed and stupid. What must they be thinking? I wiped my mouth, flushed the toilet and then just sat on the toilet lid with the door closed, staring at the lock. I just wanted to cry. What on earth had I eaten? Maybe it was just a sickness bug. I should have just stayed at home today, but no... it was like I had to prove something to the world by carrying on as normal.

I unlocked the cubicle door. I straightened my hair, washed and dried my hands and took a big deep breath before opening the main door into the corridor. Jack's classroom was on the left, he was already playing with his best friend, Joshua. Rather than disturb him, I glanced over at Lauren who caught my eye and smiled over at me. I waved at her and mouthed, 'Sorry! I must go, I'm going to be late, see you later!' I turned to walk away, down the corridor, back out of the front security door and walked the rest of the way to work. Walking made me feel slightly better, the wind blowing in my face clearing the heat and sweat from my body.

Just as I reached the corner before work, I bumped into Karen—one of the ladies from the office downstairs in admin. She must have walked as well. I didn't want to talk; I had no conversation in me, not this morning, but I could sense she wanted a chat.

'Morning, Rose. How are you? Oh...' As she looked at my face, she took a second look and must have seen how bad I looked and felt. 'Are you okay? You don't look too well.' Karen was lovely. We would often see each other in passing most mornings, she was normally hurrying off to work just like I was, but we made time to greet each other and make pleas-antries.

'Yes, I...' Before I could continue, she started talking again.

'Not saying that you look rough, I just want to check that you're okay as you look a little under the weather. Sorry, I didn't mean for that to come out like that. I...' She stopped awkwardly. I knew what she meant, I looked like absolute crap, tired and exhausted. Anyone could see that.

'It's okay, Karen, thanks for asking. No, I think I've eaten something funny. I've been up all night, but I didn't think it was fair for Jack to have to put up with me all day like this,' I replied.

'Oh, you poor thing, you aren't going to work, are you? Go home and go back to bed.' She was so sympathetic.

'Ah, thank you. I'll be alright. I think I just need work to distract me, and I'll feel much better by lunchtime. I'm sure I will.' I forced a smile.

'Okay, well, you have my number... if you need me to bring Jack back for you after work or collect him, just let me know. More than happy to help with anything.' It was lovely of her to offer but I declined politely.

'Thank you so much, that's lovely of you but Daniel should be picking him up after work.' I forced another smile, prompting her to finish the conversation. I couldn't think of anything else to talk about, every effort was being spent on not being ill.

'Take care, I hope you feel better soon'. She turned and walked ahead of me and into the main entrance of our work building.

Hurriedly, I walked into reception like a whirlwind. 'Morning, morning!' I called out to the girls on the reception desk, running straight past them and into the women's toilets. I didn't even shut the door, it just slammed behind me, kneeling bent over the toilet. I didn't even care that I was late or what anyone thought. By this point, I was just happy to be next to the toilet.

There was a creak at the main door then a young girl's voice, 'Rose? Rose, are you okay?' Emilia from reception had come in and was calling to me from outside. She sounded concerned.

'Yeah'. It was all I could struggle to say. I had only managed tiny sips of water this morning, no food at all, and I hadn't successfully kept that down either. She could hear me trying to be sick, so she pushed open the door and found me bundled up on the floor in a mess with tears in my eyes.

'Oh, Rose, what's wrong? Why don't you go home? You look terrible,' Emilia said.

'I feel dreadful. I just can't stop being sick. I haven't eaten and I can't even keep water down.' I looked at her like a help-less puppy wanting reassurance. How immature and weak I must have seemed.

'Oh, honey, it's okay. Let me go and speak to Dave. He will understand and tell you to go home and rest if you aren't well.' Emilia genuinely wanted to help.

'No, no. It's okay. I'll be fine. I...' I turned back to the toilet again to be sick.

'Rose, don't be silly. You need to go home.' Emilia got up and left the cubicle. I heard her leave the toilets and the door shut behind her. I couldn't even muster the energy to get back up. I knew the minute I stood up, I would be ill again. Less than five minutes later, I heard the door go again and a man's voice.

'Oi, Rose!' It was George. *What is he doing in the ladies?* He pushed the cubicle door open and stood in the doorway.

'Uh oh, you hungover?' He had a slightly smug look on his face as he found me on the floor. Why did he always presume that when I was ill, it was alcohol-related?

'Erm... no, I'm not, I honestly can't stop being sick, and no, I haven't been drinking.' His face then turned to one of concern.

'Oh, shit! Sorry, I just thought... Are you okay? You do look rough!' He bent down but didn't come closer.

'Cheers,' I said. I knew he meant well but I wasn't in the mood to joke with him or even talk right now. I had lost count of the number of people that said I looked rough today.

'Hey, look. Emilia has gone to speak to Dave. I thought I would just check in on you. You want me to drop you off at home? I can take you now if you want me to? I'll grab my keys.' He leaned against the cubicle door, waiting for my response.

'I don't want to trouble you, but would you mind? I think I just need to go home and sleep it off.' I had finally given in to the fact that I wasn't going to make it through the day at work. I would be totally useless to anyone.

Emilia made another appearance. *Oh wow, now I have an audience.* I knew they were only looking out for me, but I did feel slightly stupid. I should have just stayed at home and called in sick. I just didn't want work thinking I called in sick at the drop of a hat.

'I've just spoken to Dave... he was fine. He said of course you need to go home, rest up and let him know how you feel later today or tomorrow. He also said that he hoped you felt better soon. See, I told you!' Emilia nudged George, ushering for him to help me up. She handed me a wet towel so that I could wipe my mouth clean and almost leaned in to hug me.

I walked over to the basins and washed my hands.

'Do you want me to call Daniel?' George asked.

'No, I'm okay. I'll be fine, I'm just going to head home. I'll be as good as new tomorrow. Must be something I ate at the weekend.' I smiled and grabbed my bag from the floor. He put his arm around my shoulders and walked me out to reception.

'Now let's get you home so you can rest up. I'll text you later to see how you are.' He helped me into the passenger seat of his car like an invalid and drove me home. I felt defeated but if I could just get back home and get some rest, I would be brand new by tomorrow morning. I said very little to George on the way home, feeling guilty and slightly rude, I just stared out of the window.

Returning home, I unlocked the front door, hearing Harry's barks from inside the house. He ran to greet me, wagging his tail in delight. 'Hello, gorgeous,' I said as I made a fuss of him before closing the door behind me. There wasn't much else to do but get a glass of water and a blanket from the pile of washing on the dining room table. I sat on the sofa, prompting Harry to jump up and join me as I lay back, finally closing my eyes.

I spent the rest of the day still being ill, managing to get rest where I could, but the slightest movement made me feel worse. Water didn't help and I couldn't stomach food, not even plain toast. Whatever I had eaten over the weekend didn't like me one little bit.

Five o'clock came and I heard the front door go. Jack came running through the kitchen, into the dining room to find me laid out on the sofa with my blanket and Harry curled up on the end.

'Mummy!' He was so pleased to see me, hurling himself onto the sofa and giving the most welcomed hug of the day.

'Careful, Jack,' Daniel said as he stood in front of me. His face looked solemn. 'Hey, what's wrong? Jack said you were poorly this morning, I didn't hear you. Why didn't you wake me?' I sat up wearily as Daniel fired me a raft of questions.

'I don't know, it must be something I ate. I feel dreadful. Started early this morning and now I can't stop,' I replied.

'Have you had a bad stomach as well?'

'No, just sickness. I feel slightly better this afternoon, but this morning was terrible.' *That's strange...* I thought. *Normally, if I had eaten something bad, then I wouldn't just be sick.*

'Jack, can you do a huge favour for Daddy please?' He turned to our little boy with open arms. Jack jumped up and into them, clinging on whilst he carried him to the kitchen. I heard them talking away to each other. 'Can you choose a nice treat from the fridge and sit at the table for me?' Jack didn't need to reply, I could hear his rustling as he got some food out.

Daniel returned to me on the sofa and sat down next to me as though he was going to ask me the most important question of his life.

'You're not pregnant, are you?' He looked at me quizzically.

'I can't be?' I frowned.

'I'm being serious, Rose. It sounds so similar to when you were pregnant with Jack.' For once, he was serious.

'You mean we had the most amazing sex a month ago and nothing since because we have been so busy,' I corrected him.

'Yes, that's exactly what I mean.' Daniel sat there, I presumed he was thinking back to when we were in the hotel together.

'Look, Daniel, I can't think straight right now, it's not a good time.' I didn't have the energy to have a discussion, especially one facing the reality that I could be pregnant.

'Well, we need to talk about this because if you are, this isn't going to go away tomorrow or the day after, or the day after that. You know how ill you were with Jack—you could be ill for months and you will need help.' He put his hand nervously on my shoulder but almost immediately took it back off.

'Yeah, yeah, I know. Look I'll be fine tomorrow, don't worry.' I shrugged it off, just like I did with everything, but he wasn't about to give in.

'Right, I'll go to the shops and get a pregnancy test. Will you do it for me?' he asked.

'Really? You want me to do one today? Right now?'

'If it's negative, then we know it's something you may have picked up. If it's positive, then we have some talking to do.' Daniel paused and looked at me, then at Jack. 'He doesn't know what's going on either. He seemed really worried earlier in the car when he said you were poorly. I don't want this to affect him.' I saw Daniel with a little smile as if he was half hoping I was. He stood up, reached for his car keys out of his pocket and said, 'I will be back in a minute. Do you need anything else?'

'No, I'm fine thanks.' I looked up at him and watched as he walked out of the room. Jack was sitting at the table with a cheese string, playing contently, pulling each of the strings all the way to the bottom before carefully placing them in his mouth to eat.

'Daddy is just popping to the shop, I won't be long, can you look after Mummy for me whilst I'm gone?' Daniel asked Jack. He didn't say a word, his eyes fixed on his food, but nodding his head to agree and swinging his legs.

Daniel returned within minutes, clutching at a small pharmacy bag, a can of coke and a packet of mints. He passed me the bag. 'I got you a can of coke, I thought it may settle your stomach a little, and a pack of mints to suck on. It can't be nice being sick all day.' Daniel held out his hand, helping me up from the sofa.

I had deja vu. Nearly five years ago when I fell pregnant with Jack—the same feeling, the same nervousness, but this time, not as scared. I think deep down I knew what the outcome was going to be. As a woman, you just know, but once again, I tried to avoid the inevitable.

I walked to the downstairs toilet, took the test out, placed it on the back of the cistern and tried to go to the toilet but I couldn't. I was so dehydrated from being sick every time I took a sip of water that I hadn't gone all day. I had to, just a little bit. I had to give Daniel an answer one way or another. I sat patiently until I could finally go. Placing the cap on the stick, I stood up, flushed the toilet and walked back out with it in my hand. I didn't look at the display, I didn't want to. I sat back on the sofa and handed it to Daniel, he had Jack cuddled up on his lap, trying to find something to watch on the television.

He placed it display-down on the arm of the sofa until he had finished selecting the cartoon channel and then popped Jack on the floor in front of him in between his legs.

I wasn't sure I wanted to know the results. I was quite happy with us being a family of three. Daniel looked at me, then the test. It was as if he was waiting for me to tell him to look.

'Shall I?' He raised his shoulders.

'I guess so...' I couldn't even look at him, my eyes fixed on the television. Sickness swirling around my stomach again as if it was brewing. I clicked open the ring pull of the can before taking a small sip and swallowed gently. I could see that he had placed the test on his lap, face-up, but I couldn't quite make out the lines. I could feel him looking at me, but I didn't want to turn my head enough to meet his expression.

'Rose, look at me, don't block me out like you always do.' He nudged me with his hand. He waited but I did nothing. I froze. 'Rose, goddammit, you are so stubborn sometimes.' Daniel passed me the test and there it was. Once again as clear as day—two lines. A positive test. No wonder I felt as sick as I did. I was carrying his baby again.

I'm not sure my face showed any emotion at all, but many thoughts were running through my mind.

'Rose, we are in this together. It's my baby too, you know.' I'm not sure what Daniel was trying to say here.

'Look, I don't know what you want me to say. What do we do now?' I was half expecting him to be shocked like the last time, but he seemed to be more mellow, calmer, not surprised in the slightest. *Is this what he secretly wanted all along?*

'What do you mean what do we do now? We work this out together and plan for the fact that we are having another baby.' He smiled at me. Daniel looked happy.

'I don't know how I feel about this.' I looked at Daniel with watery eyes.

'Jack would love a little brother or sister.' Looking at him, I could see that, this time, it was different.

A sudden pain pierced my heart. The memory that I

thought I had erased of my night in a hotel with Steve just over a month ago flashed before me. I couldn't possibly be carrying Steve's baby instead... could I? I don't even remember using protection, I was that drunk. The night was a complete blur.

Shit. Now what? How will I explain that one to Daniel? Well, I can't. I won't

'Rose, I love you. I will always love you. Yes, you are a nightmare, but you are *MY* nightmare. I would do anything for you. I think deep down you know that.' Daniel squeezed my hand, just like he did when we were seventeen.

'I love you too, Daniel, I think sometimes you deserve so much more than me.' I looked deep into his eyes and meant every word.

'I don't want more, I already have what I want, who I want.' I had missed Daniel's heartfelt comments. Work sometimes took over our lives and we felt disconnected at times. I guess it was meant to be, and as much as this could be the second-best thing that had happened to us (Jack being the first), that niggling thought about it possibly being another man's baby would haunt me. How could I know for sure?

Jack was sitting in front of us, giggling at the television. He was oblivious to everything happening around him. I wondered what he would make of our news and having a little brother or sister to play with. It wasn't time yet to tell him.

11

HEARTBROKEN

That night, Daniel rushed around after Jack and me. He fed, bathed and put Jack to bed while I either slept or was ill. I felt so guilty and helpless but there was nothing I could do to ease the sickness. He took Jack to nursery the following day. I had to call in sick again as I couldn't leave the house, bedridden and lethargic. They were really understanding, but soon, I would have to explain to work why I was so ill. I hadn't even told my parents or family yet.

George had called and texted me several times, but I read them and ignored him. Sasha had tried popping over, but I made excuse after excuse as to why I couldn't welcome her in or come to the door.

The only upside to all of this was that the stalker had gone quiet. No letters or creepy appearances. The whole time I was at home, he couldn't reach me or have any reason to threaten me.

Day by day, I became weaker and weaker. The weight was falling from me and I felt so dizzy from dehydration. Jack wanted to be with me, to play and cuddle with his mum, but I struggled to be what he needed or do the smallest of tasks. It took all my effort just to get up and showered in the mornings. I know most women had morning sickness, but this was extreme—I couldn't function at all.

Ten days of feeling pure exhaustion, no energy and lack of vitamins or minerals to keep myself or the baby going. My mum had tried to contact me a couple of times, but I avoided her too, saying I was busy with work or with Jack and would try to pop over at the weekend. Daniel was trying to look after us the best he could, working and keeping the house going, but even he was starting to look exhausted.

Although my excitement around being a mum again was starting to peak, the way I felt just dampened any enthusiasm I had. There was a long road ahead and I had to pull myself together to get through it. I tried anti-sickness wristbands and the doctor had prescribed me tablets, but each time I swallowed them, I was sick ten minutes later. I nibbled on ginger biscuits and sipped water or tea. Nothing I tried worked, and after just two weeks, I had lost over a stone in weight. I had to tell work, and whilst they were understanding, I was worried that I would lose my customers and my job.

Daniel was beginning to grow more and more concerned and had called my mum against my wishes, asking her to pop over on Saturday morning whilst he took Jack to the park on his morning off. I couldn't let her see me like this, so I decided to get up and showered and pretend I was fine. I wanted to wash my hair and put on some makeup. It always made me feel better when I looked my best.

The warmth from the shower was lovely, I let it trickle over my face and down over my body. The steam began building in the bathroom. The heat felt like it was giving me a little energy to build myself up, so I turned it up until my skin began to glow from pink to red. Looking down, my toes were swelling from standing in the heat at the bottom of the bath, my veins raised from the surface of my withdrawn hands and arms. My body, weakened from a lack of food and water, was barely standing but it was the best shower I'd had in over a month. The hotter the water, the better I felt.

I reached down with one hand to grab my flannel, it was soaked, steam rising from it and draped over the side of the bath. With my other hand, I reached out for the shower gel, but before I managed to get there, the dizziness took hold and I felt the room spin.

I tried to steady myself on the tiles, but my hands just slid forwards. I think the lights had gone off as the room went dark and I felt myself falling.

When the lights came back on again and I opened my eyes, I wasn't in the bath. I wasn't having a steamy hot shower. I was on the bathroom floor, my dressing gown over me and a paramedic by my side. I was confused. *How did I end up here?* I groaned with pain and tried to clutch my side, but my arm wouldn't move. *Why do I ache so much?*

'Rose, can you hear me?' I flickered my eyes open and closed, trying to focus on the man in front of me. 'Rose, can you nod your head if you can hear me?' he asked again. I nodded gently with my head but the rest of me was motionless. Daniel was standing in the doorway looking concerned. I tried to get up but realised I had no clothes on, just my dressing gown draped over me. My fingers were in a clip that was monitoring my heartrate and a towel was behind my head.

'What happened?' I slowly and quietly asked the paramedic.

'You had a little bump, that's all. Can you hear me okay?' he replied.

'Yes, I can hear you.' I tried to move again but my body was stiff and everything ached.

'Try to get up slowly. It looks like your arm and side took the brunt of your fall, young lady.' He helped me up with my other arm and held the dressing gown against me so my dignity was fully covered.

The man looked up at Daniel. 'I think we need to take her in for a few checks. She looks like she may have done some damage to her arm and her pulse is a little weak. Is there anything else we should be aware of?'

'Yes, she's pregnant. We think around seven to eight weeks,' Daniel responded as the paramedic raised his eyebrows.

'Jack… where's Jack? I suddenly panicked. Daniel was at the park with Jack when I was in the shower.

'It's okay, your mum has taken him back to hers. She said she would look after him until we got you sorted. I didn't want Jack worried about your fall or seeing the paramedics turn up,' he reassured me.

'Oh, okay, as long as he is okay.' I leaned back against the bath. I still felt sick but not as bad as I had done prior to the shower.

'So, if you can help her get some comfortable clothes on, sir, I will wait downstairs until she is dressed and help her into the ambulance. Are you okay getting her down the stairs?'

'Yes, sure.' He disappeared into our bedroom. I could hear him scrambling for something for me to wear, returning with a t-shirt, the most uncomfortable bra from my drawer, the biggest pair of knickers and some jogging bottoms. Daniel tried helping, steadying me as I got to my feet, my weak hand holding onto his shoulder as I got dressed. I could hear the paramedic talking to Harry as he stood downstairs, waiting patiently for us.

I got dressed, grabbed a few essentials, threw them into a washbag and made my way out to the top of the stairs. I walked slowly and painfully down the stairs, the paramedic at the bottom and Daniel behind me. I didn't want to go to hospital, but my side and arm were throbbing. I was pregnant, that was all. I'd had a shower too hot and fainted. My stupid mistake, I wanted to be at home with Jack and Daniel, not with nurses fussing over me.

Daniel locked up the house, said goodbye to Harry and rode with me in the ambulance to the hospital. He tried to make me laugh. He talked to me the whole way there, but nothing could lift my spirits, I was miserable, my side shot with the occasional piercing pain each time I spoke, and I just wanted the sensation of feeling sick to stop. Maybe my body couldn't cope with pregnancy. Maybe it was nature's way of saying I should be grateful for the son that I had and wasn't destined to have more. I had to think positively and ride the rest of this pregnancy out. If it gave me another child as precious as Jack was, it was worth every day of illness just to have him or her.

As soon as I arrived, they wheeled me out in a wheelchair and straight up to the maternity ward at Heatherwood Hospital in Ascot. I could hear other women in the labour ward giving birth. Their wails of despair as they pushed in pain.

I only have another seven months, I thought to myself, but it felt like an eternity.

I reached the ward; the nurses took over pushing me from the paramedic. Both Daniel and I thanked him as he left, and they wished me luck. Although there was no one else on ward three, where I was, they slid the curtains shut and asked me to jump on the bed and make myself comfortable. The nurses left us together, promising to return shortly with a jug of water and monitoring equipment.

'Well, that's ruined our weekend, hasn't it?' I turned to Daniel.

'Look, your mum and dad have Jack... he loves it over there with them and the main thing is that you and the baby are okay.' He gave me a helping hand onto the bed and sat next to me on the plastic chair. It was the first time he had referred to the baby. It suddenly felt real, our growing second child. He was acting so caring towards me, I could get used to this.

The curtains swung back open, and a lovely young nurse appeared. Her brown hair swept up into a messy bun, piled up on her head and the gentlest of smiles. 'Hello, my lovely,' she said. 'So, tell me what's happened, you look like you've had a bit of a fall and we need to get you fixed.' She looked at me endearingly whilst wheeling in some apparatus and a box of plastic gloves. 'Are you Dad?' she asked.

'Yep,' was all Daniel could reply with, watching her every move.

'Okay. Do we know how far gone you are, my lovely?' She smiled.

'Erm, we think seven to eight weeks. I had gone to the doctors to get it confirmed but they told me to wait another few weeks for my scan. To be honest, I haven't been able to leave the house as I've been so poorly.' I hung my heavy head.

'It's okay, we will do a full scan while you are here and make sure everything is okay with you and baby. We also need to get your side and arm looked at. I understand you've taken a bit of a whack by the sound of it.' She lifted my t-shirt and pushed gently but I whimpered in pain.

'Oh, I'm sorry, that does feel a little tender?' she asked.

Daniel seemed shocked when I noticed his face, but I wasn't sure why. I realised he had caught side of my injuries for the first time and winced.

As I looked down, I could see my side was already black with bruising and quite swollen, painful to the touch, so too did my arm, yet I don't know what happened. I must have passed out the minute the room began to spin.

'Okay, I think we will get you scanned first for pregnancy term and then we can work out what we do with your side and arm. Does that sound like a plan?' She took my heartrate and pulse from the machine while pulling my t-shirt back in place and scribbled away, recording all my results in the flip chart at the base of my bed. 'If you could try and drink as much of the water by your bedside, someone will be up to take you to the scan room.' She pointed to the jug and glass on the roller table beside me.

The thought of drinking any liquid scared me. In the past, as soon as I drank, I knew the sickness would start again but I had to do it. I forced gulp after gulp until half a glass had gone but I couldn't manage much more. I felt I couldn't hold it for long.

In next to no time, another nurse appeared and asked me to follow her down the corridor to the scan room.

'Are you okay to walk or do you want the wheelchair?' she asked.

'No, honestly, I am fine, I can walk.' I assured her, keeping Daniel in my sight the whole time. I didn't want him to leave my side.

'Would you mind quickly jumping onto the scales for me so we can note your weight?' She walked me over to the scales and looked at the numbers flicker whilst I steadied myself. '6 stone, 11 pounds.' She pulled out a paper notebook and jotted it down before sliding it back in her pocket and continuing. I was bloated but trying to keep the water down, I could feel it working its way back up into my throat like a volcano waiting to explode.

'Can you remember how much you weighed before you found out you were pregnant?' she asked. I wondered why but I gave my answer anyway.

'Yes, 9 stone, 6 pounds,' I said. The nurse raised her eyebrows and looked shocked.

'Rose, that's over two stone you've lost in *less* than two months. That can't be good for the baby.' He now seemed worried.

We carried on to the room, Daniel next to me holding my hand the whole time. *Why do I feel nervous?* It was exciting the first time, but this time, it felt so different, almost as if I knew what was coming. The room was dark and the nurse ushered us in. Daniel looked nervous too. Something didn't feel right, I couldn't put my finger on it, maybe call it women's intuition, but I had a bad feeling.

'Take a lie down here for me, young lady.' She patted the bed beside her. 'Dad, if you would like to pull up a seat right here next to her so you can fully see the screen, then we can get you all greased up and ready to go.' She tried her best to make us feel at ease and was really enthusiastic. Daniel had a look of antici-pation on his face—I think he wanted this baby so much more than I did. Excited to hear its heartbeat, to see it moving, trying our best to make out its stage or gender but it was too early.

I lay back just like I did the first time. Peeling back my jogging bottoms to below my knicker line and my t-shirt up to just under my bra. She had my full stomach accessible to start scanning. As I looked over at her, she clicked to refresh the screen, squirted some jelly on my stomach and began moving the instrument up, down and across both sides. Daniel gently squeezing my hand with suspense.

'Okay, so this is a Doppler ultrasound, which will help us to monitor all the important things we need to find out about your baby. So, you think you're approximately eight weeks, is that correct?' she asked, turning to us both.

'Roughly,' Daniel piped up as he watched the screen tentatively. I laid there still and as quiet as I could, waiting for that familiar fast heartbeat we heard with Jack.

The nurse moved closer to the screen, squinting as she did so, her glasses dropping down her nose so she could see better. She fidgeted gently on her seat before adjusting the instrument in her hand. Daniel's face seemed to change from a smile of encouragement to confusion. Again, the nurse shifted the direction of sweep on my stomach and stared into the screen, tilting her head to one side and trying again. I held my breath.

I could hear clicking on the monitor and I could see images but there was an eerie silence. Daniel was gripping my hand tighter and tighter in frustration as he waited for her to speak, but there was still no sound. I dare not look at him this time, my eyes were firmly locked above me, tracing the lines of the dark ceiling tiles. I knew... I just knew why it was silent. My throat became drier and drier.

Finally, she gave a quiet sigh and seemed to withdraw from moving the hand instrument.

'Is there a problem?' Daniel asked, looking at me and then back at the screen. I could see his confused face from the corner of my eye and him shuffling in his chair. The room felt hot, the bed beneath me felt like it was moving but it wasn't, it was the dizziness playing tricks. I sat up quickly, bolted upright and turned to the nurse.

'I'm sorry but I'm going to be...' But before I could give her a warning, I had already tried stopping myself from being sick. The nurse grabbed a kidney bowl from the side and handed it to me as another wave of sickness erupted and gripped my entire body.

Both Daniel and the nurse looked at me with pained eyes, waiting for my episode to pass and the quiet to return to the room.

'I'm so sorry, I don't know how to say this, but I can't detect a heartbeat. The gestation period appears to be about nine to ten weeks, but it's not a viable pregnancy.' She looked like she wanted to cry as she tried explaining to both of us that our unborn baby had died. That was it, no heartbeat, not alive.

Daniel looked like he was welling up too. 'I'm sorry, I don't understand what you mean? Are you saying that we've lost the baby?' he asked.

'I'm afraid so. I can't tell whether it was the fall or due to a lack of nutrients, it could have been anything but it's not a viable pregnancy I'm afraid. I am so very sorry for your loss.' She placed her hand on my hand with Daniel's and held it there. 'The nurses will help you with what happens next, but

I'm afraid there isn't anything more I can do.' A tear rolled down Daniel's cheek as he continued to stare at the screen rather than her. I laid there motionless and emotionless. Not a tear filled my eyes. It was more painful to see him upset and in pain.

'But I don't understand. It's not possible.' Daniel looked angry like a piece of his heart had just been ripped from his chest. 'The sickness... the pregnancy test... she... I...' He wiped his teary eyes with the cuff of his sleeve, waiting for her to answer. He tried squeezing my hand again to get my attention, but it made no difference. Nothing she or he could say would change the situation. I sat in silence, ignoring them both.

'The pregnancy will still be giving out hormones causing Rose's sickness. I can't tell when or why this happened. I'm sorry, I wish there was more that could be done. Would you like me to give you some more time alone together or would you like me to call the nurse?' She genuinely looked heartbroken for us.

'Rose, say something. What do you want to do?' He looked at me, scared, like he wanted me to give him the answers.

I wished at that moment the pregnancy test had never been positive. I wished that we hadn't raised our hopes. To go through weeks and weeks of sickness and pain for the sake of having a baby to then have it completely ripped from you. I felt cheated, but no amount of upset, crying or sadness would make it feel okay. Maybe this was karma's way of teaching me a lesson. I wanted everyone to leave the room and for it to swallow me whole. Life could be so cruel at times. The only consolation that I could possibly see in this scenario was that I wasn't further along, but it still hurt, nonetheless.

'It's okay, Daniel, let's go back to the ward. My side is hurting, at least they may be able to fix that.' I still couldn't bring myself to look at him. I felt like this was all my fault. If I had stayed on the sofa this morning... if I hadn't had the shower too hot... if I had gone to see the doctor earlier maybe I could have stopped all this from happening. Yet again, it was my fault. As hard as I tried to block it, my eyes were burning with tears trying to escape, the bulge in my throat was throbbing and my heart had shattered into a million pieces.

Daniel looked distraught; it was as if he wanted me to be an emotional wreck so we could be upset together. 'Okay, let's head back.' I could hear the pain in his voice, tears rolling down his face. I knew he wanted a hug, but I knew that if I did, it would break me.

Why is it always worse when men cry?

The lady gave me a tissue to wipe my stomach before I pulled my t-shirt back down and my jogging bottoms back up. She took the small bowl full of sick from me and placed it in the sink in the corner of the room. I swung my legs down to one side of the bed, wincing in pain from my side, getting to my feet. I couldn't bring myself to look at the screen as I left the room, I didn't want to take one last look at what could have been. A screen that should have displayed a scan picture of my perfectly growing baby inside me. I felt numb once again.

Before we walked back to the ward, the nurse who was standing outside was called into the room. We were left standing there whilst they whispered between themselves. I knew what they were discussing, Daniel pulled me close to him and hugged me. My arms were wrapped around him, but it was more to console him and to make sure he was okay rather than how I felt. I couldn't cry, I was tired and exhausted. The past month had felt like a nightmare, and now for what?

Daniel released his embrace, took a deep breath and wiped his eyes again. Gripping my hand, I could feel him shaking. The nurse appeared from the room and led us back to the ward. I don't think she knew what to say. We arrived awkwardly back at the ward and she pulled back the curtains exposing the bed I was originally sat on, broken and unable to say anything.

'I'm so sorry for both of you, I really am. I'm going to leave you here for a moment whilst I go and get the doctor and I will be straight back. Is there anything I can get for you?' she asked.

'Can I use the toilet please?' I spoke quietly, the pain building in my throat, struggling to hold it together.

'Of course you can, my lovely, follow me.' She led me out of the ward to the main corridor and opened the ladies' door for me. I pushed it open, then let it close behind me, locked it and was immediately sick again into the toilet. This time, it felt pointless, like an alien inside me, still causing havoc with my emotions and stomach but it made me feel empty at the same time. It was as if I had run a race that there was no prize for. Meaningless. I had to be strong for Daniel and Jack's sake, I was still a girlfriend and a mother. That was one thing I was thankful for. I couldn't show them how hurt or upset I really was, even if I too was dying inside.

I stood up, wiped my mouth again like it was now something so normal, flushed the chain and washed my hands. I couldn't look at my face in the mirror just yet, disgusted in myself for what had happened. I wasn't ready to accept anything. Unlocking the door, I headed back to the ward and back to Daniel. He was sitting in the chair, his hands in his lab sobbing. As he noticed me approaching, he quickly composed himself, wiped his eyes and tried to smile a positive smile at me.

'You okay?' he asked.

'Uh-huh.'

Just as I was about to sit down, the doctor stood behind me. 'I'm Doctor Asban,' he said, reaching out a hand to shake Daniel's, then to shake mine. 'How are you feeling?'

'I've been better,' I replied but it was short and sharp.

'I'm sure you have, you poor thing. If you pop yourself on the bed, I would like to take a look at your side and your arm if I may?' He moved closer to me whilst I laid back and pulled my t-shirt up to expose my middle.

'Oh, deary me, that looks painful.' He pushed gently as I whimpered again. 'I think we need to get you down to x-ray. We wanted to do that first but now that...' He stopped himself, almost as if he realised what he was about to say. Did he mean now that our baby's heart wasn't beating, now that our baby was dead and decaying inside me? The x-ray couldn't hurt him or her anymore. It didn't matter. Nothing mattered.

He quickly looked up at me. 'I'm sorry, I meant let's focus on getting you better now. That's what is important,' he quickly said.

'It's fine,' I answered. 'I do have a question though...'

He looked surprised. 'Go on, ask away.'

'Now that my baby has died, what happens next?' I had to ask, I felt like everyone was avoiding the elephant in the room. 'I mean, what happens with the baby?' I felt a lump in my throat again, but I quickly coughed to quash it and tried to remain constant. Daniel looked at me like I shouldn't have said what I did.

'Ah, I understand.' The doctor shuffled nervously on his feet. 'I'm afraid there are two options now, we will have to terminate the pregnancy for you. The first is a surgical procedure where we make sure that we remove all the fetus in its entirety, the second is a tablet form that dispels the fetus, but we must scan and check you in a few weeks to make sure that it has completely gone. Either way, it is not nice for you but I'm afraid we have no alternatives.' He looked endearing. It wasn't his fault, but he answered my question.

'I want to go with the first option.' I didn't have to think twice, and I didn't ask Daniel this time. It was my body and I wanted it gone as quickly as possible. I didn't want to worry for weeks to come about whether it worked or not. I wanted this nightmare over and done with so I could move on with my life. As painful and as heartbroken as I was, for me, it was the easiest option.

'I understand,' he replied calmly. 'In that case, we will need to move you to a different ward near the theatre. I want to get you x-rayed first to understand what is happening with your side, then after that, we can plan the surgery. We may have some availability while you are still in. Is that okay?'

'Yes, okay.' I nodded back at him and prepared myself for what was to come.

'I'll just speak to the team who will prepare to take you to x-ray, and we can go from there. I'll be back shortly. Is there anything else I can do for you?' he asked before disappearing through the curtain.

'Rose, are you okay with everything? I don't know what to say. I wish I could help.' Daniel looked so sad and helpless.

'Daniel, it's fine. There is nothing you or anyone else can say that will make it okay. It is what it is. I'm sorry I couldn't carry it, I'm sorry I'm useless at carrying. I just want to get back home to Jack.' I shrugged it off as non-important.

'It's okay to cry, you know.' He leaned forward into me, his blue eyes glaring into mine, pushing me to break, but I didn't.

'Crying won't help, it never does, it's pointless.' I peered back at him and sighed. I wanted to hug him so much, I wanted to just unfold into a crying mess on the bed and let it all out, but what good would it do?

The first nurse was back in the room. 'Right, my lovely, let's take you down to x-ray. If you wouldn't mind staying here, Daniel, I will bring her back as quickly as possible and then we can take you down to surgery. If I can get you on the list, and as you haven't eaten, we should be able to get you seen this afternoon, we don't want you to be waiting any longer than necessary.' She couldn't have been nicer and more understanding. She touched my shoulder, which meant so much to me.

Straight into x-ray I went. Scanned, checked and delivered onto another ward. This time, the surgical ward. Daniel must have been sent to another waiting room as the chair beside my bed was empty. Despite all we had been through, he was my rock—with me every step of the way. I was scared about the next step. Aborting the pregnancy... *Will it hurt? What will I feel?* I wanted him with me, I needed him more than anything.

I was asked to put on a white surgical gown, remove my underwear and place string knickers on. They placed a tag around my wrist and whisked me off to theatre. A cannula was inserted into the back of my hand ready for anaesthetic and a group of nurses all stood around my bed in surgical attire. Large lights towered above me, giving off heat as they shone. My heart racing and the feeling of me about to be sick at any moment worried me. At this precise moment, all I wanted was Daniel. One last time to say goodbye, for him to reassure me or to hold my hand. I felt like I was going somewhere and not coming back. Even with multiple people in the room, it seemed so lonely.

I was placing my life into their hands—an anaesthetic and an operation for the first time. I had to be brave, everything had been so quick.

'Okay. How are you feeling? Nervous?' The nurse could read my mind. 'You are in more than capable hands so no need to worry, the procedure will take no longer than fifteen to twenty minutes and we will have you back on the ward and back with your partner. Okay?' Her hands were warm and soft as she held my arm gently, reassuring me.

I nodded helplessly.

'Can you start to count for me?' she asked as she placed a syringe into the catheter in my hand and gently released the anaesthesia. I felt a cold, weird tingle flowing up my arm as I started to count.

'One... two... three...' It was the strangest sensation, my heart was still pounding in my chest, but I did as I was told. Giving my body up to medicine.

I don't remember getting any further than that and what felt like seconds was minutes.

I slowly opened my heavy eyes and found myself back on a ward opposite a couple of other patients. I glanced up at the clock and an hour had passed since I left Daniel. He must be bored senseless waiting for me.

'Hello, my lovely.' There she was again, the same nurse who had originally greeted me on the maternity ward. 'I'm glad to see you again, I wanted to check that you were okay.

How are you feeling?' She held my hand, bending over my bed and squeezed it just like Daniel did.

'Can I get you a cup of tea, water or a biscuit? How's the sickness feeling?' I panicked, thinking I wouldn't be able to keep anything down, but I looked up at her and couldn't quite believe that the dull, aching, sick feeling wasn't there anymore. My side still hurt but I didn't feel like I wanted to vomit. I was thirsty. My mouth was dry and my cracked lips felt sore. It was the first time I hadn't felt sick in weeks, if not months.

'Can I please have a water and a biscuit if that's okay?' My voice was croaky as if I had just woken from a deep sleep. I was so hungry, it hurt.

'Of course you can, lovely.' She smiled, letting go of my hand and walked off to get them.

I felt strange, numb, almost like a limb had been removed. The air didn't quite flow in and out of my lungs as freely as it did before, but this was the best I had felt in over a month. It took me a few moments to fully appreciate my body coming around. The buzzing, whirring feeling flowing through my entire body.

'There you go.' She placed a plate filled with two custard cream biscuits by my bedside and a glass of water. I stared at them, daring myself to take a bite. I longed for food, almost salivating with temptation. My stomach had given up grumbling from hunger and had shrunk so much in size as I hadn't eaten for so long. I picked one up, my hands shaking as I bit into it, crunching as I went, the crumbs falling onto my chest. I swallowed and took another, and another until I had finished the first one. I held it down and didn't feel sick. My eyes filled with tears but I didn't cry, instead, I let them fall gently down my cheeks. I don't know whether it was a release or just a feeling of letting go but I didn't care.

I sipped the glass of water, again, I kept it down. I took another couple of sips but didn't want to drink so much that my body couldn't cope with it. In the back of my mind, I just wanted to be home, but I knew this was just the start of dealing with what had happened.

They left me to rest for another thirty minutes and then finally took me back to the main ward to see Daniel, who was waiting patiently by a bed that had been made for me. My clipboard at the end with my name on. He smiled, again with tears in his eyes, pleased to see me. Meeting someone again when you thought you'd never see them again felt like nothing on earth. I was choked and emotional.

'Oh, honey, are you okay? I was so worried! Your mum called me to see if you were okay.' He stood up as the nurse walked me to the bed and let me get settled. I had to walk slowly; the knickers now felt like a thick nappy, and I felt stiff and slow, full of painkillers.

'I'm all good. I don't feel sick so that's a good thing, I guess.' I tried to smile back at him, but it was with a painful and heavy heart.

Doctor Asban stood at the bedside. 'Rose, lovely to see you back on the ward, how are you feeling? I understand the procedure went as well as could be expected. There are a few post-surgery instructions, but the nurse will go through those with you. We have had your x-ray results back and it appears you have a couple of cracked ribs. Bruising to your right arm but nothing broken there. You will need plenty of rest to let your ribs heal but we can't operate on those, unfortunately. You are lucky you didn't pierce your lungs though.' He flicked through my papers, being careful to read all the notes.

He put his hand on Daniel's shoulder. 'I'm trusting that this young man here will be able to look after you for the next couple of weeks whilst your body repairs itself? No strenuous activities or exercise.' He glanced at him, waiting for a reply.

'I think I can do that,' Daniel agreed.

'In that case, we will need you to stay in tonight, but you should be discharged tomorrow. If you need anything else, the nurses can reach me.' He shook Daniel's hand again and tapped my hand gently.

'Take care of yourself, okay?' As he walked away, I nodded and thanked him for looking after me.

Sinking back into the bed, I buried myself in the stacked pillows behind me. I looked at Daniel, half believing what had happened but glad that it was finally over, and we could get back to being a family again. This time as a three and not a pending four.

12

WE WORK AS A TEAM

Nothing could have prepared me or us for losing a baby, regardless of how early in the pregnancy I was, but I think it hit Daniel harder than it hit me. Yes, it was my body, and I had a physical bond, but it was the emotional bond that we both shared.

Despite his pain, he had been incredible throughout it all. My coping mechanism once again was to shut it all out and pretend it didn't happen. It was like nothing had changed, I didn't want to mention or talk about it. Act completely normal and everything would be fine.

To Jack, it was like Mummy was poorly, and now that I had been to hospital, the doctors had fixed me and I was feeling so much better than before. No more sickness, that was a huge positive. No amount of crying or getting upset would change what was happening to me and I didn't want to revisit that chapter of my life.

One thing was certain, this had brought us closer together as a family unit. As a couple, we worked as a team, his strength and practicableness, I was strong in terms of positivity and encouragement. I wanted us to be better and stronger than ever. A true force to be reckoned with. I would work harder and smarter than I ever had and give Jack everything he could possibly want in life.

There was one thing in my head that I just couldn't shake and that was the situation with Steve in London. Now that I felt like nothing could break us, I couldn't help but wonder if coming clean and being honest with Daniel about what happened was the best option.

I had it all planned out in my head... what I was going to say and how I was going to do it.

If it broke us as a couple and a family, then so be it, but I couldn't live my life on a lie or a secret that I kept from him. I couldn't just blurt it out at dinner one night with Jack sitting there, so I planned the night carefully to let Daniel down gently.

I asked my parents to babysit Jack for us the following Friday night after work. My plan was to order some dinner, cook him something lovely, just the two of us, and then break the news. I was expecting an angry Daniel, I could imagine him shouting in my face, hitting walls and steaming out of the house and to the pub. I was preparing for all of that .

It had been a busy week at work and what with it being my first week back, I was conscious of having to catch up on everything I'd missed.

That Friday seemed to drag. Each hour and minute seemed slower than it had ever been before. I couldn't believe that I was coming clean, but it had to be done.

Should I tell Steve first? What if Daniel went on a rampage and wanted to speak to him? The more I thought about it, the more I had second thoughts. *Maybe I should keep quiet after all... what harm could it do, right?*

It was finally 4.50 pm and I had ten minutes to go. I started packing up everything, closing my computer down and placing everything back in my handbag at the end of the week. Just as I was about to get up and head to the toilet to waste another few minutes, my desk phone rang.

I could see it was Steve... what could he possibly want right now, just as I was about to go home and drop the ultimate bombshell?

I quickly picked up the receiver and held it to my ear, letting him say the first words.

'Good afternoon, can I speak to Rose, please?'

'This is she,' I said, giggling down the phone in the poshest voice I could muster.

'Hey, Rose, how has your week been?' he asked politely.

'Good thanks, yours?' I had missed our conversations.

'Great! Listen, Rose, I know it's last thing on a Friday, but if I place an urgent order today, is there any chance you can get it out for delivery on Monday? I know I'm pushing it, but I would be ever so grateful if you could.' He paused, waiting for my reaction.

The office was quiet, a lot of my colleagues had gone home early or booked a half-day, so talking to Steve would be a little easier than I had previously thought.

'Steve...' I tried to get his full attention.

'Yes, Rose?' he replied immediately.

'It's quiet here in the office. I'm sure I can get everything pushed through for you, but can I ask a quick question before I do as there is no one here to listen.' I had to seize the opportunity while I could.

'Um... yes...'

'So, that night in London together...' I hadn't finished.

'*The* agreement night, you mean?' Steve had referred to it as this a couple of times previously.

'Yes, the agreement night. Listen, I want to be honest and open with Daniel. I don't want to cause problems for you, but I think it's only fair that I tell him the truth about what happened between us,' I continued. He went silent for a moment, I wasn't sure if he was angry, upset or was just thinking, I had no way of reading his body language over the phone.

'Rose, are you sure? I don't think that's a good idea. George hasn't mentioned it since, so why would you say anything to Daniel?'

'George? What has...' I had no idea what Steve was talking about. *What does this have to do with George?*

'Yes, when the paramedics arrived and I left you with him.'

'The paramedics? Left me with George? I'm not sure I follow... we are talking about the night after The Pitcher & Piano, you taking me to the posh hotel? Us being together.' I wasn't sure quite how to put the last part. The bit where he was a fantastic lover and the sex was amazing. I couldn't possibly say that to Steve, but I had to know everything, to fill in the blanks and tell Daniel.

'Rose, are you okay? Have you been drinking at lunchtime?' he questioned.

'Why of course not, I'm at work, I'm sat at my desk, completely sober.' Nothing made sense.

'Okay, so you remember the bar, right?'

'Yes, I remember that, and I remember leaving to walk to the hotel. It seems to be a bit of a blur from there on. A little hazy, perhaps?' I said, hoping that Steve could fill me in from thereon.

'I only just about managed to walk you to the hotel and get you up into the lift, you were being silly, but as I tried opening the door as well as trying to hold you up, you just collapsed in my arms. I carried you to the bed, Rose. Unresponsive and out cold, I panicked and called the hotel reception. They called for the paramedics. They were quite quick to be fair, but as I ran down to the lobby to run them back up to the room, I was surprised to notice George sat in reception. I thought you were dead.' Steve paused.

I gulped, taking it all in.

Steve continued, 'He came back up to the room with me, concerned for your welfare after he saw me in a panic and I told him what had happened. They thought your drink had been spiked, but after they checked you over and made sure you were okay and no foul play was involved, they said it was probably safer if you slept it off. George agreed to stay with you, I signed the agreement and left. I felt so guilty the following day that I should have made better sure you were okay. I think it was the last drink that the bartender gave you that was spiked but I had no way of knowing.' Steve seemed to be offloading everything from that night. We had never really spoken about it until now.

'Steve, I don't understand. I...' I sat back in my chair, almost dropping the phone in disbelief. George was quizzing me about that night, about the letters from the stalker. If he knew and he was with me, why hadn't he said anything? Why wasn't he there in the morning either? I looked over at George's desk—he was also on a call. Looking in my direction, he smiled, unaware of the conversation I was now having.

'Rose, how do you not know any of this? Did you think that we...' He stopped. 'That you and I...' He seemed to be piecing together my thoughts. 'Oh, wow… hang on a second, I know we had an agreement, but after you passed out, there was no way I would touch you in that state. I would never take advantage of any woman in that state. What kind of animal do you think I am?' He instantly made me feel terrible for thinking that.

'No, Steve, I didn't think that of you. I just… I have a complete blank for the whole night, so I was trying to piece it together,' I explained.

'Why didn't you speak to me earlier? Or ask George?' He made it sound so clear and simple. This whole time I had in my head that we slept together, that we had the most amazing sex. That can't have been yet another one of my vivid dreams, the same one about Tom that wasn't real. This whole time, guilt and dread had consumed me. I rubbed my head with my hand, it was hurting.

'I don't know,' I finally replied to Steve.

'Rose, is everything okay? Do you want to talk to me in private? If you don't believe me, speak to the hotel, they have CCTV of the whole night. It was a matter of minutes from us taking the lift to me calling reception and you passing out. I know that because George was speaking to reception about getting a copy. I'm not sure why?'

Why on earth would George be asking for a copy of the CCTV? I felt cold, a shiver ran down my spine. So many questions needed answering. *Why was George in London… in the same hotel as us? Why didn't he say anything?* It was as if he was hiding something.

The thing that hurt me the most about this discovery was that I was slightly relieved when I lost my baby—relieved because I thought there was a chance that it was Steve's. George knew that we hadn't slept together but said nothing. Would it have made my loss any less or more painful?

'Rose, are you still there?' Steve's voice bellowed down the phone.

'I-I'm so sorry... it's... um... can I call you back in a second?' I needed time to process everything.

'Look, I must shoot, I'm sure you do too. Call me on Monday and we can talk.' Steve seemed in a rush.

'Of course. Sorry, Steve. And thanks for filling me in. I will get your order shipped and I'll give you a call on Monday. Have a great weekend.' I tried to sound sincere, but my glare was locked on George. This had completely changed my plans for the evening. I had nothing to tell Daniel, but I still had to figure out what the hell happened.

'You too, Rose, have a good one.' The phone line went dead. Steve was gone.

George was my best friend. He was like a brother to me. I told him everything, things that I hadn't even told Daniel, but what Steve just told me scared me. It made no sense whatsoever.

I clicked the receiver back on its base, thinking for a moment about what to do. I picked back up my handbag, just as I had done before Steve called, then scribbled a message to myself on a post-it note, stuck it to my desk, reminding myself to get Steve's order processed early on Monday morning and out the door for delivery, I then made my way over to George's desk. He leaned back as far as he could in his chair with his feet crossed on the desk—he only sat like that because Dave had left for the day.

I reached his desk, just as he finished his call and put the phone down.

'You off for the day, Rose? Have a good weekend, won't you… any plans?' he asked.

'Erm, yes, having a nice night in with Daniel tonight, just the two of us so that will be lovely. I've had another letter from that stalker again, so I'm a bit worried about going out to be honest.' I completely made that up, but I wanted to see his reaction.

'Oh, really? What did it say?' He suddenly swung forward in his chair, bringing his feet back to the floor, focused entirely on my reply.

I sat on his desk, balancing my bag next to me. 'It said that I should be more careful with my drinks in future and something about staying close to your enemies. I haven't quite worked out what it means yet. I'm confused but it's shaken me up a little bit.' I was waiting to see what George's reaction was.

'No way! Have you got the letter on you? Can I see it?' he asked

'No, I ripped it up and put it in the bin.' I had to think fast. 'What did they mean by being careful with my drinks?'

'Maybe he just wanted you to be safe, Rose. You did say that your Cosmopolitans in London tasted slightly funny… you don't want a repeat of what happened when the landlord spiked your drink, do you?' George began shuffling away his papers as if he was getting ready to leave the office too. His face had changed.

'Yes, maybe. Oh well, I better go. I need to get Jack'. I stood up from perching on the desk. George patted me on the arm as I left the office like he always did.

I left the office and made my way to the bus stop. This time, I didn't care who was watching me, who was lurking in the shadows or who was out to scare me. My thoughts had been diverted to George and his comments. How did he know that the person writing those letters was a *he?* More importantly, how did he know that Steve and I were drinking Cosmopolitans unless he was there? I was certain that I hadn't mentioned it to him because I couldn't remember the cocktail's name until he just said it.

I'm sure there was a genuine reason. After all, George had always been there for me, always looking out for me, helped me at work, with the customers and promotions... he would never hurt me in a million years.

Something just didn't add up though. What was George hiding from me? What hadn't he told me and why?

13

BEGINNING A NEW CHAPTER

W here had the time gone? I closed my eyes for a second, and when I opened them again, it was time for my baby to go to school. Wind back to my life six years ago and you would have found me at school —it didn't quite seem possible to be in this situation. I couldn't believe it.

We wanted him to go to a good school, to give him the best start in life, but I didn't anticipate the world I was walking into. Childcare while I was at work was around £1800 per month, the cost of private school was around £1300, so we figured that we were saving money and giving him a great education all at the same time.

There were many things we didn't realise until he started —the average private school had five weeks' more holiday per year, they went on super expensive holidays like skiing and The United States, and the parents were either rich or famous or both.

Of course, when you book a tour of the school, they sell you the dream. You are, after all, paying for your son or daughter to go there so they do anything they can to tempt you with freshly prepared school meals, extra-curricular activities, including swimming in their choice of heated pools, and smaller class sizes at around ten pupils in each one. *What child wouldn't want to go to school there?*

Jack was excited, a new school uniform, new shoes, a satchel almost bigger than he was and a fresh haircut. Even though he had been at nursery for the past couple of years whilst I worked, him starting school seemed to be so much more emotional. I almost cried dressing him that morning. Folding his tie around his neck for the first time, making sure he had everything packed and ready. I wanted to keep him at home for the rest of his life and not let him leave my side. I instantly knew what my mum meant when she said she wanted to keep her children wrapped in cotton wool forever.

He bounced out of the door while I tried to hide my emotions. I was proud that we had raised such a confident, bold and intelligent child. *This school will be the making of him,* I thought to myself.

We approached the big black steel gates to his impressive new school. I glanced back to check on Jack in the back of the car, and as I did, he beamed the biggest smile in my direction, his little fingers fidgeting with the zip on his coat as he looked at all the other children making their way to their classrooms. Both Daniel and I wanted to be there on his first day and be the supportive parents he needed.

'Are you excited, Jack?' Daniel asked him.

'No, Daddy,' he quietly replied.

We both turned around in shock—our little cheeky, confident boy suddenly seemed nervous. It was very unlike him.

'Oh, why, what's wrong?' Daniel asked again.

'Lilly told me that I can't make new friends otherwise she won't talk to me and that makes me sad.' Jack seemed upset and looked down at his shoes, tapping his feet together. Lilly was his best friend from nursery, they did everything together and we had to promise him that he would still see her after he started school.

'Honey, you are allowed other friends, you know that, don't you? Lilly will still be your *best* friend but it's good to have other friends too, especially at your new school.' I didn't want him distancing himself from others for the sake of what Lilly had said to him. 'I want to know all about your first day when we pick you up later, and all of the lovely new people in your class, okay?'

'Okay.' He seemed to shrug it off and looked a lot more positive.

Daniel and I parked the car in the first car park that we reached, just outside the infant block. I felt embarrassed that our car stood out like a sore thumb against the Porsches, Ferraris and sports cars that were already parked. I watched one by one as all the parents walked their sons or daughters to the main gate in their designer clothing.

I'm sure I was way more nervous than Jack or even Daniel was. Comparing us against all the other parents. Perhaps this was a bad mistake, maybe we didn't fit in here after all.

I gently opened the door, trying not to hit the car next to me and held Jack's door open as he climbed out, reaching for his little satchel. He grinned up at me, those emerald green eyes glinting in the September sun. *Don't cry, don't cry, don't do it, Rose. He's still your baby,* I said to myself.

I reached for his hand, meeting Daniel at the back of the car and we walked him to the main gate. Ten other sets of parents were waiting with their children and the teacher was talking as she leaned on the picket fence around the entrance.

I didn't need to introduce Jack; he ran up to the others and instantly started talking to them. I admired his confidence. Daniel and I, on the other hand, were apprehensive about making conversation with the others. Would we have anything in common? Would they think we were common?

'Hey, my name is Samantha, and I'm Meghan's mum, yours is?' She held out a hand to shake mine.

'Jack, nice to meet you.' Daniel nudged me but I couldn't work out why.

'Nice to meet you, Jack,' she replied in an American accent.

'Oh no, I'm sorry, our son is Jack. My name is Rose, and this is Daniel.' I laughed at the mistake she had made and pointed to Daniel so he could introduce himself.

'Hi, nice to meet you.' He also shook her hand.

'My husband is Roger... he's always travelling, so my full-time career is a mummy and a home coordinator, so if you ever get stuck collecting Jack, then I would be more than happy to help.' She smiled and waited for us to reply. Well, that is the first time I had heard it be referred to as a home coordinator, but I kept a straight face and was polite.

'Thank you so much. We both work full-time and it's always a struggle collecting him on time, so I may just have to take you up on that offer.' There were lots of other conversations taking place but both of us had to head back to work before we were late. Just as we were turning to leave, an older gentleman in a full grey suit and waistcoat walked over to us all.

'Lovely to meet you all on your children's first day. There is an assembly for all those parents that can join us in the main hall. He pointed to the large building behind us. For all the sixth formers, can you make your way to reception please, we need ushers.' He began waving his arms at Daniel and me.

We both looked at each other, confused.

'I think he believes that you are sixth formers because you're so young.' Samantha laughed as she whispered in my ear.

'Oh no, no. We aren't sixth formers... we are parents. Our son, Jack, is in reception.' I pointed to Jack playing by the playground.

'Oh, dear Lord, I am sorry,' he said in a very old English tone, chuckling and making his way closer to us. 'I do apologise. I mistook you young whipper snappers as students, haha. I'm Mr Griffiths and I am the head teacher here.' He held out his hand for us to shake.

Samantha and Mr Griffiths were two of the loveliest people we had ever met, very friendly and clearly had come from a lot of money. We tried our best to put on our best English accents when talking to them, but that sounded false and very forced.

Daniel and I both hugged Jack before leaving, but he seemed to be too busy playing with his new friends to really acknowledge us, so we got back in the car and headed to work. It felt strange having a son at school already. He was doing things that I never imagined I would see, from his first word to his first step and his first hug. I was so proud of the little person he was growing into.

I felt good about him starting school, a fresh beginning and some real friends to go through life with.

All I wanted was for Jack was to be happy in life and I was confident that this was the best starting point, surrounded by the best friends he could ever have.

14

FESTIVAL BOUND

Having Jack so young didn't necessarily mean that we had missed out on a lot—quite the opposite, in fact. Daniel and I had crammed in as much as we could into a short space of time, however, due to our responsibilities, we hadn't been quite so carefree and as wild as perhaps we wanted to be. Our saving grace meant that we had a reason to keep on the straight and narrow with a few occasions thrown in to really let our hair down.

On this particular occasion, I couldn't help but feel regret, but I guess that as life continues, there will always be times or events that we wished we could turn the clock back on.

All our friends had planned to go to a few festivals over the summer period, and we thought, what the hell why don't we join them. It was a few days away from home and Jack but something we had never experienced before, and it was better to do it while we were younger rather than older.

I had always imagined festivals to be a reincarnation of the 1970s—a free world of music, adventure, drugs and alcohol. Obviously, the drugs weren't the reason that I wanted to go, but I fully accepted there to be a lot there and people under the influence.

Our friendship group of around twenty people had been chatting and planning to go to this event for months and now it was finally here. Alcohol was the most common item on everyone's list of things to take and we planned the rest of the weekend around how much and what type we were taking with us. Clothes, money and essentials were under alcohol on the list, laughably.

We agreed to travel in a few different cars or camper vans. Strategically, we packed everything from wellies to clean underwear and hygiene products. I was apprehensive about leaving Jack behind and would miss him incredibly, but for once, I was looking forward to listening to some great bands and enjoying the atmosphere.

One by one, everyone started to arrive at our house first thing on Friday morning. I had dropped Jack at school, packed a weekend bag for him and a few other little surprises so that when my mum picked him up at the end of the day, he would have everything he needed for the weekend without his parents. I kissed him and gave him the biggest hug I could before waving goodbye and setting off back home.

I think he was more excited to be spending the weekend with my parents than I was about going away. He blew a little kiss to me, which I caught in my hand and popped in my pocket before he pushed the school door open and ran in.

'Rose, you all set?' Daniel asked, putting the last few items by the door for us to load in the car. A pile of sleeping bags, pillows and rucksacks lay in the doorway.

'Erm, I think so. I feel like I'm missing something.' I had my hand on my chin, trying to figure out what it was.

'Your son,' Alfie piped up.

'Ha, very funny. Apart from him.' It was true, it hadn't even been an hour and I missed him. I just needed to keep my mind active and start to enjoy myself.

'Get that down you and chill out.' Daniel passed me a white bottle of Smirnoff Ice, I accepted without arguing and took a quick gulp. I stopped, winked at him and then drunk the remainder in a couple of minutes. 'This weekend is going to be a blast. What we haven't got, we haven't got, and it won't matter. As long as you have a toothbrush, toothpaste and a clean pair of knickers, then you are good to go.' He chuckled out loud.

He had never been to a festival before either, so the two of us going together would be a first. With the amount of belongings we had, it looked like we were moving home for the weekend.

We threw everything into the cars parked in the car park. My sister was picking up Harry this afternoon and taking him to her house for the weekend. I gave him a big hug and said goodbye, ensuring he had enough food and water to last him, then I shut the front door and placed the spare key under the mat for her to get in.

There had never been a day since I was sixteen where I didn't have to think about organising everything in my life around my actions. A day away from home meant I had to organise Jack and Harry, plan the days, making sure things were packed and ready, where I was going to be, when I was returning, and that I was contactable in an emergency. Don't get me wrong, I wouldn't change it for the world, but sometimes when life got a little too much, the ability to just disappear for even an hour wasn't possible. I had to always be accountable.

We set off. Scott and Sasha had a bright red camper van —an old classic and authentic-looking one. Scott would be driving, so he climbed into the front seat, leaving Daniel as the co-pilot and giving us girls a helping hand into the fully overloaded back seats, piled high with every camping accessory you could imagine. He made sure we were in and then slammed the cranky metal door behind him.

'Alright, girls?' Scott shouted.

'Yep, all good,' I shouted back as I looked for a place to sit down.

Sasha was already rummaging through the cool box on the floor. 'I'm pretty sure the lemonade is in here. I put it in last night.'

'I have the vodka.' I laughed as I pulled out a large 70cl bottle of Smirnoff Red out of my bag and held it in the air for Sasha to see.

'Amazing.' She lifted two full bottles of lemonade and three plastic cups. 'Boys, are you having one?' Sasha asked.

'Hell yeah.' Daniel turned around to face us.

'Not at the moment, I need to get on the motorway first, then I will have one when we are almost there,' Scott answered. The festival was in Leeds, so it was a long four-hour drive from home.

Sasha carefully filled the cups one by one, placing them in between her legs and gently pouring. The van wasn't the most comfortable or smoothest so most of it went all over her lap, but it added to the fun of the journey. I helped by holding the bottles and cups and passing them over to Daniel in the front.

'Now for the good stuff.' Sasha had poured all three cups and placed the bottles back in the cool box, and as she did, she reached into her pocket and pulled out a small metal engraved case. I watched her tentatively. I was expecting her to get cigarettes out, but instead, she clicked it open and, from what I could see inside, were some pre-rolled joints. Around ten or so.

'All freshly rolled last night and good to go.' She chuckled, picking one up and out of the case, then popping it into the side of her mouth before reaching back into her pocket to pull out a lighter. I hadn't smoked or taken drugs in my life, but I had often wondered what they were like.

Sasha made me laugh, she delicately lit the end of the joint and inhaled gently before blowing out thick, deep smoke into the van. I couldn't see her face until it smouldered out to the rest of us. She had her eyes closed and dropped her head back against the seat rest. She looked so happy, so calm. She took another big puff of the joint and then plucked it from her lips.

The thing I loved most about Sasha was her love of life, her carefree attitude and just the way she was always so lovely. She never had a bad word to say about anyone and was the type of person that would give you her last penny. A true friend, such a beautiful soul. Jack had warmed to her instantly. Whenever she was over, he would make a beeline for her and sit on her lap while she told him stories. I was looking forward to spending the weekend with her and Scott. It would be so much fun.

'Rose, do you want some?' she slowly offered it to me as I sat opposite her.

'Erm, no. I think I'm alright at the moment.' I wanted to... I mean, I really wanted to but the only reason I declined was because I didn't want to have a coughing fit in front of her since I hadn't had one before.

'Boys, here.' She shifted in her seat to face the driver and his co-pilot. Daniel was the first to take it. Like a true smoker, he took a big, deep breath in and blew out yet more smoke into the already clouded van. He took another and another before finally releasing it and offering it to Scott.

'Cheers, Dan,' he said as he did the same. I'm surprised he could see the road ahead of him as the windscreen whirled with cannabis-scented clouds. I felt like we were deep inside a chimney as it swirled around us. After a couple more puffs, Scott passed it back to Sasha.

'Go on, Rose, just a little bit and you will feel incredible.' She held it out to me again. The red embers glowing as I contemplated doing it. Looking at hear neatly holding it between her fingers, I thought, *Fuck it, what harm could trying it do?* Daniel glared at me like a protective parent. It was cannabis for goodness sake, not a class-A drug, how bad could it be?

I took it from Sasha. Holding it gently between my lips, I took a long deep breath in and saw the end of it glow and feel warm. More smoke swarmed me, but I didn't cough. Instead, I felt calm, relaxed and a sense of heaviness landed on my eyelids as I inhaled the warm, herb-like tasting vapour. I sat back in my seat and took another puff. This time, I was more confident, blowing the smoke from my mouth but feeling it deep down in my lungs.

It felt good, sinking back into my seat, at ease and sleepy. Handing it back to Sasha, she laughed at everyone as the excitable chatter in the van had dulled to find us all just staring into the ether. Each of us smiling in a content and satisfied way.

'Happy Festivalling!' Sasha shouted and laughed as she kicked off her flip-flops and sat with her legs crossed on the seat.

It took us a while to return to our original chirpy and excitable selves. An hour from our destination and we were laughing, joking, singing and shouting about so many things. The alcohol was flowing and I felt drunk before we even arrived.

As the traffic began to build, we were only a few miles from the festival's location. A large Range Rover pulled up beside us—it appeared strange as it was a left-hand drive vehicle. Sasha smiled at the dark, rather handsome man next to her, he smiled back and seemed to be fascinated with her cuteness and good looks. Sasha had beautiful long brown hair with the most gorgeous natural waves, her chestnut eyes and big lips made her look like a stunning model. A younger Cindy Crawford or Julia Roberts perhaps. She was smart too and had a totally care-free attitude, she made me laugh all the time.

The man next to us wasn't watching the road at all, instead, he was fixated on Sasha who had taken a sip of vodka and began licking her lips as she stared right in his direction, teasing his attention. I, on the other hand, sitting opposite her could see a rather impatient wife or girlfriend sitting in the passenger seat of the vehicle nudging him with her elbow. She looked so angry, but the more fraught she became, the more Sasha enjoyed it and proceeded. She started to move everything off her lap and began crouching in the van.

'Sasha, what are you doing?' I asked, confused.

'Giving her something to be angry about.' She laughed as both her hands fell to the bottom of her t-shirt and gripped the seam. Sasha moved towards the window, and as quick as a flash, lifted her top and flashed her breasts, holding them firmly against the window of the van. In the space of two minutes, it was pure chaos. The lady in the car next to us was shouting at the man, I could see he was arguing back but laughing at the same time. The cars in the outer lanes could see what was happening and were beeping their horns.

'What the fuck are you doing, Sasha? Sit down, you are going to cause an accident, I'm trying to drive here, you absolute maniac.' Scott was trying to find out what was going on, but he couldn't see without taking his eyes completely off the road. Sasha and I laughed out loud the whole time. Like a naughty schoolgirl, she lowered her top back down and sat back in her chair, smug from the situation she caused.

The cold from the glass window had made her pert nipples stand on end. I could clearly see as she wasn't wearing a bra. Although she was my friend, I found it hard not to look at them in jealousy. Yes, I had nice breasts, but hers were pert, rounded and perfect—she hadn't had children after all.

'Miserable bastards. I was having a lot of fun.' Sasha laughed and threw her long dark hair backwards. 'I'm getting twitchy now. I've had enough of sitting in the back, I need to get out.' Like a little girl, she started fidgeting around, desperate to get out.

'Look, we have fifteen minutes maximum, you are worse than a child. Just sit tight, wait, and we will be there in no time.' Scott was sober. Trying to drive a group of drunk people for quite a few hours must have been draining.

'Pfffttt!' she answered back, blowing the air out of her mouth in a hump. She picked up the small rucksack she had kept between her legs the whole time, then leaned forwards into me and whispered, 'I'm not waiting fifteen minutes, I'm ready for fun now, are you in?'

I had no idea what she was talking about or what I was

in on as I squinted my eyes back at her. I looked down to find the tiniest white piece of folded paper. It looked like origami. Once again, she moved her hand towards me and raised her eyebrows. 'I said are you in?' She waited for me to answer.

'I... um... no, I'm alright thanks.' I knew exactly what was in that piece of paper and I equally knew why she was whispering as she didn't want the men to hear.

'Suit yourself,' she whispered back.

Sitting back in her chair, Sasha very slowly and carefully opened the piece of paper and held it cupped in her left hand, and with her right, she used her little finger and nail to push it around. As I sat up in my seat, I could make out a small pile of white powder. Cocaine—I thought as much. I watched as she moved it around a little and then using the underneath of her nail as a scoop, she collected a small amount and carefully held it to her nostril. Her eyes looked at me and she froze.

'I need you to cough, Rose,' she said, loud enough for me to hear but not loud enough for the men to hear in the front against the music.

'You want me to what?'

'Just cough, pretend to cough. When I say three, you cough, okay?' Sasha gave me the instructions; I was just carrying them out.

'Uh-huh.' I nodded.

'Okay, one... two... three...' On her three, I coughed a couple of times. Just as I did so, she sniffed as hard as she could, drawing up the powder into her nostril.

Oh, so that's why she wanted me to do that. This is all new to me.

'Sasha, where did you...' I wanted to ask where she had

got it from, but she cut me off and instead put her finger up against her lips.

'Ssshhh!' she replied, folding the paper up again and tucking it back inside the pocket of her rucksack. I had seen cocaine in films before, but I presumed it was either wealthy celebrities or homeless drug addicts that seemed to be doing it, not normal people like me... or so I thought. I wondered how long Sasha had been doing it for or who introduced her to it. Now wasn't the right time to ask so many questions, so I kept quiet and left them for a time when it would be pertinent. I wasn't snooping, just more worried about her than anything.

Other than Sasha's pupils dilating to twice the size and her inability to stop talking, I couldn't see any difference in her. I sat there wondering what she felt like, what it had done to her. Why did she feel the need to take it, was she addicted to it? I guess I should have just shrugged it off as one of those things, but my highly inquisitive mind wouldn't let it drop. I wanted to know what she was experiencing. What did it feel like? Was it amazing? Was it worth it?

We finally arrived at the venue. For as far as I could see, there were fields with cars and vans parked in neat, long rows. All the drivers and passengers were climbing out and dragging their belongings to a point far in the distance. I had never seen so many people in wellies and jean shorts carrying rucksacks and pulling carts full of crates of alcohol. I was excited, but at the same time, nervous, not knowing what to expect or when to expect it, and I was stuck here with no way of getting home till the end of the weekend.

Scott pulled up the van in the next available space, and Daniel turned to me and winked. I could tell he was as excited as I was. Jack constantly in the back of my mind, but this weekend was a chance to unwind and be like the age I was, not the age I had to act each day.

Sasha rubbed her nose and took a big sniff to clear her nostrils of drugs, then started to gather all her belongings together to leave the van. I picked up all my bits and pieces that I could find and followed Sasha like a shadow. We loaded ourselves up with as much as we could carry without having to make two trips. A rucksack, sleeping bags, carrier bags and drink, locking up the van, we joined the long line of people walking and making their way to the campsite.

I hadn't made it past the first four rows of cars before my arms began to burn from the weight. The heat of the day made me sweat profusely and I wanted nothing more than to stop and pitch the tent then and there.

'Come on, Rose, we've got miles to go, keep going.' Sasha laughed, full of energy after the drugs she had taken were starting to kick in.

'I would carry you, but I have enough already.' Daniel took the lead; he was the tallest, so we didn't lose sight of one another.

One foot in front of the other, I kept walking. My eyes focused on the flags flapping in the wind in the distance, marking the entrance. I just had to keep going. My legs buckling, my fingers turning white from the bag handles and my arms tingling. *Nearly there,* I kept telling myself.

As soon as we reached the entrance, the queues wrapped back and forth around silver security railings. Support staff stood at each section in bright high visibility jackets and stopping the occasional person to check they weren't sneaking any bottles or drugs inside. My heart began racing, not for fear of me being stopped but for Sasha instead. It would be a disappointing weekend without her and Scott.

Our bags were searched and we were let through. Wristbands were attached to us like a group of tagged animals and then left free to pitch up where we liked. Sasha breezed through the security checks as innocent as a new-born baby. All four of us made a beeline to the middle of all the tents, far enough away from the toilets but close enough to the food and drinks stands that were positioned along the edges of the campsite.

I threw the bags to the floor and laid backwards on the fresh grass looking up at the sky, giving my arms a chance to stop burning. I closed my eyes, breathing in and out as deeply as I could. Daniel kicked my foot impatiently, making me open my eyes as quickly as I had closed them.

'Up you get, we need to put the tent up first, then you can chill.' He began emptying out the tent and all the accessories, looking like he knew what he was doing. I tutted first before helping him. Almost everyone around us was struggling just as we were to erect their own tents.

With the tent up, foldaway chairs spaced out around the little area that we had commandeered, our clothes and bags neatly tucked inside the tents, it was officially time to get our drinking shoes on. I had only taken a couple of sips of my vodka and coke and felt the seat beneath me when Sasha started.

'Rose, can you give me a hand please?' she called out from her tent. Both the men looked at each other and shrugged. It was man language that meant, *'I have just opened a beer and sat down, we aren't moving.'* The two of them nodded, smiled, and continued drinking. I sank to my knees and shuffled on the grass to the opening of Sasha's tent. I found her sitting on the floor, cross-legged but facing away from me so I couldn't quite see what she was doing. I zipped up the tent behind me, just in case she needed privacy but soon realised that was the least of her concerns.

Placed on the floor in front of her was a small mirror. I presumed she used it for applying her makeup, but instead of face powder, it had a couple of lines of a different powder— cocaine. Next to the mirror was a rolled-up ten-pound note and a bank card. I stared, watching what she was doing.

'Hello, my lovely, take a seat.' She patted the blanket next to her.

I did as she wanted me to, but as I looked at the cocaine and the way she was using the edge of her card to break up the small chunks into fine powder, arranging and rearranging it into neater lines on the glass, it made me feel uneasy. This wasn't what I wanted to do all weekend; this wasn't why I came here. How would I turn her down politely if she asked me whether I wanted some?

'Right, this one is mine and that one has your name written all over it.' She took the rolled-up note into her hand, her other hand over one side of her nose, and bent down to get closer to it, taking a big deep breath in. The line disappeared up her nose like a vacuum cleaner. I sat in silence watching her. Fascinated.

'All yours.' She handed me the same note. I looked at her but no words came out. 'Here,' she said again, pushing the note into my hand.

'Sasha, look. I...' I tried shaking my head and pushing the note away, but she tried again.

'Come on, what's the worst that can happen? I've just taken it and I'm fine. See.' She smiled, lifting her shoulders up to shrug like it was completely normal. The tent smelt musty. It was hot and stuffy and the lack of air was making me sweat.

I didn't have time to think, it wasn't like my life depended on making a decision, but I looked at how normal she seemed to make it, and I had been curious as to what it felt like. Maybe if I tried just the one line, it wouldn't kill me.

Perhaps if I just...

Too late. I took the note from her and copied what she had just done. As I knelt over, I held the rolled-up money halfway up my nostril, used my other hand to hold the other side of my nose closed and sniffed as hard as I could, sliding it gently along the line until all the powder disappeared. When it had all gone, I sat up, tilting my head back so none fell out and dropped my hands. I sniffed again another couple of times till I could taste the powder. A bitter, almost chemical taste seeped down the back of my throat, turning it numb as it slid down.

I turned my head to see Sasha looking straight at me, she clearly knew it was my first time.

'Okay?' she asked. 'See how alive you will feel as soon as it kicks in, you'll love it.'

'Yes, uh-huh.' I didn't want her to think I was regretting it. I felt the urge to want to sniff a couple of more times to clear my nose, but each time I did, it just moved more powder down into my throat and repeated that chemical taste all over again.

Sasha held her finger to my lips. She had licked the tip before dipping it into the small envelope of powder and was now prompting me to lick what was stuck to it.

'Lick it, Rose, put my finger in your mouth and lick it till it's all gone.' She moved it closer to my lips.

Everyone experiments, don't they?

I wasn't stupid, I knew what I was doing. I wasn't about to get addicted, and I didn't want to be one of those druggy parents, but what harm could a little cocaine do while Jack was in a safe pair of hands, right? He would be none the wiser.

I opened my mouth as Sasha's petite finger slipped in. She watched as my lips and tongue wrapped around it, sucking it clean. The bitter, horrible taste made my mouth give the appearance of swallowing a wasp, but I continued.

My tongue went numb, so did my gums, and my teeth felt sensitive. Other than the awful taste, the numbness and the need to sniff occasionally, I felt quite normal. Why on earth did people feel so compelled to want to do cocaine, what was so amazing about it?

Even though I had licked the powder from Sasha's finger and she watched as I did it, she was one of my closest friends and it didn't feel erotic at all or in any way sexual. Had I done that with someone else, maybe things might have ended slightly differently.

'Now, we can get our dancing shoes on and rock this night.' Sasha cleared up the mirror and card, then shoved the envelope back into her jeans pocket and maneuvered her way to the zip of the tent so we could get out. She looked back, offering out a hand for me to follow.

'Hey, girls, were you okay in there?' Scott asked and then laughed. Daniel, on the other hand, didn't seem impressed by the way he looked at me—he knew exactly why Sasha had called me in there and knew I was easily led.

I tried not to make too big of a deal about it but that's when it hit me. As I got to my feet and sat back in my chair, my heartbeat was so loud and strong that I could feel it in my ears, stronger and louder than I'd ever heard it before. I was drawn to its rhythm, everything around me seemed quiet in comparison. My eyes felt alert and I was wide awake. I wanted to tell the world how alive I felt, so much energy running through my body and so much to talk about.

Sasha was chatting away with Scott and Daniel, and I joined in. I must have seemed so confident. Laughing, joking, talking, telling stories. She turned up the music on the speakers that we had brought with us, and as she did, Sasha grabbed my hand, pulling me from the chair, ushering me to dance with her.

I was so caught up in the moment and enjoying myself that I hadn't noticed Scott and Daniel disappear into our tent together, it wasn't until they both emerged that I realised they must be doing the exact same thing Sasha and I had done. I didn't give Daniel the same glaring look he gave me though. I didn't condone it, but he was his own man. He would only ignore me if I told him not to do something.

It seemed to be a reminder for Sasha that no sooner had Daniel sat down, she wanted to go back into the tent for more.

'Come on, Rose, our turn.' She bent down to make her way into the tent, but before I could join her, Daniel grabbed my wrist to stop me.

'No, Rose. You've had enough.' He gave me a fatherly glare and a look of disappointment that stopped me. Normally, I would have done the opposite, but there was something about Daniel's actions that made me think twice. He gave me a warning squeeze of the wrist and I knew full well that he wasn't playing.

'Rose, come on, don't listen to him, I've got plenty,' she continued. Daniel still had a firm grip on me.

'I think I'm okay, Sasha. I'm going to give this one a miss,' I said, wriggling my wrist free from his strong hands.

'Suit yourself, more for me.' She disappeared into the tent.

'Rose, I'm not telling you what to do but don't get easily misled. You can say no.' Usually, the need to do the opposite was so overpowering, but on this occasion, I listened. I wasn't happy with being told what to do, but it showed he cared. It was unusual for me, I'm as rebellious as hell, but for some reason, today I chose to listen.

We sat talking for so long that I couldn't remember how half of the conversations started. The longer we spoke, the more tired I got as the drugs wore off. I looked at my watch and a couple of hours had passed. The sky had dulled, ready for the evening to start. We were so stuck in a time warp of cocaine-fuelled conversations that I suddenly noticed Sasha wasn't with us.

'Hey, Sash, are you okay in there?' I called out.

Waiting for her to reply, I picked up the radio and fiddled with the stations to find some better music. It was battery-operated and the aerial was terrible, so from time to time, it would either cut out or become crackly. The music had been so loud that we were shouting over the top to hear one another.

'Sasha? Hey,' I called again but no response.

'She's probably having a snooze.' Scott laughed with not a care in the world.

I looked first at Daniel then at Scott... something didn't feel right. There was no way that Sasha was having a nap in the tent, not after all the cocaine I saw her take the first time, let alone after that. I noticed the outer tent doors flapping gently in the breeze. The tent was open. We all froze, listening out for the tiniest bit of movement from the tent right in front of us, then a mad panic to jump inside and find Sasha.

I reached the inner compartment first, but Sasha wasn't there. Where on earth had she gone? How had we not seen her come out? Surely, we would have noticed if she had left, but we were all so busy singing and drinking and the music was on loud. Knowing Sasha, she would have sneakily crept past us and out to join a better, more lively party.

The three of us stood up instantly, checking all around us to see where she was, but she was nowhere to be seen. We called out just in case she was in any of the tents next to us, but no response. Just then, as I turned my head, my eyes were drawn to the brightest blue lights in the distance. I could see the top of an ambulance by the toilet block. The lights beaming into the sky like beacons.

With my heart already racing, it began to fill with the most immense feeling of dread and panic I had ever felt. Something was wrong, I could sense it. Hoping and praying it wasn't Sasha, I ran as fast as I could towards the lights. Daniel and Scott must have felt it too as they began running. At their speed, they overtook me, fear and drugs pushing our bodies, chasing the blue lights until we reached the ambulance. Deep down, I knew it wasn't her—it couldn't be—but I had to be sure. I was expecting her to fling open one of the portaloo toilet doors as drunk as a skunk and high on life, swooping her arms around my neck and saying how much she loved me. Telling us that we were being over dramatic and that she was fine.

As we got closer and closer, I could see the crowded ring of people around a person laying on the ground covered in a blanket. The security team and medical staff were trying to move everyone out of the way. They had started to put barriers up around the body, but I was more concerned about the women stood there looking on. The noise was horrendous, the sound of female cries and tears for concern. Each with their hands over their mouths, gasping in despair for the person's fate to ensue.

As much as I wanted to continue with the search for Sasha, something was drawing me to the person on the floor.

Wait a minute... they look like Sasha's flip-flops and the bracelet on her wrist. Isn't that... her t-shirt... her...

Just as I tried reaching for Daniel's arm in shock, Scott pushed past the crowd. He was shouting something at the paramedics, but I couldn't make out what he was saying, too much was happening all at the same time.

Then the pain hit me like a sharp knife to the chest. I had never experienced anything quite like it. His shouting had turned into a tormented cry and then to a voice of distress. It all seemed to happen so fast, and before I knew it, Daniel lunged forward to stop Scott, trying to hold him back, and I followed. Scott had found her. He found Sasha on the ground, still, just lying there. It was her that everyone was crowding around.

'No, no, no, no, no, baby girl.' Scott crumbled to the floor like the ground had given way. He touched her hand and tried to hold it, but it fell back down from his grasp like a heavy weight. She was unresponsive, her lips blue and her eyes tightly closed. Daniel's face was in pure shock, he tried placing his hands on Scott's shoulders, but he threw them off. He tried again to pull him back, giving the paramedics a chance to attend to her, but we could tell it was too late. Scott was laying on her chest, sobbing into her neck.

'You have *to* give her mouth to mouth or something... anything! She isn't breathing. Help her. Do something.' The tears streaming down his cheeks and dropping onto Sasha's statue-like face. His words slurred to leave his mouth as his lips buckled under the pain. To see a man so upset was heartbreaking, let alone seeing one of your best friends laying on the floor and there wasn't a single thing you could do. Scott tried putting his hands on her chest as if he was about to perform CPR, but the paramedic closest to him reached for his hand and shook his head.

'I'm sorry, she's gone. There was nothing we could do. It won't work.' The paramedic looked solemn and sorry for Scott, trying to comfort him, but he just hung his head in disbelief.

I couldn't comprehend what was happening. I could feel my body shaking and the tears streaming from my eyes, but I couldn't move. I wanted to hug her, to shake her, but seeing Scott in so much pain was too much to bear.

I felt helpless, it didn't feel real. How could it be real? It was just like a film where they would say 'cut' and Sasha would stop pretending and we could all get back to enjoying ourselves before she went into the tent. Daniel stood up and held me back as I tried to get closer, to shake her, to slap her face and tell her to snap out of it. I was angry at her. If she hadn't left, then maybe…

What was she thinking? How dare she die on us. Daniel held me so tight, wrapped up in his big arms, trying to get me to give in.

I watched the paramedics from Daniel's arms. I could see them talking to each other, but I couldn't hear what they were saying, it wasn't clear. They began shaking their heads, almost to say enough is enough, and they needed to move her. Scott was still kneeling over her body; he didn't want to let go. I could see chaos unfolding before us as the three paramedics tried to persuade him that it was time to take her away. They didn't know how much he loved her or that they were soulmates, but they must have experienced similar incidents before at work.

All I could hear from everyone around us was the sound of crying. The pain was unbearable, and as if that wasn't enough, the groups of people high on life, alcohol and anything else they had taken that night, were stumbling around trying to get a view of Sasha, trying to take pictures of our friend lying dead on the ground.

It didn't feel real. It didn't seem right. *Why didn't I tell her not to go back in the tent? I could have stopped this from happening and I didn't. What kind of a friend am I?* Maybe I was to blame.

There were so many things we were supposed to do in the future together, so many things planned. Jack would miss her dearly. I would miss her incredibly.

If only we had seen her leave the tent... maybe she could have told us she didn't feel well, and if we had got her to the ambulance quicker, it would have saved her life. Did she take something else that we didn't know about? All I could think about was that she must have been so scared taking her last breath and the only people with her were strangers. I would never forgive myself for that.

Daniel and I stood together as tightly as we possibly could, swaying back and forth, both of us with our eyes firmly closed, not wanting to face reality. Sobbing our hearts out.

I could hear the painful tears on the floor next to us. Daniel released me from his hold, we both knelt to cuddle Scott. His knees pulled up against his chest and his head buried between them. He shook as I comforted his broken body.

The barriers had gone up. Slowly, people moved away and all that could be heard was the banging of stretchers and instruments from the back of the ambulance, trying to get Sasha into the back of the vehicle. It was eerily quiet with an occasional sniffle from us and onlookers. A security guard approached from beside the barrier and bent down to speak to us.

'Are you the next of kin?' he asked as gently and as sympathetically as he could. Scott said nothing. I think he was incapable of responding to anyone or anything since he was in such shock.

'He is, yes,' I answered for him.

'I will need to take some information from you if that's okay? Could you come to the medical tent with us please? The body will be taken for tests and her family informed.' He offered out his hand for Scott to take, but he didn't move, he just sat there motionless, his eyes red and swollen, swallowing constantly to hold back the pain. He was moments away from a total breakdown.

'Daniel, I... can you help him?' I looked up to him for guidance. Daniel was always the strongest person in the room, the pillar of strength, someone to rely on. He must have been hurting too but he was the one comforting Scott and myself. He had almost pushed his own feelings to the back of the queue until everyone else was okay.

'Scott, mate. Let's get you over to the medical tent.' He put a hand on each side of his lean body, under his armpits and tried to lift, trying to raise him to his feet, but instead of walking, Scott spun around to meet Daniel face-on and just fell into his arms like a little lost boy. Daniel hugged him as hard as he could. 'I'm sorry. I'm so sorry, mate. We couldn't save her.' The pair of them shaking with emotion and crying together, wiping tears away from their faces. I moved forward, putting my arms around them both like a group hug and just stood there huddled together.

This was the first night of the festival, we hadn't even met up with the others yet. What would we even say to them? I didn't want to think about anything right now.

They took us to the medical tent and gave each of us a space blanket—the silver foil-looking wraps that help keep you warm and stave off shock. We were handed a hot cup of tea, but to be honest, the look of Sasha on the floor had sobered me completely. Every time I closed my eyes, all I could see was her stone-cold face, her grey complexion and blue lips. A sight that I don't think I will ever forget.

Scott filled in form after form, they even offered to order us a taxi so we could go all the way home, but we decided to go back to our tents together and work out what we would do in the morning.

The three of us stood up to leave the tent. With Daniel on one side of me and Scott on the other, we walked hand in hand back to our designated area. Not a single word was spoken, we didn't know what to say... there was nothing to say. Scott didn't want to drink anymore, he wanted to go to bed but not in his own tent as it didn't feel right, not without Sasha. I moved his sleeping bag and belongings into our tent and the three of us lay side by side like mummies in our tiny two-man tent, staring up into the darkness. We could hear the chatter from other people around us and the sound of music coming from a variety of directions.

For hours, I lay there forcing myself not to cry, the bulge in my throat getting bigger and bigger and the occasional tear rolling down my cheek, but I daren't let out a whimper in case the other two were asleep and I woke them. The music made me think of her and the way she would be partying right now into the early hours of the morning if she was here. But she wasn't. She was gone forever. It seemed too hard to get my head around. I just wanted to reach out and cuddle her, just one last time.

Thinking back to the journey on the way here, *How was that earlier this morning and now she's not here?*

I must have dozed off at some point because the morning sound of someone outside our tent woke me and it was already light. I looked beside me and both the men were gone. *They must be outside,* I thought. Before I could leave the warmth of my sleeping bag, I stretched, adjusted my hair, wiped my sore eyes and threw on a jumper. As soon as I opened the zip, I saw Scott and Daniel sitting in their chairs, their heads both hung in sadness. Before I could say anything, I took one look at the empty chair next to Scott, thinking that Sasha should be there, remembering the nightmare of last night and my composure crumbled. I wished it was a dream, but it wasn't.

I clambered into my chair and cried uncontrollably. Shaking and shuddering, a blubbering mess, remembering all the events of last night.

Nothing would replace her. She was one of the nicest people I had the pleasure of knowing and she was taken too early from us. My heart broke yesterday, and it was breaking again today. The notion of living every day like it is your last and enjoying what you have would stay with me my entire life, but it also delivered to me a few home truths.

Imagine if it was me lying there on the ground instead of Sasha... what about Jack, what about Daniel? What about all the things that I hadn't yet done with my life?

The more I cried, the more Scott and Daniel cried, each one of us setting the other off. Neither of us wanted to stay, so we decided to leave. We tried to reach the others, but they were on the campsite at the other end and we had different wristbands. There was no phone signal and no way of communicating with them. We all agreed to meet them back home and let them enjoy the weekend before finding out the horrific news.

Daniel decided to drive the van home, leaving Scott in the back of the van with me. We sat there, Scott covered with blankets, cuddled up and comforted the whole journey home. Again, very few words were spoken, each of us in a nightmare, shocked and affected by what had happened, never to be the same again.

15

I'M SO SORRY

The laboratory test results had come back, they found traces of cocaine, methylenedioxy-meth-amphetamine (also known as MDMA, or better known as Ecstasy), alcohol and marijuana in Sasha's blood-stream. Not just a little bit, but ridiculously high amounts. The type of levels that would kill a baby elephant, and in this case, Sasha's cause of death was heart failure and dehy-dration.

Part of me didn't believe it or want to believe it, but also a small part of me did. She was a party animal, she was the life and soul of everything we went to, she was Sasha. The coroner said that the amount of cocaine followed by MDMA was a toxic cocktail that anybody would have struggled with. She may not have known it until it was too late, but so many young people drink so much water to rehydrate themselves that they drown from drinking too much. She must have been so scared.

Daniel and I had been over to see Scott numerous times since she left us, and he had been over to ours. They did everything together, so the first couple of weeks and months were going to be especially hard for him without her. I missed Sasha dearly but the hardest part of it all was seeing her mum and sister. Sasha had lost her dad a couple of years back—she had taken it rather badly and it hadn't helped her drug problem.

She was never the same after he went, they were extremely close—a true Daddy's girl. I guess now they were together in a better place. The only saving grace was that after he went, she became a lot closer to her mum and little sister. Sasha had almost taken on the role of protector and head of family to replace him. *What would they do now that both had gone?*

Daniel and I knocked on their front door the following day. The front room curtains were drawn and there was still post half-pushed through the letter box, so we thought we would knock, and if no one answered within 10 minutes or so, we would leave.

We stood there patiently, waiting for any sign of movement. A half-cloudy, half-misty type of day. Just as we were about to give up and turn around, there was a clicking sound, the rustling of keys and the door slowly began to open.

Sasha's mum, Jenny, was a very attractive woman in her late forties. She would always have her hair done and makeup on, she wore fashionable clothes and kept fairly trim. I was shocked... the normally glamorous-looking lady had been replaced with another similar-looking woman who appeared to have aged years. Almost unrecognisable. You could tell her eyes were red and puffy from crying. She instantly saw us and leapt forward, wrapping her arms around Daniel as he was the closest. You could hear her pain as she sobbed into his chest. I stood there waiting for their embrace to finish, I wasn't in a hurry, and it was the least we could do. His hands outstretched against her back, trying to provide comfort.

Jenny then stepped back with watery eyes and held out her arms to me.

'Rose, she's gone, my baby has gone. I'm going to miss her so much, what am I going to do?' We hugged and cried together; it was like hugging my own mum. I hadn't known her for that many years, but it felt so much longer.

There was nothing I could say or do that would take this pain away from any of us. The words 'she's gone' repeating over and over in my head.

We sat in Jenny's front room for a few hours. At first, it was difficult, we struggled to hold back the tears, choked at the very thought of her beautiful aura around us, and in a strange way, it felt like she was in the room with us. I felt somehow closer to Sasha now than I had in a long time.

After a while, we began laughing and reminiscing about all the things she had done, the silly times and the good times. I looked around the room and there were so many pictures on the wall of Sasha laughing and smiling—never miserable. She never complained and always put others first. It was as if she knew she was going early and tried to make up for it by making the most of her short life with us.

We listened to Jenny as she had ideas on how her funeral might plan out, the songs that would be played, the stories that would be told, and the flowers that she loved. Never in a million years did I ever think I would be planning a close friend's funeral. Scott had a huge part to play in the day, but he was still so devastated that he didn't want to be at Sasha's mum's house without her there. He said it was too painful to see pictures of her, knowing that he couldn't touch or cuddle her. I understood that.

Jenny had a lot of questions that she wanted answered about how Sasha went. Was she at peace? Was she in any pain and surrounded by all her friends? I felt terrible lying, but all three of us said that we were there with her, she didn't suffer and, unfortunately, she drifted away. The last thing we wanted was for her mum to think that she died in a field on her own in a panic and scared state. I hoped that if Sasha was looking down on us right now, she would believe we did the right thing.

I still couldn't help replaying the scene in my mind repeatedly, seeing her laying there motionless, her face white, eyes closed, forever sleeping like an angel.

We left, saying our goodbyes, telling Jenny that if she ever needed us for anything at all, she only had to call. I think she appreciated that. The fact that she could reach out to us meant that she was just the tiniest bit closer to her daughter.

Daniel drove us to my mum and dad's house to pick up Jack. Once again, we had to explain what had happened to my parents, the tears and emotions that came from recalling the night before was awful. My mum grabbed me and almost shook me by the shoulders.

'Let that be a lesson to you. Promise me that you won't ever take drugs, I couldn't bear losing you.' She held me so tight and cried. I looked down at Jack, who had no idea what all the commotion was for, and struggled to imagine what life would be like after losing a child. It was incomprehensible. The pain, the heartbreak. If I lost Jack, my life wouldn't be worth living, I knew that for sure.

For the next couple of weeks, things seemed to carry on. Life was slower, much heavier than before.

My mind was constantly thinking about Sasha and whether Scott, Jenny and the rest of her family were coping. In a weird way, it still hadn't sunk in. I picked up my phone on several occasions, about to text her regarding something I had seen, or that she would like or just a chat to then realise that she wasn't at the end of her phone anymore. She wouldn't be coming over at the weekend to see Jack and we wouldn't be planning what we were doing next weekend together. That was it, final, finished. She was gone. Forever. Full stop.

Her body was at the funeral parlour, but where was she? Where was her spirit? Was it true that we live on, that our souls go to heaven or hell, or some poor souls linger on in an after-world? I had often contemplated it and found myself talking to her when I was on my own, just as if she was sitting next to me.

'What do you think, Sasha? Are you up there, or aren't you? What songs would you like for your funeral?' Of course, she didn't answer, but it made me feel better somehow.

The day of the funeral came. A beautiful service planned at our local crematorium. We had promised Scott and Jenny that we would be there early to help meet and greet everyone and be there for them. So many of her friends and family had gathered, all in their black attire, tissues at the ready. I was feeling better than I thought I would. I had been speaking to myself in the car on the way to the funeral.

'Rose, you need to stay strong today, for Scott, for Jenny and for Sasha. Crying doesn't change what's happened and it certainly doesn't make you feel better. In fact, it makes your heart ache even more, so you need to pull it together and remain composed.' I had this, for once, I wanted to be everyone's rock and the burden to not be on Daniel's shoulders.

We parked the car and slowly walked to the entrance. Jenny and Scott were standing, talking to a small group of people that I had never met before. Once they finished and there was a break in the conversation, we hugged them both to let them know we were there, but then continued to greet the many people arriving.

Most people had their heads down, not wanting to talk, dreading the service ahead of us.

The crematorium was a beautiful, restful place when you took the time to notice the space around you. There were so many flowers, plants and meaningful gifts. Beside the old main building was a series of woods lined with the prettiest of bluebells, a small pathway that led to small statues and ornaments that people had left next to their loved ones. The sun was out and unusually bright. Sasha was with us... I could feel it.

Daniel held my hand—we were inseparable. Occasionally, he would look down at me to check I was okay. Feeling calm and collected, I smiled back on several occasions.

It was eerily quiet, even though the queue outside the entrance had grown, there must have been over 100 people waiting in the sunshine to say their last goodbye to Sasha. I smiled inside, thinking how nice it was that she was liked by so many people, but as I did, something made me turn, pulling my head to look behind me.

It was Sasha. The dreaded black, large-windowed hearse pulled into the main entrance and passed the wrought iron gates. The most stunning bouquet of white lilies piled high on top of the coffin and a big gold framed picture that I could only see the back of from where I was standing. My calm and collected demeanour had changed to a broken mess the minute the car steered towards us and pulled up next to everyone.

It hit me like a steam train and there was absolutely nothing I could do to stop it. The tears came, I couldn't hold them back. My throat was dry and the pain in my heart was unbearable. Her beautiful face inside the frame stood up on her coffin and was staring back at us all. A wave of mourning shook through the crowd of people and all I could hear was sniffing and wailing. One person crying made another start and so on until we were all unable to control our emotions.

I had a tissue, but the mascara from my lashes had bled into my eyes and made them sting even more. I dabbed gently, but the more I wiped, the more I cried. I sniffled, trying to catch my breath and control myself but I let go and released the mightiest wail I promised I wouldn't.

I looked over at Jenny and Scott, who were both crying uncontrollably. I couldn't bear the thought of never seeing that beautiful soul again. Gone. What I would give to have one last cuddle, a laugh, a moment... anything with her again. I had so many things left to say to her. I couldn't change what had happened, my heart hurt so much.

Two strong men, very smartly dressed, opened the back of the hearse and gently pulled her coffin to the edge of the vehicle before turning, bending down and lifting it onto their shoulders. They carried our angel effortlessly from the car to the main doors, stepping slowly in time, along to her final resting place, whilst everyone filtered into the main hall.

The sniffles and the sobbing became louder and louder as the music played. They had chosen Tiny Dancer by Elton John—such a fitting song. It instantly made me think of her. They placed Sasha gently down on the altar at the front of the room, two large red velvet curtains hung on either side.

The room was cold, I felt a shiver run down my body. I could smell a mixture of wood from the seats we sat on and various women's perfumes. I stared at her photograph, it was hard to understand that she was inside that wooden box, asleep. Such a beautiful, young woman. Life was so cruel.

I glanced over at the front row and found Scott and Jenny both broken, trying to find comfort in each other, gripping onto their soaked tissues. There were no words to describe the torture in the room, to the point that there wasn't a dry eye anywhere.

Scott had planned to speak at the service. He'd been working on what he wanted to say since it all happened two weeks back, but yesterday, he said he couldn't do it. The officiant had offered to read Scott's words for him. As soon as she did so and started the service, I knew they came from Scott's heart and how he felt about her. It was beautiful.

We sat through thirty minutes of the service, listening and learning all about Sasha. I found out things that I didn't know from her childhood and the rest of her family. Another song was played, I Will Always Love You by Whitney Houston. Again the tears rippled through everyone like wildfire.

Finally, we all said the Lord's Prayer together and the service came to a close.

I could have stayed in that room for so much longer. I wanted to stand by her and tell her how I felt, to say I was sorry and beg for forgiveness. I could have stopped it happening that night, I should have told her no more. If I had seen her leave her tent, she might still be here. Instead, a candle was lit and placed before her coffin.

I wasn't ready to let her go or say goodbye, but the curtains began to close, drawing closer and closer together until I could see her pretty face in the gold frame no more.

I whimpered before her, my lips quivering, the tears streaming.

'I'm sorry, Sasha. I'm so sorry... I couldn't save you. We were too late,' I whispered under my breath. 'I love you; I will always love you and will miss you dearly. Jack says goodbye too. Till we meet again.' I blubbered uncontrollably as everyone started to walk in single file out of the room. Daniel squeezed my hand and smiled reassuringly at me, leading me outside and away.

She was gone.

16

WHY ARE YOU SO GOOD TO ME?

The second project with my customer, Steve, was due to start again. I'd been putting it off for several reasons. Partly because of losing Sasha, it had put me in a low frame of mind and due to everything that happened last time, but if I stalled it much longer, I risked losing it altogether and I couldn't afford to do that.

Of course, we'd spoken on the phone and I sent him all the pricing and details of the new project by email, but just as the first deal had been sealed and done, Steve wanted to meet again. If the first time didn't happen, was he thinking that maybe this time I would have to sleep with him to get the documents signed? In my head, I thought that I had for so long, so would it be that bad if I went through with it this time? The fact that he didn't take advantage of me before made me feel a lot safer with him now.

I had been thinking about George and the whole scenario with the hotel and London—him not telling me that he was there. Not telling me about Steve. I think it must have been a misunderstanding and he didn't want to embarrass me by telling me what really went on. Was he trying to protect me like he always did?

'Can I come?' George said as he waltzed over to my desk and sat on the corner of it.

'I'm sorry, what?' I looked up at him, confused. I'd been avoiding him for the past couple of weeks and I think he presumed it was down to losing Sasha.

'You looked like you were in a daydream, and it seemed an awful lot better than here in the office, so I wondered if I could come too?' I realised what he meant as I sat back in my chair and tried to laugh but my heart wasn't in it.

'What's up, Rose? I'm sorry about Sasha. I know you two were close.' He smiled endearingly for once.

'I still miss her so much, the pain just doesn't go away or get easier, and to add to it, I am supposed to be out this week with Steve. I'm not looking forward to it. Dave is banking on me getting this deal in, but after what happened last time I...' I stopped and looked at George to test his reaction.

'Oh, the next big deal, right?' His eyes widened as if he knew what I was talking about but didn't want to let on.

'Yep, the biggest one in the business's history. I'm under so much pressure to get this one closed.' I smiled awkwardly, hoping that he would come clean.

'And if you don't...' George came in closer to me as if he wanted to talk without the others in the office hearing. 'It's not the end of the world if you don't, right?' It was as if he was trying to give me a get-out-of-jail card.

'I know, I know. I don't think Dave would be too happy and I could do with the commission, but...' I wanted to speak to George honestly about the time before, but it was awkward. *What would I say? What could I say?*

'Do you want me to come with you?' he asked.

'Like you did last time?' I prompted.

'Eh?' George looked confused. I also found it confusing. What didn't he understand? Was Steve right in what had happened and what he saw, or was he the one trying to cover things up?

There was nothing I wanted more than for George to come with me, but it was my mess and I had to get myself out of it. Steve wasn't dangerous and he certainly wasn't threatening, it was just the thought of doing something behind Daniel's back that pained me.

Pull yourself together, Rose, you are stronger than that. I said to myself. *You know what you must do, just get it over and done with and you can forget about it just like you did last time.*

Thursday came and it felt like deja vu. I was panicking about what I to wear... *Do I have the contracts? How do I cover for myself and tell Daniel that I wasn't coming home that night?* Dave had given me a prep talk in the office before I left to ensure that I got Steve to sign all the documents. I felt like a secret agent—all my wires were on and I was ready to complete my mission.

I got on the train to Waterloo, looking out the window the whole time. George's words whirling around in my mind. 'It's not the end of the world if you don't, right?' I had talked myself out of going a million times, and I almost stood up and got off onto the platform at each station we pulled into along the way.

The last amount of commission helped us so much as a family. We wiped our debts and our credit cards; I even had some money left over to buy us new clothes and repairs on the house that were really needed. Everything I was doing was for the family, for all of us. I tried to justify my actions should Daniel ever question me. I took a swig from the bottle of sparkling water that I had in my bag, got my phone and ticket out and checked for any last-minute messages just as the train pulled into Waterloo Station.

I had a completely different outlook this time as I walked along the busy platform. I watched as everyone walked in the same direction as groups of lemmings all heading towards their destination.

All of us in our own rat races, conditioned to living a certain way and not questioning what we were doing. We weren't living... we were existing to pay bills. To me, it wasn't the money that was important, it was the happiness that it bought. We were miserable as a family when we had no money, arguing about bills and not being able to do anything. Having a small amount of money had made such a difference to both of us, and now, here I was saying it's not about the money. *Of course, it's about money, everything forces us to think about money.*

Why can't we live in a society where money has no status? We grow our own food and family is everything. The more money you have, the more you want. This is exactly the situation I found myself in. I wanted more, a lot more, and I was willing to do anything I could to get it. Instead of calling it quits after the last deal, here I am again, after more money, pressurised by work to do it... where did it end? Would this be the last time or did my career now have me where it wanted me?

I approached the ticket turnstiles and looked up towards the tube signs, checking for any delays as I made my way to the underground steps. I tried to make my way through the crowds of people, bumping into everyone as I went. Suddenly, there he was, unannounced and in full form.

'Hello, stranger.' Steve stood right in front me, smiling.

'Oh, hi, I was...' I stopped mid-response, startled by his sudden appearance.

'Shall we get a cab instead of the busy underground? Then we can talk... clear up a few things perhaps.' He helped guide me through the busy flow of people to the main entrance of Waterloo, where the taxi rank was.

'I was going to text you but thought I would wait until I was on the other side by Bank. I felt you needed an apology.'

My hands were shaking.

'Hey, it's okay. You must be cold, Rose... do you want my jacket?' He started to remove it from his body.

'No, no, honestly, I'm okay. The train was stuffy, that's all.' I smiled back at him.

'Listen, Rose, I wanted to apologise for last time and over the phone didn't seem like the best way to do it. I left before I should have done but I made sure that you were okay and safe. I didn't want you to think that we...' He was stopped by the taxi driver before he could continue.

'Where are you heading, mate?' the taxi driver called to us through the window in a London cockney tone.

'Finsbury Square, please?' he shouted back as he grabbed the back door and clicked it open. He was a true gentleman, I would give him that. Always holding doors open and organising where he was taking me. I never at any point felt like he was creepy or pressurising me into anything I didn't want to do.

I felt like I could have said no at any point, and he would respect my decision, but me being me just carried on pushing the limits.

London seemed especially busy today, the hustle and bustle of a Thursday evening.

'So, I thought perhaps we could try again, Rose. I really

enjoyed your company last time, despite how it ended.' He smiled at me. I could see his eyes studying my entire face. *What is he thinking? What's really in it for him?* I was confused and had so many questions from last time.

'Of course. I'm sorry if I was a little drunk last time. I was a bit nervous and I... I should have watched my drinks more carefully. You shouldn't have to look after me, I'm a grown woman.' I felt the need to explain things, but equally, he had pulled me into this situation in the first place.

'Hey, what happened last time was not your fault. That low life should be accountable for what he did. Yes, you were a little drunk and you should be way more careful, but men shouldn't take advantage of women like that.' He smiled, sitting back in the seat of the taxi.

I was confused, he definitely gave me all the signs that he wanted to take advantage of me in exchange for signing a contract. How did that make him any better than someone spiking my drink?

'I have all the paperwork in my bag for you.' I showed him the papers poking out of the top of my handbag as I sat next to him, my legs folded, and hands clasped on my lap. I didn't mention any side agreement, just the papers.

'Don't worry, I assure you that I will sign them, Rose. Let's go for dinner first and then I will do it before you get too drunk.' There it was again, another reference to me being drunk last time. For me, drinking settled my nerves, did he have an issue with that?

The cab pulled up outside an expensive-looking restaurant in Finsbury Square. It was very picturesque in the middle of central London, a small green area with tall trees and benches right in the middle of a square with a mixture of three-storey homes, restaurants and a few shops sprinkled in between. A completely unexpected calm amid a bustling, built-up city full of tall buildings.

Steve stepped out, paid the cab driver and held out his hand for me to hold onto. My legs complete with stockings and high heels reached the pavement as I elegantly stood outside the restaurant. I must say, with a little money, it makes such a difference to your appearance. This time, I had the most beautiful red patent stilettos on, tan-coloured stockings and a dashing black dress. The most expensive dress and shoes I had ever purchased in my life and that was all from the commission I received from the last deal. Before, my wardrobe was the cheapest I could find on the budget I had at the time, which wasn't much at all.

Steve led me into the restaurant and up the three stone steps to the main entrance, where he stood waiting for someone to greet him. I waited patiently behind him.

'I must say, you look incredible this evening, Rose. Simply stunning,' he said as he turned around to face me.

'Why thank you.' It felt good to get such a compliment from a married man. Well, from any man. I appeared to be radiating gratitude towards him.

'I mean it, Rose, you are so beautiful and that dress you are wearing just...' A man appeared at the desk before us and interrupted his flow.

'Ah, good evening, sir. May I ask what time your reservation is for please and the name?' A smart-looking gentleman with a very sculptured moustache and gelled hair requested the booking details from Steve.

'Yes, it should be for 6.30 pm under Mr Smith,' he answered the man. I, however, sniggered behind him. I knew full well his surname wasn't Smith. The gentleman looked up at me, but soon carried on with his duties. *Mr and Mrs Smith,* I chuckled quietly to myself.

'If you would like to follow me.' He walked in the direction of the hustle and bustle of the main restaurant. It was quite busy, but it always was on a Thursday in London. It was like the new Friday evening that we all had in the south.

We did as we were told and followed him to our table. It was right in the middle of the room. Already laden with glasses, cutlery, plates, menus and a romantic white candle in its holder, right in the middle of the table.

'Erm, excuse me, could you point me in the direction of the ladies, please?' I knew my manners and my posh voice was ever-present. I had been trying to learn about this new corporate world of entertainment and how best to behave. It was just the alcohol that I had to keep under control, but tonight, I had the answer for that.

Leaving Steve to sit down at the table and order the wine that he wanted, I made my way to the ladies. As I pushed the toilet door open, I was surprised to see everything lined in gold. The taps, the door handles, mirror edges and even the toilet roll holders. It looked like real gold too. I could only imagine what price the food on the menu was and whether or not Dave would sign it off under my expenses.

I shut the toilet door, slid the lock across and hung my bag over the hook on the back, but before I sat down, I reached into the inside zipped-up pocket and pulled out a small white envelope. Yes, I had ordered a small amount of cocaine from the same source as Sasha used to. Just enough to help me through the night without getting too drunk. Since the festival, I couldn't help myself. Each time I did it, I thought of her. You would have thought that it would have put me off, but I wasn't doing it in the copious amounts that she was.

Her dealer had approached me at the funeral, worried that it was because of him that she had died, but when I said about the amounts and types of drugs in her system, she clearly had got more from the festival than he supplied. It started then... he gave me a little and his number and I couldn't help myself since.

If I did a little at a time, Daniel would never know a thing. He clearly didn't know about the dealer, or me getting his number, or the fact that I had ordered some on multiple occasions.

At least today, I would be a little more alert, not as tired and definitely not as drunk as I was last time.

I sat down on the seat, holding the envelope ever so carefully just above my lap. I gently opened the corners of the folded paper, exposing the white powder pushed together in one big clump. I used my little fingernail on my right hand to push it around a little, breaking it up as I went. Then, one big scoop, using my nail like a shovel, I lifted a mound of the powder up to my nostril, but stopping short, I stared at it. *Just a little to get me started,* I said to myself... only this wasn't little. There was as much as I could fit within the underside of my nail, and as they were currently quite long, it was a substantial amount.

'If only you knew how much I miss you, Sasha,' I whispered under my breath before continuing.

With no one else in the toilet to hear me and no sound of the hand dryer, I had to go for it. I placed the paper on my lap. My right finger as high as it would reach without spilling it and my left hand holding my other nostril closed. I sniffed as hard as I could. That horrible chemical-smelling and tasting powder hit the top of my nose, small amounts fell to the back of my throat, making it numb as it did so.

It felt like a quick boost, my heart racing. I sniffed again, that sour taste falling onto the back of my throat and making me heave, but at the same time, my eyes widening. My senses standing to attention and energy pumping around my body. Folding up the paper so that none spilled out, I tucked it as deep as I could into my handbag pocket. I then flushed the chain and opened the toilet door. I felt confident, like a new person was leaving the toilets to join Steve back at the table. A million things whirring around in my head that I wanted to say when I returned.

Looking at myself in the mirror, I checked all around my nose to make sure that nothing was remaining. I sniffed yet again and noticed the size of my pupils—they had doubled in size even though the bright lights from the mirror shone directly into my face. The last thing I wanted was for Steve to find out, especially after the last time, so I would just have to act calm. He wouldn't notice a thing.

Right, I said to myself as I washed my hands. I flung my handbag over my shoulder, fluffed my hair so it looked like I had adjusted it, and walked back to the table, the most confident I'd ever been, but I couldn't help but feel paranoid in case he noticed.

'I hope you don't mind, Rose. I ordered a bottle of red wine for us to share and some sparkling water for the table. Let's get those documents signed and out of the way so we can enjoy the rest of the evening care-free together.' He seemed eager to get them signed and done and I wasn't going to disagree with him.

Lifting them from my bag, I placed them on the table, facing him. I also pulled out a black ballpoint pen from under the table and placed it on top of the papers. Steve picked up his glasses from beside his cutlery and placed them slowly on his nose and ears, instantly looking highly professional, scanning all the words, the line items and amounts to ensure that it was exactly what he required.

I couldn't help it, but the way he looked and acted, his authority and power that he had was a huge turn-on. I wasn't expecting that, not from him. Here I was trying to convince myself that I didn't need to sleep with him to get this deal done, but the more he seemed to be backing off and not trying it on with me, the more temptation sunk deep inside me like an inner voice, encouraging me to tease him.

This deal was big, it was one of the largest deals that my company had ever done with a customer, and it was all my responsibility to bring it home. The pressure I felt leading up to this day caused me many a sleepless night, not to mention the worry of Daniel finding out.

'Uh-huh.' Steve was checking line by line. 'Yep, that's right. Ten of those and twenty of those.'

I studied his face as he worked through the document. I felt sorry for him in a way. Why did people find themselves in relationships when they didn't really love the other person, or they weren't getting what they wanted from each other? Was it through lack of talking, sharing feelings, living a lie, perhaps? I could tell that Steve just wanted someone to love, protect and look after. It was as if he had given up trying, but that someone wasn't me and it wasn't my problem, yet I still seemed to care.

'So, Rose, if I sign this right now, that's a lot of commission you will receive, isn't it?' He looked at me over the top of his glasses as he slid them further down his nose.

'Erm, yes, it is,' I nervously replied. *That's a strange ques-*

tion, I thought. *I wonder what's coming next.* I was trying not to make eye contact with him, but it was so difficult and obvious.

'So, ideally, you want this signed, done and dusted, and you get the commission. That's it, right?' He removed his glasses and placed them back on the table, crossing his hands. I wasn't quite sure where this was going now. Were we back to square one and bartering the outcome of the agreement?

'How about you share your cocaine with me, and I sign this document right here, right now, leaving us to get on with enjoying the night and I don't say a word to Dave or anyone else for that matter.' His voice went quiet so no one else could hear and he suddenly looked serious.

Shit, I thought. *This could go wrong... horribly wrong. Do I deny having any or do I offer him some? Think quick, Rose, think quick.* He must have noticed my eyes, or was it something else?

My problem is my guilty conscience kicks in when I don't want it to and disappears completely when I want it to. This is the first time that I had taken cocaine at work, for work, or anything to do with work, now it could cost me my career. *What on earth must Dave be thinking? Last time, I was spiked and today, I'm taking cocaine. Smart move, Rose... not!*

'Yes, of course,' I said, rummaging through my handbag pocket quickly, and like a professional drug dealer, I asked Steve to pass me the menu. As he did, I slipped the small white folded envelope containing the cocaine into his hand as we passed it between us. He smiled, kicked his chair back and left to go to the men's bathroom. *Game well played,* I thought.

I am either in serious trouble or this is yet another secret between Steve and I that I must erase to keep my sanity and forget it ever happened. The room suddenly felt small. It was hot and closing in on me.

Was everyone looking in my direction or was it my vivid imagination? Feeling the heat rise, I sipped some sparkling water that Steve ordered and was left on the table, but my throat was slightly numb from the cocaine. It spilled gently from the side of my mouth, so I dabbed with my napkin. I wanted the room to swallow me up whole and spit me back out. *What on earth was I thinking when I ordered drugs for me to go on a work dinner?*

Steve returned as if nothing had happened. He was somewhat more excitable and energetic, but sitting back at the table, he sat down, his hands folded in front of him. A little twinkle in his eyes as if he had just done something very naughty and unruly.

'Well, that's made my night more interesting.' He smiled at me. 'Well needed.'

'Am I in trouble?' I had to ask him, otherwise, I would worry all night.

'No, not at all. Why would you be in trouble? Besides, if you were, I would be too.' He seemed to be embracing it. 'I haven't done any in years, takes me back to my youth.'

Phew, I thought, but I was equally surprised that he would have been the type of person to have taken drugs in his younger years. I panicked for a small moment, thinking I could kiss goodbye to both my career and the project. Having dinner with Steve for the second time was different. Rather than getting to know him, it was more about catching up, continuing from where we left it last time, delving a little deeper into his personal life. It felt more like meeting an old friend, an acquaintance perhaps. I felt at ease talking to him, just like I did with George. Was it because perhaps he was independent, I knew it wouldn't go any further. Especially our last experience.

The part that I really struggled with was seeing him naked. Did that happen or did I dream and imagine the whole thing? Did he really have a well-toned, hairy body and was well endowed? I racked my brain but none of it made much sense, and I didn't have the guts to ask. Maybe after a few more wines, I would pluck up the courage. Maybe it was my imagination again that conjured up an image of what he looked like without his clothes on.

We shared a couple of bottles of red wine. Although dinner was lovely, I struggled to eat it all and Steve did too. The full effects of the cocaine had left us feeling full and unable to eat too much. A couple more trips from both Steve and I to the bathroom to sniff a few more lines up our noses and I was on such a high. The room was spinning. I struggled to make sense of exactly what he was saying but at least I was wide awake, buzzing for where the night took us next. For the first time, I didn't want to go home, I wanted to stay out and enjoy myself. I now knew exactly why Sasha enjoyed it so much.

Steve seemed to take control like a security guard with a lost child. I felt hot, my heart pounding in my chest and I was struggling to keep my head up. I needed air, I needed to get out of this stuffy restaurant and breathe freely. It wasn't a spiked drink or too much alcohol, it was everything combined, the total amount that my body had consumed. I tried to get to my feet, steadying myself with my hands on the side of the table as I did, but the more I tried, the more the room span. I felt sick, I tried blinking repeatedly to correct my vision, but it didn't work.

I could see Steve stand up and look at me, but he seemed so far away. He was just as bad as I was, two morons in a fancy restaurant. It was too late... as I stood up, holding onto the tablecloth, it slipped between my fingers, losing my balance. I heard crashing and cluttering as I fell backwards onto the floor. My chair caught the bulk of my fall but that too was sent crashing backwards as I lay there watching all the commotion around me.

The tablecloth caught on the tiniest metal hook from my watch strap sent the plates, glasses and cutlery crashing to the ground around me. There were waiters and waitresses to one side of me in a state of panic, Steve on the other side with other diners from the restaurant. I could see him struggling to keep a straight face. Close by, diners were trying to offer me a glass of water, others trying to help me sit up.

Through all the noise and confusion, I heard the restaurant owner ask Steve if he wanted him to phone an ambulance, but he reassured them that I was fine and that he had everything under control in the soberest voice he could.

'I'm fine, I'm fine. I just need some air,' I said, trying to sit up. My hand on my head, dazed, I desperately wanted to sober up and drain the drugs from my body. I looked around the room. I had caused absolute carnage. Steve, with the help of others, lifted me to my feet and placed me gently back on my chair as best as they could.

'I think we will grab the bill please and I'll take her home.' He nodded to the head waiter, organising our exit from the restaurant. I looked at Steve with what I could only imagine was a sad puppy look, one of distress, hoping he could help me in my sorry state, but he seemed to laugh and so did I, like naughty children who had been told off.

'What are we going to do with you, Miss Rose? There

seems to be a pattern of behaviour. Makes a nice change to the boring work dinners I normally have.' He gently took his hand and smoothed the hair that had gone adrift over my face, placing it back beside my cheek. 'Let's get you out of here, lovely.' He smiled in a way that I had only ever seen Daniel give me.

I was completely helpless and dependent on him. Once again, I had gotten myself into a stupid situation that could have gone horribly wrong.

Steve paid the bill, got me to my feet and we made our way to the entrance. The whole time he had my arm, propping me against him so I had his full support as I tried walking as steadily as I could.

The main entrance doors opened as we approached and the cold air from outside hit me like a steam train. A hard, smack to the face to sober me up.

Something made me look up and into the small park opposite the restaurant in the middle of the square. There he stood, just as before. A black hoodie up around his face, unable to make out his features, but I knew he was there, I knew it was him, staring back at me with the darkest of eyes. It was him, my stalker. Why was he here? How did he know where I would be tonight? I didn't even know where I was heading, only Steve did.

As if my heart wasn't racing enough as it was, seeing him only added to the panic and fear already in my body.

I raised my hand and pointed in his direction. Nervously, I looked at Steve and tried to get him to look in that direction, but the words just wouldn't come out. I began mumbling utter gibberish. Steve just pushed my arm back down and tried to get me to walk, ignoring my motions like none of it mattered.

'But... he... look... it's him... he is...' The few words I could manage made no sense whatsoever and Steve wasn't listening. He was fixated on getting me to walk, trying to keep his own body from falling at the same time.

'Let's get you back to mine. I'm staying just around the corner.' He led the way and almost pulled me along beside him. 'Rose, I'm just going to say it because I'm slightly intoxicated. You are an absolute nightmare, but I thoroughly enjoy myself when I'm with you. You make me feel like a teenager again. I haven't felt this good in years and I thank you for that.' I just looked at him, not taking in the words, but watching his mouth move as he spoke. I flung my arms around him in appreciation.

Steve hugged me back but soon turned me around to get me to walk. It felt like slow motion. I was concentrating so hard on moving one leg at a time in the most beautiful and uncomfortable high heels.

Constantly checking behind me as to where the hooded man had gone. Worrying that he was following me. I kept thinking, *That's it, he wants me dead. That's why he is here, I am far from home, no one would look for me here if I was dead or disappeared. It would be easy to kill me tonight and throw me in the Thames.*

Before long and just as Steve had promised, we arrived at his hotel. He helped me up the main steps and into the bright lights of reception. Propping me against the desk, he reached into his pocket to get his wallet so he could check in. I was trying my utmost to stand up and to act sober, but it was no use, my legs were like jelly and uncontrollable. My head was like a heavy weight on my shoulders that I just couldn't hold up and now I had the hiccups. What a mess, yet again.

Steve managed to get himself checked in. He picked up

the two room cards and helped us both over to the lift doors to lead us up to his room. The stares and the looks from other guests in the hotel didn't faze him one little bit, oblivious to people's reactions around us.

I don't remember reaching the lift, riding up to the second floor or walking the corridor to the room, I only remember reaching his room, and like a bag of weights, I fell to the floor as he opened it. The carpet felt comfy, I could have stayed there and slept on it all night, but Steve tried his hardest to help me up.

Finally, after shutting the door and kicking off his shoes, he walked over to me and lifted me with ease, walking me to the large king-size bed. He placed me there like a princess on a bed full of roses.

I had no energy to do anything other than try to say thank you and smile at him.

He sat on the bed next to me. How had I managed to get so drunk and so uncontrollably incapacitated for the second time? I clearly couldn't be trusted to go for a professional dinner with a client. Maybe I wasn't cut out for this job.

'I'm going to pour myself a drink, Rose. I would offer you one, but I think you have had more than enough for tonight.' He brushed my cheek with his hand, but he seemed to do it in an endearing manner. He was looking after me, not trying to seduce me. I looked on like an out-of-body experience, no controlled movement, a lifeless, limp woman. My limbs were frozen and unable to move. Steve lifted each of my legs in turn, working his way to my feet, and gently removed my heels, placing them on the floor next to the bed, but that was it. He stopped there... I thought he was going to undress me.

I watched as he made his way over to the mini bar. *Is this real or is this one of my stupid dreams?*

Pulling a couple of miniature drinks from the fridge and placing them and a small glass onto the bedside table, Steve then reached into his pocket and retrieved what was left from my envelope of cocaine.

He poured the contents onto the glass table, and with a credit card, he began to chop it up and divide it into lines. Before he took a sip of his drink or any of the drugs, he got up to go to the bathroom. I looked at the white lines like temptation calling out to me. I was already in a sorry state, but I thought if I had just one more, it would wake me up and I could continue the night. Like a challenge, I could say thank you to Steve, try and catch the last train home and still have the signed documents in my bag.

I mustered the energy to roll over on the bed. I picked up the rolled twenty-pound note that he left behind and inserted it into my right nostril. Without even thinking, I sniffed as hard as I could, moving it along the line until every crumb of white cocaine powder disappeared. Instantly, I felt it hit the top of my nose cavity, a burning sensation running down the back of my throat and the nasty taste of something in my mouth.

I panicked, my body was telling me that it was too much, my heart was racing, my whole body full of bad substances. The image of Sasha lying on the ground the night she died kept flashing before me. Would I end up the same way? I felt tired and exhausted, but my eyes wouldn't close, the light in the room was too much for my enlarged pupils and I didn't know what to do. I looked around the room for my bag, which was next to me on the bed. I reached for my phone, but who would I call? 999? George?

Imagine trying to explain to Daniel that I was drugged up

to my eyeballs, drunk and in a strange man's hotel room. That wouldn't go down well, so I couldn't call him.

I couldn't call my parents... they would be ashamed of me. I only had one person I could call. George, despite everything that had happened of late, was the only one I could trust to get me out of a jam.

Double vision got the better of me, I could only make out one letter at a time as I frantically scrolled through my phone's address book. From A-Z until I reached G. His name was there, my cursor was on it, and it was highlighted, but something stopped me from calling him. It was too late at night. What would I say to him? Before I knew it, Steve came out of the bathroom, his face changed from his usual smiling, happy face to instantly scared and shocked. He looked at the cocaine on the side of the table and noticed that I had taken some more.

'I'm sorry, I thought it might wake me up a little. I...' It was mine after all, but I felt I needed to somehow explain myself.

'I'm not your father, or your husband for that matter, so it's your decision what you do, I'm just worried that you are out of control, Rose. That's too much, you will end up killing yourself.' He got louder and louder.

'I'm not out of control, I know exactly what I am doing. Look.' I tried getting to my feet, standing up as straight as I could by the bed.

'Rose, I just care, that's all.' He looked both concerned and apologetic.

'See, I can do another line... I am absolutely fine.' I shrugged, trying to reach the bedside table and take another one.

'Rose, stop it now. Enough is enough, it's not funny

anymore.' He grabbed my wrist, demanding I stop. Looking down at his strong wrist, the power that he had in his arm to stop me in my tracks. I held it there for a moment and looked at him. Steve moved my arm back down beside me and held my other hand to keep me still.

'Rose, you don't need to prove anything. I would have signed those papers without you sleeping with me. I wanted to test you, to see how far you would go and whether you thought I was attractive or not for an older man. I want to feel all the passion and the lust that you talk about. My body aches for another woman to lust after me. I want what I can't have.' He opened his entire heart to me, a man that I barely knew and had only met a couple of times.

'Stop it, Steve.' I didn't want him to say anymore, I didn't want emotion or feelings in any of this, it made it so much worse. 'If I wasn't with Daniel, I would have slept with you. Not just for the money or the contracts, but because you are such a nice guy, why would I not find you attractive? The look in your eye that you've had all evening. It has kind of got me thinking. I...'

Before he had a chance to answer, he leaned forward and kissed me. I wasn't shocked, I didn't try saying anything else, I kissed him straight back. He held my arms behind my back in a place where I couldn't move even if I wanted to. His warm body pushing against mine.

His kiss was incredible, his stubble scratching against my chin, our lips sealed against each other as our tongues touched. He pushed me back again. I buckled and fell against the bed.

'Too much? Do you want me to stop?' he whispered gently into my ear. I shook my head, wanting him to carry on.

Instead of getting on top, he lifted me gently, one arm

under my back, one arm under my legs and moved me so that my head was resting on the pillows. He then leaned down onto the bed and moved closer to me. On all fours, he positioned himself right in the arm of my body. I rolled to one side to see his face hovering right above mine, my hand around the back of his neck, pulling him into me.

Steve placed his hand on my breast, cupping and squeezing gently as he looked straight into my eyes. There was something so naughty and enticing in him, touching me the way he did. His large, warm hands moving from my breasts to the bottom of my dress, up and between my thighs. I felt wet, he could feel it too as he tried to move my knickers to one side.

It wasn't that I didn't love Daniel, it was just different— unique. I couldn't say no, the feeling was just too tempting.

I moved my hands down to unfasten the belt from around his waist, unhooking the holes from the buckle and pulling the leather out to free his jeans zip. I gently slid it all the way to the bottom to expose his boxer shorts and his massive erection. Before I got completely naked, I wanted his cock in my mouth, I wanted to give him the pleasure that he so desperately needed, everything his wife wasn't giving him, and more importantly, I wanted to see his face while I was doing it.

It was my turn to take control, I pushed him backwards against the bed, my legs either side of him, and held his hands either side of his head. He was way stronger than I was, and he could have forced me off, but instead, he lay there, letting me do what I wanted to him.

At first, I kissed his face, then his neck, still holding his hands. I then shuffled a little further down, tugging at his shirt and unbuttoning it one by one until it was fully open. I stroked his hairy chest, pinching his nipples and kissing in a line right the way down to where his boxers began.

Using both hands, I peeled the top waistband back and pulled his jeans down. Shuffling again, I took his jeans and his boxers right down to his ankles but not off. By keeping them wrapped around his ankles, he wouldn't be able to make a quick move or get up—I had him right where I wanted him.

Using one hand to cup his neatly trimmed testicles, I gently but firmly massaged them, using my middle finger to slowly touch the smooth area of skin between his testicles and his bottom, and with the other hand, I wrapped it fully around his girth. Steve watched me the whole time as if he was about to cum without me even doing anything. I kneeled up, looking him deep in the eyes with tension. I licked my lips lusciously and lowered my head to take his full length all the way down my throat. He took a deep breath in as my lips were about to touch his tip.

Bang, bang.

There was a knock at the door. *Wait, what?* Surely not, who would be knocking on the hotel door at this hour? It couldn't be housekeeping and neither of us had ordered room service, had we?

Steve sat up in a panic. 'Who the fuck...' He looked at me, jumping up from the bed and trying to get to the door.

Bang, bang.

There it was again. Whoever it was, they were impatient and angry. It couldn't be Daniel... could it? It couldn't possibly. How would he...

Steve steamed over to the door angrily at whoever had interrupted his moment of pleasure. Before he could say anything, as the handle clicked, the door swung open in a rage.

'I'm sorry, sir, I tried to stop him, but he flew past reception and said that he needed to get to your room. He said there was something wrong and I couldn't...' The lady outside the room was explaining apologetically but I couldn't quite see who it was.

'Okay, thanks, you can go now. I have found them.' I knew that voice... it was George, but what was he doing here?

George entered the room in a rage.

'Rose, are you okay?' He put his arms around me and cuddled me like a lost child. Normally, I would have embraced him, but on this occasion, I was confused and angry.

'What the fuck are you doing here? I can look after myself you know,' I said, pushing him back and waiting for his reply.

'I was in town having drinks with customers. I saw you both walk past, Steve holding you up as you went.' He held his hand up and pointed it in Steve's direction. 'I was going to say hi and join you but there was a weird man in a black hoodie that was loitering behind you. He seemed quick to move on when he saw that I was on to him.'

'Wait, what? A man in a black hoodie? Was he behind us? Was he hanging around the hotel reception too?' I wasn't going mad after all, and it couldn't have been George. I had got it so wrong.

'Yes, yes, he was. I had followed you all the way from Finsbury Square when I saw you both leaving the restaurant, he was opposite, watching you from the gardens. I thought it was quite weird and wondered why he was so fixated on you.' George put his hand on my shoulder as he explained. I felt so bad that I had questioned him or that he was doing anything other than looking out for me.

'Very weird, I just don't understand. Why is he following me?'

Steve could see the worried look on my face. Why didn't George speak to the man or question why he was following me? That's what I would do.

'Who is following you, Rose?' Steve asked.

'Yes, she is okay, and she doesn't need your help. Look at the state she is in and in a married man's hotel room. Have you told her you're married, Steve? Taking advantage of someone in that state.' George put his hand up against Steve's chest as he tried making his way towards me.

'Yes, he has told me he is married and it's my fault I am in this state. I wanted to come back here... I can make my own decisions.' I know George was only trying to look after me, but it felt slightly condescending. *Who does he think he is?*

'And Daniel? Does Daniel know where you are tonight?' He stood in front of me, motioning with his hands like an angry dad trying to reason with his naughty daughter.

'Look, I don't know what is happening here, but I promise I haven't done anything that Rose didn't want me to do, and I certainly don't want to cause problems with anyone. I think it's time for me to make a move. I've already paid for the room, so you are more than welcome to stay, but I'm going to head home and see if I can get the last train back. Rose, it has been a pleasure as it always is, I'll give you a call tomorrow.' With that, he picked up his remaining clothes from the floor, shoved his wallet in his back pocket from the bedside table and got ready to leave.

'Steve... I... George... you need to leave...' I looked at them both, not knowing what to say or do, torn between the pair, not forgetting Daniel at home looking after our son.

Steve was adamant he was going. The air was filled with awkwardness, but before he left, he walked towards me. He stood before me, just looking into my eyes. I wondered what he was really thinking. With one hand on my upper arm, he squeezed gently, filling me with a mixture of emotions, then leaned forwards and slowly kissed me on my cheek. He closed his eyes lovingly like it was his last kiss and his life depended on it.

'I'll see you soon, Rose.' He smiled and left, the hotel room door crashing behind him.

I looked across the room at George, but I had no words, his solemn face looking back at me.

'Rose, I...' That was all he could say and then stopped.

'Satisfied? Seriously, what the fuck are you doing here? I get that you are looking out for me, but you can't just keep showing up like this, it's not right.'

'But, Rose I... you know I...'

'I'm tired, you need to leave.' The events of the night had started to sober me up and I was left feeling exhausted and emotional.

I left George in the room while I went to the bathroom. I stood in front of the large glass mirror, both hands on the elegant marble basin below me and tried to compose myself. What was happening right now? It all felt like a jigsaw puzzle, and I was missing the vital piece.

I'm in a hotel room that my married customer organised and paid for with a work colleague, whilst my boyfriend was at home oblivious to what was going on. *What kind of a human being am I?* I didn't deserve any of the men in my life, everything was completely my fault. I owed both Steve and

George an apology. My eyes looked tired and bloodshot from the drink and drugs and my hair dishevelled from making out with Steve. I freshened up and made my way back to the bedroom.

'You okay there, George?' I said, opening the door to find him stretched out on the bed, half-dressed, his legs crossed over each other.

'Well, I may as well make myself comfortable. He has paid for the room after all.' True, Steve had paid for the room and signed the agreement, but it made me feel bad the way the night had ended.

Twice in a row I had been a drunken mess, and instead of taking full advantage of me, which he could have done *both times*, he took me to a place so I could sleep it off. Why had he been so nice when he could have told my boss? What was in it for him? More to the point, why was George still here after the way I spoke to him? I was trying to be angry at him, but it didn't last long.

'George, you didn't tell me that you were having drinks in London tonight. What happened to the man that was following us, did you manage to see what he looked like?' More confusion riddled me as I couldn't work out why he was here.

George looked flustered. 'Err... it was a last-minute thing, a few of the team at the new customer I'm trying to break into said they fancied a drink, so I thought why not and offered to take them out. I was going to head home when I saw Steve helping you along Finsbury Square.' He fidgeted around but went back to watching the television.

'Why didn't you say hi then or stop us?' I questioned him again.

'I was going to but then I spotted the man on the other

side of the street that was peculiar, he was watching you both like a hunter. He crossed the road and picked up the pace as you both staggered along. When we reached the hotel reception, he seemed to panic as soon as he noticed that I was on to him. I tried to approach him, but he ran off,' he replied, his eyes locked on the screen, avoiding eye contact with me.

'George...' I raised my voice for him to look at me so I could test his reaction.

'What?'

'Thank you for looking out for me but I don't need you to. Why are you so good to me?' I sat next to him on the bed, trying to get his attention away from the television and to open up.

'You know why, Rose.' That was all he could say.

'Nope, I have no idea.' He sat up on the bed and grabbed my hand, pulling me closer to him.

'Just stop asking me questions for heaven's sake. You are an absolute nightmare; your drinking is out of control, there is cocaine on the side, which you have clearly been taking, but I would drop anything for you if you were in trouble. You know that.' His eyes seemed to melt; his normal comical personality changed to a sensible tone. 'And I won't tell Daniel if that's what you're thinking. If you want an affair with Steve, that's fine, but personally, I think you should stop that right now. It will only end in tears.'

'George. I'm not having an affair with Steve, and I didn't know that you would drop anything for me.' I sat like a sulking child, but I couldn't help looking into his dark and alluring chocolate eyes.

'You do know that... why did you have a text ready to send me in your phone then?' He smiled as if he had just won an argument and caught me out, but how did he know that? Did he go through my phone while I was in the bathroom? There was no way he would have known that otherwise.

I frowned, arguing back at him. 'I didn't. I...'

'Oh yes you did. I bet if I open it now, it is still on the screen.' He reached to the bedside table to get my phone and tried to flip the screen. I tried to grab it from his hand, but it was too late, he opened it and read out loud my unsent message:

GEORGE, PLEASE HELP ME. I NEED YOU. IN LONDON, PLEASE ANSWER. ROSE XX

I felt my face immediately flush with embarrassment.

'If that's not a booty call, I don't know what is.' He laughed as handed me the phone. His other hand was still holding mine.

'That is 100% not a booty call, that is a distress call... and the kisses, I definitely didn't put those, I bet you added in the love Rose part.' I tried to gain back some sense of dignity.

'Rose, just admit it, you wanted to be here with me tonight, not Steve, you just thought you would get him to pay the bill and we could enjoy it.' George laughed out loud. Despite me being angry with him, I loved the way he turned everything into a funny situation. He made me laugh even when things were really getting me down.

It then hit me like a tidal wave, our joking around on the bed had turned to a moment of seriousness.

His innocent hand holding mine now felt emotionally warm. There was silence in the room, I couldn't hear the dulcet tones of the television anymore, it was on and showing a film, but it wasn't important.

He was looking at me, and I at him, and for a moment, I noticed things I had never seen before. He always had dark stubble, but I now saw the flickering of colours from within it, from the occasional grey to red, ginger, brown and black. His nose was perfect, a small scar at the bottom had a silvery white shine to it and his beautiful, long eyelashes surrounding his gorgeous brown eyes were quite pretty for a man. He was stunning, tanned Italian skin, thick black hair and a smile that could melt your heart... and it did.

He placed his other hand on the back of my head and leaned in to kiss me. I didn't resist, I closed my eyes and felt our lips meet, but before I could really let go, I paused. It didn't feel right, it was like kissing my brother (*if I had one, of course*). Yes, he was handsome, he was funny, and above all, he was my best friend, but he was so much more than I deserved. I was kissing George... I didn't want things to be awkward between us and I just couldn't do it. I pushed back on his hand as I opened my eyes. His eyes opened too, he looked hurt and confused like a wounded puppy.

'George, I...' That was all I could say quietly to him.

'Yep, I get it. I'm your best friend.' He moved back, pursing his lips together.

'George, please... you know I love you, but not in that way.' The last thing I wanted to do was hurt him. He deserved so much more than me.

'Yep, I know.' He pulled back his sleeve, glancing at his watch. 'I better go... I have to be at work in the morning. Do you want to get the train back with me or am I too much of a friend to do that?' I didn't realise that we had been talking for hours and it was early morning.

'George, please don't be like that. Of course, I will get the train with you.' I wanted to cuddle him, but I was better off leaving it there, it would only send him mixed messages. I had to be cold for the sake of our friendship. I sat there for a moment or two just looking at him. *What did I do to deserve him as a friend?*

'I think you secretly love me and that's why you can't take your eyes off of me.' He looked at my face and laughed. I couldn't help but laugh back at him, instantly clearing the air between us. I grabbed the pillow next to me and threw it as hard as I could, hitting him directly in the face.

'Give me five minutes to quickly freshen up and I'm good to go,' I said to George. The alcohol had worn off and so had the drugs, pulling me into a hungover and sorry state. I had so much to get done today that having a hangover was the last thing I needed. I checked my bag, the contracts were in there, all signed and completed. At least that was the one success of the night, if nothing else. I looked at my phone and there were no calls or texts from Daniel, so I needed to give him a call on the way back home, and more importantly, I needed to apologise to Steve and make amends.

17

MY NEW WHEELS

I t had been 518 days since I had last driven. An 18-month ban, drink driving awareness courses, community service and an absolute headache in logistics trying to get around with a small child, without driving. I couldn't wait to get my license back, but I was so nervous about getting behind the wheel again after such a long time. The difference it would make to our family in getting around would be huge.

I have always loved cars since I was a little girl. I would look at the colours, shapes and sounds and hope that one day I would have the car of my dreams. My dad had been successful in his career and always had the latest and greatest —he would drive me around with the smell of fresh new leather and watch the mileage counter as it reached every new milestone. Nothing could beat the smell of a new car.

I had saved a little extra every month since losing my license to put towards a car when I got it back. A couple of quarters of great commission, especially the large deal that Steve just signed, had given me a top up too.

For the past year and a half, I would get the bus into town

or to work, passing the big car dealership that was along the main road, dreamily looking at all the sparkly new cars in the showroom. I knew exactly what make, model and colour I wanted. A silver BMW, 330ci, sports back had caught my eye on several occasions. I held my breath every day, hoping that it hadn't been sold and was still placed like a prize in the showroom. It only had two doors plus the boot, but it had four seats, so technically, it could still be a family car and enough room in the back for a child seat.

'Rose, you deserve it. You've worked hard, you never buy anything for yourself, and you paid the price for drink driving, so go and get the car you want,' Daniel had said to me the previous evening. It was as if I had been given the green light

The following day, I took his advice. Instead of riding the bus all the way to Jack's nursery, I decided to stop off and go into the showroom. I didn't have much time, but it was enough to quickly enquire and show my interest. After all, I didn't even know if I could afford it despite my saving attempts.

I was nervous being on my own, but I went for it anyway. Getting off the bus, my handbag draped over my arm, I was smartly dressed but I had changed into my trainers so that it was easier for me to rush around and walk everywhere.

Not wanting to draw attention to myself, I wandered through the mass of cars to the front of the showroom, gauging the prices, looking at the second-hand ones first, building up the courage to then go in and speak to them. That wasted about ten minutes in total before I moved closer to the large glass-fronted building, a large sign saying Carlson Cars hung above it.

There were a couple of other visitors. I had seen them

wander in, be greeted by the reception staff and shown around, so I was expecting the same welcome and sales assistance.

Here I go, I said to myself as I entered the impressive revolving doors into the clean, immaculate showroom. The smell was incredible, it was the same fresh leather that I remembered from my childhood. Fixated on a couple of the cars, my eyes were drawn to the back of the room where the sports models were. There she was. If a car had a gender, this one was female, beautiful in every way and gleaming in the sunlight through the windows.

The young lady at reception looked up as I came out the other side of the door and appeared at the desk. Waiting for her to greet me, I slowed down to stand directly before her. She looked me up and down as if to sum me up and then put her head back down again. No smile, no words, no nothing.

Oh, I thought to myself. *She must be busy.* So, I waited patiently by the desk.

Still nothing after five minutes but she seemed almost fidgety that I was still waiting. Her head remaining firmly down on what she was doing, clearly able to see I was there, so I cleared my throat and stared at the parting of her hair patiently, hoping to attract her attention.

'Can I help you?' She looked up at me as if I was inconveniencing her by being there.

'Erm... yes, please. I'm looking to buy a car.' I smiled politely.

'Yes, the second-hand ones are out the front, these are only the new or ex-demonstration cars in here, I am afraid.' She rudely pointed outside and then carried on with shuffling her papers around.

This type of attitude took me back to when I walked into

the estate agents to buy our first house and I was looked down on like a piece of dirt. She had taken one look at me, my age and probably what I was wearing and decided what type of car I was going to buy. Not aware of the big commission chunk I had just got from work.

'Yes, thank you, I have seen those, but I want to buy a new car please?' I remained calm and polite, smiling as soon as I had finished.

Again, without looking up, she said, 'Uh-huh. Have a look around and I will get someone over to speak with you.'

'Oh, okay, thank you,' I said and started to make my way through the strategically placed cars, hoping that she had now taken me more seriously.

I didn't touch any of them, I didn't want to leave fingerprints or hand marks on the beautifully shined bodywork, but it took every inch of willpower not to run my fingers along the side of the smooth and silky contours. Instead, I just wandered around, peering through the glass windows, admiring every button and their stunning interiors.

I spent a good fifteen minutes weaving in and out, waiting for someone to talk to me, but nobody did. In that time, two other elderly gentlemen came into the showroom. The reception lady was all over them with smiles, talking away to them, she even got a brochure from under her desk and handed it to them. I watched, feeling stupid and naïve. I had never felt so deflated in my life, buying my first real dream car had turned into an embarrassment—the story of my life.

Deciding to leave and come back another day or try another garage, I jumped back on the next bus that came along and made my way to Jack's nursery.

Disappointed and disheartened, peering out of the bus windows as it pulled away past the showroom, the lady at reception watched me leave. I knew exactly what she was thinking—good riddance.

Determined as I always was, I flipped open my phone and searched my contacts until I reached his number.

'HEY, DAD.'

He replied straight back as if he was waiting for my message to arrive.

'HI ROSE, ARE YOU OKAY?' I think he always thought I messaged him when I wanted something. Although it was the case this time, it wasn't always the reason for messaging him.

'YOU KNOW YOU LOVE CARS AND IM YOUR FAVOURITE DAUGHTER?' Of course, I was being cheeky.

'HA. YES?' He just agreed with me, I would remind him of this again in the future.

'FANCY COMING TO THE GARAGE WITH ME TO GET MINE?' I asked, hoping he would say yes.

'SURE. WHEN?' I almost fist-pumped the air.

'TOMORROW MAYBE, AFTER WORK?'

'OKAY, GIVE ME A TIME AND I'LL PICK YOU UP.' My dad was always there for me at the drop of a hat. If I asked him to cover for me because I had murdered someone, I think he would do it.

'5 PM TOMORROW? THANK YOU XX'

'NO PROBLEM, I'LL BE OUTSIDE YOUR WORK TOMORROW AT 5 PM. DON'T FORGET. LOVE DAD X.' He would always sign his name Dad, even though I was texting his number and I knew who it was, it made me laugh.

'YOU ARE A LEGEND. LOVE YOU TOO, R X.' I flipped my phone closed again and placed it back in my bag, thinking about how arrogant the lady at the car showroom had been. I shouldn't let it bother me—people always say not to judge a book by its cover, but nine times out of ten, they do. More times than not, I was judged by my appearance *and* my situation.

The following day after work, as promised, I left my desk to find my dad pulled up outside like a chauffeur. Practically running over to his car, happy to see him, I pulled up the passenger door handle and jumped in.

'Evening,' I said, leaning over to kiss him on the cheek.

'Evening, Rose. So, what are we after or is it just to look around?' he asked. Being in the car with him, just the two of us, took me back to when I was little. He would be silly in the car, race as fast as he could and make me hold on to the seat, scared for my life. Steaming through the traffic lights on amber as quickly as he could before they turned red.

'Hmm... not quite as quick as yours but I had my eye on a silver BMW, 330ci. The people in the showroom yesterday were so rude that I left.' I frowned as I began explaining.

'Rude, why?' he asked.

'Ugh... when I went in, they told me to look at the second-hand ones and then when I finally got the attention of the rude woman, she said that she would send someone over, but no one came and I ran out of time. All the other visitors were attended to, except me. I can't help but feel that they didn't think I could afford a new car.'

'We will soon sort that out.' He had an almost mischievous look on his face.

This time, we pulled into the car park by the second-hand cars. Daniel offered to pick up Jack, so we had plenty of time. Cars weren't really his 'thing' anyway, he was more excited by motorbikes.

My dad got out first and I followed behind him.

Again, we approached the revolving doors and the same

woman from yesterday looked up, beaming with a smile. She looked him up and down as she had done to me.

'Good evening, sir, how can I be of assistance today?' She stopped what she was doing, he had her full attention.

'Erm... yes. I'm after a new model. He pointed to the closest and probably most expensive car in the showroom. 'Could you call the sales manager for me, please?' Still standing behind him, I fiddled with the strap of my handbag, nervous as to what he was going to say but I let him continue.

'I'm afraid the sales manager is in a meeting at the moment, I can get an executive to help you.' She reached under the desk to get a brochure and handed it to him, then waved her hands in the air towards the direction of her colleagues. They immediately noticed her command and one gentleman started making his way over to us.

'It's okay, I can wait... I need to speak to the branch manager and not one of the executives.' She seemed taken aback but did as he had requested, nodding her head, picking up the receiver from the desk and dialled a couple of digits.

'Ah, good evening, Mr Dean. There is a gentleman at reception that would like to purchase a new car and has asked to specifically speak to you.' She nodded again in agreement with whatever his response was and proceeded to place the phone calmly down.

'Mr Dean, our sales manager will be right out to see you, please take a seat.' She pointed this time to a couple of leather armchairs to one side for us to take a seat.

Almost in an instant, a smartly dressed man came out of the glass-panelled office to our left and made his way over. He walked straight up to my dad and shook his hand abruptly.

'Good evening, Mr... and how can I help you?' He was polite and well-spoken.

'Mr Murrell,' he said, returning the handshake. 'My daughter came in yesterday and was rudely ignored, not only by reception...' He stopped and ushered me to come forward. Both men turning their heads to look at the young lady at reception. She looked at me, first in shock, I could tell she wasn't expecting me to return from yesterday, and secondly that he was calling her out, immediately hanging her head in shame.

'Then, she was ignored walking around the showroom, not one person offered to help her. Now, for a business trying to sell cars, I would treat every person as a valuable customer —young, old, male, female. As a result of your attitude yesterday, she is going to buy her brand-new car from another dealership who welcomes her. You have all lost out on not only her money but my money too. There is no way I will ever buy a car from here in the future if that's how you treat people.' The sales manager looked surprised along with the others.

'I do apologise for yesterday. The team must have been extremely busy and it was an oversight on our behalf. Let us help you find the right car and we...' He tried to apologise, shooting reception a glaring look of disapproval, but my dad cut him short.

'Not busy, just rude. We will be taking our custom else-where.' Turning to walk out of the showroom, he placed his hand on my back and guided me out. I did as I was told, just like I was a little girl being escorted out of a bad situation.

'And that, sweetheart, is how you deal with rude people. If you are in sales, like you are, then this is a valuable lesson, every customer is important.' We both laughed as we made our way back to his car and got in.

'But I wanted to buy that car, I've had my eyes on it for ages,' I said as we got in.

'There are three showrooms nearby, all with the same cars, and even if they don't have the one you want, they can ship from this one to theirs. They don't deserve a sale for treating you that way.' I understood his morals, but I lacked the confidence to be authoritative in the way that he did.

We drove to the next closest showroom and pulled up in the car park, just as we had done previously. As he got out, so did I, half-expecting to be faced with the same attitude as before.

Immediately, we were greeted by a gentleman that seemed to know him. They shook hands and talked together for a few moments before asking me what I wanted.

For the next hour, I was treated like royalty. I was taken around the cars, he made me sit in and feel the seat, the steering wheel, showed me the buttons inside and what they each did, finally taking us out for a quick test drive. The car was almost too good to be true.

Next were the financials... we went through the paperwork, the figures and terms and conditions, a rather formal-looking contract that I signed without reading. Never in my life had I bought something so expensive, apart from the house, of course, and it was all mine.

It felt good, it felt amazing, all my hard work had paid off. I owed Steve for signing this agreement and giving me the deal.

The sales manager stood up and shook my hand, a huge smile on both of our faces.

'Rose, it has been a pleasure doing business with you.' He handed me the keys and all the booklets and beamed at me.

'Thank you so much.' I shook his hand back.

Not only was this the first time I'd driven a car in eighteen months, but it was also the first time I had driven a brand-new car with only fifty miles on the clock.

'Rose, are you okay? Happy?' My dad asked, standing with me by my new car.

'Oh, I'm more than happy. Can I really drive it out of the showroom today? I presumed that there would be checks or a service perhaps before I would be allowed to take it away.'

'It was all serviced, cleaned and prepared for a sale that fell through yesterday, so it is all good to go. It was meant to be, I guess.' He shrugged and smiled again.

'Right, now be careful driving this one home, Rose.' My dad grinned at me, lovingly and cheekily both at the same time.

'I will.' I laughed as I grabbed the keys and got into *my* new car.

Nervously, I turned on the engine and listened to it purr. The smell excited me more than anything else but I looked all around the interior, this time, studying it carefully.

I couldn't quite believe it was mine, nor could I believe that I was back behind the wheel. Never again would I drive whilst drunk.

For the first time in my life, I had worked hard for something and bought it selfishly just for me.

Materialist things hadn't really bothered me before, but it felt good that people looked at what I had for once and wanted the same. It had always been me in the past looking at what others had, knowing deep down inside that I couldn't afford it. Did that make me selfish for wanting something for myself? What was I trying to prove? Surely a car is a car, right? To me, it was how I got there, how far I had come and how hard I'd worked to achieve it. I had so many things to now strive for.

If I wanted the nicer things in life, that meant I needed the job and the lifestyle to fit it. I had to keep doing my job, hitting targets and aiming for lots of commission.

I drove that car, feeling on top of the world. As soon as I got home, I ran into the house. Both Daniel and Jack were excited to see it. Jack sat in the front seat and disappeared behind the steering wheel, making car sounds. Daniel noticed the glimmer in my eyes.

Maybe things were finally starting to turn a corner for us, we didn't have to scrimp and save and cut corners on everything anymore. Life suddenly started to become a little easier. Jack would never understand the struggles we'd had in the past few years, the things that we went without or the stresses and strains that it put us through as a couple.

That first car was a reminder of everything we had learned, of all the hardship we had experienced, and more importantly than anything else, was what we had to look forward to.

18

I NEED HELP

Nobody really spoke about mental health, about panic attacks or depression. It wasn't mentioned, and it definitely wasn't understood. Stories emerged in newspapers and on the radio about successful and well-known celebrities taking their own lives, overdosing or falling into deep, dark holes of depression, unable to come to terms with the mind games that their own body was playing on them. You would frequently hear comments from the general public such as, 'They have all the money in the world, what could they possibly be depressed about?'

It's not about money, it's not about fame or fortune or even wealth, it's about how you feel inside. You could have all the riches in the world, a supportive family, good health and a million other things to make you feel special, but if your mind is in a bad place, then it doesn't make any difference.

Depression hit me like a slap in the face—unannounced, unwelcome and completely misunderstood.

It was a stage of my life where I was happy, I had a loving boyfriend, a great job, and enough money coming in that meant we had no worries. It seemed like a time in my life where I thought depression was thrown into the mix just to test how I would react to it. I began to question every little thing about me. Was I good enough for Daniel? For my son? Was I good enough at my job? Where was my life going? Was I good enough for the world I lived in or was it better off without me?

Glancing in the mirror at a body that I hated, I could pick so many holes in what was wrong with me and ignore all the parts of me that were lovely. Before long, I stopped looking back at myself because I didn't like what I saw, it was easier that way.

Regardless of how many times Daniel told me he loved me and how beautiful I was, I didn't believe him. Instead, I put it all down to him feeling sorry for me. An insecure, emotional wreck of a woman that became deluded by the vision that my own mind had conjured together rather than the true vision of others. I believed that the only reason he was with me was because I was the mother of his child.

I had a secret stash of cocaine in the drawer of my bedside table. I would take some of it most mornings for breakfast, one to keep my weight down so I didn't eat too much during the day, and two so that I could function as a person. Getting ready in the morning, getting my son to nursery, getting to work on time, working a very busy schedule and being busy and then all the chores when I got home.

It was becoming a habit—an issue. It wasn't normal, it was far from normal, but it was yet another secret that only I knew and was keeping hidden. Just as a functioning alcoholic, I needed a little boost in the morning to get me through, but my mental health was suffering. Without it, I felt tired and lethargic.

I sat at work in a busy theatre-style boardroom, listening to presentations about upcoming products and solutions that they wanted us to sell to our clients. My attention span was and still is about five minutes before I set about doodling on the pad perched on my lap, fidgeting, clicking my pen, looking out the window and anything else I could occupy myself with. Occasionally, I glanced at the projector screen so that I caught snippets of what I should be doing, but the bright light was glaring into my already enlarged pupils from my morning dose of drugs. The rest of the time I pieced together the content as best as I could.

Due to me landing one of the biggest deals in the company's history, I was a bit of a star at work. Most things that I did were overlooked and Dave had a bit of a soft spot for me. Even if they had found out that I was on cocaine at work, they probably would have given me a little warning or ignored it altogether.

The chair was uncomfortable, but thank goodness it didn't have arms as I would have made myself cosy and drifted off to sleep. Trying to concentrate, my eyes focused on the front of the room, but my balance got the better of me. I felt dizzy. Sitting up straight in my chair, I tried to correct myself and shook my head gently. There it was again... I felt the room spinning slightly so I uncrossed my legs and re-crossed them on the other leg to distract myself. I felt hot, my heart rate increasing and a burning sensation on the back of my neck. I needed air, I needed to take deep breaths, but I couldn't in a crowded room. We were in silence except for Dave talking, so I didn't want to make a scene.

I waited a few moments, attempting to distract myself with something new, but the more I tried not to think about how I was feeling, the more panicked I became. *I need to get out of here,* I thought. I rubbed my forehead in angst. Glancing around the room, everyone was concentrating, nodding their heads occasionally to the speaker. Getting hotter and hotter, I felt like I was going to faint at any minute. *Is there a window open? I need a breeze,* I thought to myself, but no windows were open.

'Are you okay?' George whispered.

'Yes, I'm good. I think I need some air.' I smiled, but inside, I was melting. I definitely wasn't okay. It was no good, I worried that everyone would look at me if I stood up and I didn't want to disturb the session, but I had to leave. It was either that or pass out and that would create more excitement in the room.

The room was shrinking, people creeping into my personal space, the droning voice of someone talking was getting quieter and quieter as my brain was getting ready to shut down. It was now or never.

I got to my feet and whispered quietly to George, 'Excuse me,' and made my way to the ladies' toilet. I shut the cubicle door behind me and sat on the closed toilet lid, trying desperately to calm myself down. I knew that all the eyes in the room were on me, but I had to forget about that and compose myself.

My heart was racing, the adrenaline pumping around my body, there was a burning sensation running down from the back of my head to my neck and through to my spine. The same as it always did, time and time again when I panicked. My hands were sweaty and I felt so dizzy. All I could think about was laying down on the cold, tiled floor and cooling down, but I sat still, waiting for it to pass. Counting quietly to myself... *One... two... three...* breathing slowly in and out, feeling sick and exhausted. What on earth was wrong with me? I felt like crying. I knew it was my mind ruling my body, but there wasn't a single thing I could do about it.

To everyone else, I was a confident, outgoing, hard-working individual that thrived in busy environments, but inside, I was a shivering, weak, shaking mess. I felt useless, ugly and stupid. Talking wasn't an option, I didn't want to. If I told someone how I really felt and how I was really functioning, they would admit me to a mental institution in a strait-jacket and take Jack away from me. I had to get through this myself, that was the only way. The last thing I wanted was sympathy. What I really wanted was to feel like me again—the real me, the old me. The one that used to genuinely laugh and enjoy myself.

I sat for a few moments more, every minute ticking away was another minute that people would be wondering where I was. I had to snap myself out of it and get on with my chaotic life. I began breathing in and out slowly, counting the numbers again in my head from four... five... six..., listening to my heart slow its pace down to normal and feeling the tingling sensation in my body slowly burn away.

'Sort yourself out, Rose,' I said to myself. 'Shut this person out, it's the only way.'

I got to my feet, took another deep breath. Seven... eight... nine... and opened the cubicle door.

'Hey, are you okay, Rose? You look like you've seen a ghost.' Amber was one of the newest office girls and was so lovely. She stood at the basins and watched as I walked slowly over and began to wash my hands.

'Yes, all good. I just felt a little sick but I'm okay now.' I smiled at her. 'Have I missed much?'

'No, they have just finished the last session, just breaking for lunch now I think.' She smiled back.

'Ah, that's good then. I was starting to doze off.' I laughed, showing her that I was happy, but knowing deep down inside that I was far from okay. I continued to wash my hands and hold them in a daze underneath the drier. I could feel the aftermath of adrenaline running deep inside my veins, unable to burn it off or let my body release its energy.

I could hear the hustle and bustle outside of the toilets from everyone finishing their sessions, waiting for lunch to arrive. I knew I had to join them and leave the comfort of the toilet, but the more I tried to move, the more I couldn't. Frozen like a statue to the tiled floor, I let the drier continue to blow on my already dry hands. How ironic that a cold, empty work toilet was now my comfort blanket, helping me to distance myself from the reality of my life outside.

It wasn't a difficult task to sit in a room and listen to someone talk for hours on end, anyone could do it. But for some reason, at this precise moment in my life, I found it hard to do the simplest of tasks, ones that I used to breeze through.

What was happening to me? Why couldn't I function? Why wasn't I in control of myself like I normally was? No matter what I did, I just couldn't shake it off. It was like I was in a deep, dark hole with no ladder and no help sign to guide me out. I had no reason, no excuse for feeling this way. Things were good... things were really good, so why now? I didn't understand it at all.

I wanted to cry. This wasn't me, I never cried, not unless I had a damn good reason to. I felt my eyes getting heavier, holding back my tears, my throat dry. I had to try my hardest not to give in.

I walked out into the corridor, joining the others, my palms clammy. The rest of the afternoon passed by and I was fine. No dizziness, no feeling panicked or hot and sweaty. It felt like a momentous occasion that I had managed to sit through an afternoon at work after what had happened earlier that day.

The evening went like clockwork, collecting Jack from nursery, cooking dinner, walking the dog, Daniel coming home from work, watching a little television, a bit of washing and finally bed. It wasn't late, about 10.45 pm, yet the minute I got into bed and relaxed, my mind went again.

Tucked under the covers, the room was dark and Daniel was snoring the minute his head hit the pillow. My eyes were closed but the burning sensation started again—a million hairs standing on end, flickering down my back like a warm electric current. My heart pounding through my chest cavity and the adrenaline pumping around my body as if it was helping me run a marathon.

The more I tried to relax, the more I felt sick, tired and emotional. I lay there as still as I possibly could but with the strongest urge to want to move. I daren't tell anyone how I felt, it simply sounded insane.

Minutes seemed like hours, staring at a tiny spider on the ceiling making its journey to the other side. I couldn't get up and walk around for fear of waking everyone, so I lay like a corpse in a closed casket, with only enough room to breathe, waiting for the dreaded feeling to stop.

I couldn't read as it is too dark, and I couldn't watch the television as we didn't have one in our room. The more I thought about how I felt and tried to reason with it, the worse I seemed to get. If this was the way my life was going to be and to constantly feel this way, then I may as well end it here. My family didn't want or need a mother or a girlfriend as weak and pathetic as me. They deserved better than this.

Once again, I wanted to escape, but to where? Even if I went downstairs, I would just sit and panic.

All night long, I tossed and turned, unable to sleep, feeling alone, frustrated and sad with no one I felt I could talk to. What good would talking do anyway?

In the morning, I woke feeling exhausted. I could have easily closed the curtains again, called in sick to work and gone back to sleep. I knew that wasn't the answer, but I couldn't help wanting it anyway.

I got up and continued with my day. I was irritable and had a foggy haze lingering over me all day. I couldn't think straight. Day after day, I continued with life like a zombie, more unemotional than normal and ignoring all the signs my body was giving me.

Friday evening came, and the one night that I normally looked forward to, arrived without warning. The hamster wheel of life suddenly threw me off and spun me into some home truths. I stood at the kitchen side preparing dinner. Jack was in the living room playing quietly in front of the television, and Daniel had gone upstairs to get changed. I chopped the vegetables, threw them in their individual saucepans, filled them with water, and placed them on the cooker stove.

Turning on the gas, I opened the main oven door to check on the roast chicken that I had put in an hour earlier. Almost ready and just waiting for the vegetables to boil, I started to get the plates out of the cupboard and onto the side. I could hear the water from the pans boiling over the top, so I moved to turn down the gas. Instead of turning it down, I stood in a daze, frozen and not moving, just caught in time watching the gas flames flicker as the water spat onto them. It had all gotten too much, coordinating everything, working to times, the thoughts going around in my head about not being good enough for anyone, work, checking in on Jack the whole time.

'Rose, what are you doing?' Daniel suddenly stood in the doorway, shouting and watching me be unresponsive.

Startled, I looked up at him.

'I was just... why are you shouting at me?' I snapped back.

'You were just watching them, not doing anything.' He seemed frustrated with me.

'Don't shout at me, I don't see you doing the dinner!' I flicked the switch and slammed the pan onto the other side of the hob.

'Here we go, blaming me for everything again.' He opened one of the cupboard doors, took out a glass and banged it onto the side. What was his problem? I felt miserable, down and lost, all he had to do was go to work and come home, I didn't ask him to do anything around the house. Who the hell did he think he was?

More importantly, what was wrong with me? My attitude wasn't just bringing me down, it was bringing us down. Our once loving, affectionate and passionate relationship was turning us into two friends bickering at even the slightest of things, and I didn't know how to change it.

That evening, we hardly said two words to each other as we ate dinner. Everything was centred around Jack and his food. We put him to bed and then still sat at either ends of the sofa, barely speaking. I was normally chatty and had a million things to say, but tonight I couldn't think of a single word—nothing.

Daniel was tired and wanted to go to bed early. I hated going to bed on an argument, but we hadn't even had one, just a few choice words, both of us exhausted, irritable and tired. Walking up to bed felt like an eternity. Step after step seemed like it took forever. I wasn't sleepy at all, my body was shattered but my mind was still annoyingly active, I knew I wouldn't be able to sleep but I went up anyway.

As soon as Daniel's head hit the pillow he was gone, fast asleep and snoring away. I turned to face him, just watching him sleep, so peaceful yet so noisy. Why couldn't I switch off like that? Why was my mind in constant overdrive? Thinking of the copious amounts of things that I either had to do or needed to do.

I rolled back over and laid there, staring at the ceiling— no spider this time, just a white-painted space of nothing. I didn't feel like me anymore, who even was I?

The once motivated, excitable, passionate person had disappeared into a protective shell that I couldn't break. A small part of my former self was left vulnerable and exposed. Always tired, angry, irritable, and more than anything else, empty. I hated feeling like this and I wanted more than anything else to shake out of it, but the more I tried, the more exhausted I was to just end everything.

Just as I expected it to appear at some point tonight, that burning, bubbling, feeling pinching at the back of my neck. The tingling sensation running down the entire length of my arms and then my heart. It picked up pace so fast that I thought it was going to pound out of my chest and onto the bed sheets next to me. My feet were burning, my toes aching.

I tried as hard as I could to contain it, but I couldn't stand it anymore. I peeled back the covers and quietly grabbed my hoodie and jogging bottoms that were screwed into a ball on the floor next to me. Tip-toeing across the bedroom carpet without any lights on, I made my way to the landing and then down the stairs. Harry greeted me at the bottom step, but he soon sniffed and then went back to bed.

There was nothing for me to do other than pace up and down the length of the kitchen and the entire downstairs. Back and forth, silently I marched, burning off the adrenaline as I went but it still wasn't making me any more relaxed. The tears streaming down my cheeks, I sobbed as quietly as I could, letting all the torment out.

I reached for the kitchen drawer, taking out the shiniest, sharpest knife I could find. With a shaking hand, I held it over the prominent veins in my other wrist. More tears rolling down my face. Just one small slice and I wouldn't feel like this anymore. *Do it, Rose, just do it. End all the pain now,* I said to myself. Harry barked, I saw him sitting on the floor next to me, looking up, watching what I was doing.

I felt guilty. I couldn't do it with him there. I threw the knife back in the drawer in a panic, closed it and made my way into the front room.

I sat on the sofa, constantly switching positions. First sitting up, then back, curling up in a ball to hopefully fall asleep. Nope, nothing worked. My heart still racing, my body exhausted. I sat up, my head in my hands crying again. I don't know why or what for, but it felt a little like release. My whole body was crying out for help.

Just as I began to feel slightly better, I heard a shuffle by the door and looked up to see Daniel standing there, rubbing his tired eyes.

'What on earth are you doing?' he whispered.

Clearing my throat, I whispered back, 'Erm... I couldn't sleep.' I tried to keep the tears back but the odd one trickled gently down my face.

'Come up to bed. It's 2 am.' He seemed distant. I know he

still cared about me, but I think his patience had worn thin. It was one episode after another.

'I wasn't feeling too well so I didn't want to wake you.' I'd never told him exactly how I felt and how I was struggling. He must have found me extremely distant and difficult too, but I wasn't one to share my feelings.

'Well, you did,' he said bluntly and left the room. He didn't give me a chance to explain or for him to see in the dark of the room that I was in tears. He didn't understand.

How was it 2 am already? I had been pacing and panicking for hours. No wonder I was tired. I couldn't go on like this, I needed help, but I didn't know where to start.

The next morning, I awoke on the sofa, cuddled up in a little ball like a child. Harry's cold, wet nose nudged me. If he was awake, so was everyone else. I stretched out, cold and tired, yawning as I did so.

After a night of emotion, crying, pacing and stress, I woke up feeling better than I had done in a few weeks. Maybe my body had given me the energy I needed to try and get myself better.

I flipped open my phone and texted the one person I knew who would know what to do.

'HEY MUM, ARE YOU FREE FOR LUNCH? R X'. It was early in the morning, but I was hoping she was awake.

'SURE, WHAT TIME?'

'12.30-ISH?' I quickly replied before Daniel appeared at the door.

'Cup of tea? Or are you still feeling sorry for yourself?' Daniel didn't wait for my response before walking off to the kitchen again. *Feeling sorry for myself, is that what he thinks I was doing?* I ignored his comment.

'OKAY, I'LL MEET YOU BY THE FOUNTAIN.' If you

lived in the town, you knew where that was. It was an old courtyard fountain that had a clock face on the floor. It stood at the bottom of the steps outside where my mum worked. Children would run in and out of the water on a hot summer's day and it was a central meeting point for most people.

'PERFECT X.' I flipped it closed and walked to the kitchen.

In previous years, I would have walked up behind him, throwing my arms around his huge, muscular body, kissing any part of his bare skin that I could find and prompting him to return the affection. Instead, I reached into the fridge, grabbing the milk out, and placed it next to the two cups he was spooning sugar into.

'Morning.' That was all I could manage to say, and it was a sarcastic morning too. 'Sorry if I woke you last night, I really didn't mean to.'

'It's fine.' That was it.

'Is Jack up yet? I need to get him ready for school.' I looked up at him but he kept his eyes fixed on making the tea. It was as if he couldn't bring himself to look at me, that once doting stare that he used to make in my direction was gone.

'I asked him to jump in the shower.' Daniel chinked the teaspoon on the side of the china mug and slid it towards me.

'Thank you,' I said reluctantly. I had hoped for more of a conversation but the lack of interaction between the two of us only made me feel worse, a deeper feeling of emptiness.

Walking up the stairs, I could hear Jack in the shower, singing away to himself. At least everything happening in his world had no effect on him, he had no idea what was going on in my life and I wanted it to stay that way.

The morning dragged on at work, it was quiet and a lot of people in the office were out. I preferred it when it was busy as I didn't have time to think, for my mind to become dangerous and uncontrollable with the most ridiculous thoughts.

My mind started to wander. *What if Jack has an accident at nursery and I'm not there for him? What if Daniel is having a secret affair at work and the real reason why he can't cope with me at the moment is because he has deep feelings for someone else? What if I'm not as insane as I think I am, and the brain fog and the sense of something bad about to happen is due to me having a brain tumour? Come to think of it, I do get a lot of headaches... Am I dying? What if I only have a few weeks to live?*

I must stop this ridiculous mind-set. It's making me ill.

I glanced up at the clock on the wall and it said 12:20. *Shit, I'm going to be late.* I stood up abruptly, shoved my keyboard forwards and grabbed my handbag from under the desk, almost running out of the door to the car park and into my car.

I was always late, In fact, it would be extremely abnormal for me to be early. My family, friends and everyone I knew expected me to be late. As quickly as I could, I drove to the nearest car park to where I was meeting my mum. I flew across the tarmac to the exit, clip-clopping down the stairs in the highest of heels, my bag flapping along over my shoulder. She was standing there waiting patiently for me to arrive, a big smile on her face as soon as she saw me racing towards her—at least ten minutes later than I said I would be there. I'm sure I had about twenty missed calls from her, chasing where I was, but I didn't have time to check my phone.

Finally, I arrived in a sweaty mess, flinging my arms

around the ultimate role model of a mother, and gave her the biggest hug.

'Lovely to see you, Rose, late as usual,' she said, muffled into my hair.

'Mmm, you too.' I kept hugging her for as long as I could before she started to wriggle free from me.

'Come on, let's go grab a coffee.' Prompting me to make our way to the coffee shop.

'How's Dad?' I asked. I knew he was fine, but it started small-talk and I missed them dearly. I moved out of home far too early.

'He's fine. I'm fine. More importantly, how are you?' She turned to smile at me, I could see out of the corner of my eye but continued to look straight ahead, avoiding any eye contact.

'Good.' That was a lie.

'Really?' she asked again.

'Uh-huh. Do you fancy doing something this weekend with Jack? Daniel has to work.' I changed the subject.

'Rose.' She stopped in her tracks and tried grabbing my arm.

'What?'

'There must be a reason for lunch today. What's wrong? Have you and Daniel had an argument again?' She held her head to one side, waiting for my response.

'Why can't I just go for lunch with my lovely mum without there being something wrong?' I tried making excuses, but my eyes were telling a completely different story. She knew there was pain behind them, they watered in the wind as I stood there looking into her loving expression.

'I'm not stupid and you know you can talk to me, so what's up? *And* you have lost weight.' The pair of us stood in the middle of a busy shopping centre, people trying to make their way around us and into the shops on either side. Staring into each other's eyes, I didn't know where to begin or what to say but I wanted nothing more than to open up and explain how I was feeling. I felt bad, the last thing I wanted to do was burden my poor mum with all my dramas, but if I couldn't talk to her, then who could I confide in?

'Okay, so are you having a tea or a coffee?' I shrugged, turned and began walking towards the large glass shop door, pulling its cold metal handle to open it for us. I held it open and let her lead the way to the small queue at the counter. I didn't want to be here in such close proximity to so many people. I wasn't claustrophobic, but being anywhere other than at home or my desk, in my comfort zone, at this stage in my life was terrifying. Glancing around the room, everyone looked so happy, chatting, talking and enjoying the company of others. Why couldn't I be like that and just relax? I was frustrated with myself.

'Rose, sweetheart. The lady wants to take your order.' I was so focused on what everyone else was doing that I hadn't noticed the queue go down and I was next in line.

'Sorry, Mum, I was in a world of my own for a minute,' I apologised.

'I can see that,' she said, putting her hand on my shoulder as we edged to the counter.

I could feel my mum's stare burning a hole in the side of my head. She was watching everything I was doing, knowing full well that as soon as we sat down, I would get the third degree. In a way, I wanted her to ask me how I was.

We sat down at the table with our mugs full of steaming coffee. I nervously removed my bag from my shoulder and sat there, stirring in the sugar, watching it gently melt away. Not saying a word, not looking up. She gently cleared her throat. I could feel the questions brewing.

'So, Rose...' I still didn't look up. 'Are you going to tell me what's wrong?'

My head still down, chinking my mug with my spoon and placing it delicately in the saucer.

'Rose!' She almost seemed to shout at me but in a quiet tone.

'I don't know what's wrong.' Looking up, my eyes began to well up, my throat restricting itself and turning dry. I didn't want to cry in the middle of the coffee shop, but my emotions had their own intentions. I couldn't stop myself. A tear rolled down my cheek, I had to take a sip of coffee to stop me from breaking down. My mum reached out her hand to touch mine, gently holding onto it and squeezing.

'Talk to me, Rose. What's wrong?'

'I don't know, that's the problem.'

'What do you mean you don't know?' She cocked her head to one side, confused.

'I wake up in the morning with the worst feeling of dread like something bad is about to happen. I'm tired, irritable and irrational all the time. I have no desire to do anything other than sit at home on my own in a dark room. It feels like there is a cloud covering my eyes wherever I go that I just can't shake. My body seems to have its own mind, I get dizzy and my heart races at the most awkward of times. I just don't feel like me and want to end it all, yet I have no reason to feel like this. Things are going great at work, Jack loves school, Daniel and I are great. I don't understand.'

Daniel and I weren't great, in fact, this was really affecting our relationship, but I didn't want to discuss that with my mum. Some things were better left unsaid.

I had managed to pour my heart out to my mum, unsure what she would reply with.

'Oh, sweetie. Why haven't you said anything before? How long have you felt like this?' She squeezed again.

'For months, I just can't take it anymore. It would be better for everyone if I wasn't here.' My tears turned into an emotional sob. My heart was aching.

'Rose, don't you dare!' She seemed angry. 'Nothing is ever that bad that it can't be fixed. You've done the right thing by telling me how you feel, now we can work on getting you better. You are depressed, your body and your mind are telling you to slow down, listen to it.'

'I can't slow down, that's the problem. I have so much to do, what with home, Jack, work… everything depends on me being efficient. I don't have time to be ill.' I don't know what I was expecting her to come back to me with, but she looked lovingly at me and smiled.

'Then let me help you. I'm sure Daniel can take on a little extra, can't he? Stop trying to take on the world, you aren't superhuman.' She pushed her mug to one side and leaned into me. 'If you are struggling with panic attacks, and I'm guessing that's what they are, then the doctor can help prescribe medication. It will allow your body to sleep at night and repair itself. As for not feeling like you, and as much as I call you a nightmare, we need to get you back to your nightmare self. That's who we all love.'

I looked around and felt as if the whole room had gone quiet and was listening in to our conversation. I shuffled nervously in my seat. I didn't want to be unappreciative of my mum's words of wisdom, especially as she hadn't called me crazy yet.

'Get some exercise, go for a walk daily, even if it's

lunchtime at work. Clear your head from everything that is filling it, and if you feel like everything is piling up, write down what you must do, and we can help you get through it all. Life does get on top of you from time to time. I've been where you are, you don't necessarily have to pin it down to an event in your life. Sometimes enough is simply enough.' I didn't think she would, but she genuinely understood what I was going through.

'Rose, you may not want to listen to me, but self-care is so important, for your own sanity and key for you to take time out for yourself rather than doing things for everyone else.' She made it sound so simple and I wished that it was, but it wasn't. If telling myself to snap out of it was the answer to all my problems, then I would have been better months ago.

'Do you understand?' Those three words and the way she said them made me feel like the little five-year-old I once was after doing something naughty. I nodded reluctantly, admitting that I had a problem and needed rescuing. It didn't make me weak or a failure, but I did have to give in to what my body was telling me.

19

THE AFFAIR

So much had happened in the past couple of months. I was so fixated on how I felt and how I was coping that I hadn't taken a moment to think about how Daniel was feeling or how everything was affecting him. The playful, loving relationship that we once had was now a combination of medication, tiredness and just getting through each day at a time.

Daniel never asked for anything. He never complained or kicked up a fuss. He just dealt with whatever was thrown at him. I looked at the calendar hung on the wall as I stood in the kitchen making a cup of tea and tried to think of the last time that we had sex, and I couldn't remember. Maybe a couple of nighttime fumbles but not the passionate, jaw-dropping and body-tingling events that we used to have.

The doctor had prescribed me Diazepam to help with my panic attacks after my mum talked me into going to see him.

The Diazepam made me calm, relaxed and sleepy. Yes, it stopped the panic attacks and the dreaded feeling that I got every time I opened my eyes in the morning, but it just seemed like the medication was masking how I really felt. A bandage was being applied to the wound, but it wasn't helping to stitch it back together. I wasn't supposed to take it all the time, just when I had a bad episode.

My normal manic episodes, my irrational thoughts and the ability to do things at a million miles an hour was no more. I did everything in slow motion. I felt trapped in my own body. Each time I popped a pill from its foil container, I looked at it and contemplated taking more than I should. A few more... a whole packet. Were they really helping me or just prolonging the inevitable? Sleeping forever in peace seemed like an option.

Daniel appeared distant. When we sat on the sofa together, he would be texting on his phone. When I tried to make conversation, it was short one- or two-word answers and his patience with me was almost non-existent. Everything I said, he would snap at. I couldn't do anything right. I couldn't help feeling the way I did, and the medication wasn't helping but it was pushing us both further and further apart. If I didn't do something about it, and quickly, I feared our relationship would be over and I couldn't stand losing him.

That night, I planned for him to come home to a nice dinner and for me wearing little or close to nothing in an attempt to salvage us. He would find something unexpected in the bedroom that would keep his focus on me and not anyone or anything else. I always presumed that sex solved everything in a relationship.

I took my lunch break earlier at work so that the shops would be quieter and less crowded. I went straight to the lingerie department of Marks and Spencer and viewed their sets of lace underwear. I was thinking of something along the lines of an underwired bodice, all black and red with flower-patterned detail, slightly padded with stockings and suspenders to match.

I wanted to go for the mistress in a boudoir-type look. I picked up my size—36DD for the bodice and a small size 8 for the suspender belt. Next on the list were the stockings, which I threw in my basket along with the rest. The only thing missing was red lipstick. I wanted the brightest, deepest red I could find so that he could see it when I was sucking his cock. *What man wouldn't want to come home to that?* I thought.

I got to the checkout and the only till that was open had a man serving. *Oh, that's great,* I thought to myself. *How embarrassing, he is going to look at me in the most awkward way.* I had no choice, I gulped and headed on over.

'Afternoon. How is your day?' he asked as I approached.

'Great, thank you,' I replied, trying to be polite.

I placed all the items on the conveyor belt as they hit the divider sign, ready for him to start scanning. Before he realised it, he picked up the bodice and suspenders in his hand and held them up to find the tag with the barcode on. He touched the cup of the bra, suddenly noticing what he was scanning and looked at me uncomfortably. I looked busy and rustled around in my purse for my card and money, trying not to look in his direction.

I could only imagine what he was thinking. *Dirty bitch,* or *I wonder who that is for?* I didn't want to know. In fact, I wanted to get out of there as quickly as I could and head back to work.

He folded them neatly, placed them in the bag and then asked me for payment. I swiped my card into the machine and waited for him to print the receipt so I could sign it. I smiled at him as the receipt slowly made its way out and he shuffled in his chair slightly.

I took the bag, thanked him and drove back to work. It felt like it used to when Daniel and I first met. Butterflies in my stomach, excitement and feeling alive. I had a lot of making up to do and I was looking forward to it. He deserved so much more than me. I needed to become the woman he deserved.

As it was a Friday, I had arranged for my mum to have Jack. I packed his favourite toys, books and a few treats in his little rucksack so that when she collected him after nursery, he would have so many of his things to occupy him at their house. He loved going there to visit and sleeping over in his room that they kept for him.

Work was busy but I managed to whizz through as many things as I could and left half an hour earlier.

I sped home as quickly as I could. Just as I was nearing our house, I turned left into our street, indicating and concentrating on the busy flow of traffic coming in the opposite direction, but as I did, I was sure I saw Daniel's car travelling on the other side of the road. I tried to take a quick second look, but the car had already gone. That was strange, why had he left work early and why was he heading the other way?

I decided to call him. I was probably imagining it and it was someone in a similar car to his.

I left it ringing but he didn't pick it up. He always answered his phone, even if it was to say that he was busy and would call me back, but this time, he didn't.

I thought it was strange, but I was more focused on getting home before him, getting ready and surprising him. I drove straight into a space in the car park by home, it wasn't straight, but I didn't care, I was in a hurry. I dumped my bags at the bottom of the stairs and quickly ran Harry around the block.

Out of breath, I returned home and ran upstairs with my bags to the bathroom. My plan was to shave every piece of hair from my body and then cover myself with baby oil so I was smooth to the touch in every crease and curve. There was something about washing and then covering my body in oil, it dried so silky soft that even I couldn't resist stroking my legs. I washed and dried my hair, put my makeup on and changed into my underwear. It was chilly, so I wrapped my silk dressing gown around my body, ready and waiting for him to come home.

I didn't want to start the dinner until he was home, but I was stuck in a dilemma. *Do we have sex first and food after, or food first and then sex afterwards on a full stomach?* My phone vibrated on the bed and I could see the screen light up. It was probably Daniel asking if I needed anything on the way home.

Picking it up, I flicked the screen and read it as I made my way downstairs.

HEY, SORRY BUT I NEED TO WORK LATE TONIGHT, NOT SURE WHEN I WILL BE BACK, YOU GUYS GET SOME FOOD, DON'T WAIT FOR ME. DX

I read it and flipped my phone closed as I approached the kitchen. It took me a moment or two to process. *Wait, what? He's what?*

I opened my phone again and re-read it. He's working late, on a Friday? There was no way he would want sex when he got home later, and why hadn't he answered his phone to me earlier when I tried to ring him? I had a bad feeling that something wasn't right, but I didn't know what. Surely people didn't work late on a Friday?

I wasn't angry, I was just disappointed. There was only one thing for it—alcohol. I opened the fridge and pulled out a bottle of white wine. Chilled and dry, just the way I liked it. I grabbed a large glass from the cupboard—it was probably a red wine glass, but who cared. There was no one here to tell me off anyway. Just as I slammed the opened bottle in frustration on the dining room table, along with the empty glass, I noticed Daniel's laptop under a pile of washing that I had folded up and placed there.

I thought about opening it and snooping but I talked myself out of it. I couldn't possibly search his personal laptop, it was private. I wouldn't like it if he snooped on me, imagine what he would find out about Steve.

I poured my wine and took a seat. As I sat, my silky dressing gown exposed my stocking-encased legs and the bottom of my suspender belt. *What a waste,* I thought to myself. Daniel's loss if he's working late. I took another sip from my glass of wine. Without dinner and a small lunch, as I had been preoccupied with my wasted underwear, it went straight to my head. Another sip, it was going down nicely. With no Jack to look after and Daniel at work, I had no one to text except George, but it felt weird texting him in the evening. I had a rule that I only ever messaged work colleagues outside of work if it was desperate.

The black corner of the laptop kept catching my eye. It's as if it was calling out to me to open it.

I couldn't. I shouldn't... but I did.

I reached over and slid the laptop out from under the washing, lifting its heavy lid to a welcome screen. I took another large sip of wine and gulped it down. So, what would his password be? My fingers ran over the keys but didn't press down on them.

I began typing the letters R-O-S-E-M-A-R-Y then 9-7, I hit enter and it let me in. Of course, it let me in, Daniel used the same password for everything. *How silly,* I thought to myself, but then again, if he wasn't hiding anything, why would he need to use a different password to the one I knew he used?

But what was I looking for, if anything? Maybe something that had Daniel preoccupied. He was definitely distant, and something was attracting him away from me, but what?

First of all, I went to his web search history. That would give me an idea of what he'd been searching recently. There was something inside of me though that was slightly worried. What if I didn't like what I found? I never thought in a million years that Daniel would do anything disrespectful to me, apart from that one time when he confessed, but I had to be sure.

I clicked on his browser and Yahoo.co.uk loaded very slowly. I worked in IT, so I knew exactly what to click on and my way around the laptop. Using his tracker pad, I moved my mouse to the top right-hand menu and clicked on the options. The history tab dropped down and gave me more options on the timeframe, I clicked the last seven days option and waited for it to return the results.

Wow, so many searches in the last week. I scanned my eyes down the list and suddenly felt ashamed of myself for snooping. Most of his searches were for hotel breaks, hotel rooms, weekend breaks and romantic getaways. Then it went onto lingerie and sexy underwear. He was thinking the same as me... our relationship needed a bit of love and attention, and he was searching for something for us. How could I ever have doubted him? But then again, that was just me all over. Instantly being selfish and thinking about myself once again.

I slammed the lid closed and took another couple of sips of wine.

I looked around the room, thinking of things I could do to pass the boredom until Daniel returned home.

Wait a minute... I thought to myself. Something still didn't feel right. Were all those searches for us? What if... No, they couldn't possibly be for someone else, he wouldn't do that. Would he? Or would he?

I kept telling myself he wouldn't but the nagging feeling in the back of my head was telling me to open it again. I spun the laptop back around, lifting the lid and finding the welcome screen displaying again. I typed the same password again, instantly letting me in.

This time, I clicked on his browser and typed in the Hotmail site to reach his emails. Surely, he wouldn't be stupid enough to leave evidence if he was cheating on me. I entered his username and password and it downloaded. Once again, I scanned the list of emails—there were so many and most of them were spam but there were a couple that stood out and Daniel had replied to them. I instantly noticed the Re: at the beginning of each message.

Taking my final sip of wine as I finished the glass, I clicked on the second email down from the top and waited for it to open.

Yes, I had been hurt in the past, and of course I had felt betrayed, but what I read next hit me like a knife to the chest. I wanted to be sick, my stomach dropped deep into my body as if it had been kicked and I felt like my heart had been ripped right out of my chest. My throat was dry, it hurt to swallow, and my eyes were burning. What I had done for work was unforgiveable, I was by no means an angel, but I did it for my family and there was no love or feeling behind it. I had never slept with anyone I had feelings for apart from Daniel. But this... this was something else. He spoke to this woman the way he spoke to me. He had genuine feelings for whoever this was, and it hurt more than anything had hurt me in my life.

I read on...

'Baby, I can't tell you how much I loved seeing you today. I will never forget this afternoon and being with you. In bed with you, in your comforting arms once again. Only five more days till I can be with you again. Forever yours, M xxx'

Who the hell was M? Can't wait to be with you again? In bed with you, in your arms once again? This wasn't the first time that Daniel had met her or slept with her. What on earth was going on? Who did she think she was? Daniel was mine.

I was now in a rage. I wasn't upset or feeling sorry for myself. I was angry.

I read more...

'Baby, being with you is like being with my best friend. You mean the world to mean, why can't we be together? I miss you so much when I'm not with you. Looking forward to next week. Same place as last time? M xxx'

[Daniel's reply]

'Yes, same place as last time. Can't stay long, need to keep it quick. Dan'

He signed it Dan... he never calls himself Dan, he doesn't like it. He was always a man of very few words though, short and sweet. It didn't make things easier. No wonder he was working late tonight, he was making up for being out of the office this afternoon with this other woman. I could barely believe what I was reading. It still didn't seem like him at all. I was his girl, his one true love, his best friend, his soulmate.

Why were we now so distant? I couldn't cope, I had to find out more. Who was this M?

How could I find out where they had met? I wasn't going to confront him or ask him. I wanted to catch him out instead. That way, I could find out who it was and why. I was angrier at her for taking him away from me.

His bank statements... that may tell me where he was this afternoon. Did he pay for a hotel room, a coffee shop or a restaurant... petrol maybe?

If I could try running through his bank account, his statements were always delivered in white envelopes. He never opened them, just threw them in the drawer with all our other papers. I could check his payments for the last month to see if it was on there.

I set to work like a detective inspector, finding clues as to what he was up to. I ran to them, gathering every unopened envelope I could find and frantically set about opening them. Reading the statement date on each piece of paper to find the latest one. Daniel forgot that I knew everything about him... well, it once seemed like I did, but this was now one thing that I didn't know about him.

His transactions were listed like a shopping cart for the whole month, up to last week, but I ideally needed today's. Wait a minute... her email said, 'same place as last time'. It took me a few moments to find it but there it was... Marlow. *Why Marlow?*

It listed the name of a hotel and another payment at a petrol station in Marlow. I saw the first hotel booking and then two other transactions for the same place followed it— one and two weeks beforehand. So, he had been there three times in total, including today. She said in her email, see you in five days. Was that including the fifth day or was it after the fifth day, making it Wednesday or Thursday next week? I was going to need time off work to catch them at their game.

How do I play it cool with him and pretend I don't know? Otherwise, I will blow my cover. I suddenly turned into Rose the unemotional person that I had come accustomed to. The strong, independent woman that despite being in absolute devastation, decided to get up and get on with it. Push everything that mattered to one side and act like nothing, and no one mattered. Except Jack, of course, he was my one true weakness.

I set to work, clearing the browsers. I shut down the windows on the laptop that I was viewing and tried putting everything back to where it was, closing the lid behind me and pushing it back under the clothes on the table. I put all the statements back into their envelopes and hid them under the other papers in the drawer.

I'm not going to lie, I felt like breaking down into a blubbering mess on the floor and sobbing my heart out, but what good would that do? It wouldn't make me feel better, it wouldn't erase what he had done, and it certainly wouldn't leave Daniel feeling sorry for me. That's not what I wanted at all, I wanted answers as to why and who.

I took the rest of the bottle upstairs with me, throwing the empty glass into the sink as it shattered into the tiniest of fragments, I swigged from the bottle, attempting to make it up the stairs in a straight line, gripping the wall as I went. I got changed back out of my sexy lingerie, pushing them right to the back of my underwear drawer and into a loose t-shirt. Sitting on the side of my bed, I fell backwards and into the comfort of the pillows, the bottle of wine neatly tucked into my arm, and closed my eyes.

'Rose, Rose, where's Jack?' Daniel shouted, shaking me. It was morning and the room was bright with sunshine.

'Ugh!' I said as I opened my morning eyes. I don't know whether I was more disgusted to see Daniel or the fact that I had a banging headache from last night's wine. I was half-expecting that last night's series of events were just a bad dream, but I knew deep down they weren't.

'Rose!' he shouted again. 'Where is Jack? He seemed agitated.

'He's at my mum's, why are you shouting at me?' I managed to reply in a husky voice.

'I thought he was in his bed last night but when I went to wake him this morning, he wasn't there. I panicked.' He sat on the edge of the bed and took a deep breath.

'Well, if you came home earlier from work rather than working late, maybe you would know,' I muttered under my breath, but he heard everything I said.

'Don't start, Rose, I don't want a day of arguing.' He sighed.

'I don't want to argue. I just...' I stopped myself, what was the point? That sordid, cheating boyfriend of mine was still thinking of Marlow. He reeked of a liar. I wanted the old Daniel back, the one that doted on me, that loved me, the one that would do anything for me.

'I'm going to get Jack from my parents, I'll take Harry with me and walk over there. Fancy coming with me?' I asked, hoping that he would join me.

'I can't. I have to work,' he said as he got up from the bed to get changed.

'Of course you do,' I replied sarcastically. I hated the atmosphere, the animosity in the room, but maybe that's what happens when you get together too young and are faced with so many things sent to try you.

'Oh, and I'll be late home one night next week. I have a customer dinner. It will need to be Wednesday or Thursday,' I called out from the bathroom to Daniel. I didn't want to see his reaction or for him to think there was anything up. There was a pause.

'I am working late Wednesday night, it's a busy week next week. I can have him Thursday though,' he shouted back to me.

There it was—bingo! He had just given me the information I needed. He was planning to meet her on Wednesday afternoon. All I had to do was get Jack looked after and drive to Marlow. I had plenty of time to figure it out but there was still one thing that I needed to find out and that was what time he was planning on being there.

It was the longest week of my life, waiting for Wednesday to arrive. Trying to act as normal as I possibly could around Daniel when all I wanted to do was scream and shout at him. Behaving like my heart hadn't been shattered into a million pieces and pretending everything was absolutely fine. I wanted to cry my absolute heart out, but I remained calm. Blotting it out like an old memory that hadn't happened.

The thing that hurt me the most was being betrayed by not just my lover but my best friend as well. It was double the deceit. There was only one thing left... I had to sort this out and put things straight for Jack's sake.

I asked Dave for the afternoon off and he approved it. Jack was at nursery and my mum was going to pick him up afterwards for me. I had worked out which route to drive to Marlow and where to park the car so he wouldn't see it. I would get to the hotel and sit in reception for a while, as far in the corner as I could, hidden but with enough of a view to see who was arriving. I would wait until they were both there and then appear.

All morning at work, I felt sick, feeling dread and anxious. I couldn't concentrate and I just wanted to go home, but as soon as the clock hit 12.30, I switched off my screen and practically ran to my car. This was the first leg of my journey. I was behaving like a crazy woman, heading to a hotel in Marlow like a spy to see if I could catch my cheating boyfriend. I got in the car and drove as quickly as I could to get there before them.

There it was... finally, the hotel that Daniel was due to be at. I was hoping that I was there before them as it would be embarrassing if I went all this way and they were already together in their room. It would mean a wasted afternoon of sitting in a hotel lobby for hours while they were having sex. I had the whole scenario made up in my head.

As I pulled into the road opposite the hotel, making sure it wasn't visible from the main entrance, I locked the car and began walking. I was beginning to have second thoughts. I should have just confronted him when I found out instead of traipsing halfway across the county to catch them. I didn't even know who she was or how they met. Was it too late to change my mind? I could quite easily stay in the car and head back home again. The stubborn side of me didn't back down, I had to go through with it.

Like a new lease of life and determination, I put one step in front of the other and walked towards the hotel foyer.

As I approached the entrance, the large revolving doors began to move. I waited for a gap and then snuck in between the panels. Inside the hotel, it was a bustling expanse of people meeting, talking and drinking tea and coffee together.

The reception desk had a short queue of people waiting patiently. If Daniel was looking for somewhere quiet and discreet to go to, this was definitely not the place. What was he thinking, or did he not care? Then again, how many people would he know in Marlow? It wasn't his hometown like Bracknell was, so the chances of bumping into someone he knew was quite low.

I chose the table and armchair furthest from the door, but I could still see the entrance. It was the perfect place to hide, sit and wait. The reception area smelled of warm bread and a lunch menu was being prepared. I could be in for a long wait, so as the waiter made his way over to me, I ordered a pot of tea for one and a ham and mustard sandwich that came with crisps.

The round, padded, blue armchair was uncomfortable. I shifted from side to side trying to get settled but it was impossible. I looked around the room to see if there were any familiar faces but there weren't, thank goodness. The waiter carried a black tray towards me with a white china teapot, cup and saucer, a milk jug and a selection of teabags in a little pot.

'Your food will be along shortly, madam,' he said as he placed everything on the small round table by my side. 'Is there anything else I can get you?'

'No, I'm all good thank you, just the bill.' I smiled as he handed me the receipt. I felt shady. The waiter and reception staff must see so many things in hotels, people sneaking into rooms, affairs, private meetings. Interesting... as long as you weren't on the receiving end like I was.

It was like waiting for paint to dry. How long would I have to wait for that dreaded moment? I glanced at my watch, it was 2.15 pm, had I missed them? I fidgeted, uncrossing and crossing my legs. My sandwich and crisps had arrived, but I wasn't hungry. I still felt sick.

I sat there in my chair, people-watching, drinking my tea and checking my watch constantly. 2.25 pm. Just as I was about to get up to go to the toilet. The revolving doors started again and something made me look up—call it intuition if you like.

I knew that face, I knew it well, but what on earth was she doing here? *What a small world,* I thought. *To see her and again here...* and then it dawned on me.

It couldn't possibly be... he wouldn't possibly... would he?

Michelle... that's what the M stood for. He was meeting Michelle. The emails were to Michelle, she had got her greedy claws into my boyfriend. How did I not see that coming? How did I not listen to Tom? Oh, it was all making sense now... the question mark from Tom. Daniel had deleted his message as it was something to do with Michelle, I'm sure of it. The dream about Tom, it was telling me something.

Maybe I was jumping to conclusions. Maybe it was just a coincidence that she was here, and Daniel wasn't meeting her, but I had a sneaky suspicion I was right. The pieces of the puzzle were all coming together now.

I could feel the same painstaking, sharp knife to the chest sensation again that I felt when I read his emails. After everything we went through, the way he said he couldn't bear seeing me with another man after the four of us were in bed together in Greece and he does something like this. I wanted to run to the toilet and be sick. The pain... the unbearable pain that I was feeling. My chest was tight, I took deep breaths in and out. I thought I was going to hyper-ventilate.

Keep calm, Rose, keep calm, I thought to myself. *Compose yourself and see what unfolds next.*

But what about the baby? Tom said she was pregnant, had she had it by now and Daniel was here to meet him or her or to perhaps discuss their plans? Maybe he was meeting her to talk about leaving me to be with his new family. I couldn't comprehend what was happening. Was I dreaming this like all the other vivid and realistic dreams I'd had of late? I pinched my arm to be sure. *Ouch! Nope, definitely not dreaming, I felt that.*

I sunk back into my chair and hid behind the pillar beside it. I needed to make sure that I could see them but they couldn't see me.

There he was. Suddenly, Daniel appeared at reception. He was talking to the woman behind the desk and she was nodding her head in agreement. Michelle had spotted him too and walked up to greet him. I watched, heartbroken, as she wrapped her arm around his back and leaned in to kiss him. He seemed to edge away but too late as her lips planted straight onto his cheek. Daniel finished the conversation with the receptionist, took the piece of paper that she had handed him and went to walk towards the lifts. Michelle tugged at his hand and tried to walk him towards one of the chairs by the bar. Daniel seemed reluctant to want to sit down but she was clearly in charge.

I knew Daniel and I knew his body language. He looked agitated, uncomfortable, angry with her possibly. I know he was in the wrong here, but I almost wanted to rescue him and hit her straight in the face. That was my man, and she was trying to steal him from me. Where was the baby? Why wasn't it with her? Had Daniel come to see it, to discuss their plans for the future?

I felt like a stalker, hidden at the back of the room, trying to conceal myself. It seemed I wasn't as hidden as I had liked. Daniel and Michelle began what looked like a heated argument. His face was red, and he was leaning into her saying something. Michelle began lifting her arms. With one hand, she seemed to be trying to reassure him. *Dammit, I wish I was closer so I could hear what they were talking about.*

Suddenly, Daniel looked straight at me as if he knew I was there. I ducked, grabbing the food menu, trying to hide my identity, but as I sunk it gently back down and peered over the top, Daniel was walking towards me. He looked panicked as he approached. I was panicking. *What do I say? What is he going to say?*

Shit, shit, shit, I thought to myself.

Daniel bounded right up to me. 'Rose, what the fuck are you doing here?'

'More importantly, what the fuck are you doing here?' I shouted back. Everyone in the room suddenly turning their attention to the two of us. 'And, what the fuck is she doing here? You have a lot of explaining to do.'

Daniel immediately realised he was in deep trouble.

'Let's get out of here and talk about it at home, I don't want a scene.' He reached forward and tried to grab my arm and pull me from the chair.

'You have created this scene, Daniel, or should I call you Dan?' I sat firmly still in the chair, not moving. By this time, Michelle had started to make her way over to the two of us.

'And you can fuck right off, Michelle, did you not think I would find out?' I had visions of hitting her straight in the face, but I wasn't a fighter, I wasn't aggressive in the slightest, she would probably hit me back and win. I had to play the victim here. *Hang on a minute... I am the victim here.*

'Rose, it is definitely not the place to talk about this, let's go somewhere and talk about this privately, let me explain.' He genuinely looked mortified that I was there and had found out. I wanted to cry, how had we ended up here together, but I had to stand strong and look like the better woman in this situation.

'I don't want your explanation, Daniel. How has this happened?' I sat there looking at him in disbelief.

'Rose, please, this isn't what you think.' He pleaded with me and tried again to grab my hand. I shook it off.

'This is exactly what I think. I've seen your emails and your bank statements. Don't lie to me.' My voice was breaking under the pain, I was choked, and it was getting more and more difficult to disguise.

'Come on, Daniel, let's leave her here. Let her think what she wants.' Michelle piped up from behind him and tried to place her hand on his shoulder.

'Get the hell away from me, you've done enough damage. I don't know why I am even here with you in the first place. Just leave us both alone.' He shook off her hand and turned his back.

He crouched down next to my chair and placed his hand on mine. 'Rose, I know you must hate me right now, but I need you to listen to me, I need to talk to you, but this is not the right place. Please come with me. I—' I cut him short.

'What, and go to the hotel room you have booked for her and you? No, thanks.' I was stubborn beyond means. I was contemplating, *Do I pick up my bag and just leave, or do I stand fast, hoping that they will leave?*

'So, you decided not to bring the baby with you then?' I shouted at Michelle. Her eyes narrowed and she looked solemn. Had I caught her out too that I knew all about their little scenario?

'Rose!' Daniel shouted at me. He was telling me off. *How dare he!*

'Sir, Madam. I'm sorry to interrupt but I wondered if you could take your conversation to a private room, it is disturbing our other guests who are enjoying a nice, quiet atmosphere.' The waiter was trying to politely get us to move our argument elsewhere. I felt sorry for him, he had every right to move us all on, but I wasn't finished.

'Daniel. Are you not going to say anything?' I wanted someone to start giving me some answers.

I stood up, grabbed my bag, placed a twenty-pound note on top of the receipt that was on the table and tried to walk past Daniel and Michelle and as quickly as I could out of the hotel, but Daniel chased after me. 'Rose, Rose, where are you going?'

'I'm going home. Well, I am going to pick up *our* son from nursery, I don't need this right now.' I dare not look at either of them, it had made me so angry.

'Rose, I'm coming with you. Where is your car?' His pace kept up with mine, leaving Michelle teetering along behind. As we approached the main doors, he stopped and turned. 'Michelle, consider this as a warning that I never want to see you again. Don't call me, text me or email me ever again. This whole thing, whatever it is, is over. Done. Finished.'

I watched as the doors rotated me around to outside. Michelle looked shocked like she was a child that had never been shouted at before. She tried to step forward as though she wanted to say one last thing to him, but Daniel held up the palm of his hand and said, 'Save it,' as he too made his way through the doors and met me on the other side.

My rage had gone from anger to upset. I held back the tears in my eyes and the pain in my heart. The only man in my life that I could ever truly love had broken all the trust I had in him. I thought he would never cheat on me again, but here I was, waiting for an explanation.

'How could you?' was all I could say. The heavens opened, rain pouring out of the sky and soaking both of us as we stood facing each other. The rain was irrelevant—like everything else in my life.

'I...' He stopped. 'You don't understand, it's not that simple.' His eyes were just as glassy as mine as he looked in pain too.

'No, I don't understand.' I wiped the rain away from my face.

'I love you more than anything, I didn't want to hurt you, but I couldn't bare you finding out.' He stepped closer to me.

'Michelle, of all people... why?' He could have had anyone, he was so good-looking, the fact that it was her just didn't make any sense.

'Please, Rose, let's get out of the rain and let me tell you everything.' He grabbed my hand and led me to his car in the car park. I didn't want to listen to his excuses. All men are after one thing and one thing only, how could I ever have been so stupid to think that he wasn't ruled by his trousers? He may have loved me, but when it came to temptation, he was willing to throw everything away. How could I have been so stupid? I would never trust again after this.

We walked in the pouring rain to the car. He unlocked it with his keys and we both climbed into the front seats, soaked through. Daniel started the engine so that he could turn on the heaters, but it only steamed up the car. We sat in silence for minutes, both of us just staring out of the windscreen with despair. I was sick of asking questions, but the suspense was killing me.

'Rose, I don't know how to begin. I'm sorry that you had to find me there with Michelle, but it's not quite as straightforward as you think. I'm...' He stopped and swallowed. He looked choked as though he was going to break down.

'Go on...' I prompted him to continue.

'It all started months ago. She kept calling and texting me, asking me to meet. I ignored her but she was relentless, saying she needed to see me and it was important. I even blocked her number several times but she just texted me from other phones.' He looked down as if he was ashamed.

'Months ago, are you serious? I knew something was wrong. How did I not see it? You should have told me, Daniel.' Another tear rolled down my cheek as I wiped it away.

'There's more. She then managed to get my work number and was put through by reception. When I answered it by mistake, she told me that she had fallen pregnant with my baby after Greece, and it was urgent that I meet her. I didn't know what to do and I didn't want it to affect us, so I agreed to meet her.' Daniel shuffled around nervously, trying to remove his damp coat and throw it onto the back seat.

'Did you meet her?' I asked, not wanting to know the answer but I already knew.

'Yes, we just met in a service station on a Saturday. I felt really bad, but when I pulled into the car park, Tom was there too, he said he was meeting a friend. Michelle had deliberately gone to the same place as Tom so he then knew I had been in contact with her. I was already in fear of you finding out but when she said she was pregnant, I thought I had another child, Rose.'

Shit, I thought. That must have been the same day and place as when I met Tom. What if Daniel had seen me there too? This was way more complicated than I thought it was.

'I asked her what she wanted from me and how she knew it was definitely mine. She agreed to get a DNA check when it was born but was adamant it was. I swear, Rose, I told her that I loved you and wanted nothing more to do with her, but the calls and texts continued. If I didn't answer my phone, she would just call my work. I think she was so desperate for a baby that I was her last hope.' He let out a cry, his eyes building with tears. He hit the steering wheel several times with his right palm.

'She then asked if she could meet me at that hotel. She had booked a room for us to meet and talk confidentially and said she needed to tell me something else. I presumed it was about the baby, so again, I agreed. When I arrived this time, she was in a mess. She said she had lost the baby after the first scan and was an emotional wreck. She had lost her job because of all the time off and didn't have any money, so I offered to pay for the hotel room. I promise, Rose, I consoled her because she was distraught, but I didn't sleep with her. The only time we had sex was in Greece when I was with you. I felt bad that she had lost the baby, but that was it.' He looked at me with the most pained expression.

'When I met her the last time, she said that she was going to tell you I had met her and to check my bank statements unless I met with her again. She had been blackmailing me for weeks. It's been torturing me for so long. I wanted to tell you, really, I did.' Daniel wiped his eyes, but the sweat was pouring from his forehead.

'But, Daniel, if you didn't do anything, what did it matter if she told me?' I wasn't sure whether I believed him or not.

'Because the bank statements looked bad. She had me exactly where she wanted me. She's obsessed. She wouldn't take no for an answer.' He turned to look at me.

'I would have understood.' I looked back at him.

'I don't think you would have done. I shouldn't have met her the first couple of times, I didn't know what to do about the baby, then it brought back memories of us and when we lost ours. I felt bad for her. The more I saw her, the deeper in I was. Last week, she tried booking a room again for us, but I said if she booked anymore, I wouldn't pay for them. It was her problem now. Today was supposed to be telling her that I had a restraining order, and that if she called work again, I would get the police involved. You saw me arguing with her. Telling her that I never wanted to see her again.'

'Why did the receptionist hand you a piece of paper?' I asked.

'It was for the car park. I managed to get a parking ticket last time by mistake. The hotel said they would get the company to waive the fees or give me a refund, so she was providing me with confirmation.' Daniel rustled into his jeans pocket and pulled out a folded-up piece of paper, handing it to me so I could read it.

Half-believing it, I opened the piece of paper, and sure enough, it was a statement of account. A refund of fifty pounds and the last four digits of his card. The description said 'Car park refund and parking waiver.'

Was it true? Or was he telling me a pack of lies and I was falling for them? I was still so hurt that I didn't know what to believe.

'What about the message from Tom, did you text him from my phone? I had a strange message come through from him with just a question mark?' Daniel suddenly shot me a look as if he had been found out yet again.

'I saw a message from Tom pop up on your phone when you were sleeping that night. I thought it was the end of us. He was telling you that I had met Michelle and that we were meeting again at the hotel, so I quickly managed to delete it and send back a text saying to stop messaging me. If you didn't see that... how did you find out I was meeting her?'

'Erm...' This time, I hung my head in shame. 'I read your emails on your laptop and your bank statement. You seemed so distant; I knew something was up. You worked late on a Friday... I saw your car driving the other way and I put two and two together and figured...'

'What that two and two makes five?' Daniel shot back a sarcastic comment.

'Kind of, what would you imagine if that was me?' Two wrongs didn't make a right, but I was hardly the bad guy here.

'Rose, look, I should have spoken to you before, but I panicked each time in case you found out. I should have never met her the first time, but I didn't know how you would feel that she was pregnant. I then thought about how it would affect Jack and whether our relationship could cope with this. Coupled with her chasing me and telling me how much she loved me, I didn't have anyone to talk to.' He held his head in his hands, the car now a hot, sweaty box of condensation and steamy windows.

'You should have spoken to me too. I just want it all to go away,' he said.

Do I say it's okay, that I forgive him? Do I believe that he hasn't done anything with Michelle? Right now, I wanted evidence. I wanted CCTV to prove it, but I knew that wasn't going to happen. Was Michelle really out of the picture now?

Was Tom trying to warn me and did he know more than what I had been told? I half felt like Tom and Michelle were in it together.

I didn't have anyone that I could turn to. I always tried to keep my personal life secret and not confide in anyone, but on this occasion, I was well and truly lost. I just stared at the other cars in the car park and up at the tall, square hotel ahead of us.

'Rose, please say something. I swear to you that nothing happened between us. I want you, not her, and I feel ashamed that I nearly let this come between us.' He held out his hand to me, wanting me to hold it. 'You and Jack mean everything to me, I mean everything.'

'Daniel, I don't know what to say. I want to believe you but...' I held his hand.

'But what?' he asked.

'I don't know. I feel betrayed. You should be able to talk to me about anything.' Even though I meant it, there was a little voice in the back of my head saying, *Well, you don't talk to Daniel about anything. You talk to George, he's the one that listens, he's the one that you confide in. Why are you any different?*

'I'm sorry I jumped to conclusions and I'm sorry that I read your laptop, I just couldn't bear losing you and I knew that there was something wrong. You have been off with me for weeks.' I squeezed his hand.

'Promise me something,' he said.

'What?' Apprehensive as to what he was going to ask.

'That in future, we both don't jump to conclusions, and we talk to each other first. Agreed?' He squeezed my hand back.

'Agreed.' I nodded my head.

'Now, let's head back and pick up Jack from nursery. I'll

make up an excuse and work late another evening to make up the time. I would rather be at home with you. I'll drop you at your car... where are you parked?' Daniel turned on the car's ignition and waited for the fans to clear the view so he could drive.

'Just across the road.' I pointed in the direction of my car.

'I'll make it up to you when we are home.' He gave me a slight smile.

The whole way home, I drove in silence—no radio, no music, just me and my thoughts. I had so many questions and thoughts running through my mind.

Was there really nothing in it with Michelle? Could I trust him? Was she that much of a psychopath that she was fixated on Daniel? I guess I would never know who was telling the truth and who wasn't.

The only thing I hadn't made up my mind about yet was whether I let it drop, or whether I took revenge on Michelle.

20

THE BEST HANGOVER EVER

I t always seemed a good idea at the time. One drink led to another and another and another. I just couldn't stop —I had no off switch. I lived for the moment and not for the hangover the following morning. Friday night was great, and I had a blast, but Saturday morning hangovers with a little boy were never a good combination.

I lay in bed. The curtains drawn and Jack cuddled up under the covers next to me. If I turned my head just slightly, my head would spin, and I couldn't stop being sick all morning. I could have stayed curled up next to him all day, but I had to get up.

'Mummy is going to get up now and get ready. Fancy going swimming?' I turned to Jack who had the covers pulled right up to his chin.

'Yeeesssss!' he said, jumping out and onto the bed. I walked slowly to the bathroom, my eyes squinting from the light of the morning and rubbing my head as if it was going to cure my headache. I felt dizzy and my breasts were unbelievably tender, but I had every optimism that going swimming would make me feel fresh.

I left Jack grabbing his swimming shorts and bag together while I had a quick shower.

I stood in the shower for a moment or two, letting the water run down my body. I started to wash my hair, my body and finally shave my legs.

As much as I wanted to take Jack swimming and spend some quality time with him, I felt dreadful. I'd had a lot to drink, but why were my hangovers so bad when others didn't get a hangover at all?

Jack was such a water baby. We taught him to swim almost as soon as he could walk. He was used to the water at a young age and would love diving underwater, he hadn't a fear in the world. I was hoping that the cold water would make me feel better, but I still had to rush back with him to the toilets a couple of times as I was so sick. Each time we did, it was an excuse for Jack to dive bomb back into the water when he returned.

Our local swimming baths weren't just a pool, it was a whole water world. They had flumes, a wave machine, a big galleon that shot water, a volcano and so many other water adventures for children that a few hours in there was not long enough. On many occasions, I had to bribe Jack to leave. His fingers would be wrinkled from being in there too long.

Back in the changing rooms, I ruffled to dry his dark brown hair, admiring his gorgeous emerald green eyes and cheeky smile. He looked exhausted but loved every minute of it.

'Thank you, Mummy, that was fun. Can we come back again tomorrow?' he asked, trying to put his own socks on.

'Haha, maybe not tomorrow but we will come back soon.' I laughed comically at his request.

It was nice spending some time together, just him and me. Quality time that I missed out on whilst I was at work during the week. I told myself that I shouldn't have regrets but it's one thing that I did regret daily. Not spending enough time with him, not being there when he really needed me, but we simply didn't have the money to survive if I didn't work.

The following morning, I awoke to a feeling like it was Groundhog Day. The same nauseous feeling, the same dizzy head. Hangovers don't last for several days, surely? I knew full well that if I ventured to the bathroom, I would feel bad, but equally, lying in bed wasn't doing me any favours either.

I didn't need to do a test—I didn't need to work out any dates. I knew instantly that I was pregnant. That same dull, sickness-inducing throbbing pain in my stomach. I was hot and sweaty; I thought my breasts hurt yesterday but today they were on fire. A dry mouth and a dizzy feeling. I could tell.

Part of me was excited—a very small part. Only because of what happened last time, painstakingly to carry a child and feel like you have a permanent hangover for several weeks if not months and then for it to end in pure heartbreak. I was sceptical and didn't want to get attached. I would love nothing more than to have lots of children, especially if they all turned out like Jack, but the thought of carrying them for nine months sent chills down my spine.

'Are you okay?' Daniel rolled over to find me awake and staring at the ceiling. Concentrating on not passing out.

'No, I feel horrendous,' I whispered back to him.

'Why, what's wrong?' he said, half-asleep and his eyes closed.

'You know last time when I passed out in the shower and things went horribly wrong?' I rolled over, watching him try to keep his eyes open and awake.

'Yeah.' It took him a moment to process my words, then suddenly, his eyes opened wide, and he stared at me. 'Really?'

'I'm certain.' I smiled.

'No way. How can you tell?' he asked.

'I just can. It's the weirdest feeling ever. I'm scared, what if...' He stopped me before I could say any more.

'Let's cross that bridge when we get there. It might be different this time.' He threw his arms over me, pulling the duvet cover over both of our bodies and cuddled up, squeezing me tight.

I closed my eyes, hoping that he was right. Maybe this time *was* different.

'Daniel,' I said.

'Uh-huh.' I think he was drifting off to sleep again.

'I'm scared. I don't think I could go through all that again. To get all our hopes up and then...' Daniel held his hands on either side of my face and looked me in the eyes before I could finish. This was the first time that I had spoken about losing the baby before. Of course, it broke my heart, but like everything else, it was brushed under the carpet and I never spoke about it again. It was a cruel world sometimes. To have a small chance of something incredible and then for it to be taken away instantly, completely out of your control.

'Rose, listen to me,' he said. 'Let's not run before we can walk. I'll go to the shops with Jack and Harry and get a test while you have a shower, *a warm shower*. Then when we are back, we can be certain that you are. This time, we can prepare for the pregnancy, get you into hospital quicker if you are unwell, maybe there is a better medication you can take that will help you this time, and if you need to be on a drip for the whole nine months, then so be it. We just need to take one day at a time. Okay?' I loved it when Daniel took control, his authority and common sense made him so attractive.

'I guess so.' I leaned forward to kiss him, closing my eyes and thanking him for his support.

What happened to the saying that you were supposed to glow when you were pregnant? Well, I certainly didn't. Maybe I wasn't pregnant after all, but I had the strongest sense that I was.

We had a little more of a cuddle in bed. I could hear Jack in the bathroom banging around and going to the toilet. Daniel got up to make sure he was okay and get him and Harry ready to go to the shops, leaving me to get up in my own time and get washed and changed.

When they left, I stood in the shower, contemplating the results of the test for the third time. This time, although I felt like I was, it seemed different. I felt stronger, calmer, more positive that no matter what, I was going to hold onto this baby. If I did it with Jack, I could do it with this one. I didn't have a big stomach, but I still held my hand on it, circling it and hoping that it was true.

Washing and towel-drying my hair, I stepped out of the bath and wrapped my dressing gown around me. I lowered the toilet lid to the seat and sat down. As soon as I did, Daniel appeared in the doorway.

'How are you feeling, beautiful?' he asked.

'Dreadful!' I smiled, looking up at him as he handed me a screwed-up chemist bag with the test inside it.

'You want me to stay with you while you do it? Jack is playing with his Lego set. I said I would be down in a minute so I can be with you.' He stood patiently, propped up against the door frame.

'Sure.' I unwrapped the bag nervously. *Maybe I should wait,* I thought. *Am I just tempting fate and that it will all go horribly wrong?* I continued anyway for Daniel's sake, unfolding the box that said Clear Blue on the side. I didn't need to read the instructions or the folded-up safety precautions, I reached straight for the test and pulled it out, holding it in my hand.

Daniel was still standing in the doorway with a look of anticipation on his face as I reached between the opening in my dressing gown, lifted the toilet seat and sat back down. I removed the plastic lid and held it between my legs. *Why is it when someone is watching you go to the toilet, or you must wee on demand, it just doesn't happen?*

I sat there for a good five minutes trying to go. I felt like a dog on a leash, where the owner was watching and waiting for them to go to the toilet before escorting them back home. Finally, I started to go, my urine drenching the stick and I think most of my fingers too. As I finished, I gave a little flick of the stick down the toilet to remove any excess and to make sure it was fully covered, I brought it up from between my legs, replacing the cap and into view. Daniel unwound some toilet paper and handed it to me. Wiping both myself and the stick, I popped it on the cistern while I washed my hands.

'I don't want to look,' I said to Daniel as we swapped places. Me standing in the doorway and him hovering by the stick.

Both of us counting in our heads for three minutes. Daniel was too impatient, he picked it up and watched as the stick window began to change, the watery line moving further and further up the window to reach the top, next waiting for the lines to appear. Watching and watching, his head didn't move.

'Well, come on, don't leave me hanging like this.' I began fidgeting.

'You said you didn't want to look?' He beamed, teasing me.

'I didn't mean it. So, one line or two?' By this time, I was desperate to know.

'Well, it's hard to tell... you see, if you hold it this way, it's not that clear.' He tilted it towards him. 'Then if you hold it this way, it's pretty clear.' He twisted it around to show me.

I threw my hand to my mouth and took a huge gasp.

'Oh my god, oh my god, oh my god.' I looked back at him. I couldn't believe what I was seeing. Two bright blue, clear-as-day lines. 100% positive. I was pregnant for sure.

'No way.' Tears ran down my face. 'I don't believe it!' I almost screamed.

'Yes way!' Daniel moved towards me and hugged me so tight, I struggled to breathe.

'Can I have a cuddle too?' Jack appeared at the top of the stairs to wonder what all the commotion was about.

'You're having a little brother or sister, Jacky,' Daniel blurted out. I looked at him in pure shock.. why was he telling Jack?

'Can it be a brother please as I don't want a sister, they smell,' he replied with the cutest comment. You couldn't help but hug him.

'We can't quite be certain yet whether it is going to be a brother or a sister. It will be a surprise, but we are going to make sure that Mummy gets everything she needs to cook this one in the oven.' I beamed at Daniel and Jack, together next to me. The two most adorable men in my life. It was going to be one hell of a ride, but we all wanted this more than anything.

The next couple of weeks were tough. I felt so ill, and I was so sick, all day every day.

Work was fantastic. My manager, Dave, said I could work from home for the foreseeable future, but I had to explain to my clients, to George, in fact, so many people had been notified and were really supportive of me taking it easy and just getting through each day at a time. Steve had sent me a congratulations card that made me cry. Both our parents were told and were ecstatic, nervous about the pregnancy but great, nonetheless. My sisters and Daniel's sister were over all the time, seeing if there was anything they could help with and generally rallying around after the three of us. I guess it made me realise just how important and lucky we were to have families like ours.

By the time I hit eight weeks, the sickness had become unbearable. My weight rapidly decreased yet again and I was dehydrated. The fear started to kick in. I was so worried about the pregnancy ending in the same way as last time, so I was admitted to hospital once again.

It felt so lonely on a ward in the maternity unit of our nearest hospital. I could still manage to work as Dave had given me a laptop but made me promise that if it was too much, then he would re-assign clients to someone else in the business to handhold them until I returned. George checked in with me all the time, asking if there was anything he could do to help or if there was anything I needed.

Wired up to a drip, on anti-sickness medication and

saline to help me get hydrated again, it made such an improvement. A scan of my pregnancy indicated that I was around eight to nine weeks and with a strong heartbeat, so all was well.

Only another six to seven months to get through and I was there. It felt so far away.

21

YET ANOTHER WHITE LIE

I t was around 08.00 am and I opened my eyes to the most unbelievable wave of sickness.

Again and again, it hit me in waves and I could do nothing to control it. The nurses brought in multiple bowls for me, but you could see that they didn't know what to do. Just as I'd had enough and wanted to give up, the doctor came walking into the ward.

'Rose, I'm so sorry that you are feeling this way and the drip doesn't seem to be helping. I've been speaking to the nurses and they are going to give you some medicine that will hopefully alleviate the sickness. It won't stop you feeling sick, but it will definitely stop the stomach contractions.' He patted me on the shoulder as I leaned over the side of the bed again.

As soon as the nurses arrived with the small glass bottles, he left the room. *Thank goodness for that,* I thought. *I will take anything to stop this.*

'Right, my lovely, let's hope this will make you feel a little better.' The nurse used the syringe to collect all the medicine from the bottle, placing it gently on the side and then started to administer it via my catheter.

'Fingers crossed...' I started to say before I felt my wrist start to burn, then my arm. The heat began radiating up my body, my fingers tingling and throbbing. I looked at the nurse in panic... what was happening to me?

'Oh no, what's wrong?' the nurse quickly asked as the heart monitor beside me began to beep and flash. My heart rate rocketed—my arm was itching like crazy and my head was pounding.

The nurse suddenly slammed the emergency alarm button behind my head and snapped back the bed so I was lying flat down on the bed. Three other nurses and the doctor came running in. There was chaos in the room—it all seemed to happen so quickly. I didn't know what was going on.

My head began spinning, all the commotion in the room was hurting my ears and the speed of my heartbeat was pounding in my chest. I closed my eyes, the clenching of the bed eased, I relaxed, and the room went dark.

'Rose, Rose, how are you feeling?' Doctor Wheeler appeared by my bed as I opened my eyes.

I looked around the room, there were two nurses and the doctor stood beside me, looking on tentatively.

'What happened?' I asked wearily.

'It looks like you had an allergic reaction to the anti-sickness medication—metoclopramide—so we have given you a counter medication and some sedatives. Don't worry, it won't affect the baby, but hopefully, it will make you a little sleepy today so at least you can get some well-earned rest.' He smiled, tapping my arm. 'You scared us a little there, Rose.'

I didn't really understand what he was saying, so I just nodded and smiled slightly.

After four days of being in hospital, hooked up to machines and pumped with all kinds of medication so my body could balance everything that was going on, I was feeling fed up and just wanted to go home. Why couldn't I carry a pregnancy? Why was I so ill? It was as if I was carrying a foreign object that my body tried rejecting time and time again.

The following morning, the doctor came again to check on me, but I felt so far away from home. I wanted to be with Jack, Daniel and Harry and the rest of my family or even back at work, at least it kept my mind busy. Being in hospital was lonely and boring, I guess I had to learn to give my body time to repair itself.

'Good morning, Rose. How are we this morning? Your vitals are starting to look much better.' He smiled, looking at the figures on my chart at the end of the bed.

'Much better, thank you, I would rather be at home, but you are all looking after me so well,' I replied in a fed-up tone.

'I know you would, but first things first, we need to get you stable so that you don't keep coming back in.' He tilted his head reassuringly as he looked at me.

'Thank you, the nurses have been amazing, I'm just missing my boys, that's all.' I shuffled a little in bed so that I could sit up and listen to what he had to say.

'So, we now know that the saline is improving your hydration. Metoclopramide is now not an option and you have a red wrist tag for this, but I'm still not happy with why your sickness is so severe. We took some bloods yesterday and I am hoping that this afternoon we will be able to analyse the results and see if there is a deficiency somewhere that may be causing the issue. Just to confirm, you are blood type B RhD negative, is this correct? The father is A RhD positive. Hmmm, okay. Well, like I said, we will run some checks and hopefully have some answers this afternoon before releasing you. Is that okay?' His eyes still focused on my clipboard, flicking between the papers attached to it.

'Uh-huh. All fine with me.' I nodded my head to agree with him, after all, he was the specialist, but there was something nagging in my head from what he had said. *I'm pretty sure that he said I was B RhD negative blood type. How could that be possible? I am almost certain that both of my parents are A RhD positive. I'm not an expert but I don't think that is quite right?* Puzzled, I sat back in bed and tried to think about what he had just said. Perhaps he made a mistake and it was somebody else's notes.

'Okay, any questions?' He flicked the papers back down and latched the clipboard to the end of my bed.

'I'm sorry, did you say B RhD negative was my blood type?' I sat patiently waiting for his answer.

'Yes, that's correct, unless the lab has made a mistake.' He shuffled over to the end of the bed and re-read the paperwork. 'No, that's right, definitely B RhD negative. Is there a problem?' he asked.

'No, no, just checking.' How on earth had I not ever known what my blood type was before? Twenty-three years old and oblivious. How had I not given blood before or had anything checked?

Something wasn't right... something didn't add up. A sudden feeling of confusion hit me like a lead balloon. Was I still dreaming and hadn't woken up yet? I pinched the skin on my arm with two fingers. *Ouch,* I thought to myself, that hurt but at least I knew I was awake. I studied the room around me. The only one on my ward—it was quiet. Had they given me another medication that was making me hallucinate?

'Are you okay, Miss Murrell?' the doctor asked, watching me.

'Yes, I'm fine. Erm... what day is it today?' I asked.

'It's Wednesday. It is the 13th of September 2003. Is there a problem?'

'No, no. Everything is great.' He didn't seem convinced.

'Okay, I need to go now as I have surgery in an hour. I will get one of the nurses to check in on you before breakfast is brought around.' He turned to walk away and left the ward.

I sat up quickly in bed and reached to the end to get my clipboard. Grabbing it from the rails, I studied the information on the first page. My name, address, and date of birth was all correct. The data was all correct, but something that stood out in big glaring letters was my blood type. *They must have it completely wrong and mixed my results up with someone else's as I am almost certain that that is not my blood type.*

Just as I was studying the rest of my details, the nurse walked in. I panicked, dropped the clipboard on the floor, tangled the drip in my arm with the bed covers and looked at her in shock.

'It's okay, I will get it.' She rushed over to the bed, picking up the clipboard and placing it back at the end. Untangling the wires above the bed and plumping up my pillows, I sat back, holding my head down looking all sorry for myself.

'Sorry about that,' I said without looking up.

'Is there something wrong?' she asked, looking at the monitor at the side of the bed. My heart rate was high, the screen was beeping as it rose over the higher line on the graph.

I could have stayed quiet, I should have let it stew on my mind, but I needed clarity for my own sanity.

'I'm so sorry, I'm just... I'm confused,' I said.

'Confused about what?' the nurse asked.

'The doctor said my blood type was B RhD negative, but I am confident that both my parents are A RhD positive. How is that possible?' I looked up at her caring face, it seemed to turn to confusion as well.

'Well, it's not possible. Two parents with A RhD positive can't have a child with B RhD negative blood type. You may want to check that with them again as you may have it wrong.' It didn't seem to bother her in the slightest. Why would it? That must be it, I had their blood type wrong the whole time.

'Breakfast is yoghurt and pancakes... would you like a fruit or plain yoghurt this morning? Don't worry if you can only manage a mouthful but do try something little.' She asked me this question every morning. *Just try something little* as if it was the easiest thing in the world. Food just hadn't been the same for the last month because I knew the minute I ate something, it would make me sick for the next twelve hours.

'Fruit yoghurt and a glass of water, please. Thank you,' I replied.

'You're welcome.' She smiled and left the ward.

Now that I had this in my head, I couldn't let it go. I had to find out what the hell was going on.

I reached into the small drawer in the cabinet beside the bed and got out my mobile phone. I tried to keep it in there as much as possible unless I heard it bleep when someone texted me.

I began typing.

'MUM, QUICK QUESTION... NOTHING SERIOUS BUT WHAT BLOOD TYPE ARE YOU AND DAD? R X'. She was normally very fast at responding. I must have definitely got it wrong, and they were both B RhD negative as well. Then I could put my mind at rest and get on with the rest of my boring day in bed.

My phone began ringing. She was calling me.

'Rose,' she said as I pressed the green button to answer.

'Yes... I can't talk right n—'

She stopped me abruptly. 'I'm with your father right now, can I call you later to talk?' She seemed agitated and in a hurry.

'I just need to know your blood type, Mum. We can speak later, I'm sure that—'

Again, she cut me off. 'Rose, I will call you later. What time are visiting hours and we will pop in?' she asked.

'Mum, just your blood type. That's all I...' I tried to quickly ask but it was too late.

'Okay, darling, see you later.' She hung up.

I looked at my phone—that was weird. I only asked a quick question. Why didn't she answer me?

I text again.

'VISITING HOURS 5-7 BUT I NEED TO KNOW YOUR BLOOD TYPE. WHAT IS YOURS AND DAD'S AGAIN? R X'

I sat looking at the phone for a response, but I didn't get one. I flicked up the front and placed it beside my bed again. There is nothing more dangerous than an overactive mind. When you don't have anything to occupy it, you find yourself in all sorts of imaginable situations. My imagination was incredible at times. That's why I was always busy, always running at a million miles an hour because the minute I stop, it had terrible consequences.

Why couldn't she just answer my question? I had the most horrible feeling.

'MORNING, HONEY. MISSING YOU GUYS. HOW'S JACK?' I picked up my phone and started texting Daniel. No response, so I put it back on the side.

I looked out the window at the trees blowing in the gentle breeze outside, it was a cloudy, murky day and the sun had all but vanished since the week of sunshine we had in the summer. That wasted another five minutes of my time before I began thinking again.

What if my parents are blood type A, and I am blood type B, what does that mean?

My breakfast arrived and it was all I could do to keep the tiniest of mouthfuls down. The nauseous feeling in my stomach and the pending visit from my parents meant I had about two spoonfuls and then gave up. At least I'd had something, I guess. The cup of tea was good though. I hadn't managed to keep a whole cup of tea down for weeks.

'Okay, do you want the good news or the good news, Rose?' Doctor Wheeler appeared from nowhere.

'Erm, I'm guessing the good news then, please?' He looked extremely pleased with himself.

'We all knew that it was extreme morning sickness that lasted all day, and we knew that it was a condition called Hyperemesis Gravidarum or (HGD) as it is known. You have experienced this before. What we didn't know before was what caused it. Research now shows that HGD is caused by a few factors, mainly genetics, body chemistry, foetal gender and high levels of cortisol. Genetic causes are the biggest factor here and they are the GDF15 and PGR genes.' He looked up at me as if to make sure I was following what he was saying, but I was completely puzzled.

'What I am trying to say here, Rose, is that we know you have HGD. A severe form of morning sickness, believed to have been caused by certain proteins in the body. The only way we can help you is by prescribing a different anti-sickness medication. It won't completely cure your symptoms, but they will be manageable. Meaning, you may be sick once or twice early in the morning, but as the day progresses, it will move to a dull, nagging sensation of wanting to be sick.'

He occasionally looked up at me from his notes to ensure I was listening and following him.

'This means that, hopefully, you should be able to keep down small amounts of food and liquid and enable you to provide all the vitamins and minerals necessary to feed your unborn child. Don't worry too much about how healthy the food is, just try and keep something down. Even if it is a piece of toast or a biscuit. Anything you can supply your body is better than nothing.' He reassuringly smiled at me.

'Thank you, does that mean I'll be able to return home, or will I have to stay in longer?' I asked.

'I would like to start you on the medication straight away. Let's monitor your condition and see how you are tomorrow, and if successful, you can go home. If it's not, then we need to go back to the drawing board and rethink how we manage this, but we will get you home.' He looked like he had just returned from surgery, the remaining marks of indents on the bridge of his nose from wearing glasses and he still had a surgical hat on and a face covering wrapped around his neck.

'Thank you, Doctor Wheeler, I really do appreciate it,' I replied and was thankful they were doing their best for me. I just missed my family so much. Trying to keep still and occupied was difficult for me.

'You're welcome. The nurse will bring you in the new tablets. Small round yellow ones that you insert under your top lip against your gum and slowly let them dissolve.' With that, he left the ward.

That afternoon, I read a Women's Health magazine that I found totally boring. I did a Sudoku puzzle that was easy and took me around two minutes to complete, I then checked my phone for about the 15346 time that day but had no messages, and I overthought so many things in my mind until I heard that amazing voice coming running down the corridor—Jack.

Holding hands with his dad, Jack came running up to the bed and gave me a huge hug. Ah, it felt so good.

'Hello, Mummy, I did something for you today.' He passed me a beautifully drawn card that he had made for me. It had a picture of what looked like two adults, a child, a dog and a box on wheels.

'That is beautiful. Thank you very much, Jack, can you tell me what you have drawn?' I asked, waiting for his explanation as it was so much easier than me guessing. He pointed out all the things on the card and talked me through it.

'So, this is Daddy, and this is you, that's me and Harry, and that is my baby brother in the pram.' He pointed to the box with wheels on.

'Oh, okay, so Mummy is having a little boy, is she?' I smiled as I asked him the question.

'Yes, and he is asleep in your tummy right now, isn't he? That's what Daddy said.' Daniel helped him to jump on the end of the bed with his feet swinging over the side. He sat there with a huge smile on his face, as he always did.

I laughed. 'You do make me laugh, Jack. And what should

we call your little brother?' I asked, looking at Daniel to see what his response was as well.

'Hmmm.' Jack put his little fingers on his chin and looked up to the ceiling as if he was thinking long and hard about my question. 'I... quite like Harry,' he said.

'We can't call him Harry as the dog is called Harry. We can't have two, otherwise, they will be confused.' I laughed again at him.

'Okay, Luca!' he shouted. 'I like Luca. That's a nice name.'

'Luca... oh, okay. Where did that come from?' I asked him. He just shrugged, swinging his legs and looking around the ward, taking in everything.

'Luca. Well, that's one for the list.' Daniel smiled and turned to me.

'How's my girl?' he asked.

'I'm all good.' I leaned into him so no one else could hear me, not even Jack. 'Please get me out of here, I'm going crazy and want to come home.'

'You're in the best place, Rose, if I take you home now, you will just be back in again next week. Stay, relax and get yourself better. We've got everything covered at home. Chill and look after my second little boy.'

Wow, there's a lot of pressure for this to be a boy. What if she turns out to be a girl?

'Rose, your tablets.' The nurse handed me a small white pot with two little yellow round tablets placed strategically right in the middle at the bottom. They must have only been about 5mm in diameter, but even that seemed to worry me that they might make me sick.

'Okay, thank you.' I smiled as I took the pot from her.

'Pop them under your top lip, keep it against your gum so it slowly disintegrates, and then take a small sip of water. The doctor says he will pop back first thing in the morning, but you need to take another as soon as you wake in the morning. I will bring it to you later tonight so you have it ready.' She smiled both at Daniel and Jack in turn as she left.

'Thank you,' I said, looking at the tiny little pill.

'More medication,' Daniel said. 'Is it working though?'

'Well, I haven't been sick for twenty-four hours, so I'm hoping so. I still feel rough but at least I'm keeping food and drink down, I guess.' I smiled at Daniel with all the effort I could muster.

He leaned forward and kissed me on the head.

They both stayed for around an hour, long enough for Jack to start getting bored and fidgety. He didn't understand why I was in, nor did he get the concept that he couldn't talk as loudly as he normally would and had to keep his voice down.

Just as they were leaving, I could hear my parents' voices. Maybe finally I would now get to the bottom of my blood group after it had been bugging me all day long.

'Hello, sweetie. Oh, I'm sorry, we can come back later if you want to spend time with Jack and Daniel.' She was so apologetic.

'No, it's okay, we were off anyway. Jack is getting fidgety and I need to get him home to have his dinner and get ready for bed, so we will leave you to it.' I didn't want them to go but I knew that they had their routine to get back to. Daniel helped Jack down from the bed. They both gave me a kiss and said their goodbyes and left. I placed Jack's handmade card right next to my phone on the bedside table.

My mum came over to the bed and squeezed my hand.

'Are you okay? I hate to see you like this. How are you feeling? Is there anything we can do?' So many questions that

I didn't have a chance to say anything. My dad stood fidgeting just as Jack had done at the end of the bed. What on earth was the matter with them both? It was as if they were about to drop a bombshell.

'I'm fine, I'm fine. I'm hoping these new tablets will work and I can go home tomorrow.' I smiled at my mum, then my dad.

'Oh, that's great news,' she said, over-enthusiastically.

'Mum, Dad. I need to ask you a question as it has been driving me insane all day.' I looked at them both, but they had their heads down, avoiding eye contact. Something was very peculiar.

'See, the doctor said I am B RhD negative, but I think they have my results wrong because I am almost certain that you are both A RhD positive. That can't be right, can it?' I looked my mum straight in the eye, her still holding my hand. Her hands almost began to tremble. Her eyes looked watery and sad, and her bottom lip quivered, but she said nothing.

'Mum... I don't understand. It's not possible, is it?' My eyebrows frowned and I moved my gaze to my dad. 'Dad, what's going on? What...' I stopped talking, I think I knew the answer deep down but didn't want it to be true or acknowledge it.

'Mum...' I said again, hoping to prompt her into telling me.

'Rose, darling.' She sobbed.

'Mum... what is it?' I could feel a bulge in my throat. To see her cry made me cry.

'The thing is... it is possible.' She looked at me, right into my eyes, into my heart.

'It's possible because your parents are B RhD negative too. Well, one is.' She had tears falling down her cheeks, she looked in pain like someone had stabbed her chest a million times. Her bottom lip was all creased and torn.

'I don't understand, you are my...' *Oh my god!* I stopped in my tracks. *No, this can't be happening.* I suddenly realised what she was saying. I tore my hand from hers and threw both my hands over my eyes, I let rip. My whole body and my chest were shaking as I sobbed my heart out. *This can't be happening, not now, not ever. How could this be true?* I felt her hand rest on my shoulder.

'Rose, please, sweetie. I meant to say your biological parents. We are your parents, we always will be, and we love you so much, we wanted to tell you so many times but there never was the right time to tell you. We...' I couldn't open my eyes or take my hands away from my face, but I could hear them both sobbing and sniffling as they cried. No wonder she didn't want to tell me over text. My whole life was a lie.

'Rose, darling. Please say something.' I could feel her teary eyes waiting for a response from me.

I slowly withdrew my hands from my face to look at the parents I once knew and loved, I was instead sitting in front of two complete strangers. Who were they? Were they even related to me? How could I not even know this? Would they have told me if I hadn't found out? So many questions running through my mind. Was this actually happening to me?

My dad walked around to the other side of the bed to where my mum was standing. The two of them held my hand like I was a five-year-old little girl. 'Please let us explain,' he said, almost begging me to listen and perhaps understand what he had to say.

I looked at him, deep into his eyes, into his soul. I could tell he was hurting just as much as I was, but he had a story to tell, and I owed it to him to listen. Confused, upset, angry, hurt and emotional all at the same time, I agreed to hear them out.

'Let me start at the beginning.' My mum pulled the chair beside the bed closer so that she was sat right next to me, still gripping onto my hand like her life depended on it.

'I never told you I had a sister, Rose. I never told you because she reminds me so much of you and I miss her so much.' Tear after tear rolled down her face. I was still so confused but I let her continue anyway. What did her sister have to do with me?

'She was ten years younger than me and such a wild child, but her heart was the biggest heart that I ever had the pleasure of knowing. She had the most beautiful green eyes, just like yours, and her spirit so free. The love that she and James had for each other was incredible. Just like you and Daniel but...'

She paused to wipe her teary eyes on the tissue she had pulled from the box on my bedside table.

'I just don't understand.' I sat there on the hospital bed like a lost puppy.

'Rose, you are my niece, not my daughter!' she bluntly answered my confusion. 'We should have told you earlier, but the pain just didn't go away, and it got harder and harder to tell you.'

'Then where is my mum, what happened?' I think I knew the answer but didn't want to accept it.

'Your mother, Scarlett, she was just twenty years old at the time. You were only two.' She began to sob, finding it hard to produce the words. My dad reached his other hand across the bed in front of me and held hers too, I could see him squeezing it with encouragement.

'I still remember the call. Your sister and her were so close. She was just finishing work. I said I would have you for the day and take you to the park with your sisters. James went to pick her up, but the car kept breaking down. This time, the car failed at a red light and a lorry didn't stop as it was dark. Their lights had failed. There was nothing the paramedics, the police or fire brigade could do. They died instantly, together.' My mum looked down to the floor, her lips quivering, her tears soaking the sheets.

I felt numb—completely cold. There were no words, nor could I think of any. I sat in silence, motionless, frozen. More tears rolling down my face and onto my chest.

'Rose, we have always loved you like a daughter since the moment we met you. You are your mother's daughter, the wild side, the beauty, the free spirit and the loving nature, but the love we have for you is just as strong as the love she had for you. The only saving grace on that day is that you weren't in the car with them.' My dad squeezed my hand too. I had never seen him cry before, he was such a strong man, my rock and my absolute protector. The look of him now sent me into shock. He had turned into an emotional mess, crumbling in my presence.

Of course I loved them, my feelings for them hadn't changed despite the news, but I was struggling to come to terms with the fact that they weren't my real parents, my biological mum and dad. I had so many questions.

'Do you have any pictures of them?' I asked. My mum instantly looked up at me.

'We have so many. I kept a cardboard box of all her keepsake items that I wanted to eventually give to you one day. Your nan was so distraught when she passed that she wouldn't even mention her name, so we collected all pictures of her into a box to keep them safe. It was as if she vanished that day.

I remember it like it was yesterday. Friday 14th May, 1982. Of course, James' parents wanted custody of you, but they knew how close you were to your cousins that they gave us their blessing to adopt you.' She gave a slight smile, one of pure endearment.

'So, my sisters aren't my sisters, they are my cousins?' I asked.

'Technically, yes, but they don't know your history either. We didn't think it was fair to tell them without you knowing. Well, Karen remembers it a little, but Ashley has no idea.' My mum glanced over at my dad, he looked completely drained.

That explained a lot. Karen, my eldest sister, was like a second mum to me. Always there, supportive, authoritative and super protective over me. Any time I needed her, she was there, checking I was okay.

She always seemed to be the sensible one, but the older I got, I realised that she appeared to be a little more relaxed and like me in many ways.

'So, what happens now?' That was a question that I didn't know myself let alone expect them to answer.

'I guess it depends on you,' my mum replied. 'I can understand that you are probably angry and upset with us for not telling you sooner, Rose, but it was never meant to happen this way. There was never a good time to tell you. Then when Jack came along, we didn't want to lose you and him. She would have been so proud of you all. I can remember the day you were born and the day that Scarlett and James brought you home.' She sniffled.

Both my hands were hot and sweaty, tight from the pressure of my mum and dad's grip. I looked up to the ceiling. *Do*

I even call them Mum and Dad now? Should I be calling them Aunty and Uncle? I felt cheated that I didn't get to meet my real parents, but surely my real parents were the ones that raised me, loved me, nurtured me, put up with all my tantrums, mood swings and heartache? I couldn't have asked for better parents. They didn't have to take me under their wing.

Still, in the back of my mind, I was struggling to deal with everything they had told me. It was as if I was going to wake up any minute and it would all be a horrible dream.

I began to withdraw both my hands from their grasp. *Should I hug them? Do I shake their hands and say thank you for an amazing upbringing?* It shouldn't make a difference, but it did. I felt like a different person, suddenly lonely as if someone had shut one door on me but offered me another couple of doors to choose from. I looked around the room for clues, it felt like minutes had passed yet it was only seconds.

'We have so much to tell you and show you if you'll only let us?' She edged forward, making my decision as to whether to hug her or not all the easier. Our embrace felt like one where we were saying goodbye, tight, strong and with so much feeling. Eventually, she let go and it was my dad's turn. His big arms wrapped around my back and were holding me so tight.

'I don't care if you aren't my biological daughter,' he whispered in my ear. 'I love you just like you are my own and there is nothing anyone can do or say that will change it. You are still my beautiful Rose, and I will do everything in my power to protect you, even if you are twenty-three. I'm sorry if we hurt you by not telling you sooner, but we didn't want to lose you.' His hug became tighter than ever, my ribcage under pressure, before letting me go and staring at me.

'Visiting time has five minutes left, please.' The nurse entered the ward and gave us notice that visitors had to leave to make way for dinner and allow rest for myself as well as the other patients.

Stunned and shocked by the whole situation, I turned to them both. 'I guess I'll see you tomorrow then,' I said.

'Of course you will, Rose,' she replied. She had an air of disappointment in her voice, but instead of saying anything, she sniffed, wiping her nose with the screwed-up tissue in her hand, collected her handbag that had been placed on the floor by my bed and ushered for my dad to leave.

'Get some rest, you hear?' Dad said as he followed Mum out of the ward.

I slammed my body back against the bed and just stared up at the ceiling.

'What's the matter, Rose?' the nurse asked as she wheeled the bed table over towards me and popped my dinner on it.

'Uh, if it doesn't rain, it pours!' I shrugged. 'Have you ever been told something that makes you question literally every-thing about your entire life?' I sat up, looking straight at her.

'Erm, kind of,' she replied. She clearly had no idea what I was talking about but interpreted it in the best way she could.

I wasn't very hungry; I used the fork to push the food around my plate. Roast beef, mashed potatoes and vegetables with gravy. It sounded nice but I wasn't in the mood for eating anything at all. I just wanted it all to go away. That wasn't happening anytime soon.

I rolled to one side so that the rest of the ward and the nurses couldn't see me and just closed my eyes, crying with pain. I shook and shuddered; my whole body distraught from the news. So much of this didn't make sense, but in a way, there were a few things that now made perfect sense. Pieces of my puzzle were suddenly fitting into place.

I still loved my parents, there was no doubt in my mind about that. It wasn't as if I could speak to my biological parents and meet them to ask lots of questions I had. They simply weren't there. There wasn't anything I could do about it, and it wasn't my mum and dad's fault either. They didn't have to take me on. I felt even worse about the heartache I had caused them now. What an absolute pain in the backside I must have been growing up. They could have told me at any time and given me up as their responsibility, but they didn't. They loved me unconditionally. To throw that all back in their faces now would be an absolute insult.

Yes, I had so many things I wanted to know about my biological father and his family, but to be honest, that wasn't important anymore. What was important was my mum and dad, and I wanted to continue calling them that. They weren't my aunty and uncle... they were *MY* mum and dad. The two people in my life that had always been there for me, regardless, raising me as their own and giving me everything I could have ever wanted.

22

BABY BLUE EYES

I tried every old wife's tale I could think of from drinking castor oil, eating pineapple, spicy foods, sex... you name it, I did it, but nothing would make my baby hurry up and enter the world. Day by day, I was getting more and more frustrated. I was heavier than I'd ever been, weighing in at 11.5 stone—4.5 stone more than when I was admitted to hospital eight months ago.

I couldn't sleep, I couldn't breathe, and my stomach was so stretched, it felt like it was going to tear. I was, however, thankful that I had made it almost to full term.

I took a walk earlier that day and played a game with Jack. I asked him how many steps he could walk up and down, and we would count as we went. The idea was to hopefully get my bump engaged and I was hoping it would bring on contractions, but still nothing.

I had a hospital appointment at 4 pm with the midwife for a membrane sweep—it was my last resort. Ten days overdue, and if he didn't come soon, I couldn't take it anymore. I was at my wit's end. I had been told that the sweep was previously successful as it released hormones (prostaglandins) that would hopefully start the labour. I had my fingers, toes and everything crossed. Surely, they wouldn't let me go any longer than ten days, I would burst for sure. There was no physical room left inside me.

I sat in the waiting room as patiently as I could. Even my clothes felt stretched and under pressure. I was uncomfortable when I sat, so I stood. Daniel grew impatient as I fidgeted around, trying to find some form of comfort.

A petite nurse with short, dark hair opened the room door and called out my name. I almost ran to her as Daniel gathered his belongings together and followed me.

'How are we?' she asked.

'Fed up,' I replied.

'Uh-huh. Nearly there.' She didn't seem phased at all by my response. I was probably the one-hundred-and-first woman that day who had said the same thing. She patted the bed, prompting me to get onto it, but because of the size of me, I needed a hand. Daniel came to my aid, holding my hand with his and holding onto my arm to help lift me into place. I was the size of a whale.

'Much movement?' I wasn't sure if she was asking me the question or about the baby.

'I'm sorry, you mean the baby?' I thought I would check first.

'Yes, of course the baby.' She was not the chirpiest of midwives I had met during my pregnancy. Almost military in style.

'Erm, yes, a fair bit. He seems very active at night, kicking and moving around, but a little quieter during the day. Do you think the sweep will help to bring the labour along?' I looked at Daniel with hope in my eyes.

'Oh, yes. The sweep will bring on the baby. You should see something in the next couple of days. If there are still no signs in forty-eight hours, you need to ring the hospital again and we will induce you. Break your waters.' The midwife was busy searching in all the medical drawers. I'm not sure what she was looking for, but she seemed very preoccupied.

'Oh, that's good. So, hopefully, he should be here in a couple of days,' I almost muttered under my breath as I squeezed Daniel's hand. He seemed quite content, sat in the chair next to the bed. He looked up at me and smiled. I think he was just as fed up as I was and my constant moaning about being uncomfortable and tired.

'Okay, make yourself comfortable while I find some gloves. If you would like to remove your clothes from the waist down and put the blanket over your waist. I will give you a few moments to get ready.' She had her back to me the whole time but was writing some notes on a piece of paper.

There was nothing dignified about any of the checks during my pregnancy.

Total strangers have a look and a feel around your private area. I have lost count of the number of times that someone said to me to take a seat on the bed, remove your clothes and lay there with your legs wide open. To be honest though, at this precise moment, the only thing I cared about was getting this baby out and me being able to walk and breathe again with ease.

They say that having your second baby is easier than your first because your birth canal has already been used and stretched and everything is more relaxed. For me, I thought it was worse as now I knew what to expect, I knew exactly how much it hurt and how exhausted I was. The saving grace was that, in the end, I would have a beautifully perfect baby, my baby, our baby, that suddenly made the whole thing so worthwhile. All the pain and fear disappeared from last time. I would do it a hundred times over if it meant having a precious baby like Jack at the end.

The room went quiet, Daniel sat in embarrassment as the midwife carried out the sweep. He looked around the room to look less awkward, but I sat there laughing at him.

'Right, I want you to go home, make sure you have a substantial meal and get some rest. He or she could be here before you know it,' the midwife declared as she started to remove her gloves.

'Oh okay.' I seemed quite shocked it was all done and I was free to go home. I think I was secretly thinking that suddenly my waters would break and my labour would start. This baby wasn't budging, completely happy inside and in the warm.

I wrapped my arms around my bump like I was helping to lift him up, and said to myself, 'Come on then, little one, today isn't the day, it's home we go.' Daniel got up and helped me from the bed like an old woman, incapable of doing anything myself right now.

'Hey, they will come when they are ready. Let's get some sleep in while we can, I'm shattered.' Daniel held my hand as we walked, and I waddled down the corridor, leaving the hospital to go home.

That evening, it was as normal as it could have been. I couldn't eat a huge amount, every mouthful I swallowed felt like it was just sitting in my chest, and my stomach had no room to hold anything more. We both put Jack to bed together, read him a story and sat on the sofa watching television, but I couldn't settle. My back ached and my stomach was in pain.

As I looked over at Daniel, his eyes were getting heavier and heavier, he nodded off a couple of times as I sat there watching him.

There it was. That feeling I knew oh so well. A tightening of my sides, my whole lower body clenching like it was getting ready for something to happen. *I'm pretty sure that was a contraction,* I thought to myself, but I sat still waiting for it to happen again. Maybe I was just hoping it was as I patiently watched the clock, counting the minutes in case another appeared. Ten minutes and nothing. *Oh well, I'm sure they will come when they are good and ready.* I stood to get a glass of water and felt it again.

That was most certainly a contraction, I could remember them from Jack's labour. Excited but nervous at the same time, I held my stomach and took a deep breath, waiting for the feeling to pass. I didn't want to wake Daniel until I was certain that it wasn't a false alarm. Another couple came and passed, I just paced up and down the kitchen and into the dining room. They weren't painful yet, just uncomfortable, but they seemed to be quicker and faster than when I had Jack. It was 09.02 pm and Jack had only been asleep for a couple of hours.

'Daniel, Daniel,' I whispered. Shaking his shoulder to wake him up. 'Pssttt.'

'Huh?' Sleepily, he opened his eyes and looked at me. 'What?'

'I think it's time. I can feel the contractions have started.' I smiled, a bubble of excitement rose up and through my body. Daniel shot up instantly, his eyes burst wide open like he had been hit by an electric current.

'I'll get the bag. I need to wake Jack up and take him to

your mum and dad's. Are you ready? What do you need?' He went into overdrive, panic mode, itching to go.

'Slow down, it's fine. We have hours. I'll call the labour ward... can you call or text my mum and let her know?'

Daniel was suddenly rushing around like a whirlwind, yet this was the second time we were going through this. I, on the other hand, was treating it like the first time and thinking I had all the time in the world.

We woke up sleepy-eyed Jack from his bed and helped him to get his dressing gown and slippers on, packing a little overnight bag and some clothes for the morning. Instead of dropping him off, my mum had agreed to come over to ours and pick him up.

I could then concentrate on my own bag, which I hadn't packed or organised. Ten days overdue and you would have thought that I had it all planned out, but no, in true Rose style, I left everything to the last minute as per usual.

What did you need anyway? Spare pair of clothes, some new underwear and baby nappies and clothes. It wasn't as if I was going on holiday for a week. *Pack the bare minimum,* I thought to myself.

'Oh, that's strange,' I muttered under my breath. Watching the chaos unravel around me, Jack was crying, he wanted to go back to bed and was tired, Daniel was trying not to lose his patience, and Harry was barking at the door. I was guessing that my parents had just turned up.

'What's strange?' Daniel must have heard my confused mumble.

'Oh, nothing.' I could feel the contractions getting harder and stronger a lot quicker than the first time around. How bizarre, maybe I didn't have as much time as I thought I had with Jack. I didn't want to worry Daniel, he would be speeding me to the hospital, zooming me up to the labour ward in a wheelchair the moment we arrived.

'Hello, darling, are you okay?' My mum's familiar voice came from downstairs. Things were still a little strange between us.

'Yep. Oohhh...' I cried out to her, I doubled over, holding on to my bump as it all tightened.

No matter how old you are, there is always something so comforting in your mum being there when you are poorly, sick or in pain, despite our situation. I needed her, just as she was always there for me, but this time, Daniel and I wanted to experience our second child enter the world together, just the two of us—calm and relaxed. Something special between the two of us. Besides, I wanted to make sure that Jack was being looked after.

'Go and get yourself to hospital. This one may be quicker.' She smiled and looked up to me as I made my way down the stairs, one step at a time.

If you have ever experienced the late stage of pregnancy, you will relate to me when I say that trying to manoeuvre yourself down a flight of stairs is not the easiest of tasks, especially during contractions. The baby is so big and heavy that you feel them resting right at the centre of your opening, pushing down, pinching your spinal nerves, making every movement such a mission to achieve. Weirdly, though, I wasn't tired, I felt full of energy and ready to meet my new little love.

We said our goodbyes to Jack and to my parents as if it was the last time I was going to see them.

I thought I was prepared to breeze through this labour like I did with Jack. Don't get me wrong, it was incredibly painful, but this time, it seemed so much more painful, quicker and stronger. I didn't tell Daniel, but he could see that I was gritting my teeth and clenching my fists more frequently with the pain's intensity. If he wasn't careful, this baby was going to arrive in the car.

We arrived at the hospital, Daniel in panic mode.

'Do you want me to get you a wheelchair?' he asked.

'No, I can walk.' Fed up with all the fussing.

'Let me give you a hand.' He wrapped his arm underneath mine as I climbed out of the car.

'I'm fine, I can manage.' My patience was running thin with him and I pulled my arm away.

'Let me grab your bag then.' Daniel looked like a lost puppy, not knowing how he could help or what he could do.

'Oooh...' I bent down, the contractions squeezing my sides and pausing me for a moment.

'Are you okay?' Daniel bent down with me by my side.

'Yep, fine.' My pain threshold was normally high, but even this was testing me. If I did it the first time with gas and air, I could do it the second time. I took a big deep breath in and out, getting to my feet. One step in front of the other as I approached the main entrance.

The hospital was quiet. It was the middle of the night, but I was still expecting it to be busier than it was.

Following the maternity ward signs, we walked the corridor together, quietly. I couldn't think of much to say in the way of a conversation. Instead, I kept wondering what my little one was going to look like and how heavy he would be. I couldn't wait.

There was still that thought in the back of my mind though... what if something was wrong, what if there were complications, would I lose him before I had even got to meet him? Some things were out of my control, but it didn't stop me from worrying about him. I had to concentrate on the here and now and get this baby out the best I could. I had my mind made up, just as I did with Jack, that I wanted no pain relief apart from gas and air. He was coming out as naturally as possible. That's what we were made for, to reproduce, so unless I really, really needed it, I was going to do this on my own.

As soon as we arrived outside the maternity ward, Daniel pressed the security buzzer and waited for someone to come.

'Oohhh.' Another contraction hit me like a tidal wave, my whole body in lockdown. I had a feeling that I didn't have that long. A strong sense of needing to push but I had to hold it as much as I could until I got to the ward.

'Hold on, honey, we are nearly there. Squeeze my hand.' Daniel was only trying to help but I slapped it out of the way, gripping hold of the door handle, dealing with the pain.

Daniel glared at me but didn't say a word. He didn't dare to, he knew I didn't mean it but was just in pain and frustrated.

'Okay, my lovely, let's get you into labour room six for assessment.' A lovely midwife answered the door and walked us through the corridor.

It was now 11.06 pm. Over two hours had passed by the time we had left the house and got to the hospital. The contractions were harder and faster than I had ever experienced, especially with Jack, but I was adamant about pain relief. Maybe it was just because I had forgotten how intense they were.

Before we reached the room, she asked a couple of questions, which Daniel answered consecutively.

'Have you been timing the contractions? Have you felt much movement of the baby?' He was on the ball with the answers that I didn't even need to say anything, so I focused on the pain.

'Would you like to go in the birthing pool? It's vacant at the moment?' she asked.

I had never thought about having a water birth before, but several questions rang through my mind... *What happens to the baby when they are born? Will they not drown in all that water? Is it safe? Is it dangerous?* I looked up at Daniel to see what his reaction to her question was.

'Up to you, honey, what do you want to do?' He referred the decision straight back to me.

'Erm... okay. I'll give it a try.'

'Our ladies all say that it is so lovely, more relaxed, a calmer birth, but it is entirely your decision. Let's fill her up and see what you think, you can always change your mind.' She smiled and led the way.

She approached the next door on the left of the corridor and opened it wide so that we could both step in. I gripped the doorframe as yet another contraction took hold and stopped me in my tracks. The room distracted me slightly from the pain as I looked around.

Half-expecting a clinical, medical space that most labour rooms were like, I was surprised to find it looking more therapeutic like a wellbeing centre. Right in the middle of the room was a large round bath—the birthing pool. It looked big enough to have five or more people in, more like a small swimming pool. A bed with a side table against the wall on the left-hand side and sideboards with equipment on to the right (what you would normally expect). The two windows on the back of the wall were blacked out with dark blinds drawn, and as I looked up, the ceiling was painted in either dark blue or black, I couldn't make out which it was, plastered with glow-in-the-dark stars. The room seemed almost magical. *Why didn't I think of having this type of birth before?*

The midwife began filling the bath, small bouts of steam filled the room.

'Make yourself comfortable. It's up to you, you can either remove the bottom half of your clothes or take everything off. You may find that you remove the bottom half first, then when you are hot and relaxed, you can remove the rest.' She continued to fill the pool until it was about halfway and then twisted the taps off slowly. 'I hope that is a nice temperature, but again, we can adjust it to suit you.'

She seemed like a lovely lady, short bobbed blonde hair, dark eyes and a calming aura about her. I wanted her to stay and guide me through the birth. I wasn't one for covering up, but at the same time, I wanted a little dignity. I removed my leggings and underwear, placing them in a neat pile at the end of the bed. Daniel popped my bag on the chair in the corner and walked over with me.

I climbed up onto the first step of the two-step platform to get in, but just as my foot lifted to dip into the water, I felt a gush of water from between my legs. I gasped. 'Aahhh... I think my waters have broken, what do I do now?' I looked at Daniel in panic and then, in turn, to her. He held my hand.

'It's okay, it's fine. Let's get you in, sit down and we will take all your details, I will buzz to the others to get that cleaned. Baby is on its way.' She smiled reassuringly but I still couldn't help feeling anxious. My waters didn't break with Jack, it was a completely different birth to last time. I know I was a grown woman, but I wanted my mum, she always made everything okay.

The water was so pleasant, not too hot that I was sweating but not too cold either that I was shivering. One foot in, the water trickling down my thighs, the second foot in. Daniel holding my hand and arm to help me steady myself into the pool, my overstretched, tired and aching body lowered into the water and I sat down. The large t-shirt that I still had on was half wet and half dry, my back against the wall of the pool, it felt good, probably the best I had felt in days.

'I still need to check you and the baby through the whole process as the pool could slow the contractions down and we don't want that. We want it to be as comfortable as possible for you but ultimately move it along so that the baby is out as soon as possible.' She reached for my hand so that it was draped over the side and connected me to the blood pressure monitor. She listened, checked all my figures, and appeared to be happy.

'Let's give baby a quick check. My name is Jess, by the way, and I will be with you the whole night.' Thank goodness for that, I smiled back and let her do her job. Jess placed the baby monitor on my stomach and listened. We could hear the heartbeat. Daniel's eyes welled up; he looked like he was going to cry but composed himself. I, on the other hand, kept thinking that the worst was yet to come. Getting them out and safe was when I would be happy.

'Sounds like they are quite happy in there, not stressed or worried, so let's keep things going.' Jess stood up, taking the monitor with her, walked over to the equipment bench and came back with a small face towel, passing it to Daniel. 'If she wants to, and if it helps, place this on her forehead or wipe her face so she feels okay.' I wasn't sure if that was such a good idea or not, or whether it would annoy me, but if it gave Daniel something to do, then so be it.

There were two large blue gym balls against the wall in

the room. She bounced them both over next to the pool and gave one to Daniel whilst she sat on the other.

'I know it looks like we are about to do a workout, but trust me, by the end of the night, without one of these leaning over the pool, your back will feel like it won't ever work again. These have been a lifesaver with the last couple of births.' She laughed at Daniel who looked slightly confused.

The two of them wobbling around in front of the pool, I suddenly sat up, another contraction started, but this time, in the water. It didn't feel quite as bad as the last few. I gripped the sides, let my body do what it needed to do, and went with it. Breathing steadily as it progressed.

'Ooohhh. I want to push, it feels so near...' I said, straining.

'Go on, push... listen to your body,' Jess said, sitting up and holding my hand.

'Come on, sweetheart, you can do this.' Daniel had hold of my other hand as I pushed with every muscle in my body.

'I think I need gas and air.'

'I'm afraid you can't have any painkillers whilst in the bath in case you are dizzy, we don't want you passing out while in the pool, it could be dangerous to you and the baby. If you want gas and air, we will need to get you out.' She looked at me like she was telling me some bad news.

Ah okay, I wasn't expecting that, I thought to myself. *Do I stay in the pool and ride it out or do I get out?*

'Okay. I want to stay in here then.' Daniel looked at me in such a proud way. *I've got this,* I thought. *I can do it.* Determined as ever.

Another contraction, another push. This time, I could

feel my whole lower body burning, my opening stretching as I clenched down, then it slowly faded to a dull throbbing.

'Let's see what's going on.' Jess stood up and reached along the side to a mirror on a large arm. My eyes widened as I wondered what she was going to do with it.

'Daniel, take this.' She handed it to him. He looked curiously at her. 'I want you to place this in the water. Rose, if you can remove your top so we have a clear view of the mirror, kneel up for me and, Daniel, you place it between her legs to see where baby is.' He did as he was told, I took off my top, throwing it on the floor outside the pool. One arm around Daniel's shoulders and the other arm around Jess's, I kneeled up. All three of us looking in the mirror, only I couldn't see as my stomach was so large that I hadn't seen downstairs for about six months.

'Okay, we have the crown showing so they are nearly there. I need you to give a hard push, the hardest you can, and a squeeze on the next contraction and their head should be out.' I looked at Daniel and wanted to cry.

'Oh, Rose, good girl. Come on. Let's do this.' It felt like a marathon with the two of them cheering me on at my side.

There it was, another contraction started. I squeezed, I pushed and moaned with pure strength. The burning sensation grew as I could feel such tension, the stretching of my body to get them out was incredible.

'Uuughhhhh...' I sounded like a woman in distress. I *was* a woman in distress.

'Come on, keep going,' Jess said.

As I pushed down even further, I felt a quick release but as if something was stuck. Jess and Daniel looked in the mirror again.

'Okay, we have a head, one more push and they will be

out. Good girl.' Jess was so encouraging but I could feel tears in my eyes. I was so tired, physically. I was panicking. If their head was out, it would be in the water, and he would be drowning in the water. I couldn't hear him crying, why? Something was wrong, my heart began racing, I needed to get him out desperately.

'Come on, baby, I'm so proud of you. One more push and they are here. You ready?' Daniel whispered in my ear, squeezing my hand gently with support.

I sniffled, wiped my running nose, and took a big deep breath in, building myself up for what was to come. Here it was, I could feel it building and I felt the need to push once again.

'Uuuuggghhhh...' I pushed as hard as I could, my whole body squeezing as hard as it could. I held my breath, my chin on my chest, concentrating on the one thing I had to do.

'Go on, Rose, nearly there, push, push, push.' Jess's focus was between my legs, watching in anticipation. The same incredible burning, stretching sensation and then my body almost took over as a gush of blood and water swirled, and they were out.

Jess leaned into the pool, used the mirror as a paddle to clear the water and held them, floating in her arms. Instantly, the pain ceased, I couldn't feel a thing apart from pure dread. My body shattered. Instead of kneeling, I lowered myself down, the room was silent. Daniel had a look of dread in his eyes that I had never seen before, looking back and forth at me and then Jess. My body shook, I was crying both with relief but also in worry, but Jess didn't seem to share the same distress as us.

'He's okay, Rose. He won't breathe until we cut the cord and remove him from the water, it's still like he is inside, so relax, I can feel his strong heart beating. Take a moment to get your breath back and we will get him out.' She smiled at both of us.

'Oh, Rose, a boy! He's so beautiful, you are so clever.' A small tear fell from Daniel's eye and rolled down his cheek as he gazed at him with pure love.

'Do you want to cut the cord, Daniel?' she turned to ask him as she placed the umbilical scissors halfway down his cord. Daniel looked apprehensive but agreed.

'Okay, are we both ready? As we both nodded our heads, the next few seconds were a blur, but I could hear his little lungs blaring out with cries as she pulled him from the water and placed him on my naked chest. 'Meet your new little baby boy. Congratulations to you both, he's adorable.' She smiled like a proud parent at us. Daniel moved around to be by my side, and with his hand, stroked his dark, wet hair.

I glanced up at the clock, it was 01.32 am on the 14th of April. He was finally here, we did it. He was perfect in so many ways, both of our boys were perfect... how was I so lucky?

So strange, though, the 14th of April was the same day that my biological mother had left me at the age of just two years old.

23

THE SAME BUT DIFFERENT

We had considered so many names by the time he was born but we couldn't decide on the final one. Once again, we looked at his precious little face and couldn't make up our minds.

'Maybe we should think about it for a while before we choose,' I said to Daniel. It didn't feel right referring to him as it, but I wanted it to be the right one, so Luca it was.

For nine months, I was expecting the same child as Jack. What I mean by that is, for six years, Jack had been my world, my everything, I couldn't love another human being as much as I did him. Yet, here I am on the labour ward staring over at Luca in his crib, wrapped in blankets, fast asleep, and I love him exactly the same as Jack.

No favourites, no difference, just pure maternal love for both of my boys. I made the same promise to Luca as I had to Jack that very first day—that I would do everything in my power from this day on to love them and protect them for as long as I was alive.

Daniel was asleep in the chair next to the bed. I was tired too, both emotionally and physically, but the adrenaline pumping inside me wouldn't let me sleep. I didn't want to take my eyes off Luca, not even for a split second. The midwife had told Daniel to go home for some rest, but I didn't want him to leave my side, so he snuck a blanket and made himself comfortable in the chair.

I couldn't wait for Jack to meet Luca, although I did have my concerns. What if Jack was jealous? What if he didn't love his brother? How would I divide my attention between them?

The sun was beaming in through the ward. I was certain that Luca would wake at any moment, but before he could, Jess began walking towards my bed, and instead of coming over to me, she stood beside Luca and looked down at him.

'I'm afraid my shift has finished, Rose, so I will be leaving shortly. Once the doctor has done the rounds and come to see you, unless there are any complications or any concerns you have, you should be free to go home, so I wanted to take this opportunity to say that you did an amazing job and congratulations on your perfect little boy. He's gorgeous.' She stroked the blanket so gently that Luca remained sleeping, and so did Daniel.

I thanked Jess for everything, her support and her calming nature. I'm sure not every labour was as calm and relaxed as mine was.

As soon as I found out I was pregnant, I began having nightmares, panicking about what-ifs. What if he had something they couldn't pick up on the scans? What if he didn't make it to labour? What if I lost the pregnancy halfway through? What if he was stillborn? There were so many what-ifs that I would wake most mornings in a sweat. I'm sure that every woman experiences the same, it is what makes them protective over their child, and having carried them for so long, the attachment, the fear of losing them. Now that he was finally here, and was so perfect, I couldn't help but just stare at him.

He was like Jack in so many ways, but also different. Unique.

Luca was slightly bigger than Jack, weighing 8.5lbs. He did have the same chubby cheeks and the cutest set of fingers and toes. I saw a little flicker of movement as he began to stir, moving both hands above his head almost like a stretch, and suddenly, his eyes slowly opened. There was no smile yet, but he appeared to be looking all around. I'm sure he was trying to work out what this new world was that he had been rudely awakened to.

'Hello, my sweet little Luca,' I murmured, stroking his velvet-like cheek. His eyes met mine, but I couldn't tell if he could see me or just a blurry image.

Luca had slightly lighter hair than Jack, blonde eyebrows and the tiniest button nose. I glanced over at Daniel still in the chair fast asleep. Our little family was complete. I didn't have the desire to want more children, nor did I want girls. Being the tom girl that I was, having a brood of boys was perfect.

Daniel woke up startled to see me leaning over Luca. 'What, what's wrong with him. Is he okay?'

'He's fine, I was just admiring how perfect he is.' I smiled lovingly at Daniel.

'Oh okay.' He stretched, just as Luca had done five minutes earlier.

As soon as the doctor visited the ward and completed all

his checks, I was given the all-clear that I could leave and go home. For once, we were prepared and dressed Luca ready for the outdoors. Being April, he didn't need the layers that Jack did to go outside but it was still colder than he would have been used to. We bundled him into his car seat and strapped him in so he was safe. Daniel carried him whilst I collected all the bags and belongings and followed him out of the maternity ward and across the car park to the car.

We arrived home, and before we had even made it through the front door, all my family were there and waiting to see Luca. Everyone except Jack. I thought he would be first in line and so excited, but I found him in the front room playing Lego.

Leaving Luca with Daniel and the rest of the family for cuddles and to make a fuss, I joined Jack and sat on the floor next to him. After giving birth the previous day, it wasn't the easiest of things to do, and sitting down was a little more delicate than before.

'Hey, baby, what are you building?' I asked as I nudged up a little closer to him.

'Um, a new house that has just two bedrooms,' he replied.

'Oh, just two? Who are they for?' Hoping he would tell me.

'That's Mummy and Daddy's room and that's my room.' Jack pointed to each of them.

'Where's Luca's room?' I looked down at Jack.

'He doesn't get a room.' I got a sense that he wasn't happy about Luca's arrival and that the jealousy had already kicked in.

'Jack, sweetheart. You know that you are still my boy. Just because Luca is here, it doesn't mean I love you any less and he will love you lots and lots too. Plus, I will need your help. You have lots of things you need to teach him.' He looked up at me, confused.

'Teach him?' he asked.

'Yes. Well, you are the master of building Lego and who better to teach him than you? Then there is rugby and football and feeding Harry. They are all really important things that you will have to show him. Being a big brother is a really important role. Imagine if you had a little sister. I mean, yuck, that would be horrible, wouldn't it?' I tickled Jack on both sides as he threw himself backwards and laughed.

'Come on, let's go and see him together. I think he's got something for you as well.'

'He has?' Jack looked a little brighter.

I took his little hand. He had to help me up from the floor and get to my feet, but we walked to the kitchen to find Daniel holding him. Jack looked up and smiled as Daniel crouched down to greet him.

'Hello, my big boy, what do you think of your little brother? Isn't he cute? He's already the best at choosing Lego. He bought you something on the way home. Look in that bag over there and give your brother a kiss to say thank you.' Jack ran quickly to the bag and looked inside. His face lit up as he took out a Lego set, then ran back over to Luca and Daniel and very gently gave him a cuddle.

That was my biggest fear that the boys wouldn't get on, or at the very least, would rival one another. Although Luca was tiny, I made sure that I treated them both exactly the same, like twins in the hope that one day they would be as close as they possibly could.

It was harder having two children than one, but as the age

gap was six and a half years, it meant that Jack could help me and was a lot more self-sufficient than Luca was.

I had the pleasure of Daniel and my mum having a few weeks off work to help with a few things. I was planning on making the most of the time with them and with Jack and Luca together.

24

I CAN'T DO THIS

I was sitting on the edge of my bed, the curtains drawn, looking down at Luca in his Moses basket. He was crying, not just a little whimper, a full-on loud, hysterical screaming type of cry. Tears rolling down his face. He'd had his first bottle of the morning, he'd been changed, winded and cuddled all morning. I rocked his cot gently with my foot but nothing I did seemed to make a difference. I brought my legs up close to me, wrapping my arms around them and started to move back and forth as if I was rocking myself back to sleep.

My eyes started to water, the tears flowing down my cheeks. I didn't even wipe my eyes, I just let them stream, and before I knew it, I was sobbing. My mouth open, face scrunched up and ugly-type of crying, but I didn't know why. I was just staring into his helpless little eyes when what I should have been doing was picking him up in my arms and rocking him for comfort.

Any decent mother would have whisked him up by now. A good mother would have stopped him crying and he would be fast asleep. Maybe I wasn't cut out for this. He deserved a better mum.

The curtains were drawn but the room felt so much darker than it normally was. I felt a ringing in my ears and then silence, not even Luca crying, but I looked at his face and he showed all the motions of screaming. It felt like the room was closing in, like I was in a deep black hole and there was no way of getting out. Just me rocking back and forth and silence.

As if in slow motion, Daniel entered the room. He looked at me and then looked at Luca.

'What the fuck are you doing?' He was in a rage, his face red with anger.

'He's fucking crying, sort yourself out!' He shouted at me.

It didn't make me move, it just made me cry even harder and continue rocking as he walked out of the room with Luca in his arms. It just proved a point—I was useless, not cut out for motherhood.

Perhaps it would have been better for everyone if I wasn't here anymore. I only seemed to mess up things anyway and Daniel could handle things while I was gone. I had done the hard part of giving birth, now was the easy part of raising the children. Daniel was the best dad in the world, the same couldn't be said for me. Too busy previously with a career and partying to be a good mum.

Daniel came back into the room, this time, with Luca fast asleep in his arms. He gently lay him back down in his crib, pulling his little blanket up over his chest and quietly moving back so he didn't wake.

'Go and have a shower, for goodness sake before he wakes up,' he whispered to me but still in an angry tone. I felt like a naughty schoolgirl who had been told off by her teacher. I did as I was told, I stood up, tears still pouring out of my eyes like a hysterical teenager. I just couldn't stop. My towel was draped over the corner of the door, unhooking it, I wandered slowly to the bathroom.

It was as if I was possessed, my body couldn't function. Every simple task seemed to be an absolute mission. A big hazy cloud was fogging my mind, my heart was in a constant state of panic and adrenaline, yet I had zero energy to do anything. To be honest, I just wanted to be locked in a dark cupboard somewhere and left to my own devices.

Throwing my towel into a ball on the floor, I turned both the hot and cold bath taps on full pelt. I put the plug in the bottom and simply stared at the running water in a complete trance. It got higher and higher. I knew it was way more than I needed, but I let it continue to fill. Painstakingly, I turned them off just before they reached the brim. Peeling off my nighty, one foot after the next, I lifted it into the water, sinking them to the bottom of the bath, but as the rest of me entered the water, my calves, my thighs and finally my bottom as I sat down, the water just poured over the sides. I didn't care, I couldn't even feel the temperature of the water and whether it was hot or cold.

More thoughts were running through my mind...

I could just end it all here and now, I thought to myself. *I'm fed up with feeling like this, it's no way to live. What happened to my former, happy self?*

Waking up in the mornings and feeling good had been replaced with dread and fear like something bad was about to happen. *I can't take this anymore, nor is it fair for Daniel to have to cope with me being like this as well as having to look after the children. I'm such a burden.* Exhausted, I couldn't eat or sleep and my nightmares were getting worse. The thought of leaving the house filled me with dread.

I am the nightmare. I didn't want to go back to medication and how I felt before. I just couldn't do it.

I could end it all right here, right now. It would be quick and painless. I looked around the room for something I could use. I had seen it in films, a quick nick of the veins on the wrists, letting the blood pour from my body wouldn't hurt and I could just lay back and let all the pain in my life disappear. Daniel's nightmare would end and it would be just him and his two beautiful boys.

I picked up the shaver that was resting on the side of the bath and studied it. *If I could remove the blades one by one...* I thought. I held the tweezers in my hand and tried to snap the blades free from the end of the shaver. One snapped easily. The second and third were harder but I managed to do it. I placed the tweezers back down then held the small, silver piece of sharp metal between the fingers in my right hand and lifted my left wrist to face me. *So many veins to choose from... Do I cut one, deep long line down, or multiple cuts to make sure? I'm going to count... one... two... three.. then take a deep breath and...*

Daniel burst through the door. 'What the fuck, Rose! No, what are you doing? Stop!' But as he shouted, I panicked, blood pouring into the water. I began crying louder in shock, I looked down at what I had done.

'No, no, no, no.' Daniel grabbed the towel from the floor, wrapped it around my wrist, yanked at the plug so the bath emptied and tried to pull me out. We were both in tears, panic and pain filled the bathroom.

'I'm sorry... I... you and the kids are better off without me.' I tried to apologise to Daniel but felt lightheaded.

'What are you talking about? I can't live without you, nor can the boys. We need you.' Daniel looked into my eyes. He looked distraught, he looked scared. Sitting me on the toilet, he grabbed another towel from the back of the door, wrapping me with it as I began to shake.

Daniel applied pressure again to stop the bleeding, but it was no good, it kept soaking through the towel.

'I think we need to go to A&E. What the hell were you thinking? You know I can't live without you. You're sick, Rose, you need help.' He cuddled me, squeezing my wrist with pressure as he leaned in. I couldn't say anything, I just sat there sobbing, trying not to pass out. I felt cold.

'I'll get the boys ready, stay completely still with your hand on that and I'll quickly get you some clothes.' Daniel rushed off and reappeared seconds later.

'Once again, I'm a pain. A burden on you and the kids having to take me to hospital,' I apologised to Daniel.

'Rose, you're not a burden. We need you to get better, so let's get you dressed and some help.' Daniel picked up Luca, disturbing him from his sleep. He watched me the whole time like I was his third child. Making sure I was holding my hand, getting ready at the same time.

'Jack, Jack, can you come here, please?' He called down to him as he was watching television in the front room. 'Can you do me a huge favour, please?' he said as Jack came running up the stairs.

'Don't panic, Mummy has cut her hand, so I need you to walk her downstairs while I quickly go and clear the bathroom. Get both your shoes on so we can jump in the car and take her to hospital. Can you do that for me like a good boy?' He bent down, smiled at Jack and rustled his hair.

'Yes... uh... huh...' he replied. The look on Jack's face said it all. He looked extremely concerned and worried. He took it all in. The blood on the towel wrapped around my arm. My red face and watery eyes from crying. His dad in a fluster—he wasn't silly. He knew exactly what was going on and it broke my heart that I had done this to him, to Daniel, to our family.

Daniel went to the bathroom, Luca in his arms and carrying the towel that he had used to keep me warm. He didn't want Luca seeing the bathroom in that state, with the blades around the bath or the blood everywhere. I didn't realise that the water had dripped through the ceiling downstairs from overflowing the bath and that was what made Daniel come to check on me. If he had been a second later, if the water hadn't gone through to downstairs... it could have been too late.

I noticed that, in the panic, it wasn't my wrist it was my hand that I had cut. A huge gash in the bottom of my palm, the blood was pouring out, soaking the towel. I was thinking I had minutes to live.

Daniel bundled us all into the car. The children in the back. I sat in silence. He tried to make conversation with Jack and make out as if everything was completely normal. I, on the other hand, had no energy, no sense of feelings. I had self-doubt and felt like I was a burden to everyone around me. *How is that a good mother or partner?* I thought to myself.

By the time we arrived at the hospital, my hand had slowed bleeding a little, but the towel was drenched from dark blood, even my clothes were stained. It looked like a crime scene.

'I'll park, get the kids out and then walk you in, but I may have to leave you as Luca needs feeding,' Daniel explained. I nodded.

Getting out of the car in shame, I got to my feet. Jack was

so lovely. 'Are you okay, Mummy? I don't like it when you are poorly.' His little face looked sad as I shut the door and spoke to him through the window.

'I'm okay, sweetie, just managed to cut myself. I'll be fine,' I reassured him.

'Can we go to the park later when they have fixed you?' he asked.

'Of course we can,' I said as I tried getting him out of the car with one hand and walked to reception.

'Sit down there with the boys and I will speak to the front desk.' Daniel ordered me to sit down like a child with our boys, but he had every right to. I did as I was told, Luca in his car seat, still asleep on the floor in front of me, and Jack perched on my lap.

'Can I see what you have done, Mummy?' Jack tried tugging the towel.

'Oh, I don't think you need to see that, why don't we read a book instead?' I answered as I took the first book I could find from the pile in the corner of the waiting room and began reading to Jack. He was quite good at reading himself, but it helped me to concentrate on something other than how I was feeling.

Daniel seemed to be talking to the staff for quite some time. Surely, it didn't take that long to give them my name, date of birth and to say I had cut my hand.

'Rose Murrell.' My name was called by a nurse standing by the front desk. She smiled as I stood up.

'I'll wait here with the boys. You carry on... unless you need me?' Daniel asked as he walked back over to sit with Jack and Luca.

The nurse took me straight into a cubicle on the assessment ward.

'Gosh, what have you done?' she asked. 'Pop yourself onto the bed and I'll take a look.' She peeled a pair of fresh plastic gloves so she could examine my hand. After the amount of time I had spent in hospital, pregnant with Luca, I wanted to be in and out as quickly as I could.

'I cut myself cutting up some food in the kitchen earlier.' That was a complete lie, but it sounded better than me trying to end it all in the bath.

'No worries, we will have you fixed in no time but that will need quite a few stitches I'm afraid.' She turned to the trays behind her and pulled out a pulp dish, a couple of syringes and some other materials to dress the wound before repairing it.

I didn't look down while she was doing it. Instead, I studied the room around me. The posters on the wall, the curtain rail, even the ceiling tiles that looked worn and needed replacing. My hand was throbbing, I could feel her gentle hands cleansing and the gentle warmth of liquid before a sharp prick.

'Ooh!' I squirmed a little.

'Sorry about that. Now you won't feel a thing,' she explained.

In what felt like minutes, I had my hand stitched, bandaged and all good to go. I felt so guilty that I had left Daniel and the boys waiting in reception for me, but I didn't feel guilty for what I had done. Imagine I had gone through with it. Imagine I wasn't sitting here with this nurse and I had ended things. How would I feel about not seeing them again or never having the chance to see what the rest of my life had to hold? I wasn't thinking straight.

I was in a moment of madness this morning. Unable to cope and feeling suffocated. You might think I was selfish, there were other people a lot more unfortunate than I was, and that I should be appreciative of having what I had, but it wasn't about what I had. It was how I felt inside. I didn't like myself very much and I worried about what others thought of me. My intention was that Daniel and the boys would be better off without their nightmare of a mother and partner. I sat on the hospital bed waiting for the nurse to discharge me. It was feeling all too frequent, a trip to the hospital.

'Oh, before I forget, the doctor wants a quick word with you before you leave.' She smiled and placed all the items back on the side before drawing the curtain back and getting the doctor.

Oh, really? Just for a cut hand? I thought to myself.

The doctor appeared. A slim, young doctor who looked about the same age as me. Short blonde hair and glasses and had a stutter as he spoke.

'Miss Murrell, is that correct?' he asked.

'Yes, that's correct.'

'How is your hand?'

'It is much better now, thank you.' I looked down at my rather elaborate bandage.

'I understand it could have been much worse.' He raised his eyebrows and looked straight at me.

'I'm sorry, I...' I wasn't sure what he was getting at, and I wasn't about to explain what had happened this morning.

'I spoke to your partner. He is very concerned about your welfare. This is a completely confidential conversation, but I must make sure that you aren't a harm to yourself or others. How are you feeling at the moment?' He seemed quite caring, but I didn't want to explain to him exactly how I was feeling. It hurt too much to admit it to anyone.

'I'm fine,' I sheepishly answered.

'Do you mind me calling you Rose?' he asked.

'No, that's fine, you can call me Rose.' I smiled positively.

'Having a small child at your age is a task. Having two children at your age is an even bigger task for any woman. I know you have the support of your partner, but the point is, many women suffer from post-natal depression. Feelings of low self-worth, doubt, anxiety and many other symptoms are all quite normal. It is how you deal with them that matters.' He took a step closer to me and put his hand on my shoulder as if he was trying to attract my attention.

'I know, I understand but I'm fine,' I said again.

'I'm sure you are fine and I'm also sure that you are quite a strong young lady, independent and struggles on regardless. Is that right?' He was pushing for a response.

I felt myself suddenly welling up again, just as I had done this morning. What was happening to me? I had turned into a weak, juddering mess of a person and unable to control my emotions.

'I just... I...' I couldn't quite get the words out, but I found my eyes watering again, struggling to remain composed.

'Go on, Rose, talk to me. I want to try and help you.'

'I had a moment this morning,' I blurted out. 'I couldn't stop myself; it would be better for everyone if I just...'

'If you just what?' His eyes turned to a sad and helpful look.

'If I wasn't here anymore. I can't stand the way I feel, from the moment I wake up until I go to bed. I wish I could sleep forever so that I didn't have to feel like this anymore. I can't function and everything gets on top of me.' I blabbed as the words fell out of my mouth.

'How long have you been feeling this way, Rose?' A stranger to me but he seemed so understanding. Maybe that's why I was telling him. Somebody independent and non-judgemental.

'Weeks, days... I don't know, I can't remember not feeling this way. I can't seem to get the old me back.' I sobbed uncontrollably once again. My heart was hurting but I couldn't explain why. There was a lump in my throat and my eyes were so sore. I was tired. The whole pregnancy, birth and now this had drained me.

'You must understand that you will feel like you again. This is a stage in your life, which most people go through. The first stage to fighting depression is by realising that you have it.' He squeezed my shoulder in a sympathetic way.

'Depressed?' I looked at him confused. I didn't think I was depressed again—*I've just had a baby. I've been depressed before and this feels different.*

'Your body is a strong old engine; it powers on when you need it the most. Like pregnancy, or like a coping mechanism, then when you relax or your body can't take anymore, it starts to give you warning signs or shuts down. The heart-racing palpitations and the sensation of having run a marathon in the middle of the night, that is called a panic attack. We call it the fight or flight response in medicine.' He stopped to check I was still listening.

'Imagine you were in danger of being chased by a predator, your brain pumps your body full of adrenaline so that you can run or get away. Now, imagine that you wake in the middle of the night, or you are over-stressed, your brain suddenly pumps adrenaline but there is no way of you burning it off, so it just flows through your veins like a toxin in your bloodstream and scares you. What we need to do is help you with some medicine that stops your mind's ability to release this. They are called beta-blockers and will help to calm you down. They will also relax you a little so that you can gradually build yourself back up as a person and get back to your former self.' He explained it in such a way that it made total sense, but I felt like I was going crazy.

'If I take these tablets, will I be on them for the rest of my life?' I asked, worriedly.

'Of course not. We will start with a small dose, say 10mg of Cipramil or Citalopram as some pharmaceutical companies call it, every other day. You may experience headaches the first couple of days and feel a little hazy, but that just means it's working. If we feel like you need a stronger dose, then we can increase it. After fourteen days, increase the dose to every day. Do not, and I repeat, do not just stop taking them as the side effects will be so much worse. Your doctor will need to see you for a review in a few weeks to see how you are finding them and avoid heavy drinking as alcohol will just fuel the way you feel.' He looked at me like a father looks at a daughter when he is trying to talk some sense into her. 'Okay?'

'Okay?' Admitting defeat, I agreed with him. My tears had subsided and I felt a little hope.

'There are so many people you can talk to and will be in the same position as you. Don't be afraid of how you are feeling, okay?' He was waiting for me to concur.

'I know and thank you. Sorry for the outburst.' I couldn't thank him enough.

'Not at all. Right, I am going to write out your prescription. If you give me five minutes, you can collect them from the main reception where you came in. Now focus on getting yourself better, those cute little boys in reception need you right now.' He squeezed again and turned to leave.

'Thank you again.' How did he know that I had boys

waiting in reception? *Ah, Daniel spoke to him.* Maybe these tablets will help. I don't want to feel this way anymore, so if it meant taking them then I guess that's what I had to do.

I picked up my belongings, pulled my sleeve half over the bandage on my hand to disguise it but it was so big that only a fraction was covered. I looked over at Daniel in the corner of the waiting room. He looked stressed. Jack was hanging from his arm and Luca was on his lap feeding from a bottle.

What did I do to deserve such a man? If it wasn't for him, I wouldn't be here right now and I owed him everything—my life, my children, my heart.

I collected my prescription. Daniel placed Luca back in his seat and I walked back to the car with Jack holding my unbandaged hand.

'Are you okay now, Mummy? You look like a mummy now!' He chuckled as he walked, looking at my bandage.

'I do, don't I? No swimming for me for a while.' I laughed back. It was the first time I had laughed in a long time.

In the car on the way home, Daniel was itching to talk to me. I could see him uncomfortable in the driving seat and occasionally looking at me to check I was okay. I felt too embarrassed to say anything.

'Rose...' he finally said.

'Yes...' I knew what was about to come.

'Why didn't you tell me how you felt?' he asked shamefully.

'I didn't want to bother you,' I answered.

'Bother me? You can always bother me. You're my world. I couldn't imagine you not being here. What you did this morning scared the hell out of me. I can't believe that you would ever think that me or the boys would be better off without you.' Daniel looked so emotional. I felt horrendous.

'I just... I don't know what I was thinking.' I looked at him, but his eyes were concentrating on the road. It was as if he was trying to keep it together for fear of Jack listening or watching our conversation.

'I want you to make me a promise.' He sounded stern.

'Okay...' I agreed without knowing what that promise was.

'I want you to never ever do anything like that again. No matter how bad or down you feel, you come to me first. You are not leaving me yet. You hear? You're my best friend and my soulmate, being without you is unimaginable. I've told you before and I will tell you again. Yes, you are an absolute nightmare, but you are my nightmare. Together, we make a great team—don't break it up.' His voice was emotional and heartfelt.

'I promise.' I couldn't think of anything else to say. I agreed with everything he said. He was my world too, but I felt numb. The day had been so traumatic, I was tired and exhausted. 'Without you, I wouldn't be here,' I slipped in.

He held one hand on the steering wheel, the other he dropped to my lap and held it out. I reached out with my right hand and fit it snug inside his, clasping his fingers over the top of mine and sealing them both together.

'I mean it, together forever.' He looked into my eyes and smiled.

'Together forever,' I returned and smiled back.

25

I'VE MISSED YOU

The following day, I awoke feeling like a new person. Yesterday felt like a nightmare. My head still a little hazy and in a low mood, but nothing compared to then. Luca was sound asleep in his crib and Daniel was snoring on the pillow next to me. The sunshine was creeping through the smallest of gaps between the curtains, enough to fill the room with a little light. The box of anti-depressant tablets was on my chest of drawers next to the bed and a half-filled glass of water that I always took to bed with me.

I opened the packet and popped out a pill. A tiny little tablet with the number 10 engraved into it. I felt like Alice in Wonderland about to swallow a magical dose. If it was going to make me feel better, then this was the way I was going to start my mornings. I was trying to be quiet, but the rustle of the box and the packaging made Luca stir. Instead of crying, his little dark blue eyes shone back at me. I think he was starting to recognise who I was and began studying my face.

'Come here, beautiful,' I said, lifting him out and cuddling him up into my arms. He was fascinated with the sun's rays bursting in. He started fidgeting as I glanced over at the time—he was due a morning feed. To not wake Daniel, I went downstairs into the kitchen and got out a bottle of milk that he had prepared the night before. My bandaged hand was throbbing in pain.

He guzzled away, and before long, had finished the bottle. He twisted and murmured away so I placed him over my shoulder and gently patted his back to release any wind that had become trapped. A couple of quiet burps emerged but he sat there, content.

Jack had been a fantastic older brother. He seemed nervous when he held him, afraid to break his precious little body, but he always ran to fetch things to help us like nappies or cream or bottles, so it made our lives so much easier with a little helper. I think Jack was super eager for Luca to play with him, but as there was six years difference between them, he may be waiting a while.

I made a cup of coffee and carried it back upstairs to the bedroom, placing it next to Daniel's side of the bed so he would wake to it. He was regular as clockwork when it came to waking up, so I knew he wouldn't be asleep for long. Jack was already rustling away in his room, so I got him up, dressed and we had breakfast together. Why couldn't every morning be like this... calm, collected and stress-free?

Maybe this was what I needed, to slow down, to reconnect with the family and the world around me. I constantly tried to cram as much into each day, I was like a whirlwind of chaos, trying to balance a million spinning plates and moving from thing to thing. Now was the time to enjoy the time I had off work for maternity leave and focus on getting better so I could be the best mum to those children.

I put Luca back in his crib whilst Daniel took over with Jack, so it gave me the opportunity to have a refreshing shower and get changed. I was quite scared going back into the bathroom. The images of yesterday's aftermath were still imprinted in my mind. I could still see the red water I was sitting in and the blades on the side. I think Daniel was worried as he asked me to keep the door open and all the shavers and razors had been removed from the bathroom. I felt humiliated in a way, but it was what I needed. No temptation, no thought-provoking items and a boyfriend that cared for my welfare.

'Rose, Rose, you nearly done?' I could hear Daniel shouting at me.

'Yes, I'm fine,' I shouted down.

'No, Rose, have you finished?' I couldn't hear what he was saying so I finished washing the soap from my body, stepped out of the bath and towel-dried my hair.

'Coming.' He clearly wanted something, so I hurried along.

With no plans for the day, I wrapped the towel around my hair and piled it high on my head, then pulled on some jogging bottoms and an old t-shirt. I had to wear a bra as I hadn't long finished feeding Luca so they would leak if I didn't put something on. I looked down thinking, *Gosh, how unattractive a body is not long after having my second child.* Hopefully, it would return to its semi-former glory in the months to come.

As I reached the bottom step of the stairs, I could hear Daniel talking and another man's familiar voice.

'You have a visitor,' Daniel said as I appeared.

Oh wow, I was instantly embarrassed. He had never seen me looking such a state before.

'Hello, stranger,' he said before walking up to me and giving me the biggest hug.

'George. What are you doing here?' I blushed as he let go of me.

'Well, I've come to see you, haven't I? If I can't annoy you at work, then I'll come to your house and annoy you instead. Congratulations on number two. How's things? Wow, what have you done to your hand?' He stared at me with concern.

'Oh, this?' I held up my hand to him. 'This is nothing, just a cooking incident that went slightly wrong.' I smiled, shrugging it off but he knew that I wasn't telling the truth, he could see it.

'Oh, okay, as long as you are alright?' He took another concerned stare at Daniel, but he looked away.

'I'm not exactly looking my best right now but it's nice to see you.' It was really good to see him, and he looked so well, almost as if he had been working out. He wouldn't have the foggiest what we went through yesterday, so it was nice to see someone and to think about something else for a change.

'I can see that, but it's not every day that you push something the size of a melon out of the size of a grape, is it?' he cheekily replied.

Daniel almost spat his coffee out, he wasn't quite used to the comments that George would come out with on a daily basis, let alone them being aimed at me. I just raised my eyebrows, his comment didn't faze me in the slightest, in fact, they were refreshing and made me laugh. I chuckled back.

'Look, Mummy... look what George got me.' Jack appeared at the door with an action man.

'Oh, wow, how lucky are you? Did you say thank you?' I smiled at George—that was sweet of him.

'He did,' Daniel confirmed. Jack nodded but was fascinated with his new toy. It was Aquaman, he had a mask, a snorkel, flippers and a diving outfit on so he could take him in the bath and play with him.

'Well, it's not every day that you become a big brother, is it? It's an important role. Lots of bad things to teach your little brother, you are going to have to be on your A-game, Jack,' George said to him as he bent down to see the figure.

'George, I don't want you teaching him bad things either.' It was so nice to see him, but he was such a bad influence that I could see Jack picking up all sorts of things.

Daniel was quiet, it was like he was jealous. He had met George before, but I don't think he realised how well we got along. It felt quite awkward with them both in the room together. Daniel was polite and had made him a coffee, but I couldn't help feeling that he was watching us and looking at how we interacted, how we were looking at each other and every time George touched me or was near to me, Daniel would change the subject or get in the way. He was behaving like a jealous boyfriend.

He doesn't think that me and George like each other, does he? Oh no, he wouldn't... would he? That is disgusting, I wouldn't ever, I mean, he's like a brother to me.

'I'm going to go and change Luca while you two catch up, I'll be down in a minute or two.' Daniel peered at me as if asking my permission.

'Okay, thank you,' I replied and carried on mid-conversation with George.

We sat on the sofa, Jack playing with his new toy and cars next to us both. It was so good to see him. I had missed George. I loved Daniel but I genuinely missed George, just like I missed Sasha. It felt easy talking to him, I felt at home like I had found my comfort blanket.

'I got you some flowers, they are on the table. Nothing extravagant, just something to say well done and all that.' He had a way with words.

'Ah, thank you, they are beautiful,' I said. A gorgeous bouquet of white lilies and added foliage, tied with pink ribbons and tissue paper. He knew that cala lilies were my favourite, even if they were supposed to be the flowers of a funeral. I didn't know whether I should hug George to say thank you or kiss him, but Daniel appeared in the doorway, and it killed the moment.

'Sorry, mate, I feel guilty that I didn't get you anything, but then again, you have the best girlfriend in the world, so you don't need anything else,' George said to Daniel. *I can't believe he said that.* I think he was in shock; Daniel just stared at him and didn't smile or anything. If anything, he looked angry. I sat between the two of them awkwardly.

I think George knew he overstepped the mark a little, and with that, he stood up.

'So, I best be making a move. I just wanted to drop in quickly to make sure everything was alright, to wish you well and say hurry up and get back to work because I don't have anyone quite as fun as you to wind up.' With that, he leaned forward and kissed me on the cheek. He ruffled Jack on the head. 'Look after Aquaman,' and then shook Daniel's hand as he made his way to the door.

'I'll see you out,' Daniel said as they walked together quietly back to the front door.

I heard the door slam and then cups clang and spoons chink a lot louder than normal as Daniel sounded like he was making a cup of tea.

'Wow, aren't you lucky, Jack? Aquaman is cool, we will

have to play with him in the bath later.' I smiled and watched him playing with his toys.

'There's a tea for you.' Daniel slammed the cup down on the nest of tables next to the sofa. I glanced up quickly to see the look of disgust on his face.

'Hey, what's wrong?' I asked.

'Nothing, nothing at all,' Daniel replied.

There clearly was as he wouldn't be behaving like a child if there wasn't.

'Nice flowers,' he prompted back.

'They are lovely, aren't they? My favourite,' I beamed. I was refusing to fuel Daniel's rage and let him get over his jealousy.

'So, you and George get on like a house on fire then. Didn't realise you were quite so close?' Daniel was clearly fishing.

'Like a house on fire? We are work friends, that's it,' I stated.

'Didn't look like just work friends. I saw how he looked at you. He clearly likes you.'

'Daniel, I'm not sure what you are getting at. I like George, he's lovely, but he's like my big brother, he's a complete windup, he annoys the absolute hell out of me, but more importantly, he has my back and would do anything for me,' I tried explaining.

'Oh, would he now?' Daniel butted in.

'Not like that. You know what I mean.' I tried reassuring Daniel as he sat down next to me. 'Nothing has or ever will happen between us. I really like George, but I love you and they are two completely different things. I need friends outside of our relationship and he just so happens to be male. I know where I stand, and he says things as they are. Look at what we have—a house, a dog and two beautiful boys together. You have all of me and I love you.' I couldn't have been more explicit if I tried.

'Uh-huh.' Daniel sat on the sofa like a sulking child. His jealousy was incredible at times. It was as if he wanted me all to himself and hated anyone coming anywhere near me. In control of me at all times.

I had a feeling this wasn't the last of Daniel being jealous of George, but it wouldn't stop me from seeing or working with him—nothing would.

26

TOO CLOSE FOR COMFORT

D aniel and I could only afford three months of maternity leave. I wished it was more, but it was either we had to cut back on everything, go back to not being able to pay our bills, mortgage and other items, or Luca had to go into full-time childcare. It broke my heart, but in the big scheme of things, I thought I was giving our children everything they needed in exchange for being left in the capable hands of a nursery nurse for a few hours of the day.

Jack had been in full-time childcare, and he was turning out to be one of the most loving, confident and friendly children I'd ever known. I just needed to make sure that it was worth it, making every minute count as soon as I was home from work.

We had interviewed so many people, yet no one was good enough to look after our handsome little boy until Ellie came along. She was the friend of a friend, only twenty-five years old, so a similar age to us, but she had come with a glowing report. She was great with children, qualified and had the loveliest, sweetest of nature. We both instantly warmed to her.

As money was tight and she needed a place to stay, it worked out for all of us that she could stay in the spare room (it was currently decorated as a nursery for Luca) and make it her own. We moved his cot in with us and put a new bed into her room. It was perfect, she was there first thing in the morning to help me get him ready, fed, and I could leave her at home during the day while I was at work. She even did some cooking and cleaning on days when either Daniel or I were late home from work. Jack simply adored her and asked us if she could pick him up from school.

It was an absolute dream. Things were great, the kids loved her and so did we. I guess some things are too good to be true...

I woke one morning to the sound of Luca crying gently, but it seemed different, his cry was more distant than it normally was. As I opened my eyes, he wasn't in his cot. I looked around the room to see if Daniel was holding him, but he too was fast asleep. I sat bolt upright, panicking as to where he was but followed the sound.

Ellie was sitting at the dining room table, Luca cuddled up in her arms, giving him his morning feed.

'Ah, thank you so much,' I whispered to not wake the others.

'It's okay, I heard him murmuring and thought you could do with a lay-in.' She smiled and continued feeding him, but as she looked up again, her eyes fell on my chest and stayed there, her focus locked in.

As I looked down, my dressing gown had fallen slightly to the side and I hadn't realised that my nipple was half-exposed. I had only just finished breastfeeding Luca about two weeks prior, so my breasts were still slightly swollen, large and voluptuous.

'Oh, I'm so sorry, I ran down the stairs, so they must have...' I apologised, quickly adjusting my dressing gown.

'No, it's okay. I was looking at how lovely they still are. Daniel is a lucky man,' she said in such a way that I blushed. She gave me a compliment that I wasn't expecting. I hadn't thought of Ellie that way before, especially as she was looking after our children, but if I had seen her on a night out, she would be my type of woman.

Ellie had mid-length dark brown hair, dark eyes, almost Spanish-looking. A curvy figure, large breasts, slim waist and a bubbly personality. Her features were striking—big lips, a small nose, high cheekbones and lashes that were so long and pretty, you would mistake them for being false.

How should I reply to that?

'Why thank you, your boobs are lovely too.' *What the fuck? Why did I say that?* I flustered and pretended to head back into the kitchen and look for something in the cupboards. As I peered back around and into the dining room, she had a big smile on her face as though my comment had made her laugh.

'Morning, ladies,' Daniel appeared in the doorway holding Jack's hand. Both with scruffy, messed-up hair and still in their pyjamas. You could have cut the air with a knife. Daniel must have sensed that he had just walked into something but pretended that everything was normal.

'Okay, Jacky, what are we wanting for breakfast?' Daniel asked him. It was a Saturday morning so the usual hurry and lack of time that we had during the week was restored with a little bit more ease.

'Morning, Ellie. Morning, beautiful.' He kissed me on the

back of the head as he walked Jack through the kitchen and to the table for his breakfast. Ellie seemed to watch Daniel as he did—it was almost as if she was jealous, that she longed to be the one that Daniel kissed, but I hadn't noticed any chemistry with them before now.

'Morning, Daniel.' She smiled and looked over at him, studying his messy hair and good looks. Was I jealous? Maybe it was in my head as I'd just had a baby, my body wasn't quite back into its former place and Daniel and I hadn't had sex since Luca was born. He was a little bit funny about hurting me and us not wanting to ruin things too soon. Maybe now was the right time. He was starving with sexual tension; he must be, and I wanted to make sure that he didn't fall into the arms of another.

'Hey, I was thinking that maybe we should have a few drinks and a takeaway tonight. Luca's nearly four months now and I haven't drunk since I found out I was pregnant... I could do with a wine or two?' I asked, looking over at Daniel to see his reaction, but before he could answer, Ellie spoke up.

'Oh, that would be lovely, I was thinking yesterday that I could do with a drink. Obviously, I will only have one or two so that I can listen out for Luca and you can enjoy yourself.' Ellie gave me the biggest smile. I don't think she was being manipulative—I think it was an honest mistake—but my suggestion wasn't meant to include her as well, it was supposed to have been directed at Daniel. I didn't make it clear though and she was living with us, so I was mainly to blame.

'Sounds lovely, ladies. I'll just watch.' Daniel spoke before he thought about what he had said and was flustered. 'I mean, sounds lovely, I'm in, I mean... oh, whatever... sounds lovely.' He laughed out loud, I looked at Ellie and we both laughed too. It was quite funny in a way to see him squirm with embarrassment around the two of us, and apart from anything else, it was quite nice to have a bit of girl company in the house for once.

'Perfect, I'll get some menus together, and later on, I'll order what everyone fancies,' I said.

'Pizza. I want pizza!' Jack shouted.

'Me too.' Ellie high-fived Jack. 'I can grab a couple of bottles of wine when I'm at the shops later. White okay with everyone?'

'All good with me. Thank you,' I replied.

I think Jack saw her as an older sister, I loved that they got on so well and I didn't have to worry.

That Saturday was just an average Saturday like any other. Daniel and I went to the park with Jack while Luca was in his pushchair and Harry strapped by his lead to the side. Ellie went off with her friends and family for the day. I caught up on housework while Daniel had the kids and we all regrouped around five in the evening.

For the first time since Ellie had stayed with us, I noticed her. I noticed her in a sexual way that I hadn't before. She had a tight white bodysuit on, it clenched to her body like a second skin, and I could see the outline of her underwear beneath it. Her high-cut jeans were held up by a thick belt and added to the curves around her bottom. She had a great figure, and I found my eyes glued on her when she arrived back home, standing in the kitchen talking to Daniel.

You must not think naughty thoughts, Rose, I reasoned with myself as I tried to peel my eyes away from her.

'Hey, Rose, I got a couple of bottles of white, I hope you like them.' She brushed past me, heading to the fridge to chill them. She had the most alluring perfume on, it smelled expensive and enticing. It knocked me from my trance, bringing me back into the room.

'You okay, honey?' Daniel asked.

'Sorry, I was miles away there. Thanks, Ellie, that's very kind of you, I am sure they will be lovely.' I had a quick snap of my former self take control of me. The naughty, funny Rose that everyone liked. It had been a while. The tablets I was taking for my depression had made me subdued, almost characterless, but they helped me in so many other ways, especially from stopping my wild side.

The evening arrived and I wanted that glass of wine more than anything. I craved its dry, crisp taste in my mouth and the feeling that you get when you are drunk. I hadn't had it for so long that I couldn't wait.

'Ellie, time for a glass or two,' I said as I chinked the glasses out from the cupboard.

'Steady on, Rose, it's only just gone six and the kids are still up,' Daniel chirped back.

'Quite right, quite right,' I said, pushing them back on the kitchen counter.

'It can't hurt having a small one maybe?' Ellie looked at me and winked without Daniel seeing.

'Exactly, just a small one.' I edged the glasses back towards me like they were yo-yos before Daniel could disagree. I grabbed one of the cold bottles from the fridge and filled each of the three glasses half full, handing them out like they were treats to Ellie and Daniel as they sat at the dining table. I sat down to join them while Luca slept in his pram in the corner of the room and Jack played happily with his Lego in the front room. The television blaring out cartoons in the background.

'I'm thinking, just to mix it up a little bit tonight and to make it funnier, how about we get the playing cards out and have some fun?' It didn't sound much but Daniel's suggestion was a good one. We had always got the playing cards out when friends came over and it turned into a very funny night. We all nodded and agreed, laughing and joking about which card games we had played in the past and which ones we should try tonight.

I liked Ellie, she seemed like such a warm and caring person. She didn't have a bad bone in her body, but I was slightly jealous of just how lovely she was. You couldn't hate her if you wanted to.

'I just want to say thank you again to both of you for being so lovely to me, for letting me stay here, for looking after your gorgeous boys. You are such a lovely couple.' She got up to give me a hug. A sweet innocent hug that lasted way longer than it should have done. We were stuck in a moment that didn't stop until Jack came running over, shouting, 'Group hug! Group hug!' Ellie and I laughed as we broke free.

Ellie then moved over to Daniel and did the same, hugging him. Her large breasts pushed up against his neck as he sat on the chair. He looked at me with that look—the look where he wanted me to tell him that it was okay even though he felt slightly uncomfortable, but I smiled and just watched as his face flushed and he patted her on the back.

There seemed to be a growing tension between the three of us, but nobody said a word. I felt it and I was sure the others did too.

We sat around the table laughing and joking with each other. Jack occasionally came up to us with the creations he had built until there was a knock on the door and the pizza arrived. The four of us ate like ravenous teenagers until we couldn't eat anymore. The first glass of wine had gone to my head and Jack was starting to get tired and grumpy, so I said I would take him to bed and read him a story before I had drunk too much.

Just like clockwork, Jack stood on the bathroom stool, looking into the mirror on the wall, trying to sing while he brushed his teeth. I laughed back at him in the reflection. He went to the toilet and jumped into bed, ready for his favourite book. The wine helped me play the character voices in his book and he chuckled away as I read. His eyes sleepier with every page that turned until he drifted off and I had to peel myself back off the floor next to him and back downstairs.

As I turned the corner into the kitchen, I found Ellie had changed Luca for us and was giving him his last bottle of the night. I caught Daniel watching her feeding him, but I noticed his eyes weren't on Luca... they were on her breasts, his gaze locked on them like the most delicious pair he had ever seen. Ellie knew he was staring at her but continued anyway.

I entered the room, Daniel quickly changing his stare to me, flustered yet again like a naughty schoolboy who had been caught masturbating in his room.

'Was Jack okay?' he asked quickly.

'Yes, all asleep.' I smiled with a naughty grin, showing him that I knew what he was staring at and I didn't mind. He smiled back.

'Then that means one thing... it's card time once Luca has finished.' Just as he said that, Luca finished the last dribble of milk from the bottle. Ellie pulled it from his mouth as he suckled and placed it on the table. She wiped his mouth and placed him gently over her shoulder and began patting him on the back so he could get rid of any wind he had. She would make an amazing mother to her own children one day —we were so lucky to have her.

I cleared the pizza boxes from the table, wiping the surface clean with a cloth from the kitchen and refilling our glasses while Daniel started shuffling the cards.

'I'll only have one more. You two can enjoy yourselves, then that way I will look after Luca.' I trusted Ellie implicitly with him.

'Thank you so much, Ellie.' I touched her on the arm that was free from Luca, her skin so soft and delicate.

'So, what game do we want to play? Twenty-One? Rummy?' Daniel asked, shuffling them again.

'Ride the Bus!' I shouted. That was always a favourite with friends, but it tended to end rather messy.

'Okay.' Daniel began dealing out the cards to each of us in turn. Ellie placed Luca back in his pram.

We played a couple of rounds, proceeding to get louder and louder as we went and the more drunk we became. Occasionally stopping to settle Luca and making sure we didn't wake him.

'I'm bored of this game now. What other one can we play?' I asked, slightly slurring my words. A year of not drinking had turned me into a lightweight but it felt so good to be back again.

'Poker.' The words suddenly fell out of Ellie's mouth.

'Poker, okay?' Daniel looked taken aback.

'Yes, strip poker,' she said again.

Daniel and I both looked at her. *Is she being serious?* The room went silent.

'Okay,' I replied, confirming her request. 'Dish them out, Daniel, let's see who loses.' By losing, I wasn't sure whether I meant the person who had the least clothes on or the person with the most cards, but I was up for it.

'Okay. Here goes.' Daniel shuffled the cards more frantically than he did the first time, almost as if he couldn't believe his luck, throwing them back on the table as quickly as he could. There was more sexual tension in the room than ever before, but we were all laughing.

Have you ever had the feeling where something feels so naughty and so wrong, but the more you think about it, the more it grips you and makes you want to do it? I felt attracted to Ellie, but almost as if I was taking advantage of her if we did anything. She was twenty-five, for goodness sake—an adult. She knew exactly what she was doing, just like we did. She wasn't a child, and I was the adult, it was just the situation with the children that we were in, and I didn't want that to affect things. *What the heck?* I thought to myself. *You only live once, and she suggested it to us, not the other way around.*

Round one, and guess who lost—Daniel. Ellie and I laughed as he stood up to remove his shirt, but instead of taking it off seriously, he undid each button in turn, pulling it from side to side like he was in a show, teasing us as he did it. The pair of us staring at his masculine chest with wide eyes. Laughing as he did so.

'Right, round two. I want to see you ladies lose next.' He sat down, dealing the cards once again.

Our poker faces were incredible, like true professionals, we lifted our cards, studying them but gave nothing away. Round two and I was next. Ellie clapped but I wasn't sure if it is relief or she was just happy that it was me and not her.

I did the same as Daniel and pulled my tight white t-shirt up slightly to reveal the bottom of my bra, teased it back down again, and then crossed my arms, pulling it right up and over my head. I didn't know we were going to be playing this game, but for some reason, I had chosen my underwear wisely. I sat in a cute black and red-laced sexy push-up bra, my breasts shoved together, presenting the most amazing cleavage that even Ellie looked impressed with.

'Nice!' They were both looking at me up and down. The room was alive now—all we needed was Ellie to be next.

I was half-expecting Daniel to have cheated and rigged the cards so that Ellie lost time and time again, but round three was Daniel again, leaving him in just his boxers and socks, and round four with me in my underwear. Ellie was still fully dressed.

'Right, if Ellie doesn't lose in round five, then she has to do a forfeit.' Daniel laughed but I think he was being serious.

'Fair enough.' She took it like it was a dare.

The cards were dealt. Before we all checked what we had, we sat there staring at each other, seriousness in our eyes like our lives depended on it. Tension mounting.

'One, two, three... go,' I counted us down.

Yes, finally Ellie had lost the round and had to remove her first item of clothing. Rather than taking it off straight away, she sat back in her chair and sat with her legs apart like she was contemplating her situation.

'Do I take off my jeans first to show my panties, or do I take my top off? You guys decide.' She was talking dirty with us, I was sure of it. She encouraged us to make the decision for her, I liked how naughty she was being.

Daniel looked at me in shock, not wanting to say the wrong thing.

'Hmmm,' I thought for a moment, wondering what the naughtiest answer I could think of would be and then I went for it. 'What if you aren't wearing any panties?' I asked.

'Oh, I definitely have some on.' She looked at me in a wicked way.

'What colour are they?' I was enjoying the tease.

'The naughtiest colour you can get—red,' she answered, licking her lips.

Daniel sat up. I could tell he was getting aroused but was watching what was about to happen next.

There's a baby in the corner of the room, should we be doing this? I thought to myself. It didn't feel right.

'Guys, I don't want to ruin such an incredible moment, but I feel weird with Luca in the room. I know he's fast asleep, but something just doesn't sit right with me. Let me take him up to his cot, I'll put the baby monitor on, and we can continue. I'll be back quicker than you know, and by that time, Ellie will have made her decision.' I made my apologies and carried Luca carefully upstairs, placed him in his cot, making sure that the monitor was on, and we would be able to hear him okay.

As I switched it on, I could hear whispering downstairs between Ellie and Daniel, but I couldn't make out what they were saying. *Why are they whispering?* They weren't going to wake up Luca from down there, now that he was upstairs. I wanted to know what they were saying. Taking one final check on Luca and with the monitor in my hand, I raced down the stairs.

Entering the room, I found Ellie back in her chair, one leg bent up in front of her but without her jeans on. Her tanned, well-toned legs bare next to Daniel. Her bodysuit was still on, but it may as well have been taken off as it was so transparent, you could see everything. They both sat there laughing but what were they whispering about?

'What did I miss?' I asked.

'Oh, nothing.' Daniel shrugged it off. 'I was just saying what a nice bottom Ellie had and that she should have it out more often.'

Why did Daniel's comment not bother me? If someone had complimented me on my bottom, Daniel would have had such a rage that he would have knocked them out. I guess that was the difference, him saying it to someone else and him being jealous of me.

'Right, I can concentrate now. Back to the fun... next round.' Like a game of Russian Roulette and our lives depended on it, we all watched the cards fall in front of us, eyes eager like hawks, we lifted and then our eyes turned to each other.

'Dammit!' I shouted as I knew that it was my turn again. The first time I had removed my knickers in a sexual way for months, and not only for my boyfriend but for our nanny as well. I was confident in my body, but I wanted to make it as seductive as possible. I wanted Daniel to like my bottom more than Ellie's and I was damn sure about flaunting it. I immediately threw my cards and got to my feet. My eyes glued on hers, I moved to stand in front of her and slid my fingers between the waistband of my knickers and my skin. Eagerly teasing them down but then back up again, I could see Daniel out of the corner of my eye watching with bated breath.

'Shall I help you with those?' Ellie offered as I nodded.

Her cold fingers touched my stomach. She ran them down my sides and to the top of my knickers, but they didn't stop there, she outlined the pattern before going further down to the start of my pussy and between my legs. She looked up at me as she could feel the want in me for her to touch me. I moved my hips forward, making it easy for her to gain access, but her hands moved back to my bottom cheeks, and she pulled my knickers down to my knees. I sighed quietly but just enough for her to know that I was excited.

Ellie stood up, looking at Daniel as she did. She bit the bottom of her lip before levelling her face with mine, leaning in to kiss me. I kissed her back, my naked breasts against her body. I moved my hands down to the bottom of her bodysuit, unfastening the clips between her legs, freeing it and then started to pull it over her shoulders. She wasn't lying when she said she had sexy red lingerie on. Her bra was incredible, her breasts were big and beautiful as they rubbed against mine.

Daniel stood up, his erection trying to break free from his boxers. He couldn't contain his desire for the two women beside him and moved to be closer to us. He kissed me while Ellie began stroking his cock, removing his boxers and leaving him standing there naked.

'Ellie, you are stunning, and I want you, but I have to do Rose first, it's been months and I need to feel her.' Daniel grabbed me, lifting me off the floor and sat me on the edge of the table, just enough so that he could fuck me standing up. I was nervous like it was our first time, but I had never wanted it more than I did right now. He edged forward, the tip of his cock resting on my entrance as he slipped it gently forward and in. I let out a gasp of pleasure, it felt good, his large shaft slowly entering all the way right down and inside.

'You okay?' he asked, checking if it felt good enough to continue.

'More than okay,' I said, pulling Ellie in closer so Daniel could kiss her while he was fucking me. I reached around and undid her bra, freeing her perfect boobs as I cupped and fondled them, pulling gently on her nipples to heighten her desires. She groaned but I could tell she wanted more. It only took me a few minutes before my whole body shook with my first orgasm in months, my vagina pulsing, sending a current up the small of my back and filling my body. I pushed back on Daniel before he could cum and switched positions with Ellie.

She lifted her legs up and around his waist, gripping onto him as he entered her, leaning back on her arms with her breasts bouncing with each thrust that he gave. I didn't touch them both, I stood there watching him fuck her, his bottom cheeks clenching with each movement in and out, harder and faster.

I could see the sensation on her face as she leaned forward, holding onto him and biting his shoulder. Daniel threw his head back in pain but closed his eyes and continued until the pair of them came together. He slowed his pace and they locked into each other as if paralyzed. Their breathing slowed until Daniel opened his eyes, he looked at me, but I didn't know what he was thinking. I smiled at him to tell him I was fine, but I was sore. Ellie took a deep breath and closed her legs as Daniel pulled out.

We were all quiet until Daniel broke the silence.

'So, I think I won the last round.' We all laughed but I couldn't help but wonder what everyone else was thinking. What was wrong with me? Was it bad that I didn't mind sharing my boyfriend with other women? Surely it wasn't normal, but it wasn't the sort of question I asked other women.

We sat back at the table as if the moment hadn't just happened, except Ellie looked distracted. She shuffled around, trying to put her underwear back on and step back into her jeans that she had earlier dipped out of whilst I was upstairs.

'I... um... think I will head up. I'm quite tired and I want to make sure I'm up early in case Luca wakes up.' She looked embarrassed. I felt bad in case it was because of the situation —I didn't want it to ruin the relationship we had or how she was with the children.

'Okay, Ellie, have a lovely sleep and don't worry about Luca. I've only had a couple of glasses and I think I've sobered up to be honest, so I will get up for him early, but thank you anyway, you're an angel.' I tried to touch her on the arm as a gesture, but she brushed past it and made her way upstairs.

Daniel looked at me from the other end of the table but didn't speak, there were no words, and we were good at not talking about our feelings after situations like this. I guess it was our way of brushing it under the carpet and moving on with our lives.

'I think I might go up too, Daniel, if that's okay?' I asked for permission before letting Harry outside in the garden quickly before leading him back into his bed for the night. The poor dog had remained curled up in the corner asleep while Ellie, Daniel and I had played our seeded, sexual games on the dining room table. Not disturbing us for even a minute.

That night, I lay in bed listening to the sound of both Daniel and Luca snoring on either side of me. Daniel's loud and unsettling nasal snore and Luca's more gentle purring sound like a small animal. I tossed and turned, staring at the ceiling, thinking about the night's antics. Had we fucked it with Ellie? For all I knew, she was the same as me and was in the room next door wide awake, thinking the exact same thing. I didn't regret it, not one single piece of me. Her taste, her scent, the way she touched me, the way I touched her, watching her with Daniel, you couldn't beat the feeling or the sensation of what we did.

I must have dozed off as the next time I turned my head, there was a small, thin glimmer of light reaching in through the gap in the curtains of the room. Luca was as quiet as a mouse just looking around the room. His beautiful sparkling blue eyes glistening in the morning light. As I peered over at him, he gave me the cutest of smiles, his sweet little dimples showing on either side of his mouth and he gurgled away.

'Good morning, angel,' I whispered to him.

Glancing at the clock, it displayed 07.02 am. That was late for Luca, it was also a lay-in for Daniel and me. A midweek wake-up call for us was anytime between 5.30 am and 6.30 am. I felt refreshed, relaxed and as though I had slept for eighteen hours or longer. Yawning, I swept my long hair out of my face and stretched my arms up into the air before dragging myself out from under the covers. Daniel rolled over, taking the covers with him and continued to snore.

'Come on, gorgeous, let's go downstairs for breakfast.' I quickly grabbed a nappy from the pile next to his cot, un-popped his baby grow, changed him, and buttoned him back up. Luckily, it wasn't the worst nappy I had changed, so we were quick. I lifted Luca up and out of his cot, placing him on my waist like a kangaroo placing their baby Joey in their pouch. That's what women's hips were made for, wasn't it? So that they could carry their babies around with them easily.

Luca was getting heavier by the day, he weighed 8.5lbs when he was born and had continued to gain weight rapidly ever since. His cute arms and legs had rolls of skin, he had a double chin or maybe even a triple chin and the chunkiest of bottoms, simply adorable, just like his older brother was when he was a baby.

I crept downstairs to not wake the house up, but Harry came bouncing through the dining room and into the kitchen to greet me, his claws tip-tapping on the laminate wood flooring. He was so pleased to see me that it was hard not to say hello to him. Then I noticed that Ellie was sitting at the table, a mug of tea in her hand and reading a book. She was in the same seat as last night and resting on the same table that Daniel had fucked her on. I don't know why that popped into my head, but it did.

'Morning, Ellie, good night's sleep?' I asked. I think I startled her, despite Harry bounding past her.

'Oh, good morning, Rose. I'm not going to lie but I couldn't sleep a wink last night, so I thought I would get up early. I was going to see if you wanted me to feed Luca, but everything seemed so quiet, so I guessed you had him under control.' She smiled beautifully at me.

'He was a quiet boy this morning and only just woke up. Are you sure you didn't slip some wine into his bottle last night?' I tickled Luca with the hand that wasn't holding him and smiled back at Ellie. It wasn't awkward, it didn't seem different at all. What was I so worried about? I had been up all night thinking the worst when, in fact, everything was fine.

'I've only just made my tea so the kettle should still be hot if you want a cuppa.' Ellie pointed to the milk and tea bags that were left on the side. 'Sorry I haven't put everything away; I wasn't sure whether to make you both one and bring it up for you, but I was so engrossed in this book that I got carried away.'

'What book are you reading?' I asked, trying to read the front cover.

'Jayne Eyre by Charlotte Bronte, it's wonderful.' Ellie seemed hooked on the book, but I couldn't help but feel how ironic it was. The book was about a young lady that overcame her traumatic childhood to then find herself in a new home at Thornfield Hall and falls madly in love with Mr Rochester, the man that she worked for.

I know our house isn't quite Thornfield Hall and Daniel isn't Mr Rochester, but it does sound a little too close to home, I thought to myself.

'It is a wonderful book, I studied it for my A Levels,' I replied.

Ellie looked up at me. Was she surprised that I had read it? Perhaps she was thinking the exact same thing I was and that it was ironic.

Daniel appeared at the door with Jack holding his hand, an exact same repeat of yesterday morning apart from different pyjamas, and Daniel looked a lot more tired and hungover than he was yesterday.

'Morning, ladies,' Jack said in a funny and cute voice, mimicking what Daniel said yesterday.

'Morning, boys,' Ellie and I said in tandem.

'Daniel, I'm going to pop over to my parents shortly and take the kids with me, it's been a while and they are desperate to see the boys, do you fancy coming with me?' I asked him.

'Oh, I would love to, but I need to fix the guttering in the garden, it's leaking down the side of the house every time it rains and I'm worried that it's going to cause damp in the back bedroom and the front room. It's a nice day today so I could do with getting it done before it rains again. Say hi to your mum and dad for me.' He ruffled the hair on Jack's head as he made his way back upstairs to the bathroom.

That's a bit of a lame excuse, I thought to myself. They aren't his parents I guess, and he was a man that liked to repair things around the house rather than me having to nag him to get things done, so I left him to it and Ellie to read her book.

I gave the boys their breakfast, got them both dressed as well as myself and said goodbye to Ellie and Daniel. I took the pram, Luca bundled up inside, and Jack helped me to push. We walked the ten-minute walk to my parents' house. I started chatting away with Jack and talking about what he planned at school the following day, but something didn't sit right with me. There was a thought niggling away in the back of my mind that I couldn't shake.

I had left Daniel and Ellie alone together in the house. Now they had slept together, he had fucked her while I watched. *What if he fucked her again without me there, without me watching, just the two of them?* Jack tugged at my coat to gain my attention

'Mummy, Mummy... look.' He pointed up to the sky so I could see a huge Red Kite bird in the sky swooping and soaring below the clouds above us.

'Wow, look at that, isn't it beautiful? He's looking for food, I suspect.' I bent down to hug Jack as we stood still and watched it for a moment together.

What if the two of them are undressing each other right now as I stand here with his children? The thought of it made me so jealous, I wanted to run back to the house and walk in on them. To catch them before they went too far. I had it playing out in my head. Daniel would be in the shower getting ready,

Ellie would hear him, the scenes from Jayne Eyre playing around in her mind...

She walks upstairs to find Daniel (aka Mr Rochester) naked in the shower and offers to join him. Of course, he obliges, drawing back the shower curtain and watching as she undresses, her beautiful naked body from last night steps delicately into the running water and...

My mobile phone began vibrating from my pocket, I snapped out of my vivid imagination, Jack still holding on to me as I scrambled in my pocket to reach my phone.

Daniel was calling. *Is he naked in the shower with Ellie?*

'Daniel?' I answered

'Hey, Rose, can you pick up some lunch on your way back please?' he asked.

'Lunch?'

'Yes, lunch... the food you eat around midday,' he said sarcastically.

'Erm, yes, okay. Where are you?' I asked another question. Intrigued to find out if my imagination was reality.

'I'm at home, you know that... you left me here. I'm going to fix the guttering.' He seemed confused.

'Where is Ellie?'

'She just left, said she was going to see a friend or something. Why's that?' he asked. 'Do you need her?'

'Oh, no reason, I just wondered. I was going to ask her something.' I wasn't, I just wanted to check. I didn't want Daniel thinking that I was jealous or didn't trust him, but the truth was, I didn't. I wouldn't trust myself if I was a man, so why was he any different?

'Rose, are you okay?'

'Uh-huh, sorry I better go, Jack is on at me to go to the park before my parents' house and I don't want to be out too late as Luca will be due a feed soon. Love you.' I hung up, breathing a sigh of relief. I didn't have to rush back home to find my boyfriend having sex with our nanny.

That moment of passion with Ellie and the two of us eventually turned from a one-night stand to something more casual. It wasn't the only time it happened, and it became more frequent. She would deliberately brush past me, her breasts touching up against my arms or her hand would stay that moment longer as she was trying to reach something out of the cupboard. Each time we greeted or left each other, we would kiss and hug. She and Daniel did the same. Ellie would make him a cup of tea, but their hands would meet. If she passed him something, her hand would rest on his leg for far longer than normal.

Twice she had knocked gently knocked on our door late at night and snuck into the bed between us. For hours, we would touch, kiss, stroke and fondle each other. I lost count of the number of times that the three of us had sex, but we never spoke a single word or mentioned it to one another, or even how we were feeling about it all. It was something that happened frequently but was never discussed, almost like a dream that wasn't dreamed until that one morning changed it all.

Jack came running into the room crying and rubbing his eyes. 'Mummy, Mummy, I had the worst...' He stopped in the doorway, staring as all three of us sat up in bed looking at him. All of us were naked with just the covers over our bodies.

'Daddy?' Jack looked both confused and shocked. 'Ellie?' He stood there still. We all went to get out of bed, but I was the only one with a dressing gown beside my bed. I reached down to collect it and draped it around my body as I stepped out, approaching Jack in the doorway to comfort him. He must have had a nightmare.

'It's okay, honey, it was just a bad dream. I'll come back to bed with you.' I held his hand as I walked him back to his bedroom. Very rarely did he have nightmares and he never woke in the middle of the night, so I knew it must have been a bad one.

'Mummy, why is Ellie in bed with you and Daddy? Can she stay in my bed too?' He looked up at me as he jumped onto his bed.

'I... um...' I had to think fast, and it had to be good. He wasn't stupid, and I didn't want him repeating this to his school teacher or family.

'She had a bad dream just like you and she wanted to quickly show us something, that's all.' I was hoping that was the last he would ask.

'Oh, does she want a cuddle too?' He went to get back out of bed to go and see her, but I stopped him in his tracks.

'No, no, don't be silly. Daddy has given her a big cuddle and she's fine now.' *Wasn't that the truth,* I thought to myself. I spent a few moments talking to Jack, stroking the hair on his head to soothe him back to sleep. When he finally dropped his eyelids and I made sure he had gone back to sleep, I tucked him in and made my way back to the bedroom, but I wish I hadn't.

I crept quietly back to the room, so quietly that Daniel and Ellie hadn't heard me return. I wasn't in the doorway, I stood back a little in the corridor with just enough of a view that I could see them both. The room was quite dark but there was enough light for me to see what they were doing.

My heart sank, I felt cheated, like a punch to the chest. I didn't disturb them, instead, I stood there watching, frozen, unable to move. Daniel was lying there, Ellie on top. They were kissing, she was rocking back and forth so I knew they were fucking each other again. They looked so happy, so content with each other, but this time, I wasn't a part of it. I had been forgotten. This wasn't the agreement. Not once had I slept with or touched Ellie without Daniel there, it would feel like I was cheating on him, but there they both were without me. This had to stop, Daniel was starting to have feelings for her, and before long, I wouldn't be his girl.

I stood in the hallway watching them, waiting for them to finish, tears rolling down my face, a mixture of anger and pain but I couldn't let Daniel or Ellie know I had seen them. They finally finished, she rolled off him in a quivering mess, whispered something to him and then started to get out of the bed. I stepped backwards as if I was just leaving Jack's bedroom, wiping away the tears from my eyes. Walking down the corridor to my bedroom, she appeared and stopped still.

'Rose, I'm sorry, I'm a bit tired. I'm going to jump back into my own bed and get some sleep, I hope you don't mind,' she whispered, kissing me on the cheek, opening and shutting her door quietly behind her.

I bet you are tired, I thought to myself. *You just fucked **my** Daniel and now you're going to sleep.* We should never have started this whole thing, I wish we had never invited her into our home, trusted her with our children and now she was falling for Daniel. I couldn't let it happen. It was partly my fault, I had encouraged the whole scenario.

I climbed back into our warm bed.

'Mmmmm.' Daniel rolled over to lay behind me, his arm draped over my side and his head resting on the back of my shoulder. Within minutes, he was snoring and fast asleep. I tried my hardest not to cry, to not let this affect me, but it did.

Monday morning hit me like a car crash. 06.00 am and Luca was screaming for his feed, Daniel snoring in my ear and Harry banging around downstairs. The toilet flushed in the bathroom, which meant that Jack was up... which meant that the whole house was up.

I didn't sleep at all last night, constantly thinking about Ellie and Daniel together. How would I approach it? What if Daniel didn't want things to end and he still wanted to see her? Imagine if he chose her over me. There it was again— my vivid imagination getting carried away.

I acted like everything was normal. Daniel got ready and left for work, Jack came with me, and I dropped him off at school before I got to work, and left Luca with Ellie for the day. All his bottles and washing ready and waiting for her. The worst part of my day was kissing both Jack and Luca in the morning and having to leave them behind for the day while I went to work.

I sat at work preoccupied, trying to make myself busy to forget about last night, but how could I?

I had watched Daniel with women before, but this one got to me. Was he falling in love with Ellie? Did he have feelings for her? It made it weird that I saw them, but I didn't say anything to him, now to go back and ask him questions seemed odd.

'Hey, miserable.' George appeared by the side of my desk.

'I'm not miserable, I'm just busy.'

'No, you're not, you've pushed the same piece of paper around for about an hour now and you haven't eaten your lunch,' he said, pointing at the left-over sandwich next to me.

'That's weird.' I looked up at him as he sat on the corner.

'What is?' he asked.

'You watching me?' I laughed.

'I simply can't take my eyes off of you, Rose... I'm besotted.' He punched me childishly on the shoulder. He was joking, but I knew he wasn't as I often looked up and his eyes were on me. Not in a creepy way obviously, but weird nonetheless.

'Ouch!' I laughed again.

'So, are you going to tell me what's up or am I going to have to sit here all afternoon before you speak? You and Daniel fighting again?' He moved in closer as if I was about to pour my heart out to him. I think he loved listening to the gossip.

'I dunno. Maybe. Maybe nothing.' I shrugged and sat back in my chair, swivelling from side to side.

'I'm all ears.' George propped himself up on the desk with his hands either side of his legs and sat there staring at me, waiting patiently.

'The childminder... the nanny...'

'Ellie?'

'Yes, Ellie.' He had a good memory.

'I'm having second thoughts, maybe it's best if she didn't stay with us and Luca went to a nursery with other children.' I placed my hand on my chin, thinking out loud.

'Oh my god, you slept with her, didn't you? Does Daniel know?' George's eyes widened as he waited for me to continue.

'George, how the hell did you get that from what I just said?'

'It's obvious, I can read you like a book. You slept with her while Daniel was out and now you are worried he's going to find out. See, I know everything.' He laughed out loud as the whole office turned to look at us.

'Okay, no... that is not what happened.'

'Oh... that's a shame, I was looking forward to hearing all about that.' George looked disappointed. 'Daniel slept with her behind your back?' He guessed again.

'Kind of...' I watched as he suddenly perked up.

'Go on...'

'Okay, so we got drunk one night, we were playing cards and the three of us sort of—' I tried explaining but George cut me short.

'I knew it. You two are terrible.' He laughed again, but this time a little quieter to not draw attention.

'Let me finish. It turned from one night, to another night, and another. Before we knew it, she's been sleeping in our bed, she turns up in the middle of the night and it's as if there are three of us in this relationship. Neither Daniel nor I wanted to rock the boat because she's so good with the children, but last night I went to put Jack back in bed as he had a nightmare, and they carried on without me. I saw the whole thing and now I'm worried that Daniel may have feelings for her. What if they have sex without me all the time? The next thing you know, he leaves me, and Ellie is the children's new mum.' The whole story just fell out of my mouth and onto George's shoulders.

'Wow, that is so cool.' He sat there with his mouth half-open just looking at me, waiting for more. I had no idea what was running through George's mind.

'No, George, it is not cool. It is not cool in the slightest.' I shoved my papers into my inbox, slid my keyboard so it was perfectly straight with my monitor, and crossed my arms like a small child throwing a tantrum.

'Okay, okay, so let me get this straight... you guys have both been sleeping with the nanny but now you are jealous that they are doing it without you?'

'Yep. That is about the full of it.' I'm not sure what I was expecting George to say or do, but I felt better just getting it off my chest and talking about it.

'Can I watch next time or be involved?' George asked, trying to hide his smile.

'You are not helping in the slightest. I'm going to the toilet.' I went to stand up and slide my chair under my desk, but George stopped me.

'Seriously, Rose. I'm only joking with you. You know that, right? If you aren't comfortable with the situation, talk to Daniel, not me.' He jumped down from the desk and gave me a hug that seemed to last a lot longer than it should have done. 'And if Daniel isn't happy with that, he can run away with Ellie, and I'll look after you.' I sighed, pushing George gently back, smiled at him and made my way downstairs to the ladies' toilets.

Sitting there for a moment or two in complete silence, the cubicle door shut, I thought about what I needed to do. I had to speak to Daniel, tell him how I felt about what I saw.

That evening after picking up Jack from school, I got home to a very happy Luca and a giant bunch of flowers in a jar. Dinner was cooking, it smelt incredible—a scrummy roast dinner with all the trimmings and an over-friendly Ellie. It was all too good to be true, it would be hard talking to Daniel, but in a way, I felt like it wasn't real. The bubble had to burst for the sake of our relationship.

I gave Ellie a hug, kissed her on the cheek, said thank you for everything she was doing and relieved her of holding Luca. He smiled and babbled away as I held him in my arms. Jack ran straight upstairs to get changed out of his school clothes and into something more comfortable.

'Why the flowers?' I asked, trying not to be too suspicious.

Did she feel guilty for sleeping with my boyfriend last night without me?

'Oh, just to say thank you for being so lovely and welcoming to me. I do need to speak to you both when Daniel is back from work though, I have some news,' she announced.

'Oh?' Now I was highly suspicious.

Just as she was about to say something else, the keys turned in the front door and Daniel walked in.

'Evening, ladies...' He looked at both of us as if it was his turn to walk in on an awkward situation... only, it was completely innocent, we were just talking.

'Evening, Daniel, there is a bottle of rum on the side for you. Your favourite, next to Rose's flowers.' She carried on cooking the dinner.

'Thank you, that's very kind of you, but am I missing something? It's not my birthday. Are we celebrating something else?' He turned to me and mouthed, 'What's going on?'

I shrugged. I was just as clueless as he was.

'No, no special occasion. See, the thing is, you have both been so lovely and the children... well, I adore them, but...' She paused and looked at us. I thought she was going to cry.

'The closer I have got to the two of you, the more I realise that this whole thing isn't quite right. I'm sleeping with a couple in their house and looking after their children. I have feelings that I shouldn't have.'

I knew it, I thought to myself. *She is falling for my Daniel.*

'I love you both, really, I do, but I can't live like this anymore. I need to find my own place, my own partner in crime. I'm the outsider here and one of us is going to get hurt eventually—probably me. I hope you understand but I think it's best that you find another nanny for Luca.' Ellie looked sad, and whilst I wanted to comfort her, I couldn't help but feel slightly relieved. To be honest, I felt extremely relieved that it was coming from her rather than me.

Daniel stepped forward and hugged her. 'Ellie, I am truly sorry it has come to this. I feel bad that we are partly to blame. The children love you, but we understand.'

'You do?' She looked up at him in shock, then turned her eyes to me to see my reaction.

'Oh, Ellie, I am sorry too. It is going to be hard finding another you.' I stepped forward and hugged her. Jack came running down the stairs just as I did and joined in.

'Group hug,' he said, but he had no idea what the group hug was for, it made us all laugh and clear the air.

We ate dinner together, I helped Ellie with the rest of the preparation, dishing it up and setting the table. Daniel spent some time with the children, and we had the loveliest meal together for the last time. Ellie packed her bags that evening. She gave us a couple of weeks' notice, but she felt it better that she moved back in with her parents whilst we found an alternative to look after Luca and her to find another job.

Daniel and I sat in bed together after she left. Side by side, we lay staring at the ceiling rather than at each other.

'Daniel,' I said, still looking up at the light.

'Yep?' he answered.

'I know it makes me sound horrible, but I think it will be for the best that Ellie is going.' I had to be honest with him and myself.

'Really?' he replied. *Oh god, what must he think of me now I have said that?*

'Yes, I was so jealous. I dreaded leaving the house with the two of you together in case... well, you know... in case you had sex without me.' I turned my head to look at him.

'Thank goodness for that. I was starting to feel that way too, I was starting to think that you liked women way more than you liked me and that I would be left out. I had been rushing to come home from work in case you got there before me, but I didn't know how to tell you.' Daniel also turned his head to look at me.

We were both thinking the same thing—that we had taken the situation way too far. There wasn't room in this family for another person, I wanted Daniel all to myself. Without rolling over, Daniel slid his arm sideways along the sheets, his hand open. I did the same and held his hand. His grip seemed harder and stronger than it had been in a long time. I guess we needed that extra person to realise that the two of us still loved and cared for each other in a way that couldn't be matched by anyone else. Our relationship was fine with just the two of us.

I had wasted the whole day worrying about the situation rather than speaking to him.

'Rose.'

'Yeah?'

'I love you.'

'I love you too.'

'Let's get married.' I wasn't sure if Daniel was joking or being serious, but either way, I knew deep down what my answer was.

'No, I like things the way they are.' I squeezed his hand.

The pair of us laid there, still on the bed, holding hands together. The children in bed asleep, silence in the house. We fell asleep, fully clothed, on top of the bed sheets, a smile on both of our faces.

27

LEAVE ME ALONE

A t times, I felt like my life was one big drama, so to suddenly have nothing going on, no worries or challenges to contend with, felt incredible. Just to be able to enjoy life for what it was. Two beautiful and healthy sons, one amazing boyfriend. I was lucky and appreciative for so many things.

Daniel and I were getting on so well and work was going great. My mental health seemed to be improving, and although I missed Sasha terribly, I was learning to live without her. I think you have to go through a lot of turmoil in life to appreciate when things are good. It gives you a sense of balance.

In fact, work was going so great that I had been put forward for a promotion. I had the biggest year on record. Dave was so pleased that I had smashed all my targets and he was looking at increasing my basic salary and potentially working in London on some great accounts one or two days a week.

I was excited at the opportunity and so was Daniel, but

George was worried that it would be a lot more hours, taking into consideration the commute, and I would also have a new manager. I wouldn't see him in the office as much as I was currently, so maybe he was just feeling a little down in the dumps.

It was the turning point in our lives—the hard work was paying off. Better money, more perks, more holiday allowance to enjoy, it made complete sense. I knew what I had to do and that was to take the job.

That afternoon in the office, everything seemed to be against me. My computer kept turning off and the fire alarm had sounded, everyone in the building had to evacuate and stand in the office car park whilst the designated safety officers checked for fires and potential hazards before it was safe to let us all back in. Outside in the office car park, it was freezing standing without a coat. I had left my jacket on the back of my chair, there was no time to grab it as we were ushered out through the fire exit as quickly as possible.

My handbag was on the floor under my desk—everything including my purse, mobile phone and car keys were in it. I wasn't thinking about the building going up in smoke, I was thinking selfishly about my personal belongings.

I looked all around at everyone amongst the commotion but couldn't see George... *Where on earth is he?* I turned to the ladies next to me and asked, 'Where's George? Has anyone seen George?' but no one had.

The safety team were members of staff that had been trained to deal with emergency situations. It was their responsibility to ensure the safety and wellness of employees, to document and follow procedures. They stood at the front of the building wearing yellow high-visibility jackets, holding clipboards and counting everyone in the crowd, marking each person off against their list of names.

There he was. George came bumbling through everyone to where I was standing. He looked flustered, his dark hair slightly out of place and a sweat on his forehead that he wiped away frantically.

'Where did you go, Superman?' I laughed.

'What do you mean?' He seemed confused about my comment.

'Well, Superman always disappears when there is an emergency. I was expecting you to show up wearing a cape and a costume having rescued people from a burning building.' I laughed again, but this time, he didn't find it funny, he wasn't his normal self.

'Very funny, Rose. I got stuck in the stairwell and the door was jammed.' His eyebrows frowning.

That was strange as he wasn't in the office when the alarm went off and we all made our way down the stairwell. I didn't see him, nor was the door jammed. Oh well, we must have crossed paths without knowing. Maybe he went back up to get something, even though we weren't allowed.

'Oh well, as long as you're safe.' I stood next to him, patting him on the back like a lost and found child at a fairground.

George stood there in silence, he seemed preoccupied. Normally, he would be making jokes and causing a scene—it wasn't like him at all.

'Are you okay, George?' I looked at him, worried.

'All good, I feel a little under the weather if I'm honest. I think I might go home if the building is all clear, get a little rest. As long as everyone is safe. I'll be right as rain tomorrow.' He wiped his forehead again with his sleeve and blew the air to move his hair from his face. His usually glistening, chocolate eyes looked worried. Something wasn't right but he didn't seem in the mood to talk to me.

'I have some paracetamol in my bag if you want it?' I offered him.

'No, no, I said I'm fine.' He gave me a fake smile and watched as the safety officers gave the thumbs up and ushered us all to go back into the building. George was almost fascinated with watching what was going on.

'Okay. I hope you feel better soon.' I looked at him with a worried face.

I turned to follow the others and made my way back in. I presumed that George would follow but just as I stepped forward, he grabbed my arm and stopped me. I spun around quickly to see what he wanted.

'Rose...' He stopped what he was going to say and paused.

'Yeah?' He was acting strange.

'Can you tell Dave that I have gone home as I'm not feeling well, and I will be back in tomorrow?' He let go of my arm.

'Of course, are you sure you're alright? You don't look well.' George nodded, smiled and walked in the opposite direction to the building, making his way to the car park.

Everyone around me was chatting and laughing whilst walking back upstairs. It must have been a false alarm or maybe just a practice run for the real thing, but as we got closer to the office on the first floor, I began to hear gasps. People holding their hands over their mouths in shock, but I wasn't close enough to see what had happened.

As I got closer, more focused on George and if he was okay, I started to see the carnage unfolding in front of me. The normally tidy office looked like it had been hit by a whirlwind. There were papers and documents all over the floor, chairs on their sides, the watercooler had been knocked over and water was everywhere, keyboards hanging by their wires. None of it made sense. Who would burgle the office? There wasn't anything of value to take... or was there?

Kaye, the office manager, was talking to Dave.

'Everything has gone,' I could overhear her saying to him.

'What do you mean everything?' He had his hands on his hips, looking around, confused.

'The money from the safe, my bag and a few other belongings. Colin said he saw a man in a black hoodie running down the stairs and out the back exit, but he couldn't make out who it was.' Kaye seemed in a panic.

'Do we have CCTV?' Dave asked.

'We aren't sure, we are trying to check but we counted outside, and everyone is there, it must have been an inside job... who would have known the safe combination and where we keep everything? Unless...' She quickly turned and ran back downstairs.

I walked back to my desk, looking at all the mess—that's when I noticed it. My bag wasn't under my desk either. Papers were everywhere, my desk drawers were both empty and the letters that I had hidden from my mystery stalker were on the desk, opened, right on top of everything else.

In a panic, I grabbed them, stuffing them back in their envelopes. I scanned the office to see if anyone had noticed them. Everyone was too busy worrying about what items of theirs were missing or if any of the office items were gone.

Dave left the office before I could tell him that George had gone home sick. Kaye flew into the office and headed straight in my direction.

'Rose, Rose!' she called.

'Yes...' I asked, wondering what she was going to say.

'I found your bag... I presume it's your bag as the keyring has a picture of your boys on it.' She held it up and handed it to me so I could confirm it was mine.

'Oh, yes, it is mine. Thank you, Kaye, where did you find it?' I asked as I rummaged through the contents, trying to figure out what was missing.

'Very strange but it was just behind the door in the stairwell, behind the door that had been wedged open for everyone to leave when we had the fire drill. How we didn't notice him leave is beyond me.'

'But you caught him on CCTV, right?'

'No, afraid not. The power cut this morning cut the power to the machines. It looks like the tapes have been taken, so whoever did this knew where everything was, and exactly what they were doing. All we know is that Colin in the warehouse said he saw a man with a black hoodie leave the building via the back exit and into the alleyway. He tried to run after him, but he was moving pallets, and by the time he reached the door, the man had vanished. It's all very peculiar.'

She shrugged her shoulders and walked off.

I sat down in my chair trying to piece the whole thing together. A man in a black hoodie, just like the man that had chased after me, the same man in my dreams, the same black hoodie that I thought I saw in London. It can't all be a coincidence, but why would Jim be ransacking the office unless he was really trying to shake me up this time? How would he know when and where I was in London? What did he still want with me? It surely couldn't have still been about the house—that was years ago.

I searched and searched. My keys were still there so at

least I could get home, but my wallet was nowhere to be seen, including my driving license, my bank cards, money, you name it. Even my phone wasn't in my bag, all my numbers and messages were on it. I didn't know whether to cry or have a hysterical fit right in the middle of the office. The one person that I would normally turn to would be George and he wasn't here.

I picked up the desk phone and dialled Daniel's work number, praying that he would pick up.

'Hello, Daniel speaking. How can I help you?' he answered instantly.

'Daniel, it's Rose,' I said bluntly.

'Are you okay? What's up?' I very rarely disturbed him at work, I would normally text so he would have known something was up.

'No, not really. We had a fire alarm at work, but while we were out, the office was ransacked. They stole my bag, my purse and my phone. Well, I have my bag back now, but I can't find my purse or my phone.' I wanted to scream—it was such an inconvenience.

'What? Someone burgled the office during the day whilst you were all still there? That's weird, have they caught them?' he asked, but before I could reply to him, Kaye came back in the office and clapped her hands loudly.

'I have an announcement, everyone, can you all please stop what you are doing and listen.' She sounded like a teacher trying to draw attention to her children.

'Daniel, I better go, I can't hear a word. I'll meet you at home after picking the boys up, I just won't have my phone so you can't get in touch with me.'

I hung up just as I could hear him saying, 'Okay.'

'I have spoken to Dave. He has had to report the break-in

to the police and is dealing with a few other matters. He has asked me to relay the message that the office is far too chaotic to get any work done this afternoon, and it may potentially be a crime scene, so can you all please leave your desks as they were and go home for the day. Management will take care of the rest of the office, the clean-up, and restore the office to its former state by tomorrow morning when you are all back. If you notice any missing items or anything else has been taken, can you please email the list or details to your line manager. Any questions?' Kaye looked around the room as everyone stood there, listening to her, shaking their heads to confirm no further questions.

Everyone was in a state of shock at who would do such a thing.

My heart was thumping away, the adrenaline rushing around my body. Could I feel another panic attack swirling through my veins or was this just anger at who had done this? Was he back? Was it him? What did he want from me? Could he be wanting to kill me or just scare me? Whatever he was after, it was working, I was really shaken up and I didn't know what to do.

There was only one thing for it. I cleared all the letters from my desk (even though I was told not to) and slammed them into my handbag, heading straight to the stairwell and leaving the building. If George wasn't here, then I would go to see him. He would help me figure this whole thing out, and he wouldn't have known about what happened in the office. I couldn't text him because I didn't have my phone.

I knew where he lived because we had shared a taxi previously that had dropped him off first, I'd just never been inside before.

I made my way out of the building, rushed across the car

park and got in my car. I felt better knowing that I was on my way to see him. It only took me ten minutes to reach his house. He lived in a beautiful mid-terrace, 1920s cottage-style house. I remember it well as it was number thirty-one and that was my birthday.

I pulled alongside the curb out the front of his house, but all his curtains were pulled. He must be really ill and asleep, the poor thing. *Maybe I shouldn't disturb him,* I thought to myself.

No, that's what friends are for, to see if they are okay and to be there when they need them. I've lost count of the number of times that George has been there for me, and turned up unannounced, so now it was my turn to be there for him.

I grabbed my bag and got out of the car, but as I turned to walk up his driveway, an old doddery man said something to me, walking in the opposite direction.

'I'm sorry?' I said, turning to face him.

He was a well-dressed gentleman wearing brown corduroy trousers, a smart brown and green patterned waistcoat, nicely polished shoes and leaning on his walking stick. He needed a bit of help with his grooming as he had hairs coming out of his ears to match the curly whiskers that he had on his face. His cloudy brown eyes, however, looked kind and gentle.

'Sorry, my sweet, I didn't mean to startle you,' he said as he hobbled over to me. 'I just said not another one.'

'What do you mean?' I asked.

'That one at number thirty-one, many a woman coming and going at all hours in the morning. Oh, what it is to be young again.' He sniggered under his breath.

'Lots of women? All hours of the night?' I questioned. Surely he can't be talking about George... that's not like him.

'Oh, yes, lots of women.' And off he carried on walking.

That's strange, I thought. *I know that George is a charmer, but it doesn't sound like him to have lots of women at his home late at night. The little devil, I will have to ask him about that.* I half-smiled, but I also felt slightly jealous. Why would I be jealous? We were *just* friends.

I watched as the old man continued along the road as I walked up the path to George's front door. Very in keeping with the style of the house, a black gloss painted door with pretty, stained-glass windows on the top half and a big brass knocker. I gave it a loud tap so that he could hear. Hopefully, he wasn't sleeping, and I had just woken him up. I stood there waiting.

I knocked again. Nothing. I didn't want to seem impatient, so I waited a few moments and knocked again, but this time, louder.

I saw a scuffle of movement from inside and George shout out, 'Who is it?'

'It's only Rose,' I called back.

I then heard what sounded like a series of bangs, movement and shuffling around like he was tidying up. The shadow of a man flitted past the door and then it was all quiet again. Surely, he wasn't tidying up for me?

'I don't mind if it's messy, I've come to see you,' I shouted out to him. If the old man was right, maybe he had women over last night and he was hungover. I now had so many things I could wind him up about.

Finally, George approached the door and opened it slightly, just enough for him to show his face.

'Rose, what are you doing here?' he asked.

'I came to see you... how are you feeling?' I said sympathetically. He looked dreadful as if he hadn't slept all night. His normally well-groomed face was covered in dark black stubble, his hair ruffled like I had never seen before and his eyes red and bloodshot.

'Shouldn't you be at work?' He seemed off with me.

'Rude!' I said. 'I have genuinely come to see you, aren't you going to invite me in? I want to tell you what happened in the office after you left.' I inched forward, hoping he would open the door and let me in.

'Okay, fine,' he said, opening the door wide enough for me to come in. 'I'll stick the kettle on, and you can tell me all about the burglary. Do you want tea or coffee?'

'Tea, please... white, one sugar. How do you know about the burglary?' I asked, shutting the door behind me and following him down the short hallway to his kitchen.

He stopped and stood still but didn't look back at me. 'I... um... Dave called and told me all about it. Chaos, I hear.' George carried on walking.

His house smelled of alcohol and the faint smell of cigarettes, which surprised me. I expected his house to be immaculate, just like his appearance at work most days. It wasn't a mess but just different to how I imagined him to live.

I looked around as he grabbed everything to make the tea and began clicking the kettle on. He wasn't talking. It made me more uncomfortable when people were quiet because I had to think of a conversation topic, rather than when people spoke aimlessly at me.

'So, how are you feeling? Better?' I asked again.

'Not quite myself, if I'm honest, but I am better for seeing you.' He gave a faint smile for the first time since I had arrived. No sarcastic or funny comments yet so it wasn't quite the real George from work.

'Take a seat and I will bring them over.' George pointed to the small round wooden kitchen table with matching chairs, but as I stepped back to sit down, I accidentally tripped up on something behind me. I heard a loud meow and noticed a black cat with the prettiest emerald green eyes had snuck in and was sitting there looking up.

'Oh, I'm sorry.' I bent down to stroke it to say sorry, but it hissed back at me, so I stopped.

'Stupid cat. He doesn't like anyone,' George said as he went to move the cat out of the kitchen, but he too tripped over the cat as it ran off. Instead of falling to the floor, he tripped and used the kitchen door to hold on to. It swung closed and the black hoodie that was hanging there fell to the floor.

'Oh shit, are you okay?' I stepped forward to help George up from the floor, but he shot me the most scared look I had ever seen. *What is wrong with him?* He was acting the strangest I had ever seen. I picked up the hoodie and hooked it up on the back of the door. George got up and I sat back down.

'What do they say about a black cat crossing your path? It's meant to be good luck, isn't it?' I laughed, thinking that George might come back with something witty, rude or sarcastic, but he didn't. He just looked at me like he had seen a ghost.

'I'll just have my tea and make a move, George. You really don't look well. I shouldn't have come, I just wanted to make sure you were okay and to tell you what happened in the office.' I pursed my lips back together, waiting for him to reply, but he didn't say a word.

He drained the tea bag, stirred the brew and chinked the side of both mugs. He seemed to hesitate before giving me mine.

'Oh, I forgot sugar.'

'I'm sorry?' I didn't quite hear what he said, hoping he would repeat.

'I forgot to put sugar in, silly me,' George said, but I was too busy looking around his kitchen to watch what he was doing. Finally, he walked towards me, placing both mugs on the table and sitting down opposite me.

'George, what's wrong? Talk to me. You're always there for me, I want to be here for you. I can't help but feel there is more to this than you feeling poorly.' I picked up my mug, blowing the steam away to sip, and took a couple of mouthfuls. It tasted funny but I thought maybe it was a different brand of tea.

'Nothing, Rose, I just... are you sure you want this new job in London? I...' He watched me as I took another sip.

'Really, George, is this what it's all about? You are in a mood with me because of the promotion. Why didn't you say?' I rubbed my forehead to try to re-engage in our conversation. I suddenly felt dizzy, the room spinning a little and quite hot.

'George, can I use your bathroom?' I asked, trying to get to my feet but my legs were wobbling and weak—how strange.

'Yes, it's the last door along the hallway, just before the front door. The last door,' he said again and watched as I walked slowly out of the kitchen.

It took me so much longer to walk than it should have done. I had to concentrate heavily to put one step in front of the other. I saw the door in front of me and opened it. It wasn't the toilet door, but I stood there for a moment trying to steady myself between the door frame. I felt drunk, the room was spinning, everything was blurry. What was happening to me?

I could make out a small office in a tiny room, a desk with a chair and computer, a small bookshelf to one side and a bean bag on the floor. There was a pinboard on the wall, but I couldn't make out the photos.

My heart suddenly jumped into my mouth—my stomach dropped. I instantly panicked at what I had just seen. Fear grabbed hold of me. There on the desk, next to the keyboard was a driving license. That driving license looked like mine, but I couldn't be sure. It had my picture on, I think, but everything was so blurry. *Why did George have my driving license when the office burglar had taken it?*

Oh my god. Oh my god. It was... it's him... he... I was trying to speak but the words were just in my head.

It suddenly dawned on me. It was George all along. The black hoodie on the back of the kitchen door, my purse had gone and he had my driving license. The stalker knew my home address, my work location, where I was every day, when and with whom.

The burglar at the office knew where everything was, the location of the CCTV, the safe... George was nowhere to be seen and then he appeared looking all flustered. He needed to do it during the day whilst we were all there so that he could take our personal belongings, but why?

George knew everything about me. I told him everything. More than Daniel ever knew. *He couldn't possibly, he wouldn't... would he?* Anyone could have a black hoodie, that didn't make him guilty. *The letters... oh my god, the letters, why would he torment me in such a way?* He was my best friend, my closest friend.

The hotel room, him turning up at such short notice and in London. He must have followed me there too.

I looked up at the pinboard in front of me and moved closer so I could see who the photos were of. *Oh no. This is so much worse than I could have imagined. Every single photo is of me, there are so many! How? When did he take all these?*

This couldn't be right.

I'm scared. I need to get out and quick, before he finds me in here. I tried reaching forward to get to the driving license, but as my grip left the door frame, my legs were too unstable.

I heard a noise. Turning my head, I saw George standing behind me in the doorway.

The door slammed shut.

The room went black.

I felt myself falling, then a thud.

My eyes closed as I hit the floor.

THE YEARS YOUNG COLLECTION

15 Years Young

The first book in the series featuring Rose and Daniel as the main characters, as they embark along their lifelong journey together. This novel sets the scene, introduces the background to their chaos, and unveils dark secrets.

20 Years Young

Rose and Daniel continue along their epic journey called life. Painful losses cause grief and turmoil. A dark secret spills into their relationship causing shockwaves of emotion. Big business decisions mean consequences. Constant torment from a shady character and the biggest lie of all is out in the open.

25 Years Young

Rose's need for excitement and adventure causes problems. How naughty can she really be without losing everything that means something to her? Her true identity is causing problems.

THE YEARS YOUNG COLLECTION
CONT'D

30 Years Young

Times are changing. Dirty thirties have arrived. Years have passed but history has a habit of repeating itself. The skeletons in the closet keep presenting themselves. So much has changed but have they?

40 Years Young

Naughty forties sound exciting. Interesting events take a turn for the worst. A new character causes a big wave. The grass isn't always greener, but it was fun while it lasted…

ESMERALDA KING COLLECTION

THE ESMERALDA KING COLLECTION

A new series of books featuring Esmeralda King (aka Esme) as the main character. Her family and friends think that she has a boring office job but, little do they know that she runs an investigation business. Each book uncovers a case of mystery, deceit, infidelity and conspiracy as she helps her clients get the closure they need...

Coming soon for 2023

All books are available in paperback, hardback, ebook and audiobook. Collect or download your copy in all major bookstores including; Waterstones, Foyles, Barnes & Noble and Independent bookstores as well as all online platforms - Amazon, Google, Apple, Kobo, Audible and others.

ABOUT THE AUTHOR

Kathryn Louise is an emerging author of drama and adult fiction based novels. She is well known for the rebellious female characters in each of her books.

Born in Berkshire in 1980 as Kathryn Louise Murzell, she married in 2007 changing her name to Bennett but used her first and middle as her pen names. She still lives in Berkshire, UK with her family.

English language and literature has always been a passion for Kathryn Louise. She aspired to be an English teacher from a young age but deviated careers to support her family.

Now in 2022, almost twenty five years later, she has emerged with two collections; The Years Young and Esmeralda King.

The first two books have received outstanding reviews, star ratings and incredible feedback.